BKM

JAMES LEE
BURKE

HEARTWOOD

Published by Random House Large Print
in association with Doubleday
New York 1999

Library of Congress Cataloging-in-Publication Data

Burke, James Lee, 1936–
Heartwood : a novel / James Lee Burke.
p. (large print) cm.
ISBN 0-375-40849-5
1. Large type books. I. Title.
[PS3552.U723H39 1999]
813′.54—dc21 99-34270
CIP

Random House Web Address: http://www.randomhouse.com/
Printed in the United States of America
FIRST LARGE PRINT EDITION

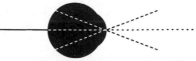

This Large Print Book carries the
Seal of Approval of N.A.V.H.

To Margaret Pai
and in memory of her husband, Walter Pai

HEARTWOOD

1

IT WOULD BE EASY TO SAY WE RESENTED EARL Deitrich because he was rich. Maybe to a degree we did. He grew up in River Oaks, down in Houston, in an enormous white mansion set up on a hillock surrounded by shade trees. Its size and seclusion separated it even from the Midas levels of wealth that characterized his few neighbors. But our problem with him was not simply his money.

He was an officer, on leave from the army, when he came to the town of Deaf Smith, up in the Texas hill country, where the working classes wrestled drill bits and waited tables and the new rich chewed on toothpicks at the country club. He used his wealth to hold up a mirror to our inadequacies and take Peggy Jean Murphy from our midst, then brought her back to us as his wife and possession, almost as though she were on display.

Peggy Jean Murphy, who was heartbreakingly beautiful, who lived in our dreams, who commanded such inclusive respect the roughest kids in the West End dared not make a loose remark about her lest they be punched senseless by their own kind.

Earl Deitrich made us realize that our moments on the dance floor with her at high school proms and the romantic fantasies we entertained about marriage to her had always been the vanity of blue-collar kids who had never been in the running at all. Maybe even the high school quarterback she'd loved before he'd been drafted and killed on the Mekong had not been in the running, either.

But that was a long time ago. I tried not to think about Peggy Jean anymore. She and Earl lived abroad and in Montana much of the year and I didn't have occasion to see them, or to regret the decisions that led me into law enforcement on the border and the months of unrecorded and officially denied nocturnal raids into Coahuila, where a playing card emblazoned with the badge of the Texas Rangers was stuffed into the mouths of the dead.

But try as I might, I would never forget the spring afternoon when Peggy Jean got down from the back of my horse and walked with me into a woods above the river and allowed me to lose my virginity inside her.

When I rose from her hot body, her pale blue eyes were empty, staring at the clouds above the pine tops. I wanted her to say something, but she didn't.

"I don't guess I got a lot of experience at this," I said.

She ran her hand down my arm and held my fingers. There were blades of grass on her shoulders and breasts.

"You were fine, Billy Bob," she said.

Then I knew she had not made love to me but to a soldier who had died in Vietnam.

"You want to go to a movie tonight?" I asked.

"Maybe tomorrow," she replied.

"I like you a whole lot. I know when you lose somebody, it takes a long—"

"We'd better go back now. We'll go to the movie tomorrow. I promise," she said.

But no one competes well with ghosts. At least no one in our town did, not until Earl Deitrich arrived.

EARL AND PEGGY JEAN'S HOUSE was rumored to have cost twelve million dollars to build. It was three stories high, concave in shape, inset in a scooped-out hillside, the yard terraced with tons of flagstone. The front was filled with windows the size of garages, framed by white-painted steel beams. Ninety-foot skinned and lacquered ponderosa logs were anchored at angles from the roof to the ground, so that at a distance the house looked like a giant, gold-streaked tooth couched in the hills.

It was spring, on a Thursday, when I drove my Avalon out to their house for lunch. I had never felt comfortable around Earl, even though I did my best to like him, but she had left a handwritten note in the mailbox at my law office, saying they were back in town and would love to see me.

So I drove across the old iron bridge on the river, back into the hills, then through a cattleguard and down a long green valley whose fields were covered with buttercups and bluebonnets and Indian paintbrush. As I approached the house I saw a sun-browned, blond man in khakis and scuffed boots and a cut-off denim shirt setting fence posts around a horse lot that had been nubbed down to dirt.

His name was Wilbur Pickett and he had failed at almost every endeavor he had ever undertaken. When he tried to borrow money to start up a truck farm, his own mother told everybody in town Wilbur couldn't grow germs on the bottom of his shoe.

He wildcatted down in Mexico and set fire to a sludge pit next to the rig, then the wind blew the flames through a dry field and burned down the local police chief's ranch house. Wilbur barely got back across the border with his life.

In the Flint Hills of eastern Kansas, after a blistering 110-degree day, he unloaded an eighteen-wheeler full of hogs in rest pens without noticing the rails were down on the far side. Then watched them fan across the hills into three counties under a sky spiderwebbed with lightning.

But when it came to horses and bulls, Wilbur could come out of a rodeo chute like his pants were stitched to their hides. He broke mustangs in Wyoming and went seven seconds with Bodacious, the most notorious bull on the professional circuit (Bodacious would pitch the rider forward, then rear his head into the rider's face and crush the bones in it). Wilbur's face had to be rebuilt with metal plates, so that it now looked chiseled, the profile and jawline faintly iridescent, as though there were chemicals in his skin.

I stopped my car and waited for him to walk over to the window. His gray, shapeless cowboy hat was sweat-stained around the base of the crown. He took it off and wiped his brow and smiled.

"I got a pipeline deal down in Venezuela. Twenty or thirty grand can get you in on the ground floor," he said.

"I bet," I said.

"How about sluice mining in British Columbia? I'm talking about float gold big as elks' teeth, son."

"How's the weather up there in January?"

"Beats the hell out of listening to rich people tell you how much money they got," he said.

"See you, Wilbur."

"Jobbing out like this? Temporary situation. I'm fixing to make it happen."

He grinned, full of self-irony, and pulled his work gloves from his back pocket and knocked the dust out of them against his palm.

PEGGY JEAN AND EARL had other guests that afternoon, too—a United States congressman, a real estate broker from Houston, a member of the state legislature, their wives, and a small, nervous, dark-haired man with a hawk's nose and thick glasses and dandruff on the shoulders of his blue suit.

Peggy Jean wore a white sundress with purple and green flowers on it. She had always been a statuesque girl and the years had not affected her posture or figure. There was a mole by the side of her mouth, and her hair was the color of mahogany, so thick and lustrous you wanted to reach out and touch it when she walked by.

She saw me looking at her from across the room. I went into the kitchen with her and helped her make a pitcher of iced tea and a second pitcher of lemonade. She washed a bowl of mint from the garden, then trimmed the sprigs with scissors and handed me two of them to put in the lemonade. The tips of her fingers were wet when she touched my palm.

"Earl's going to talk business with you," she said.

"He can talk it all he wants," I said.

"You don't do civil law?"

"Not his kind."

"He can't help where his family's money came from," she said.

"You're looking great, Peggy Jean," I said.

She picked up the tray and walked ahead of me onto the side porch, which was furnished and built to look like an eating area in a simple home of sixty years ago. The walls were unpainted slat board, the ceiling posts wood and lathed with bulbous undulations in them; the long plank table was covered with a checkered cloth; an old-time icebox, with oak doors and brass handles, stood in the corner; a bladed fan turned lazily overhead. I stood by the open window and looked at Wilbur Pickett dropping a shaved and beveled fence post into a hole.

"Last year I inherited half a city block in downtown Houston," Earl said to me, smiling, a glass of iced tea in his hand. He was a handsome man, at ease in his corduroys and soft burnt-orange shirt, his fine brown hair combed like a little boy's across his forehead. There was nothing directly aggressive about Earl, but his conversation always had to do with himself, or what he owned, or the steelhead fishing trips he took to Idaho or up on the St. Lawrence River. If he had any interest in anyone outside his own frame of reference, he gave no sign of it.

"But it's my worst nightmare," he went on. "A failed savings and loan had the lease on the site. The government seized the savings and loan, and I can't do anything with the property. The government doesn't pay rent on seized properties and at the same time I have a six-figure tax obligation on the land. Can you believe that?"

"This has something to do with me?" I asked.

"It might," he replied.

"Not interested," I said.

He winked and squeezed my forearm with two fingers. "Let's eat some lunch," he said.

Then he followed my gaze out to the horse lot where Wilbur was working.

"You know Wilbur?" he said.

"I've bought horses from him."

"We'll invite him in."

"You don't need to do that, Earl," I said.

"I like him." He cut his head philosophically. "Sometimes I wish I could trade places with a guy like that," he said.

I was soon to relearn an old lesson about the few very rich people I had known. Their cruelty was seldom deliberate, but its effect was more injurious than if it were the result of a calculated act, primarily because the victim was made to understand how insignificant his life really was.

An elderly black man, whose name was John, went out to the horse lot to get Wilbur, who looked uncertainly at the house a moment, then washed his hands and forearms and face with a garden hose and came in through the kitchen. He pulled up one of the cushioned redwood chairs to the table and nodded politely while he was introduced, his shirtfront plastered against his chest, his neck cuffed with fresh sunburn.

"Y'all pardon my appearance," he said.

"Don't worry about that. Eat up," Earl said.

"It looks mighty good, I'll tell you that," Wilbur said.

But Earl was not listening now. "I want to show y'all a real piece of history," Earl said to the others, and opened a blue velvet box, inside of which was a huge brass-cased vest watch with a thick, square-link chain. "This was taken off a Mexican prisoner at the battle of San Jacinto in 1836. The story is the Mexican looted it off a dead Texan at the Alamo. I have a feeling this was one day he wished he'd left it at home."

The men at the table laughed.

Earl opened the hinged casing on each side of the watch and held it up by the chain. The watch twisted in a circle, like an impaired butterfly, a refracted, oily light wobbling on the yellowed face and Roman numerals.

"That come from the Alamo?" Wilbur said.

"You ever see one like it?" Earl said.

"No, sir. But my ancestor is supposed to have fought at San Jacinto. That's the good part of the story. The bad part is the family says he stole horses and sold them to both sides," Wilbur said.

But no one laughed, and Wilbur blinked and looked at a spot on the wall.

"John, would you bring a second glass for everyone so we can have some wine?" Earl said to the elderly black man.

"Yes, sir, right away," John replied.

"Y'all have to come up on the Gallatin in Montana," Earl said. "We catch five-pound rainbow right out the front door."

Wilbur had picked up the watch from the velvet case and was looking at the calligraphy incised on the case. Without missing a beat in his description of Montana trout fishing, Earl reached out and gingerly lifted the watch by its chain out of Wilbur's hand and replaced it in the box and closed the lid.

Wilbur's face was like a pink lightbulb.

I finished eating and turned to Peggy Jean.

"I have to get back to the office. It was surely a fine lunch," I said.

"Yeah, we'll talk more later about that real estate problem I mentioned," Earl said.

"I don't think so," I replied.

"You'll see," Earl said, and winked again. "Anyway, I want y'all to see the alligator I dumped in my pond," he said to the others. Then he turned to Wilbur and said, "You don't need to finish that fence today. Just help John clean up here and we'll call it square."

Earl and his guests went out the door and strolled through a peach orchard that was white with bloom. Wilbur stood for a long time by the plank table, his face empty, his leather work gloves sticking from his back pocket.

"You go on and finish what you were doing out there. John and I will take care of things here," Peggy Jean said.

"No, ma'am, I don't mind doing it. I'm always glad to hep out," Wilbur said, and began stacking dirty plates one on top of another.

I walked out to my car, into the bright, cool air and the smell of flowers and horses in the fields, and decided I couldn't afford any more lunches with Earl Deitrich.

But the lunch and its aftermath were not over. At four that afternoon Earl called me at my office on the town square.

"Have you seen that sonofabitch?" he said.

"Pardon?" I said.

"Wilbur Pickett. I put that watch on my office desk. When Peggy Jean's back was turned, he went in after it."

"Wilbur? That's hard to believe."

"Believe this. He didn't take just the watch. My safe door was open. He robbed me of three hundred thousand dollars in bearer bonds."

2

TEMPLE CARROL WAS A PRIVATE INVESTIGATOR who lived down the road from me with her invalid father and did investigations for me during discovery. Her youthful looks and baby fat and the way she sometimes chewed gum and piled her chestnut hair on top of her head while you were talking to her were deceptive. She had been a patrolwoman in Dallas, a sheriff's deputy in Fort Bend County, and a gunbull in Angola Penitentiary over in Louisiana. People who got in her face did so only once.

I stood at the second-story window of my law office and looked across the square at the sandstone courthouse. High above the oak trees that shaded the lawn were the grilled and barred windows of the jail, where Wilbur Pickett had remained since his arrest last night.

Temple sat in a swayback deerhide chair by my desk, talking about East Los Angeles or San Antonio gangbangers. Her face and chest were slatted with shadows from the window blinds.

"Are you listening?" she said.

"Sure. The Purple Hearts."

"Right. They were in East L.A. in the sixties. Now they're in San Antone. Their warlord is this kid

Cholo Ramirez, your genuine Latino Cro-Magnon. He skipped his own plea-agreement hearing. All he had to do was be there and he would have walked. I picked him up for the bondsman behind a crack house in Austin and hooked him to the D-ring on my back floor, and he started telling me he was mobbed-up and he could rat out some greaseballs in San Antone.

"I go, 'Mobbed-up, like with the Dixie Mafia?'

"He goes, 'They're taking down rich marks in a card game, then messing up their heads so they can't report it. What I'm saying to you, *gringita,* is there's a lot of guys out there scared shitless and full of guilt with their bank accounts cleaned out. That ought to be worth my charges as well as something for me to visit my family in Guadalajara.'

"I go, 'All you had to do was show up at your plea. You would have been out of it.'

"He says, 'I had a bad night. I slept late. I didn't get paid on that last card-game score, anyway. Those guys deserved to get jammed up.'"

When I didn't respond, Temple picked up a crumpled ball of paper from the wastebasket and bounced it off my back.

"Are you listening?" she said.

"Absolutely."

"This is how it works," she said. "They bring the mark into the card game, at a hunting or fishing lodge somewhere up in the hill country. The mark wins two or three nights in a row and starts to feel like he's one of the boys. He even knows where the house bank is. Then three guys with nylon stockings over their faces bust into the game. Of course, one of the guys in a stocking is the thinking man's goon, Cholo Ramirez.

"One by one they take the players into the basement and torture and execute them. The mark believes he's the only one left alive. By this time he's hysterical with fear. He tells the three guys where the bank is. They clean it out and tell him one guy in the basement is still alive, actually a guy who was decent to him during the games. They take the mark down the stairs and make him fire a round with a nine-millimeter into the body that's on the floor. So now the mark is an accomplice and can't tell anybody what he saw.

"A week or two goes by and the mark thinks it's over and nobody will ever know what he did. Except he gets a call from a greaseball who tells him he gave away the mob's money and he either writes a check for all of it or he gets fed ankles-first into a tree shredder.

"Cholo Ramirez says they got one guy for four hundred grand and bankrupted his business."

"The guns had blanks in them? They were all in on it?" I said.

"Gee, you were listening all the time," she said.

I looked at the tops of the oaks ruffling in the breeze on the courthouse lawn. The clock on the courthouse tower said 8:51.

"The only reason I told you the story is it'll never see the light of day. The kid Cholo stabbed dropped the charges and Cholo's home free again," Temple said. "You going to take Wilbur Pickett's case?"

"I think I ought to stay away from this one." In the silence, I could feel her eyes on the back of my neck.

AT NINE O'CLOCK I walked downstairs, out of the cool lee of the building into the sunlight, then up the shaded sidewalk past the steel benches and the Spanish-American War artillery piece on the courthouse lawn. The wood floors inside the courthouse gleamed dully in the half-light, the frosted office windows glowing like crusted salt. I walked to the elevator cage in back and rode up to the jail and stepped out into a stone and iron corridor that was filled with wind blowing through the windows at each end.

Wilbur Pickett lay on an iron bunk in a barred holding cell, his shirt rolled under his head for a pillow. His shapeless Stetson hung from the tip of one boot like a hat on a rack. Gang graffiti had been scorched onto the ceiling with cigarette lighters. The turnkey gave me a chair to carry inside, then locked the door behind me.

"I took his watch, but I didn't steal no bearer bonds," Wilbur said.

"What'd you do with the watch?"

"Dropped it in the mail slot of the County Historical Museum," he said.

"That's brilliant."

"I allow I've had smarter moments." He sat up on the bunk and started flipping his hat in the air and catching it by the brim. "I ain't gonna be riding in that prison rodeo, am I?"

"I can't represent you."

He nodded and looked at the floor, then brushed at his boot with his hat.

"You don't want to take sides against Deitrich's wife?" he said.

"Excuse me?"

"Her boyfriend got killed in Vietnam. She went through a bunch of guys before Earl come to town. Ain't no secrets in a small town."

I felt the blood rise in my throat. I stood up and stared out the window at the old Rialto Theater across the square.

"It looks like you've got everything figured out. Except how to keep your hands off another man's property," I said, and instantly regretted my words.

"Maybe I ain't the only one that's thought about putting my hand where it don't belong," he said.

"Good luck to you, Wilbur," I said, then called for the turnkey to open up.

After the turnkey locked the door behind me, Wilbur rose from the bunk and stood at the bars. He pulled a folded and crimped sheet of lined notebook paper from the back pocket of his khakis and handed it to me between the bars.

"Give this to my wife, will you? We ain't got a phone. She don't know where I'm at," he said.

"Okay, Wilbur."

"You don't know her, do you?"

"No."

"You got to read it to her. She was born blind."

WHEN I GOT BACK to the office, Kate, my secretary, told me a man had gone inside the inner office and had sat himself down in front of my desk and had refused to give his name or leave.

"You want me to call across the street?" she said.

"It's all right," I said, and went into my office.

My visitor's head was bald and veined like marble, his seersucker suit stretched tight on his powerful body. He was bent forward slightly in the chair, his Panama hat gripped tightly on his knee, as though he were about to run after a bus. He turned to face me by plodding the swivel chair in a circle with his feet, and I realized that his neck was fused so he could not change the angle of his vision without twisting his torso.

"Name's Skyler Doolittle, no relation to the aviator. I have been a salesman of Bibles, encyclopedias, and Fuller brushes. I won't deceive you. I have also been in prison, sir," he said, and gripped my hand, squeezing the bones.

His eyes were between gray and colorless, with a startled look in them, as though he had just experienced a heat flash. His mouth was pulled back on the corners, in either a fixed smile or a state of perplexity.

"What can I do for you, Mr. Doolittle?" I said.

"I seen the picture of this fellow Deitrich in the San Antonio paper this morning. That's the fellow cheated me out of my watch in a bouree game. I didn't know his name till now. I come to get my property back," he said.

"Why are you coming to me?"

"I called over to the jail. They said you was the lawyer for the man done stole it."

"They told you wrong."

He glanced about the room, like an owl on a tree limb.

"This fellow Deitrich had a trump card hidden under his thigh. I didn't find that out till later, though. That watch belonged to my great-great-grandfather. You'll find his name on that bronze plaque at the Alamo," he said.

"I wish I could help you, Mr. Doolittle."

"Ain't right. Law punishes a poor man. Rich man don't have to account."

"I can't argue with you on that."

I waited for him to leave. But he didn't.

"What were you in prison for, Mr. Doolittle?" I said.

"I stole money from my employer. But I didn't burn down no church house. If I'd done something that awful, I'd surely remember it."

"I see. Can you walk down to my car with me? I have to run an errand."

"I don't mind at all. You seem like a right nice fellow, Mr. Holland."

WILBUR PICKETT LIVED out on the hardpan in a small house built of green lumber with cheesecloth curtains blowing in the windows and zinnias planted in tin cans on the gallery. It was treeless, dry land, with grass fires in the summer that sometimes climbed into the blackjack on the hills and covered the late sun with ash. But Wilbur had a windmill and grew vegetables and kept chickens behind his house and had planted mimosas by his small three-stall barn and irrigated a pasture for his Appaloosa and two palominos.

I HAD HEARD THAT WILBUR had married an Indian woman from the Northern Cheyenne reservation in Montana, but I had never met her. She came to the door in a pair of jeans, brown sandals, and a denim shirt with tiny flowers stitched on the pockets. Her face was narrow, the nose slightly flat, her hair fastened in a ponytail that hung over one shoulder. But it was her eyes that transfixed you. They had no pupils and were the color of blue ink flecked with milk.

I told her Wilbur was in the county jail and would not be home until his bail was set. I stood in the center of the living room and read his penciled letter to her.

"'Dear Kippy Jo, Earl Deitrich is a damn liar and I didn't take no bonds from his safe. Ask Mrs. Titus to carry you down to the IGA to stock up on groceries. Charge the groceries if you can, but if you can't there is a one-hundred-dollar bill under the paper liner in my sock drawer. Don't fret over this little bump in the road. I have lived here all my life. People know me and ain't going to believe the likes of Earl Deitrich.

"Keep all the mail in a safe spot. The pipeline deal in Venezuela is about to come through any day. Or else the gold deal up in B.C., which is just as good although a lot colder. Me and you are going to make it happen, hon. That's a Wilbur T. Pickett guarantee.

"When this is over I aim to stick Earl Deitrich's head in a toilet bowl.

"Your husband, Wilbur.'"

"You're his lawyer?" she asked.

"No, ma'am, I'm afraid not," I replied.

She seemed to look at a thought, or a question, inside her head.

"I'll get you some coffee. It's already made," she said.

Before I could answer, she walked into the kitchen

and picked up a blue, white-freckled coffeepot off the stove with a hot pad and poured into a cup, one fingertip inset just below the cup's rim. She went to the cabinet and brought a sugar bowl and spoon to the table and sat down with me, her eyes fixed on my face as though she could see.

"This man Deitrich, he's got millions of dollars. Why's he doing this to Wilbur?" she said.

"He says Wilbur stole his bonds," I replied.

"If you're my husband's friend, you know he didn't do it."

"He shouldn't have taken the watch."

Her face darkened and her sightless eyes remained fixed on mine, as though she had transferred an image of me from the external world to one inside her head that she could examine, an image that bothered her. Unconsciously I wiped my palm on my trouser leg.

"Money and people are a bad combination, Ms. Pickett. I'm never surprised at what people will do for it. I'm not necessarily talking about your husband," I said. Outside, the windmill was pumping water into a corrugated metal tank that had overflowed on the ground.

The wind puffed the screen door open. Her head turned toward the sound, then back at me. "How much is it for a lawyer?" she asked.

"In a case like this, you'll probably need a few thousand. Sometimes you can pay it out."

She nodded again, then she said, "Ms. Titus, the

neighbor he mentioned in the letter, is down sick. Can you drop me off at the IGA? I can get somebody to bring me back."

"Don't y'all have some family hereabouts?"

"His mother was the last one. She died a couple of months back."

I could hear the horses nickering out in the pasture, the windmill shifting in the breeze, the blades ginning furiously.

"Tell you what, Ms. Pickett. I'll carry you down to the grocery and wait for you, then I'll go back up to the jail and talk to Wilbur again."

Her face showed no expression.

"He thinks growing up here means people will take his word over a rich man's. That's why he loses out in all his business deals. That's just Wilbur. But this time it's different, isn't it?" she said.

"Well, you never know," I lied, then waited for her out by my Avalon.

Dust devils were blowing out of the hills in the distance and the wind was hot and dry and thick with grasshoppers.

I LIVED BY MYSELF in a three-story purple-brick Victorian home in the west end of the county. It had a wide, screened-in gallery and a veranda on the second floor, and the front and back yards were framed by poplar trees and blooming myrtle and the flower beds planted with hydrangeas and yellow and red roses. I parked the Avalon in back and fixed a chicken sandwich and plate of stuffed eggs and potato salad and a glass of iced tea for lunch and ate it at the kitchen table.

The interior of the house was oak and mahogany, and the wind seemed to fill every room with the presence of all my ancestors who had lived there. From my window I could see my barn and horse lot and my Morgan named Beau rolling on his side in the pasture, the windmill ginning on the far side of the barn roof, the fields of melons, corn, strawberries, cantaloupes, beans, and tomatoes that a neighbor farmed on shares, and a two-acre tank, or lake, that the state had stocked with bream and big-mouth bass.

At the far end of my property was a stand of hardwoods, then the bluffs over the river, which was slate green in late summer and roiling and full of mud and cottonwood bloom in the spring.

The sun went behind the clouds and the wind was cool inside the house, as though it were being drawn through the windows by a huge attic fan. But I could not concentrate on the fine day or the fact that where I lived had always been for me the best place on earth. Instead I kept thinking of Wilbur Pickett and the uncomfortable reality that I had never come to terms with my feelings for Peggy Jean Murphy, who was another man's wife now, or with the memory of what it was like to feel her hand slip down the small of my back, her thighs cradling my hips, while I came inside a woman for the first time and the fecund odor of damp earth and bruised grass and wildflowers rose around us in a green envelope that for a moment seemed to hold together the vanity of my passion and her unrequited love for a dead soldier.

I picked up the phone and called Marvin Pomroy at the prosecutor's office.

"I'm representing Wilbur Pickett," I said.

"That's funny. I just talked to him. He said you told him to drop dead," Marvin said.

"Must have been a bad echo in the cellhouse."

"Let me warn you beforehand, Billy Bob. Earl Deitrich wants Wilbur's head on a pike."

"Really? Say, I had a strange-looking fellow named Skyler Doolittle in my office this morning. He said something about doing time and burning down a church."

"He was pestering me, too. You don't remember him?" Marvin said.

"No."

"He got drunk and plowed into a church bus outside Goliad. The bus burned. Four or five kids didn't make it out," he said.

"Wilbur's wife is blind and by herself. Let Wilbur go on recognizance."

"We're talking about a three-hundred-thousand theft," Marvin said.

"According to Earl Deitrich. Has anyone ever seen those bonds?"

"Yeah, his wife. Is she lying, too?" When I didn't answer, he said, "You still there?"

"I'm going up to see Wilbur now. I don't want anybody questioning him unless I'm there."

"You ought to take a nap, get more rest. Your moods . . . Never mind. Have a good day," he said, and hung up.

THAT NIGHT THE PHONE RANG during a terrible electric storm. The rain was beating against the windows, and the yard was flooded and quivering with lightning and the barn doors crashed back and forth against the jamb.

"That young man, Pickett, is he still in jail?" the voice said.

"Who is this?"

"I think perhaps a degree of wrong is being done here."

"A degree of wrong?" I said.

"Yes."

Then the voice came together with an image, that of a small, nervous, dark-haired man, with a hawk's nose and thick glasses, in a blue suit with dandruff on the shoulders. What was the name? Green? Greenberg?

"You're Mr. Greenbaum. The accountant. You were at the Deitrichs' luncheon yesterday," I said.

The line went dead.

3

THE NEXT DAY WAS SATURDAY, AND THE STREETS in town were rain-washed, the sky blue and the air shining. I did some work in my office, then drove out to Val's for lunch. Val's was the drive-in restaurant on the north side of town, equidistant between the West End and East End of Deaf Smith, a neutral territory where the children of the rich and those of oil field and cannery workers put their hatred and fear of one another in temporary abeyance.

I went inside and had just ordered when I saw Jeff Deitrich, Earl's son, pull into the parking lot in a yellow convertible with a Mexican boy and girl next to him. They parked under the awning, and Jeff walked across the lot toward the entrance, his partially unbuttoned silk shirt filling with wind.

We were told he was the child of Earl's brief first marriage to a Cajun girl when he was stationed at Fort Polk in Louisiana. Jeff was larger, more handsome and athletic than his father, with dark brown hair that had natural waves in it and wide shoulders and long arms and big-knuckled hands. He was bright in a limited way and confident and always ingratiating and had done well for two years at the University of Texas, then had quit, either to learn his father's business or just out of indifference toward what he saw as the necessary province of others.

But I always had the sense that Jeff's manners were the natural ones of his class and that he used them only as the situation required him to. Three years ago I had witnessed a scene in the same parking lot, one I had tried to forget. But I had never looked at Jeff quite the same afterwards.

It was a lovely fall night after a football game, with a yellow moon as big as a planet hovering right over the hills. The lot was filled with convertibles, customized 1950s hot rods that glowed like hard candy under the neon, chromed Harleys, and Cherokees and Land-Rovers and roll-bar Jeeps. Then a beery oil field roughneck, in Cloroxed jeans and steel-toe boots and a T-shirt still spotted with drilling mud, got into it with Jeff Deitrich.

They fought between cars, knocking serving trays onto the pavement, then went at it in an open area, both of them swinging hard, connecting with skin-tearing blows in the face that made the onlookers wince.

They fought their way between two cars in the front row, then Jeff caught the roughneck hard above the eye and knocked him across the curb against the side of the building. The roughneck was down on one knee, his eyes glazed, the fight gone out of his face, a self-deprecating smile of defeat already tugging at the corner of his mouth. When he started to rise, propping his fingers against the pavement for support, Jeff drove his fist into the hinge on the man's jaw and fractured the bone like pecan shell.

The restaurant owner had to hold the roughneck's jaw in place with a blood-soaked towel until the ambulance arrived.

"How you doin', Billy Bob?" Jeff said expansively as he passed my booth on the way to the men's room, not waiting for an answer before he pushed the door open and went inside.

Outside, the Mexican couple in his car were ordering from the waitress. The boy's hair was as black as paint, cut short, oiled and combed back on his head. The girl's skin was biscuit-colored, her hair a dark reddish color, as though it had been washed in iodine. She was smoking a cigarette, tipping the ashes over the side of the door, her eyes lingering suspiciously on the people in other cars. She and the boy next to her sat apart from each other, not talking.

Jeff came back out of the men's room and sat down in my booth.

"You curious about the cuties in my car?" he said.

"They look like gangbangers," I said.

"The guy is. That's Ronnie Cruise. Sometimes they call him Ronnie Cross. Leader of the Purple Hearts. His squeeze is Esmeralda Ramirez."

"What are you doing with them?"

"My dad's funding a youth program in San Antone and Houston," he said, and smiled at me with his eyes, as though we were both privy to a private joke.

"You know where I could find an accountant named Greenbaum? He's a friend of your folks," I said.

"Max? Sure. I put him on a plane to Houston this morning. What's up?"

"Nothing important."

"It's funny how they run of a type."

"Pardon?"

"The Tribe. It's like somebody writes a script for them. Guys like Max must read the material and walk right into the role."

I set down my fork and looked at him. His grin never wavered. His confidence in the health and good looks that seemed to have been given him along with his family's wealth was such that my stare at his bigotry and callousness had no more meaning to him than the fact a waitress was standing by his elbow, ready to take his order, reluctant to interrupt him in midsentence.

"We're all right here," I said to her.

"You want to meet Ronnie Cross? Two guys tried to pop him on a rooftop. Both of them took the fast way down. Six floors into the concrete."

"I'll pass. He's wearing a rosary around his neck. Tell him for me that's an act of disrespect," I said.

"Tell him yourself. It's my father who wants to send these guys to Taco U. I just drive them around once in a while, like Operation Outreach or something." He winked at me, just as his father had. "Gotta boogie. See you around."

Later, they drove out of the lot past my window. The boy named Ronnie Cruise passed a quart bottle of Lone Star to Jeff. The girl named Esmeralda, who sat by the passenger window, looked straight ahead, an angry light in her face.

I GOT UP EARLY Monday morning and brushed out Beau, my Morgan, in the lot, put some oats and molasses balls in his trough, watered the flowers in the yard, then went upstairs and showered. Through the window I could see the long, gentle roll of the green land, seagulls that had been blown inland, plots of new corn in a hillside, oak trees planted along a winding two-lane highway that had once been part of the Chisholm Trail.

The phone rang. I wrapped a towel around myself and picked up the receiver in the bedroom.

"I guess this is foolish to ask, but can we take you to lunch after Wilbur's arraignment?" Peggy Jean said.

"Y'all are going to be there?" I said.

"Earl's upset. But that doesn't mean our friendship has to be impaired."

"Another time, Peggy Jean."

"I thought I'd ask."

"Sure," I said.

After I replaced the receiver in the cradle I felt a strange sense of loss that didn't seem warranted by the conversation.

In the closet mirror I saw the welted bullet scars on my left foot and right arm and another one high up on my chest. Loss was when they put you in a box, I told myself.

But the feeling wouldn't go away. I looked at the framed picture on my dresser of my mother and father and me as a child. In the picture I had my father's jaw and reddish-blond hair, just as my illegitimate son, Lucas Smothers, did. Next to my family picture was one of L.Q. Navarro, in his pinstripe suit and ash-gray Stetson, a bottle of Mexican beer in his hand, his Texas Ranger badge on his belt, a dead volcano at his back. L.Q. Navarro, the most loyal and handsome and brave man I ever knew, whom I accidentally killed on a vigilante raid into Coahuila.

I blew out my breath and rubbed the bath towel in my face and dressed by the window, concentrating on the blueness of the sky and the dark, steel-colored rain clouds that were massed on the hills in the distance.

AT TEN O'CLOCK Wilbur Pickett was arraigned and released on five thousand dollars' bail. Earl and Peggy Jean had been sitting in the back of the courtroom. Earl got up from his seat and banged loudly on the doors.

When I walked outside he was standing by his maroon Lincoln, in the shade of the oak trees, his anger replaced by an easy smile. Peggy Jean sat inside the car, her elbow propped on the windowsill, her fingertips rubbing one temple.

"Marvin Pomroy owe you favors?" Earl said.

"On the bail? It doesn't work that way, Earl," I replied.

"That boy steals a historical relic and three hundred grand and gets released on a five-dime bond? You telling me y'all aren't working together?"

"Yes, that's what I'm telling you. Wilbur's not going anywhere, either," I said.

"Did I say he was?" He reached out and pinched me in the ribs.

"Excuse me, but don't do that again," I said.

"Whoa," he said, grinning broadly.

"Earl, I recommend you stop clowning around and give some serious thought to what you're doing," I said.

"Clowning? Trying to recover a six-figure theft?" he said.

"A man named Skyler Doolittle says you cheated him out of that watch in a bouree game. If we go to trial, he's going to be a witness for the defense. Your accountant, Max Greenbaum, is too."

"Greenbaum? What's he got to do with anything?" Earl said.

"Run your bullshit on someone else," I said.

I walked across the street toward my office. When I looked back, Earl and Peggy Jean were arguing across the top of their car.

• • •

TEMPLE CARROL WAS WAITING inside my office.

"What's wrong?" she asked. She wore a pair of jeans and a silver belt and a yellow cotton pullover.

"We need to find out more about Earl Deitrich's finances. See if he's filed an insurance claim," I said.

"The Deitrichs stoke you up out there?"

"No."

"Is it true you and Peggy Jean were an item?" She straightened her shoulders, her hands in her back pockets, her eyes not quite focusing on mine.

"I thought we were. I didn't know a whole lot back then," I replied.

"Don't let a prissy buttwipe like Deitrich get to you."

"He doesn't."

"Oh, I can see that," she said.

"I told him the witnesses I'd use against him. Not too cool," I said.

She kept her expression flat and let her eyes slip off my face.

"Why would he try to involve me in his real estate and tax problems down in Houston?" I said.

"He wants to buy your good name." When I didn't reply, she said, "He hangs heads on walls. You were in the saddle with his wife. Stop thinking like a tree stump."

• • •

TWO DAYS LATER the sheriff, Hugo Roberts, tele-
phoned the office and asked me to walk across the
street.

"What for?" I asked.

"Got a man in here tells quite a story. Maybe you
ought to hear it, counselor," he said.

"I'm busy, Hugo," I said.

"You gonna be a lot less busy when this ole boy
blows your defense for Wilbur Pickett out the water."
He was still laughing, wheezing with pleasure, when
he hung up the phone.

The sheriff's office was behind the courthouse in
the original sandstone and log jail that had been built
when Deaf Smith was a frontier village in the 1870s.
Hugo Roberts had not been elected but promoted
into the office after his predecessor was murdered
with an ax last year. He was pear-shaped, potbellied,
and smoked constantly, even though one of his lungs
had already been surgically removed. When I entered his office, the air was layered with smoke, the
light through the windows a sickly yellow. Hugo sat
behind a huge oak desk; the log walls were festooned with antique guns and the black-and-white
photos of convicts our county had sent to Huntsville
for electrocution or death by injection.

Hugo leaned back in his swivel chair, one booted
leg on his desk, and aimed a finger at a tall, raw-
boned man with sideburns and a drooping left eyelid

who sat in a straight-back chair with a straw hat hooked on one finger.

"This here is Bubba Grimes," Hugo said. He sucked on his cigarette and blew a plume of smoke into the air. "Picked up Bubba for smashing beer bottles against the side of Shorty's last night. Why would you do something like that, Bubba?"

"Hell, I don't know. Seemed kind of dull. The music on the jukebox would make a corpse stop up his ears," the man named Grimes said. His skin was grained and coarse and it creased like a lizard's when he grinned.

"Tell Billy Bob what you told us," Hugo said, and rested his eyes on me with anticipation.

"Ain't much to it. Last Thursday I got a call from Wilbur Pickett. He said he had a mess of bearer bonds he wanted to get rid of. Said he was calling from the IGA pay phone by his house," Grimes said.

"Why would he call you in particular?" I asked.

"I do a few investments for folks, mostly for working people don't trust banks or brokerages. Not the kind of transaction Pickett had in mind, though. That's what I told him, too—to take his business somewheres else," Grimes said.

"We already checked with the phone company. There was a call made Thursday afternoon from the IGA to Mr. Grimes's home in Austin," Hugo said.

Grimes wore alligator boots, western-cut, striped slacks, and a dark blue shirt with roses sewn on it.

The skin around his drooping left eye looked dead, like a synthetic graft, and I couldn't tell if the eye had vision in it or not.

"I know your name from somewhere," I said.

"I'm a pilot. Out of the country most of the time. I doubt we've met," he replied.

"It'll come to me," I said.

"Billy Bob was a Texas Ranger and an assistant U.S. attorney. Got a memory like flypaper," Hugo said. A column of dirty sunlight fell on his desk. His hand, which was round and small and the color of a cured tobacco leaf on the blotter, cupped a cigarette whose smoke leaked through his fingers. He grinned at me, his lips purple in the gloom, his eyes full of gloat.

I pulled open the door and stepped back out into the afternoon breeze and dappled shade and closed the door behind me and heard the metal tongue on the latch fall into place. The breeze felt wonderful in my face. Then I remembered the name. I pushed the door open again. The glare fell like a dagger across Grimes's face.

"You were mixed up with a televangelist preacher and the Contras down in Nicaragua. You were shot down dropping supplies to them," I said to Grimes.

"I told you, boy's an encyclopedia of worthless in-formation," Hugo said.

"Then you made the news again. Flying for the same preacher in Zaire. Except you were diverting mercy flights to his diamond mines," I said.

"I bet a local jury will get on this like stink on shit," Hugo said.

"They sure will. That's where all Earl Deitrich's money comes from," I said.

Hugo's cigarette paused halfway to his mouth, the smoke curling upward like a white snake.

EARLY THE NEXT MORNING the air was unseasonably cold and a milk-white fog blew off the river and hung as thick as wet cotton on the two-acre tank behind my barn. As I walked along the levee I could hear bass flopping out in the fog. I stood in the weeds and cast a Rapala between two flooded willow trees, heard it hit the water, then began retrieving it toward me. The sun looked like a glowing red spark behind the gray silhouette of the barn.

I felt a hard, throbbing hit on the lure. I jerked the rod up to set the treble hook, but the lure rattled loose from the bass's mouth, sailed through the air, and clinked on the water's surface. Behind me I heard someone tapping loudly on my back door, then a truck engine grinding past the barn and through the field toward me.

Wilbur Pickett got out and walked up the levee in a pair of khakis and cowboy boots and a denim jacket cut off at the armpits.

"They're flopping out there, ain't they?" he said.

"There's a pole and a coffee can of worms by that willow," I said.

"Lordy, this is a nice place. I aim to have one like it someday," he said, squatting down to thread a night crawler on his hook.

"You doing all right?" I said.

He swung the cork and weighted line out into the fog.

"My wife sees pictures in her head. It scares me sometimes. She says you got dead people following you around," he said.

"I don't see any."

"She said these are people you killed down in Old Mexico. I told her I never heard no such thing." He looked straight ahead, a nervous flicker in the corner of his eye.

I reeled in my line and rested my rod against the trunk of a redbud tree. I watched a cottonmouth moccasin swimming through the shallows, its body forming and re-forming itself like an S-shaped spring.

"Billy Bob?" Wilbur said.

"They were heroin mules. They got what they deserved," I said.

"That don't sound like you."

"I've got to get to work," I said.

He rubbed his palm on his forehead, and his eyes searched in the fog, as though looking for words that weren't part of his vocabulary. I saw his throat swallow. "She says you're a giver of death. She says it's gonna happen again."

"What will happen again?"

"She says there's spirits that want revenge. It's got to do with human heads in a garden in Africa. It don't make no sense. I ain't up to this. I ain't never hurt nobody. I don't want to have nothing to do with this kind of stuff," he said.

He dropped the cane pole across a willow branch and got into his paint-skinned truck and began grinding the starter.

"Wilbur, get down here and talk," I said.

His engine caught and he twisted his head back toward me as he turned the wheel with both hands.

"You killed people and you ain't sorry? That ain't the Billy Bob Holland I always knowed. Why'd you tell me that?" he said, his eyes wet.

He roared through the field, the tall grass whipping under his front bumper, trash blowing from the bed of his truck.

4

LATE THE NEXT AFTERNOON I RECEIVED A PHONE
call from Kippy Jo Pickett, Wilbur's wife.

"They tore up our house. They ripped the floor out
of the barn," she said.

"Who did?" I said.

"The sheriff and his men."

"Did he have a search warrant?"

"He said he did. He kept rattling a paper in front
of me. He smelled like liquor," she said.

"Where's Wilbur?" I asked. "They drove him
out to the hills. When they brought him back, he
wouldn't come in the house," she replied.

A HALF HOUR LATER I parked in Wilbur's dirt drive
and walked around the side of the house to the back,
where he was burning trash in an oil barrel. His shirt
hung on a fence post and his skin looked like warm
tallow in the yellow and red light of the fire. The
kitchen window was at my back. I turned and looked
through the screen into the sightless eyes of Kippy
Jo.

"I'm sorry. I didn't see you there," I said, regain-
ing my breath.

She walked away from the sink without answering.

Wilbur glanced up from his work, then went on shoving a stack of splintered boards into the flames.

"Hugo Roberts drove you out in the hills?" I said.

Wilbur sucked in one side of his mouth. "He showed me what was left of a cougar that got caught in a hoop wire. He said the more it fought, the more it cut itself up."

"He threatened you?" I asked.

"He said we live way out here on the hardpan. He said Mexican dopers go through here at night sometimes. He wouldn't want none of them to catch Kippy Jo home alone, 'cause some of them ain't half human."

I waited for him to go on, but he didn't. His face looked flushed in the heat of the fire.

"You're not telling me something, Wilbur," I said.

"Hugo said he'd like to have a good boy like me as one of his deputies. He took his nine-millimeter out and stuck it down in my pants. Like this." Wilbur shoved the flattened ends of his fingers down under his belt buckle. "He pushed it on down till it was pressing against my privates. He told me, 'You're a natural-born lawman, Pickett.' His deputies was grinning from behind their sunglasses, like I was some kind of geek in a carnival."

"Hugo fears and hates people who have courage, Wilbur. That's why he's cruel," I said.

He speared a board into the flames, his eyes avoiding mine.

"He offered you a deal, didn't he?" I said.

"He said it don't matter if Deitrich gets the bonds back or not. I can say a fence burned me and took off without giving me no money. The insurance is gonna take care of it, anyway."

"Listen to Hugo Roberts and you'll be chopping cotton on Huntsville Farm."

"He's the man with the power."

"Goodbye, Wilbur."

I walked back out to my car. The scrub oak on the rim of the hills looked like stenciled black scars against the molten sun. I started the car engine, then turned it off and got back out and slammed the door. I stepped up on the gallery and opened the screen door without knocking. Kippy Jo was tucking in a fringed bedspread on the couch. She turned and stared in my direction.

"Did you tell your husband I was a giver of death?" I asked.

She folded her fingers in front of her, her eyes like white-flecked blue marbles, her very skin seeming to absorb the sounds around her. But she didn't speak.

"I not only killed drug transporters, I accidentally killed my best friend. If people want to talk about it, that's fine. I just don't want to listen to it," I said.

I let the screen swing back on the spring behind me. But my angry words brought me no comfort.

THAT NIGHT I DROVE down the road to the convenience store for a loaf of bread. I heard the car behind me before I saw it, its twin Hollywood mufflers rumbling off the asphalt. It was a customized 1949 Mercury convertible, with a grille like chromed teeth, the deep maroon finish overpainted with a tangle of blue and red flames blowing out of the hood. I turned into the convenience store and went inside, and the customized Mercury turned in after me and parked in the shadows by the side of the building.

When I came back out, two kids with baseball caps inverted on their heads were sitting in the convertible's front seat. A third kid stood on the pavement, throwing a tennis ball against the store wall.

He was bull-necked and thick-chested, his brown hair cut short, his T-shirt and beltless slacks as limp as rags against the hardness of his body. When I got into my Avalon, he threw the tennis ball against the front windshield. I opened the door and stood up, one foot still inside the car.

"Is there something I can help you with?" I asked.

"Yeah, Earl Deitrich's doing good for a lot of kids in San Antone. Why you bringing a crazy guy out of the woodwork to hurt him?" he said.

"Crazy guy?"

"Yeah, this guy burned kids up in a school bus, looks like a penis stuffed inside a suit, what's his name . . ." He snapped his fingers at the air. "Skyler Doolittle, he's telling lies about Earl Deitrich. We don't like that, man."

He leaned over and picked up his tennis ball, then stepped closer to me, kneading the ball like a sponge in his palm. There was a tattoo of a death's head on one side of his throat and on the other side a knife that was made to look like it had cut into the flesh and was dripping blood. The wind had dropped, and the heat rising from the pavement carried his odor into my face, a smell like reefer and unwashed hair and motor oil.

"Put it in a letter, bud, and I'll get back to you on that," I said.

"Bud? Who you think you're fucking with, man?" he said.

"You got me."

"My name's Cholo Ramirez. You heard of the Purple Hearts?"

"Cholo the warlord, right? There was a gal around here last Saturday by the name of Ramirez. She was with Earl Deitrich's son and a kid named Ronnie Cruise. You related?"

"Esmeralda? What you mean she was around here? She's going to the Juco. She don't have nothing to do with—hey, man, don't try to sling and bing with me. I can break your sticks."

I sat back down behind the wheel. But he grabbed the window jamb before I could pull the door shut.

"You telling me my sister was with Jeff Deitrich?" he said.

"Stand away from the car. I don't want to hit you backing out," I said.

"You pick the shit out of your teeth and answer me."

I dropped the Avalon into reverse, cut the wheels in a circle, and backed out into the light by the gas pumps, leaving Cholo Ramirez staring at me with his fists clenched by his sides, the veins in his arms pumped with blood.

EARLY THE FOLLOWING MONDAY I tapped on the frosted glass of Marvin Pomroy's office on the first floor of the courthouse. He sat behind his desk in his rimless glasses and blue suspenders and immaculate white, starched shirt, his hair neatly combed, his jaws ruddy and closely shaved, his eyes as placid and secure as a Puritan theologian's.

"Hugo Roberts redecorated Wilbur Pickett's house late Friday afternoon. He also stuck a nine-millimeter down Wilbur's fly," I said.

"I see Hugo Roberts five times a day. You don't have to tell me about his potential."

"I think he's more interested in a confession than in recovering stolen bonds."

"You're saying Hugo is on a pad for Earl Deitrich and Earl Deitrich is running a scam on the insurance company?"

"You know, that actually crossed my mind," I said.

His eyes rested calmly on my face. "We both know why you don't like Earl," he said. "But Peggy Jean asked you out there for that lunch, didn't she? How many women ask their old boyfriends to their husbands' business lunches? That doesn't strike you as peculiar?"

"Not with Peggy Jean. She's a decent and fine person."

Marvin got up from his chair and pulled open the window. He leaned on the sill and looked out at the oaks on the courthouse lawn and the mockingbirds flying in and out of the shade. "I'm coaching American Legion this year," he said. "For some reason I can't teach those boys not to swing on a change-up. Meanest pitch in baseball. The pitcher holds the ball in the back of his hand and messes up your head every time."

FOR LUNCH I WALKED OVER to the saloon and pool room next to the barbershop and ate a sandwich and drank a cup of coffee at the bar. The saloon was dark and had wood floors and an old mirror over the bar and was cooled by electric fans mounted on the walls.

Skyler Doolittle walked in from the glare of the street and stood at the end of the bar, twisting his torso one way, then another, his fused neck turning with his shoulders, until he saw me in back.

"This fellow Deitrich is trying to have me sent to the asylum. I want to hire you. Ain't nobody else around here gonna represent me. I want my watch back, too," he said.

"Why would Earl want to send you to an asylum, Mr. Doolittle?" I asked.

"The fellow's a cheat. I confronted him with it. In the Langtry Hotel dining room. In front of all them businessmen."

"I'm primarily a criminal defense lawyer. I don't know if I'm the right man for you, sir."

His eyes looked about the saloon, wide, frenetic. The pool players were bent over the tables in cones of light.

"I knowed your daddy years back. You was river-baptized," he said. "Immersed both in the reflection of the sky and the silt from Noie's flood. That means the earth and the heavens got you cupped between them, just like the hands of God. I ain't no crazy person, Mr. Holland. On a clear day like today I see everything the way it is. I'm haunted by them children. A crazy man don't walk around in Hell."

"The children in the bus accident?" I said.

"They talk to me out of the flames, sir. I don't never get rid of it."

The pool shooters nearby did not look in our direction, but their bodies seemed to hang motionlessly on the edges of the light that enveloped the tables.

"Why don't we walk on over to my office, Mr. Doolittle?" I said.

He fitted his Panama hat back on his head and stepped out the front door into the heat like a man braving a furnace.

• • •

I WORKED LATE in the office that evening. My air conditioner had broken and I opened the window and looked down onto the square at the cooling streets, the scrolled pink and purple and green neon on the Rialto Theater, the swallows dipping and gliding around the clock tower on the courthouse. Then I saw the sheriff's tow truck hauling Cholo Ramirez's customized 1949 Mercury through the square toward the pound.

The tow truck was followed by two cruisers that stopped on the side of the courthouse. Four uniformed deputies got out and escorted Esmeralda Ramirez, her wrists cuffed behind her, into the squat, one-story sandstone building that served as the office of Hugo Roberts.

I went back to my desk and tried to resume work. But I could not get out of my mind the image of four men dressed in khaki, their campaign hats slanted forward on their heads, the lead-gray stripes on their trousers creasing at the knees, marching a manacled girl into a building that looked like a blockhouse.

It started to sprinkle while the sun was still shining. I put on my coat and Stetson and walked across the street, then around the side of the courthouse lawn to the entrance of Hugo's office. Two of the deputies were smoking cigarettes by the door, their faces opaque, my own reflection looking back at me in their sunglasses. Out of the corner of my eye I saw

Temple Carrol carry a sack of groceries from the Mexican store on the side street to her Cherokee.

"What's the deal on the girl?" I said to the deputies.

"What's it to you?" one said.

"The '49 Mercury you were towing, a kid named Cholo was driving it the other night. He tried to give me some trouble," I said.

"We got a 911. The girl was weaving on the highway out by the Deitrich place. We found a vial with two rocks in it under the seat," the same deputy said.

"Is Hugo inside?" I asked.

"Yeah, but the office is closed."

"I'll just take a minute," I said, and went between them and pushed open the heavy oak door.

Hugo Roberts was sitting behind his desk, bent forward, his elbow propped on his blotter, toking on his cigarette while he watched a deputy shake down Esmeralda Ramirez against the wall.

Her palms were high up on the logs, her ankles spread, her midriff exposed above her jeans. Her dark hair hung down on both sides of her face. A uniformed deputy ran his hands down her armpits and ribs, his fingers brushing the edges of her breasts, then over her buttocks, up her thighs, until one hand came to rest firmly against her genitalia.

"You better get a female deputy in here, you sonofabitch," I said to Hugo.

"And you'd better get your ass out of here," he replied.

"Fuck you," I said.

"*What? What* did you say to him?" the deputy shaking down the girl said, straightening up now, his right hand clenching and unclenching. When I didn't answer, he shoved me in the breastbone with three fingers. "Boy, I'm about to turn you into a serious Christian."

Hugo's head was wreathed in cigarette smoke. "Kyle won't abide interference with an officer in the performance of his duty. I won't, either, Billy Bob," he said.

The deputy named Kyle snipped the cuffs on Esmeralda Ramirez's wrists again, this time in the front, and stuck his hand inside the back of her blue jeans and panties, knotting the fabric, his knuckles wedging into her buttocks, and pulled her toward a chair.

I grabbed his upper arm and spun him toward me. The skin of his face tightened against the bone, his teeth showing, his eyes glinting. He pulled a lead-weighted blackjack from his back pocket and wrapped his palm around the braided grip. I swung with my right and caught him just below the eye, snapping his head back, driving him into the wall.

Then I felt the old curse have its way, like kerosene evaporating on hot coals and igniting in an enclosed space, a yellow-red flash that burned away all restraint and always left me numb and shaking and unable to remember what I had just done.

I felt my fist sink to my wrist in his stomach, then

my boot arched into his face, the heel raking his mouth and nose, splitting the back of his head against a log in the wall.

But three other men were swinging at me now, with fists or batons or both, the blows showering across my back, and I knew I was about to slide into the bottom of a dark well where I would be safe from the angry faces that shouted down at me from above.

Then suddenly the room was still, speckled with blowing rain, the only sound that of the deputy named Kyle, on his hands and knees, spitting blood on the oak floor. Temple Carrol stood in the doorway, her extended arms and rounded shoulders and chestnut hair etched with the sun's last fiery glow.

"Ah, the testosterone boys in uniform at work and play. Hugo, you sorry sack of shit, please give me an excuse to blow your other lung out," she said.

AT THE SAME TIME that I, an officer of the court, was brawling with rednecks, a small man with thick glasses named Max Greenbaum was leaving a synagogue in the old Montrose district of South Houston. The rabbi, who had known Greenbaum for years, waved goodbye from the doorway. Greenbaum stopped at a post office and picked up a priority envelope, then drove into Herman Park and stopped by a tree-shaded lake and was writing on a legal pad when three cars filled with Mexican gangbangers pulled into the parking area, sealing off Max Greenbaum's Jeep.

It was dusk now, and the only other people at the lake were an elderly black couple and their grandchildren picnicking on the grass. The gangbangers' stereos roared with such ear-pounding volume that the water in the lake trembled. A kid who wore a bodybuilder's shirt deliberately scissored into strips threw a beer can in the direction of the picnickers.

"Hey, man, the park's closing," he said.

Then they pulled Max Greenbaum from his Jeep, lifted the cellular phone from his hand, and crushed it on the pavement.

"Y'all leave that man alone. He ain't done you nothing," the black woman yelled.

"Time to haul yo' black ham hocks out of here, mama," the kid in the scissored shirt said.

The elderly black couple loaded their grandchildren into their car and backed out into the road, their faces staring in bewilderment at the scene taking place before them.

One of the gangbangers tore Max Greenbaum's priority mail envelope and the sheet of letterhead paper it contained into shreds and threw them in his face. Then they formed a circle around him and began pushing him back and forth as they would a medicine ball.

But the terror that Max Greenbaum probably felt turned to anger and he began to fight, flailing blindly at the gangbangers with his fists, his glasses broken on the pavement. At first they laughed at him, then his finger scraped across someone's eyeball. A gang-banger reeled backwards, the heel of his hand pressed into his eye socket as though it had been gouged with a stick.

The circle closed on Greenbaum like crabs feeding on a piece of meat.

5

THE HOUSTON HOMICIDE DETECTIVE WHO called the next afternoon was a woman named Janet Valenzuela.

"The early word from the coroner is it looks like heart failure," she said.

"How'd you get my name?" I asked.

"The gangbangers picked up most of the pieces of the priority envelope. But a couple were under the victim's Jeep. We could make out your zip code and the last five letters of your name. Do you know why he would be writing you?"

"I think he had knowledge that would exonerate a client of mine," I said.

"Does this have to do with stolen bonds?"

"How'd you know?" I said.

"Greenbaum told his rabbi an uneducated workingman was being set up in an insurance claim. It's a muddy story. It has something to do with a guy being provoked at a luncheon, then stealing a watch, and a rich guy claiming hundreds of thousands of dollars in bonds were stolen, too. Are the gangbangers tied into this somehow?"

"I'm not sure."

"You were a city cop here?"

"That's right."

"Keep in touch."

An hour later Cholo Ramirez pulled his customized Mercury to the curb in front of my office, the stereo thundering. His sister, Esmeralda, got out and walked into the portico on the first floor.

A moment later she was standing in my office, dressed in the same jeans and maroon shirt, now thoroughly rumpled, she had been arrested in the day before.

"You're sprung?" I said, and smiled.

"They're not filing on me."

"How about the rock under the seat?"

"The cop was lying. Who'd be crazy enough to drive around in Cholo's car with crack in it?"

"They're bad guys. Who sicced them on you?" I said.

"I just came to thank you for what you did."

"Sit down a minute, will you?"

"I'm not feeling too good. There was noise in the jail all night."

Her face was pretty, her eyes turquoise. She pushed her hair up on her neck with one hand. A package of cigarettes stuck out of the front pocket of her jeans.

"You had a reason for being out by the Deitrichs' place?" I asked.

"I want Mr. Deitrich to leave my brother and Ronnie . . . Ronnie's my boyfriend . . . I want Mr. Deitrich to leave him and Cholo alone."

"You were going to tell him that?"

She blew her breath up in her face and sat down on the corner of the chair. "Look, he's a bullshit guy. Guys like him didn't make their money worrying about people who eat refried beans," she said.

"Earl Deitrich's got another agenda?"

"Hey, I'm glad you weren't hurt too bad yesterday. That's it," she said, and walked out of the office without saying goodbye.

TEMPLE CARROL COULD FIND a chicken feather in a snowstorm. Early Wednesday morning we drove out of the hill country toward San Antonio. She had already put together a folder on both Cholo Ramirez and Ronnie Cruise, also known as Ronnie Cross.

"Ronnie is a California transplant. He came out here with his uncle in '88. This customized car business they run may be a front for a chop-shop operation. Boost them here and sell them in Mexico," she said. "Anyway, Ronnie was in Juvie once in L.A. County, but that's his whole sheet."

"Jeff Deitrich says he threw a couple of guys off a roof," I said.

"My friend at San Antonio P.D. says two Viscounts got splattered all over a cement loading dock about a year ago. The word on the street is Ronnie did it. Supposedly the Viscounts had tried to molest Cholo's sister in a movie theater. Ronnie 'fronted them on the roof because Cholo was his warlord. Later Ronnie and Esmeralda developed the hots for each other. The stuff of great romance."

"I still don't get the tie to Earl Deitrich," I said.

"Maybe Earl's just helping out disadvantaged kids, Billy Bob. Maybe he's not a total bastard, even though some people would like to think so." She gave me a deliberate look.

I kept my eyes straight ahead. The country was rolling and green, and red Angus were grazing on a hill. A moment later I heard Temple take some papers out of a second folder.

"This kid Cholo is a walking nightmare," she said. "The mother's boyfriend threw him against the wall when he was a baby and probably damaged the brain. He has epileptic seizures and refuses all medication. He's been in the reformatory three times and a mental ward twice. My friend at San Antonio P.D. says every cop in the city treats him with extreme caution."

"What about that story Cholo told you, the one about taking down rich marks at a phony poker game?" I said.

"Nobody seems to know anything about it. He's been on crystal and acid half his life. He probably sees snakes in his breakfast food," she said.

The car garage where Ronnie Cruise worked for his uncle was in a Mexican neighborhood just outside of town, one with dust-blown streets and untrimmed banana and palm trees and stucco houses with tin roofs and alleyways that groaned with un-emptied garbage cans.

Ronnie Cruise was taller than he had seemed at the drive-in restaurant in Deaf Smith, his arms heavy with muscle, his bare chest flat, his lats thick, taper-ing away to a narrow waist. The inside of the shop was filled with antique cars that were either being re-stored or customized and rebuilt with high-powered, chromed engines. Ronnie Cruise walked outside with us into the shade, away from the noise, wiping his hands on a rag. He wore a red bandanna wrapped around his hair. His upper left arm was ringed with scar tissue like a band of dried putty.

"I had barbed wire tattooed there. Bad example in a time of AIDS. I had a doctor take it off," he said.

He leaned against the side of the building, one work boot propped against the stucco. He stuck an unlit cigarette in his mouth.

"Smoking bother you?" he said.

"Go ahead," Temple said.

He played with his lighter, then dropped the ciga-rette back in the package and put the package in his pocket.

"What's between the Purple Hearts and Earl Deitrich?" I asked.

"Nothing," he answered. He looked down the alley at a banana tree moving in the breeze.

"You just drive up to Deaf Smith to hang around with Jeff?" I said.

"How'd you know I been with Jeff?" he asked.

"I saw you and Esmeralda with him at Val's Drive-In," I said.

"Oh, yeah," he said, and nodded absently. "Look, my uncle don't want me taking off too long."

"Some gangbangers caused the death of an accountant down in Houston. You and Cholo hear anything about that?" Temple said.

"I don't get to Houston much. Anyway, I'm signing off on this stuff. So excuse me and maybe I'll see you some other time," he said.

"Cholo got Esmeralda out of jail. You didn't want to be there for her yourself?" I said.

"We're not getting along real good right now," he replied.

Then I took a chance.

"Is Jeff getting next to your girl? She got busted out by his house," I said.

He looked at the tops of his hands, his face impenetrable.

"I heard you took some whacks for her. That's the only reason we're talking now. But anything between me and Jeff is private business. I don't mean nothing personal by that," he said.

He untied the bandanna from his head and shook it out and walked back into the garage.

Temple watched him go back to work on the shell of a 1941 Ford, the flats of her hands inserted in her back pockets.

"That kid's a piece of work. You see him throwing two guys off a roof?" she said.

"With about as much emotion as spitting out his gum," I said.

THAT AFTERNOON I walked over to Marvin Pomroy's office in the courthouse. His secretary told me he was at the Mexican grocery store that was located just off the square. When I cut across the lawn toward the store, I thought I saw Skyler Doolittle walking on a side street, in his Panama hat and wilted seersucker, his upper torso bent forward, as though he wanted to arrive at his destination sooner than his body could take him.

I found Marvin Pomroy at a table under a wood-bladed fan in the back of the store, eating a taco while he read a book.

"I hope this is about baseball," he said.

"Was that Skyler Doolittle out there?" I asked.

"He came by and gave me a book. About Earl Deitrich's great-grandfather. Evidently the great-grandfather was an Alsatian diamond miner and slaver for the Belgians."

A uniformed deputy sheriff came in and bought a package of Red Man at the counter. He gave both of us a hard look before he went out.

"Esmeralda Ramirez isn't bringing sexual battery charges against Hugo's office, provided they don't charge you for punching out the deputy. Did you know that?" Marvin said.

"No, I didn't," I said. Marvin lifted his eyes into my face when I pulled out a chair and sat down without being invited. "Cut Wilbur Pickett loose."

"The state attorney's office seems to think he's a guilty man. I've gotten calls from a few other people, too." His eyes left mine and looked at nothing.

"Tell both them and Earl Deitrich to get lost," I said.

"Oh, yeah, that kind of statement makes people with money and power go away every time," he said.

We stared at each other in the silence. The breeze from the overhead fan ruffled the pages of the book he was reading. Marvin Pomroy was a good man who believed the system represented a level of integrity that somehow transcended the people who constantly manipulated it for their own ends. No amount of arguing or the personal battering of his soul had ever affected that faith. I knew nothing I said now would change that fact.

"Why'd Skyler Doolittle give you the book?" I asked.

"Hell if I know. I guess the great-grandfather was a genuine sonofabitch. He even wrote a handbook for the Belgian government on how to capture starved natives at night when they snuck into their gardens for food. Take a look at this picture. He used human skulls to border his flower beds . . . You all right?"

"Wilbur Pickett's wife talked about the same

thing. She saw the picture inside her head. It has something to do with spirits that want revenge."

He pinched his temples gingerly, then signaled the waitress for his check.

"I think I'll stroll on back to the office. Don't get up. Stay and have some iced tea. It's on me. Really," he said.

6

THAT EVENING I HAD AN UNEXPECTED VISITOR, my son, Lucas Smothers, who was finishing his first year at A&M. He parked his stepfather's pickup in the driveway and walked into the barn, where I was raking out the stalls and loading a wheel barrow for the compost heap. His snap-button cowboy shirt was open on his chest and his straw hat was slanted down on his head. He squatted on his long legs, pushed the brim of his hat up with his thumb, and squinted with one eye at the sun setting over the tank, as though a great philosophic consideration was at hand.

"I can think about a whole lot more fun things to do this evening," he said.

"Aren't you supposed to be up at school?" I asked.

"I got exams next week. You want to wet a line?" he said.

"How about I buy you a barbecue dinner out at Shorty's instead?"

"I ain't got no objection to that." He stood up and removed a Mexican spur from a peg on the wall and spun the rowel with one finger. It was one of the spurs my friend L.Q. Navarro had worn the night he died down in Coahuila. "I hear you been messing with the Purple Hearts," he said.

"Who told you this?"

"I saw Jeff Deitrich at Val's Drive-In."

"You know why his father would want to get mixed up with Mexican gangbangers?"

"I don't know about his old man. I know about Jeff, though."

"Oh?"

"His reg'lar is a gal named Rita Summers. I said to him once, 'She's sure a nice girl. In fact, she's got it all, don't she?' He goes, 'So does vanilla ice cream, Lucas. That don't mean you cain't try chocolate.'"

He spun the rowel on the spur, then hung the spur back on the peg.

We drove through the hills in the cooling shadows to Shorty's and ate dinner on a screen porch that rested on pilings above the river. The water was high and milky green, and it flowed around the edge of a hill and dropped over boulders into pools that were white with cottonwood seeds. The air was cool now and smelled of fern and wet stone, and when the sun set, Shorty, the owner, turned on the electric lights in the oak trees that shaded his picnic tables.

The country band on the dance floor was just warming up.

"Got me a job roughnecking this summer. Got a bluegrass gig in Fredericksburg, too," Lucas said.

"You've done great, bud," I said.

He smiled but his eyes were looking beyond me, through the screen, at the shadows of the trees on the cliff wall across the river.

"Be careful with Deitrich," he said.

"I don't think Earl's a real big challenge."

His fork paused in front of his mouth. Then he set it in his plate. "I ain't talking about Earl," he said. "Jeff used to go down to Austin to roll homosexuals. Not for the money. Just to stomp the shit out of them. I always been too ashamed to tell anybody I seen it."

His eyes were downcast when he picked up his fork again. His face looked curiously like a girl's.

PEGGY JEAN DIDN'T HAVE TO FLIRT to attract men to her. Oddly, a show of fatigue in her face, a buried injury, an unshared problem, made you want to step into her life and walk with her into the private places of the heart. Her vulnerability wove webs that allowed you to enter them without shame or caution.

On Thursday morning I saw her by her pickup truck at a farm supply and tack store on the edge of town. A clerk was carrying a western saddle from inside the store to the back of the truck while she waited by the open tailgate, a platinum American Express card held loosely between two fingers.

"Oh, hello, Billy Bob," she said when I walked up behind her. She wore tight riding pants and a checkered shirt and sunglasses, and she pushed her glasses more tightly against her face when she smiled.

"Beautiful saddle," I said.

"It's for Jeff's birthday." She kept one side of her

face turned from me, as though she were waiting for someone else to emerge from inside the store.

"You already paid, Ms. Deitrich?" the clerk said, looking at the credit card in her hand.

"No, I'm sorry. I'll go inside and take care of it," she replied.

"Let me have your card and I'll bring the charge slip out here for you to sign. It ain't no trouble at all," the clerk said, and took the card from between her fingers before she could reply.

Peggy Jean looked away awkwardly at the loading platform. Her skin high up on one cheekbone was heavily made up with rouge and powder.

"Everything okay, Peggy Jean?" I said.

"Oh yes, just one of those days," she said, then smiled, like an afterthought. "It's so windy out here today." She took a bandanna from her back pocket and tied it around her hair, knotting it under her chin.

"It's too bad about the accountant, that fellow named Greenbaum. He seemed like a nice man," I said.

"What are you talking about?"

"He's dead. He was jumped by some gangbangers at Herman Park in Houston."

"*Max?* When?"

"I'm sorry. I thought y'all knew."

"No . . . I heard nothing . . . You're talking about Max Greenbaum?"

She seemed to look about her, as though the answer to her confusion were inside the wind.

I stepped closer to her, my fingers touching her elbows.

"I'll drive you home," I said.

"No . . . Absolutely not . . . Billy Bob, please,
just . . ."

She walked away from me and stood in the shade
by the driver's door of her pickup, her arms folded in
front of her, as though she were creating a sanctuary
that I couldn't enter. The clerk came out of the store
with her credit card and charge slip attached to a
clipboard. Then he saw her expression and his face
turned inward and he lowered his eyes.

"If you'll just sign this, ma'am, I'll take care of
everything and you can be on your way," he said.

"Peggy Jean—" I began.

"I'm sorry for my lack of composure. *Max?* No,
there's a mistake about this," she said, and got in her
truck and scoured a cloud of pink dust out of the
parking lot.

I SAT IN THE HALF-LIGHT of my office and drank
a cup of coffee. On the wall, encased in glass on a
field of blue felt, were the .36-caliber Navy Colt
revolvers and octagon-barrel lever-action '73 Winchester rifle that had been carried by my great-
grandpa Sam Morgan Holland when he was a drover
on the Chisholm Trail. In his life he had also been in
the Fourth Texas at Little Round Top, a violent
drunkard who shot five or six men in gun duels, and

finally a saddle preacher who took his ministry into the godless moonscape west of the Pecos.

The bluing on Sam's weapons had long ago been rubbed off by holster wear, and the steel now had the dull hue of an old nickel. In Sam's diary he described his encounters with John Wesley Hardin, Wild Bill Longley, and the Dalton-Doolin gang, all of whom he loathed as either psychopaths or white trash. But in his account of their depredations there is never an indication that the worst of them ever struck a woman.

In the historical South the physical abuse of a woman by a man was on a level with sodomy of animals. Such a man was considered a moral and physical coward and was merely horsewhipped if he was lucky.

But today a woman who did not flee the batterer or seek legal redress was usually consigned to her fate, even considered deserving of it.

I wondered what Great-Grandpa Sam would do in my situation.

I set my empty coffee cup in my saucer, opened my Rolodex to the "D" section, and punched a number into my telephone.

"Earl?" I said.

"Yes?"

"Who hit your wife?"

"What?"

"You heard me. On the right side of her face."

"You've got some damn nerve."

"So it was you?"

"You keep your carping, self-righteous mouth off my family."

"Touch her again and I'll catch you out in public. Everything you own or you can buy won't help you."

He slammed down the phone. I sat for a long time in the pale light glowing through the blinds, the fingers of my right hand curling into the oil and moisture on my palm.

THAT EVENING a lacquered red biplane dropped out of an absolutely blue sky, circled once over the river, and landed in the pasture beyond the tank. I got into the Avalon and drove past the chicken run and barn and windmill and out through the tall grass that grew at the foot of the levee. When I came around the willows at the far end of the tank I saw the man named Bubba Grimes, who had claimed that Wilbur Pickett had tried to sell him bearer bonds; he was leaning against the fuselage of his plane, pouring from a dark bottle of Cold Duck into a paper cup.

"You tend to show up in a peculiar fashion, Mr. Grimes," I said, getting out of the Avalon.

He set down the bottle on the bottom wing of his plane and grinned at the corner of his mouth. His drooping left eye looked like gray rubber that had melted and cooled again.

"Got an offer for you. Wilbur Pickett is about to have some bad luck. Price is right, I can change all that," he said.

"Wilbur's a poor man, Mr. Grimes. That means I'd have to give you money out of my own pocket. Now, why would I want to do that?"

"To bring down Earl Deitrich. The word is you topped his wife."

"I think it's time for you to get back in your plane."

He drank his paper cup empty and tossed it in the weeds. "The man's weakness is gambling. You want my hep, here's my number. The two of us can mess him up proper," he said, and shoved a penciled piece of notepad paper in my shirt pocket with two fingers.

"Get off my property," I said.

He cut his head. "I cain't blame you for not wanting to know your own mind. That woman's special. She's got a fragrance like roses. In Africa once, she'd been out working in the heat and she come in the tent, and the smell was like warm roses. It's too bad rich men always get the pick of the brooder house."

In the red light his face was filled with a glow that was both saccharine and lustful. When he took off, he raised his bottle in salute; his plane clipped the top of a willow tree and scattered leaves behind him like green bird feathers.

FIVE DAYS LATER Lucas Smothers came to my office and sat in the swayback deerhide chair in the corner and took off his hat and gazed out the window. He had been working in the fields with his stepfather, and I could smell an odor like grass and milk in his clothes. He had his mother's blue eyes, and the light seemed to enter and hold inside them as it would inside tinted crystal. His expression was deliberately innocuous, as it always was when he felt caught between his need to instruct and caution me and at the same time protect me from the knowledge of what his generation, with its rapacious addictions, was really like.

"A guy who runs around with Jeff? He told me this crazy story about him, about how Jeff ain't always in control like he pretends. It's a little off the wall, though," he said.

"I'll try to handle it," I said.

"That Mexican girl who got busted out on the highway, Esmeralda? It was Jeff called the cops on her. His friend says Jeff did a one-nighter with her. Except she won't go away and the truth is Jeff don't want her to, no matter what he tells himself and everybody else."

I had to be in court in twenty minutes and I tried not to let my attention wander or my eyes drop to my wristwatch.

"So a couple of nights ago Jeff drives his girlfriend, Rita Summers, down to this Mexican restaurant north of San Antone where Esmeralda works. Jeff's gonna show Esmeralda there's nothing between them and Rita is his reg'lar and he ain't afraid to get it all out in the open, if that's what it takes.

"All his buds are there, cranking down tequila sunrises and Carta Blanca, after they been smoking dope all the way from Deaf Smith. When Esmeralda walks by with a tray, some guy goes, 'I never thought I'd like to have sloppy seconds on a pepperbelly.'

"Jeff's face looked like he'd eaten a tack. Rita Summers don't say anything for a long time, then she calls Esmeralda over and goes, 'Excuse me, but this food tastes like dog turds.'

"Esmeralda looks back at her real serious and says, 'I know. That's why I don't eat here.'"

"Pretty funny story," I said.

He sat forward in his chair and folded his hands between his knees, his eyes staring at a place on the rug.

"Jeff can be a rough guy. But getting it on with Ronnie Cross's girl? Three white guys jumped Ronnie after a football game. He beat them up so bad one of them got down on his knees and begged," he said.

"You worried about me?"

"Ronnie's girl was in your office. You had a run-in with Cholo. Something real bad's gonna come out of this. It's like the feeling I had when I was a kid. I'd wake up in the morning and there was a sick feeling around my heart, like a hand was squeezing it."

"These kids don't have anything to do with my life, Lucas," I said.

He looked out the window at the trees blowing in the wind, his skin puckered under one eye.

"Wilbur Pickett started all this. Now he's dragging you into his bullshit," he said. "You older people don't have no idea what goes on in this town. Y'all ain't never known."

He stared down at the frayed bottoms of his jeans to hide the anger in his face.

THAT NIGHT IT STORMED and the house was cool and filled with wind and the smell of ozone. On nights like this I used to hear the tinkle of L.Q. Navarro's spurs, then he would be standing next to me in the library, the lightning flickering through the window on his grained skin and his lustrous black eyes.

L.Q. lived in my memory—in fact, was always present in some way in my life—but I didn't feel guilt about his death any longer and I seldom saw him during my waking hours. I kept his custom-made, blue-black .45 revolver and his holster and cartridge belt in the top drawer of my desk, and sometimes I removed it from the leather and opened the loading gate and turned the cylinder one click at a time, peering through the whorls of light in each empty chamber, my palm wrapped around the yellowed ivory handles that seemed warm and sentient from his callused grip.

But L.Q. knew me better than I knew myself. On his visitations he would chide, *"Tell me it wasn't fun busting caps on them Mexican dope mules."*

And when I thought too long about our nocturnal raids into Old Mexico, I became like the untreated drunkard who has renounced whiskey, until in his denunciation he unconsciously begins to rub his lips with the flats of his fingers.

And just as I always did when these moments occurred, I drove to the small stucco church in a rural working-class neighborhood where I went to Mass and lighted a candle for L.Q. Navarro, for whom I converted to Catholicism after his death, as though somehow I could extend his life by taking on his faith.

Then I went next door to a clapboard cafe that served buffalo burgers and blueberry milk shakes and sat by the screen window and watched the lightning flicker on the pines in front of the church and listened to the thunder roll harmlessly away into the hills.

Lucas Smothers had tried to warn me about the youth culture, if one could call it that, of south-central Texas.

Why should he even have felt the need?

The answer was that Lucas, like L.Q. Navarro, knew me better than I knew myself.

I should have been able to walk away from the complexities surrounding the defense of Wilbur Pickett.

But the problem was a fragrance of roses. Bubba Grimes, the pilot with the drooping left eye, had said it. When Peggy Jean perspired she smelled like warm roses. She smelled like roses and bruised grass in an oak grove and skin that's sun-browned and cool and warm at the same time. All I had to do was close my eyes and I was back there in that heart-twisting moment with my face buried in her hair, unaware that she and I were creating a memory for which I would never find an adequate surrogate.

THE NEXT MORNING Hugo Roberts left a message on my office answering machine.

"We just made a second trip out to Wilbur Pickett's place. Guess what? That poor li'l pecker-wood had a couple of them bonds hid in the panel of his wife's dresser. Thought I'd just keep you up to date. Have a good day."

7

My son, Lucas, had told me that the other people of Deaf Smith had never known what really went on in our town. He was right. We talked about younger people as though they were no different from the generations of years past. Somehow the eye did not register the kids who were stoned by second period at the high school, the girls who had abortions, the kids infected with hepatitis and herpes and gonorrhea, or the ones who passed their backpacks through a window so they could get their guns past the school's metal detectors.

A kid upon his knees in front of a toilet bowl, strings of blood hanging from his broken lips, the jean-clad legs of his tormentors surrounding him like bars, is a sad sight to witness. The fact that the teachers know better than to intervene is even sadder.

But if we saw younger people as they were, we'd have to examine ourselves as well. We'd have to ask ourselves why we allowed people like Hugo Roberts to dwell in our midst.

By the time I had listened to his voice on the message machine and walked over to his office, he had another revelation to make. The only light in his blockhouse of an office came from the desk lamp;

the upward glow from the shaded bulb made his face look like a wrinkled tan balloon floating in the gloom.

"We picked up that ole boy Skyler Doolittle. He says he's your client," he said.

"Not exactly. What'd he do?"

"Hanging around the playground at the elementary, trying to give them kids candy bars."

"We have an ordinance about giving away candy bars?"

"You can be cute, Billy Bob. But I've dug children out of leaf piles and garbage dumps. Y'all do that in the Rangers?"

"I came over here for only one reason, Hugo. You planted those bonds in Wilbur Pickett's house. You'll wish you didn't."

He grinned and picked up a pen from his blotter and popped off the cap. He worked the head of the pen in and out of the cap.

"You seen that Mexican girl lately, what's her name, Esmeralda something?" he said.

I WALKED ACROSS the lawn to the main courthouse, where Skyler Doolittle was sitting on a wood bench inside a holding cage between the jailer's office and the back elevator. In his long-sleeve white shirt and wide red tie, his bald head and fused neck looked exactly like the domed top of a partially repainted fire hydrant.

"I'll have you out of here in about a half hour. But I think it's a good idea you not go around the school yard again," I said.

"I wouldn't harm them kids," he said.

"I know you wouldn't," I said. His eyes that were between gray and colorless seemed to take on a measure of reassurance. "By the way, my investigator checked around and didn't find any indication Earl Deitrich is trying to put you in an asylum. So maybe you were worried unduly on that score, Mr. Doolittle."

"Those sheriff's deputies called me a sex pervert. They said they'd had their eye on me. They said the state's got a special place for my kind."

I laced my fingers in the wire mesh of the cage. He looked like the most isolated and socially and physically rejected human being I had ever seen.

"Some Mexican gangbangers made mention of you to me, Mr. Doolittle. Maybe they're the same kids who caused the death of a Jewish man in Houston. I think you're a decent and good man, sir. I suspect your word is your bond. In that spirit I ask you to leave Earl Deitrich alone," I said.

He seemed to study my words inside his head, his mouth flexing at the corners.

"If you ask it of me. Yes, sir, I won't give him no more trouble," he said.

When I walked past the elevator, one that looked like a jail cell on cables, two uniformed deputies were struggling with a waist-chained black inmate in county whites. The inmate's left eye was cut and white foam issued from his mouth.

"What are you staring at? Sonofabitch drank out of a fire extinguisher," one deputy said.

The second deputy looked at me with recognition, his arm locking simultaneously around the black man's struggling head.

"Hey, your client, the freak in the cage? We pick him up again on the same beef, he's going out of here a steer," he said.

THAT EVENING a tornado destroyed an entire community south of us and killed over thirty people. I rode Beau, my Morgan, out into the fields and watched the dust blowing on the southern horizon and the rain clouds moving like oil smoke across the sun. I turned Beau back toward the house just as the rain began to march across the fields and dimple the river.

The sky turned black and the temperature must have dropped twenty degrees. I turned on the lights in the barn and tied on a leather apron and pried a loose shoe off Beau's back left hoof. A car turned off the highway into my drive, paused for a moment by the side of the porch, then rolled slowly to the front of the barn.

Its headlights were on high beam and shone directly into my eyes.

I picked up a hammer off the anvil and stood just inside the opened doors of the barn. The headlights went off and I saw a chopped, sunburst 1961 T-Bird, with chrome wire wheels and an oxblood leather interior, full of Mexican kids. Ronnie Cruise cut the engine and walked through the rain into the barn.

He wore baggy black trousers and a form-fitting ribbed undershirt and a rosary with purple glass beads around his neck; his shoulders looked tan and hard and were beaded with water.

"That's quite a car," I said.

"Me and Cholo built it. I done a lot of custom work for people around here," he said. His eyes dropped momentarily to the hammer in my hand. "You think we're here to 'jack your Avalon, man?"

"You tell me."

"I didn't mean to dis you at the garage. But see—" He held his fingers up in the air and looked at them as he spoke, as though they held the words he needed. "See, I heard what the lady said when my back was turned, about two guys going off a roof. Like, that's the story somebody told you. But you didn't have the respect to ask me about it. I don't think that's too cool, man."

"So maybe it's none of our business."

"Yeah, well, I'll clear it up for you. A couple of Viscounts put their hands all over a girl in a theater. Then when they had to explain theirselves they got scared and like the punks they were they pulled a nine. Maybe the guy they pulled it on got it away from them and chased them across a couple of roofs. So the two Counts decided they were gonna jump to a fire escape. They almost made it. But the guy didn't throw nobody off a roof . . ." His eyes searched my face. "Why you keep looking at me like that?"

"Because I don't have any idea why you're here."

He cut his eyes sideways and exhaled through his nose.

"There's a tornado out there and I couldn't get back home," he said.

"Y'all want some coffee?"

He pawed at his cheek with three fingers. "Yeah, I think that'd be nice," he said.

I went into the house and brought back a pot of coffee and a paper sack full of tin cups. His friends, two girls and two boys, all of them wearing caps backwards on their heads, sat on hay bales or walked idly through the stalls, touching saddles, coils of polyrope, rakes, hoes, mattocks, bridles, a pair of chaps, axes, and fire tongs as though they were historical artifacts.

I rasped Beau's hoof smooth and reshoed it, then led him toward his stall. Ronnie Cruise stepped behind him to get to the coffeepot, and Beau's back hooves slashed into the air like jackhammers. Ronnie grabbed his shinbone, his face white with pain, his shirtfront drenched with coffee. I grabbed him by one arm and eased him down on a hay bale.

"You all right?" I said.

"Oh yeah. I always like getting my spokes broken." He rocked forward, squeezing his shin with both hands.

"Let me show you something. You can walk be-hind a horse all you want as long as you let him know what you're doing," I said.

I ran my hand and arm along Beau's spine and rump and let my body brush close into his when I moved across his hindquarters. "An animal is just like a human being. He fears what he doesn't under-stand. Here, step up beside me," I said.

Ronnie Cruise rose to his feet, then hesitated, his tongue wetting his bottom lip. I picked up his hand by the wrist and set it on Beau's rump, then pulled Ronnie toward me. Beau twisted his head once so he could see us, then blew out his breath and shifted his weight on the plank floor.

"See?" I said.

"Yeah."

"Your leg okay?"

"Yeah, no problem." His face was inches from mine now.

"Do me a favor, will you?" I said.

"What?"

"Don't wear a rosary as a piece of jewelry."

Raindrops as big as marbles clattered on the tin roof. He stared back at me, his mouth cone-shaped with incomprehension.

IN THE MORNING the San Antonio and Austin and local newspapers were filled with news about the tornado that had scoured an entire town out of the earth. But they also carried a wire story about a fire that had burned down half a city block in Houston later the same day.

Before I could finish reading the newspaper's account of the fire, the phone next to my kitchen table rang. It was the Houston homicide detective whose name was Janet Valenzuela.

"Why is it people from Deaf Smith keep showing up in my caseload?" she said.

"You've lost me," I said.

"It's not a good story," she said.

The fire had started in the bottom of an empty office building that had once housed a savings and loan company. The rooms had been filled with stacked office furniture, rolled carpets stripped from the floors, jars of paint thinner, and paper packing cases left behind by the movers. The fire rippled across the exposed dry wood in the floors, snaked up the walls, flattening temporarily against the ceiling, then blew glass onto the sidewalks and curled outside onto the brick facade.

Five minutes later the ceiling collapsed and the second- and third-story windows were filled with a yellow-red brilliance like the marbled colors inside a foundry.

A fireman inside the fourth-floor stairwell used his radio to report what he swore was the voice of a child. Three other firemen went into the building, and together they worked their way from room to room on the fourth floor, ripping open doors with their axes, their heavy coats and the inside of their face shields starting to superheat from the flames crawling up the walls.

Then a fireman yelled into his radio: "It's a doll. A talking doll. Oh God, the tiger's got us . . . Tell my wife I . . ."

The fire, fed by a sudden rush of cold air, turned the brick shell of the building into a chimney swirling with flame. The roof exploded into the night sky like a Roman candle.

"The doll was one of these battery-operated jobs. We think a homeless woman left it in there and the heat set it off," Janet Valenzuela said.

"How'd the fire start?"

"Winos and street people live in there. Somebody saw some Hispanic kids hanging around earlier. The place was filled with accelerants. Take your choice."

"Why are you calling me?"

"The building belonged to a savings and loan company before it went bankrupt and was seized by the government. But the land it stood on is owned by a man named Earl Deitrich. That's the guy Max Greenbaum was an accountant for. Funny coincidence, huh?"

"Come up and see us sometime. Widen your horizons," I said.

"If it's arson and homicide on federal property, you'll get to meet us as well as the FBI. Say, does this guy Deitrich know any Houston gang members?"

"You ever hear of a bunch called the Purple Hearts in San Antone?" I asked.

"Say again?"

AT LUNCHTIME I WALKED from my office to our town's one health club and sat in the steam room with my back against the tiles. The bruises from the baton blows I had taken in Hugo Roberts's office looked like purple and yellow carrots under my skin. I dipped a sponge in a bucket of water and squeezed it over my head, then lay on my back and stretched my muscles by pulling my knees toward my chest.

When I walked into the shower two of the men who had beaten me were lathering themselves with the showerheads turned off. Their bodies were tanned and hard and streaked with soapy hair, their eyes malevolent and invasive. I put my head under the shower and turned on both faucets and let the water boil over my face.

TEMPLE CARROL MET ME in the courtroom, where a client of mine, a twenty-year-old four-time loser with alcohol fetal syndrome, was being arraigned for holding up the convenience store where he used to work. He had used no mask or disguise and his weapon had been a BB pistol.

The judge's name was Kirby Jim Baxter. His face

was furrowed and white, like a bleached prune, and it stayed twisted in an expression of chronic impatience and irritability.

"You back again? What the hell's the matter with you? You want to spend the rest of your life getting pissed on by a prison guard's horse?" he said.

My client, Wesley Rhodes, had a harelip, a flat nose, an I.Q. of eighty, and wide-set reptilian-green eyes that seemed to contain separate thoughts at the same time. He stuffed socks inside his fly and wore motorcycle boots with elevated soles and two heavy, long-sleeve shirts that made his upper torso splay from his Levi's like a cloth-wrapped stump.

I began to run through the same old shuck that every judge hears when people like Wesley have their bail set. "Your Honor, my client has entered an alcoholic treatment program and is attending A.A. meetings daily. We'd like to request—"

"Did I address you, counselor?" Kirby Jim said.

"No, Your Honor."

"Then shut up. Now, you listen, young man—"

It should have been a cakewalk. Kirby Jim was annoyed with the planet in general, but he wasn't a bad man. He was sympathetic to the fact that people like Wesley Rhodes had no chance from the day they were born. He also knew that inside the system Wesley was anybody's bar of soap.

"It wasn't armed robbery 'cause there wasn't no BBs in the gun. I was in there to buy a magazine. My daddy said to tell y'all that and to kiss my ass. I ain't afraid to go back. Horses don't piss on people unless you get under them, anyway. So that shows how damn much *you* know," he said, and turned his grinning, pitiful face on me, as though his wit had forever destroyed the Texas legal system.

"Bail is set at ten thousand dollars. Bailiff, take him away," Kirby Jim said.

That's what most of it is like.

OUTSIDE, TEMPLE AND I SAT under the trees on a steel-ribbed bench by the Spanish-American War artillery piece. It was warm in the shade and the trees were full of jays and mockingbirds.

"It's not your fault. That kid had a millstone around his neck when he was born," she said.

"I was thinking of something else." I told her of the visit to my house by Ronnie Cruise the previous night and the fire that had burned down the empty savings and loan building on Earl Deitrich's property in Houston.

"You think these Mexican kids did it and Ronnie Cruise was setting up an alibi?" she asked.

"Maybe."

"Who cares? They're street rats. It's not related to defending Wilbur Pickett, anyway."

"I don't like getting used."

She straightened herself on the bench, pressing the heels of her hands against the metal. I felt the edge of her hand wedge against mine.

"You want to feel these kids aren't all greaseballs. The truth is they are," she said.

"You're too hard, Temple."

"It's a habit I got into down in Fort Bend County after I let a gangbanger ride in the back of my cruiser without cuffs. He paid back the favor by wrapping his belt around my throat," she said.

I looked at her profile. She lifted a wisp of her chestnut hair off her forehead and fanned her face with a magazine. Her mouth was red and small, her skin moist and pink with the heat. Her eyes had the same milky green color as the river that ran through our county, and they often had shadows in them, just the way the river did when the current flowed under a tree. Her uplifted chin and the parting of her lips made me think of a flower opening in the shade.

"You staring at me for a reason?" she said.

"Sorry. You're a real pal, Temple."

"A pal? Oh yes," she said, standing up. "Always glad to be a pal. See you later, cowboy. Don't let your worries over the Purple Hearts screw up your day."

I STILL HADN'T EATEN LUNCH and I walked over to the Langtry Hotel. It had been built of sandstone in the nineteenth century, with a wood colonnade over the elevated sidewalk that was still inset with tethering rings. Supposedly the Sundance Kid and his schoolteacher mistress, Etta Place, had stayed there, as well as the vaudevillians Eddie Foy and

Will Rogers. The upstairs rooms were boarded up now, but the old bar, with its white, octagon-tile floor and stamped tin ceiling, was still open, as well as the dining room, which was paneled with carved mahogany and oak and hung with chandeliers that when lighted looked like yellow ice.

Diagonally parked in front of the entrance was Earl Deitrich's maroon Lincoln, its chrome wire wheels and immaculate white sidewalls blazing in the sunlight. The velvet curtains were open in the dining room and I could see Earl and Peggy Jean at a long, linen-covered table with some of the town's leading businesspeople. Peggy Jean, whom I had never seen drink, had an Old-Fashioned glass in her hand.

Don't go in. Leave them alone, I thought.

Then, with all the caution of a drunk careening down a sidewalk, I thought, Like hell I will.

I sat at a small table by the window, across the room from them, and ordered. Earl and his friends were in high spirits, garrulous and loud, Earl's laughter even more cacophonous than the others, as though it welled up from some irreverent and arrogant knowledge about the world that only he possessed.

I listened to it for five minutes, then could take it no longer. On the table next to me was an abandoned copy of the morning paper. I folded it in half and walked to Earl's table and set it by his elbow, so the headline about the fire in Houston could not escape his vision.

"Too bad about those four firemen who got burned to death on your property last night," I said.

The mirth in his face died like air leaking from a balloon.

"Yes. It's a terrible thing. I've been keeping in touch by telephone," he said.

"Hugo Roberts's trained cretins picked up Skyler Doolittle on a bogus beef. I think you know what I'm talking about," I said.

"No, I don't," he said.

"You cheated him at cards. He got in your face about it. So you had Hugo's Brownshirts roust him."

Earl smiled tolerantly and shook his head. The other men at the table looked like they had been frame-frozen in a film, their hands poised on a napkin, a water glass, their eyes neutral.

"Go back to your table, sir," the owner, a California entrepreneur, said behind me.

"No, no, he's invited here. You sit down with us, Billy Bob," Peggy Jean said, her throat flushed, her mouth stiff and unnatural and cold-looking from the whiskey and iced cherries in her Old-Fashioned glass.

I put one hand on the table and leaned down toward Earl's face. His fine brown hair hung on his brow.

"You paid Hugo Roberts to plant evidence on Wilbur Pickett. Then you shamed and humiliated a handicapped man. I'm going to take what you've done and shove it up your sorry ass," I said.

"You went to night school and earned a law degree

and are to be admired for that. But you're still white trash at heart, Billy Bob. And that's the only reason I don't get up and knock you down," he replied.

I turned and walked stiffly past my table, left a dollar for having used the place setting, and went up the stairs through the old darkened lobby, past the empty registration desk and pigeonholes for guest mail and room keys and the dust-covered telephone switchboard, into the shade under the colonnade and the wind that blew like a blowtorch across the asphalt.

I was a half block down the street when I heard Peggy Jean's voice behind me. "Billy Bob, wait. I need to talk with you. Don't go away like this."

She was on high heels, and when she started toward me she twisted one ankle and had to grab on to a wood post. Then Earl was on the sidewalk beside her, and the two of them began to argue with the attempted restraint of people whose lives are coming apart on a stage. I stood in the middle of the sidewalk, under a candy-striped barbershop awning, like a foolish and impotent spectator who cannot bring himself to either flee or participate in the fray.

"You're tight. Go sit in the lobby. I'll have some coffee sent out," Earl said.

"You had that handicapped man arrested? Over a card game?" she asked incredulously.

"I didn't. He's demented. He's been in prison for killing schoolchildren, for God's sake." Then Earl waved his hands in the air and slapped them against his hips in exasperation. "I give up," he said, and went back into the hotel.

But he didn't stay. He was right back out on the sidewalk. "To hell with it. Just to hell with it. Go back inside and eat something. I'll send Fletcher with the limo," he said, and got into his Lincoln and backed out into the street while Peggy Jean propped herself against the colonnade's post and pulled off her broken high-heel shoe.

"You want a glass of iced tea?" I said to her.

"Tea. Aspirin. Heroin. Anything. I feel like a train wreck," she said.

"Why don't you sit down on the bench? I'll get my car."

I told myself my gesture was an innocent one. Perhaps it was. You didn't abandon an impaired friend in a public place and leave her to swelter in the heat and her own embarrassment while she waited on the mercies of an irresponsible husband.

Yes, I'm absolutely sure I thought those thoughts.

We drove north of town toward her home, then she asked to stop at a steak house that was built on an escarpment overlooking a long valley. When she got out of the car she deliberately knocked the heel off her other shoe on an ornamental boulder by the restaurant door, then put her shoes back on as flats and went in the ladies' room and washed her face and put on fresh makeup and came back out and sat at a table with me by the back window.

The restaurant was cool and softly lit and deserted

except for a bartender and a waiter. Clouds covered the sun now, and the valley below us was blanketed with shadow and the wind blew the grass and wild-flowers in channels like the fingers of a river.

The jukebox was playing an old Floyd Tillman song. Her face seemed to go out of focus with a private thought or maybe with an after-rush from the Old-Fashioneds. Then she fixed her eyes on me as though I were walking toward her out of a dream.

"Dance with me," she said.

"I'm not very good at it," I said.

"Please, Billy Bob. Just one time."

And that's what we did, on a small square of polished yellow hardwood floor, balloons of color rippling through the plastic casing of the jukebox. She placed her cheek against mine, and I could smell bourbon and candied cherries and bitters and sweet syrup and sliced oranges on her breath, as though all the blended, chilled odors of what she had consumed had been refermented and heated inside her heart's blood and breathed out again against my skin.

Then her head brushed against my face and I smelled a fragrance of roses in her hair. Her loins, when they touched mine, were like points of fire against my body, and I knew I was entering a country where the rules that had always governed my life were about to be irrevocably set aside.

8

AT SUNSET THAT EVENING I DROVE OUT TO Wilbur Pickett's place on the hardpan. The sun had dropped behind the hills in the west and the afterglow looked like fires were burning inside the trees on the hills' rim.

Wilbur and his wife, Kippy Jo, had moved their kitchen table out into the middle of the backyard and were eating ears of corn they had roasted on a barbecue pit. His pasture was dimpled with water and had turned emerald green from yesterday's storm, and his Appaloosa and two palominos were drinking out of the tank by his windmill, their tails switching across their hindquarters. Parked by the barn was an ancient snub-nosed flatbed truck loaded to the top of the slats with rattlesnake watermelons.

"I'm trying to put your trial off as long as I can. A guy like Earl Deitrich eventually sticks his hand in a porcupine hole," I said.

"Don't matter to me. I got these ole boys down in Venezuela just about sold on this pipeline job. You still got time to get in on it."

It was like talking to a child.

"Good-looking melons," I said.

"I went on down through Rio Grande City and got

me a mess of them. I'm gonna flat clean up on that li'l deal," he replied.

"You went to Mexico?"

"Yeah, what's wrong with that?" he said.

"You're on bail. You don't go to other countries when you're on bail," I said.

"You want some corn?" he asked.

"Wilbur, I think Earl Deitrich is into some very bad stuff. I'm not sure what it is, but you're his scapegoat. Stop playing his game," I said.

He looked at me from under his shapeless cowboy hat with a private, ironic expression, then flung the coffee from his metal cup and wiped it clean with a napkin.

"You were going to say something?" I asked.

"Not me, son," he replied. After a moment, he said, "Kippy Jo, tell him what you been seeing in your dreams."

She turned her blue, sightless white-flecked eyes on me. The wind was blowing at her back and it feathered her hair around her throat.

"A winged man is coming. His teeth are red. He's killed Indian people in another place. I don't understand the dream. He's very evil," she said.

I didn't respond. She turned her head slightly, as though the creak of the windmill or the horses snuffing and blowing at the water tank meant something. Then her eyes came back on me and her head tilted, her mouth parting silently, her cheeks slack with a thought that confused her.

"But you already know him. How can you be around a man this evil without knowing it?" she said.

"Don't that blow your head?" Wilbur said.

When I walked out to my car with Wilbur I wished I hadn't come. I had wanted to caution him, but it did no good. Wilbur had been born in the wrong century. His kind became the tools of empires with glad hearts and an indefatigable optimism. When their usefulness ended, they were discarded.

But he was not the only one who was naive.

"You were fixing to tell me something back there," I said.

He took off his hat and pressed the dents out of the crown. Against the fire in the western sky his chiseled, surgically rebuilt profile looked like a Roman soldier's.

"Me and Kippy Jo was selling our melons out on the state road today," he said. "I seen your Avalon coming hell for breakfast around a truck. I thought, Now, there's a man badly in need of melons."

His eyes held mine. I could feel my face burning.

"I ain't gonna tell a man of your background about milking through the fence, but if that wasn't Peggy Jean Deitrich in your car, then ole Bodacious headbutted me a lot worse than I thought," he said.

That Saturday afternoon Lucas and his band played at Shorty's out on the river. Shorty's, with its screened porches and lack of air-conditioning, might have been a ramshackle nightclub and barbecue joint left over from another era, but either out of curiosity or need every class of person in our area came through its doors.

They scored dope and on one another. Bikers got swacked on crystal; forlorn oil field wives went up the road to the Super 8 Motel with college boys; rednecks broke their knuckles on one another's faces out in the trees; and Hollywood film people from Fredericksburg took it all in like happy visitors at a zoo.

Jeff Deitrich's birthday party had started at his house, then had moved in a caravan of Cherokees and roll-bar Jeeps and sports cars to Shorty's. Jeff and his friends occupied both the side and back screen porches. They drank daiquiris, Coronas with lime, and B-52s. As the evening wore on, the joints they toked on along the riverbank glowed like fireflies among the darkening trees.

A yellow Porsche convertible pulled into the lot and two men, one young, the other middle-aged, went inside and sat at the bar. The younger man was too thin to be called handsome, but his delicate facial bones, bright eyes, and guileless manner gave him a boyish charm and vulnerability that drew older men to him.

The middle-aged man with him wore creamcolored pleated slacks and white shoes and a navyblue shirt. He had a dissolute face and thick, salt-and-pepper hair. His hips and lower stomach swelled over his belt slightly, and his soft buttocks splayed on the barstool when he sat down. He crossed his legs and smoked a gold-tipped cigarette with his wrist held in the air, surveying the dance floor, letting his smoke leak upward whimsically from his open mouth.

When the band took a break Lucas went to the end of the bar for a cold drink. The younger man, whose name was Leland, kept twisting his head so he could see through the side door onto the screen porch where Jeff Deitrich, his shirt unbuttoned on his brown chest, was standing at his table, entertaining his guests, and downing a B-52, a jigger of whiskey dropped into a schooner of draft beer.

Then Jeff caught Leland's stare. His dark eyes blazed and his throat and the gold chain and St. Christopher's medal that hung from it were ropy with sweat. He set the schooner down on the plank table and walked to the bar, standing three feet from Leland. He waved the bartender away, scooped a handful of peanuts out of a dish, and ate them with his fingers, one at a time, looking at the bottles on the bar. He breathed audibly through his nose.

"I told you not to come around here again," he said.

"We were just passing by, Jeff. I guess birthday congratulations are in order," Leland said.

"In three minutes you and the queen better be the fuck out the door," Jeff said.

The middle-aged man pursed his lips and said, "Aren't we the excitable one?"

Leland's hand immediately touched his friend's wrist.

But Jeff let the remark pass and walked toward the men's room. He stopped at the end of the bar, as though seeing Lucas for the first time.

"What do you think you're doing, Lucas?" he asked.

"I work here. I'm taking a break. What's it to you, Jeff?"

Jeff grinned, his face oily in the reflected glow of the bar's lacquered pine paneling, the curly brown locks on the back of his neck stirring in the breeze from the electric fan. "It's nothing to me. Come on back to the table. We still have champagne and cake left," he said.

Three minutes later Leland and his friend were gone from the bar.

But not far enough.

Jeff had gone back out on the screen porch and rejoined his party. Then his attention strayed. He stood at the screen, his hands on his hips, watching Leland and his friend walk between the parked cars toward their yellow convertible. Jeff rubbed the sweat off his chest on the flat of his hand, his fingers kneading it idly in his palm. A lump of cartilage flexed in his jaw.

He followed the two men into the gravel parking

lot. He hooked one finger under the middle-aged man's arm and turned him in a slow pirouette toward him.

"I called you a queen in there, sir. I shouldn't have done that," Jeff said.

"I've answered to worse," the man replied, unconsciously feeling the wet spot on his sleeve where Jeff had touched him.

"What's your name, sir?"

"Mike."

"It's a pleasure to meet you, Mike. You like cake, Mike?"

"I'm on a diet. You eat it for me."

"How about the icing? I mean, when you eat it with ice cream, what do you think about when you stick it in your mouth with a spoon?"

"I was in the navy, kid. I've heard it all. So have a happy birthday."

"I've really tried to go the extra mile, but I think you're laughing at me, Mike. I really do."

"Not on your life, kid. You got a hard-on you could break walnuts with. I hope you get rid of it for your birthday. But it's not gonna happen on me."

"See, you're talking down to people. You pick up young guys to go down on you, then you insult people you don't know. You probably pissed on the toilet seat, too. Don't walk away from me. I'm talking to you . . . Mike? . . . Listen to me now . . . Here, see how this feels," Jeff said, and spun the man who called himself Mike back toward him and buried his fist in his stomach.

Mike fell to his knees, his mouth strangling for air. Jeff grabbed his hair in both hands and drove his head into a door panel, again and again, then wiped his hands on his shirt as though his skin glowed with an obscene presence.

The man named Mike was on his hands and knees now and accidentally touched the tip of Jeff's shoe. Jeff kicked him in the mouth, gashing his lips against his teeth, convulsing his face with shock.

Jeff's friends pushed and cajoled and held him, circling him so he couldn't get at the weeping man on the ground. Then he broke free from them, his arms flailing at the air.

"All right, all right! I'm cool! It's not me got the problem! This guy came on to me at the bar!" he said.

"Jeff, honey, you're right. Everybody saw that. But the cops are gonna be here. Come back inside. He's just a queer," a girl said.

Jeff walked unsteadily toward the state road, his shirt pulled out of his slacks, his body etched with car lights as though it were razored out of scorched metal.

"Jeff, get away from the road!" someone yelled.

He stopped, as though finally accepting the cautionary words of his friends. But he wasn't thinking about his friends now, nor of the road or the trucks that roared by him in a suck of air brakes and a swirl of beer cups and diesel fumes. He stared stupidly at the maroon '49 Mercury, its hood and doors over-painted with rippling blue and red flames, the grille like chromed teeth, that had just pulled into the parking lot.

The sole occupant, Esmeralda Ramirez, cut the engine and got out and stared at him across the top of the roof. She wore an organdy dress and earrings and makeup, and the car's interior light seemed to bathe her cleavage with both shadow and the flesh tones of a painting.

"Why are you here?" Jeff said.

"I brought you a present. You look terrible. What have you done?" she said.

"Nothing. A guy tried to put moves on me. I never saw him before."

"Get in the car."

He remained motionless. She looked back down the road where the emergency lights of a sheriff's cruiser were coming around a bend.

"Did you hear me? Get in the car. Now," she said.

He sat down in the passenger seat and closed the door and did not look back at his friends. His body seemed to press back into the leather seat, as though it were dead weight gathered into foam rubber, when Esmeralda fishtailed the Mercury out onto the asphalt.

9

SUNDAY MORNING I SHINED MY BOOTS AND PUT on a suit and saddled Beau and rode up a slope that was humped with blackberry bushes. Then I was inside the sun-spangled shade of pine trees, Beau's hooves thudding softly on the moist carpet of pine needles, and a moment later I came out into the hard-packed dirt backyard of a half-breed Mexican boy named Pete who went with me to Mass every week.

Pete was eleven years old and had a haircut like an inverted shoe brush. Even though he had an alcoholic mother and no father, he had already skipped one grade in school and could think circles around most adults. I leaned from the saddle and pulled him up on Beau's rump.

"I got a good one for you," he said. "An old man was playing checkers on the front porch of his store with a cocker spaniel. This California guy pulls in for gas and says, 'Mister, that must be the smartest dog that ever was born.'

"The old man says, 'I don't think he's so smart. I done beat him three games out of five.'"

Pete howled at his own joke.

We rode along the crest of the slope that bordered my property. Our shadows flowed horizontally along the ground through the vertical shadows of the trees, then we came out on a dusty street, where the tile-roofed church and Catholic elementary school stood. Beyond the pines in the churchyard I could see the small white cafe where Pete and I always ate breakfast after Mass. Ronnie Cruise's sunburst T-Bird was parked in the lot, the front door open for the breeze. Ronnie had reclined the seat and was stretched back on it with his forearm across his eyes.

"Take Beau into the shade. I'll be along in a minute," I said to Pete.

"You know that guy?" Pete asked.

"I'm afraid so."

"He's a gangbanger, Billy Bob. He don't belong here."

"He probably wants to go to confession," I said, and winked.

But Pete saw no humor in my remark. He walked with Beau and the tethering weight into the pines, repeatedly looking back at me, as though somehow I had made an alliance with an enemy.

"You want to see me?" I said to Ronnie.

"Yeah, that lady you come to the shop with, she was jogging by your house. She said I'd find you here. Esmeralda didn't come home last night."

"I'm supposed to know where she is?"

He scratched his face. "Do you?" he asked.

"No."

"I went out to Jeff Deitrich's place. Some guy

named Fletcher stopped me at the gate. He said if I was interested in the gardening job, I could come back tomorrow. He said not to knock on the front door."

He took his sunglasses off the dashboard and clicked the wire arms together.

"Anything else you want to tell me?" I said.

He gave me a quizzical look. "You bent out of joint about something?" he asked.

"Four firemen were burned to death on Earl Deitrich's property. I think you came by my house the other night to cover your ass."

He got out of the car and put on his shades.

"You calling me a bullshit guy, right?" he said.

"No, I'm saying it's Sunday morning and I'm not in the mood for somebody's grift. If that offends you, go fuck yourself."

I walked out of the sunlight onto the church lawn, into the pine trees where Pete waited for me. I heard Ronnie start his car and back out onto the dirt street and head toward the state road. Then he slowed and made a U-turn through the portico of a deserted Pure station, the Hollywood mufflers reverberating off the cement. He stopped in front of the church and left the car running in the street. He jumped across the rain ditch onto the grass and caught my shirtsleeve with two fingers, oblivious to the stares of people going inside the church.

"I ain't burned no firemen, man. And *nobody* don't talk to me like that. That means *nobody*."

• • •

WHEN I GOT BACK to the house I walked Beau into the barn and unsaddled him and turned him out. As I walked toward the house I saw Temple Carrol jog past the front of the driveway, then pause in mid-stride and stare back at me, as though unsure of what she was going to do next.

She walked up the drive toward me, her hair tucked inside a baseball cap.

"You look like you've been pouring it on," I said.

"I've got a problem. This friend of mine has his head up his butt. But I really don't know how to tell him that," she replied. She wore a pair of faded pink shorts, and the tails of her shirt were knotted under her breasts. Her skin was glazed with sweat, her eyes blinking with the salt that ran into them. She blotted her face on her shirt.

"What is it, Temple?" I asked.

"If you want to be an idiot in your private life, that's your business. But I'm part of Wilbur Pickett's defense team. You don't have the right to do what you're doing."

"Doing what, please?"

Her hands were in her back pockets, her face tilted up into mine now, the whites of her eyes shiny and pink. Her breasts rose and fell against her shirt.

"It's a small town. Peggy Jean had a fight with her husband in front of the Langtry Hotel. Then the two of you boogied on down the road," she said.

"She twisted her ankle. I took her home."

"Well, twist this. You've managed to publicly involve yourself with the wife of the man who's brought charges against your client. You piss me off so bad I want to beat the shit out of you." She shoved me in the breastbone with her hand. Then she shoved me again, her face heating, her eyes watering now.

"Nothing happened, Temple. I promise."

She turned and walked away from me, then ripped the baseball cap off her head and shook out her hair. The faded rump of her shorts was flecked with dirt.

"Come on back, Temple," I said.

But she didn't.

I WENT INSIDE the house and turned on the television to fill the rooms with as much noise as I could to drown out Temple's words.

A Houston televangelist was sitting on a stage with his two co-hosts, a middle-aged blonde woman and a white-haired black man who looked like a minstrel performer rather than a real person of color. The three of them had joined hands and were supposedly receiving telepathic pleas for help from their electronic congregation. Their eyes were squeezed shut, their faces furrowed with strain as though they were constipated.

I stared in disbelief as the pilot Bubba Grimes took a seat among the latticework of plastic flowers. He talked of mercy flights to Rwandan refugees, or missionaries who risked their lives in jungles that swarmed with wild animals and tropical disease. Grimes's face broke into thousands of fine wrinkles when he grinned, like the lines in a tobacco leaf. The televangelist was bent forward in his chair, his unctuous voice modifying and directing Grimes's peckerwood depiction of Western humanity at work in Central Africa.

The blonde woman and the black man, whose skin looked like greasepaint and whose hair was as white as new snow, nodded their heads reverentially.

Grimes poured into a glass from a pitcher filled with ice and Kool-Aid and drank until the glass was empty.

"Bubba loves his Kool-Aid," the televangelist said.

Grimes grinned at the camera, his lips as red as a wet strawberry.

It was sickening to watch.

I WENT TO MY DESK in the library and punched in Earl Deitrich's number on the telephone.

"What is it now?" he said when he recognized my voice.

"I drove your wife home the other day because you left her on the sidewalk with a sprained ankle. That was the extent of it. I hope we're clear on that."

"Oh yeah. That's why y'all were dancing in a bar

the same afternoon . . . You there? No smart-ass remarks to make?"

I looked stupidly out the window at the blades of my windmill ginning beyond the barn roof.

"Your wife didn't do anything wrong, Earl. If there's any blame involved, it's mine," I said.

"You got that right."

I started to ease the receiver down, to let go of pride and anger and all the vituperative energy that had clung to me like a net since I had run into Ronnie Cruise by the church. But for some reason I kept seeing Bubba Grimes's red smile on the television screen.

"That sociopathic pilot, the guy you paid to lie about Wilbur Pickett? He landed his plane on my pasture. He wanted to hang you from a meat hook. I'd hire a better class of lowlife, Earl," I said, then hung up.

I walked down to the bluffs above the river and threw rocks at a beached, worm-scrolled cottonwood until my arm throbbed.

JEFF DEITRICH didn't return home that morning or even by that afternoon. Hugo Roberts and his deputies began searching the county for Cholo Ramirez's 1949 Mercury, questioning truck stop and filling station and motel operators, cruising through Val's Drive-In and campgrounds and the wooded promontory high above the river, called the Cliffs, where teenage kids smoked dope and made out.

Hugo Roberts and his deputies were obviously grunts for Earl Deitrich and would exercise damage control for him, but unfortunately for Earl the Texas Department of Public Safety would not. When the homosexual whom Jeff beat at Shorty's filed charges against Jeff, the highway patrol picked up the description and license number of Cholo's car.

At dusk on that same Sunday Jeff was asleep in the passenger seat of the Mercury when a highway patrolman parked in a roadside picnic area saw Esmeralda roar past him on the two-lane. The patrolman hit his flasher and siren and chased the Mercury for five miles through hills and a one-redlight town, the two of them sweeping onto the shoulder to pass a poultry truck, careening around a wide gravel turnout on the river's edge, showering rocks like bird shot into the water.

She crossed a narrow concrete bridge at ninety, the backdraft blowing bait cups and fish-blood-stained newspaper into the air like confetti. Then the road straightened along the river and Esmeralda got serious. The Mercury's engine roared with a new life and pushed the car's body back on the springs. Rocks from her tires broke car windows on the opposite side of the road and rang like tack hammers on metal road signs.

The highway patrol cruiser slowed behind her but not out of defeat.

Up ahead, just inside the county line, Hugo Roberts and his deputies had set up a roadblock.

Around a bend, behind bushes and a signboard, so that a driver approaching it at high speed from the south could not see it until the driver was right up on it.

Esmeralda swerved onto the shoulder and was airborne going across the irrigation ditch into a tomato field. The Mercury slid sideways for a hundred feet, scouring clouds of cinnamon-colored dust into the air, trenching a path through the tomato vines like the tail of a tornado.

The engine killed and the hood crackled with heat. As soon as Esmeralda opened the car door Hugo's deputies were on her like flies, pinning her across the hood, pressing her cheek into the hot metal, running their hands like spiders down her sides and hips and thighs.

One of the deputies leaned his mouth close to her ear. "You just wrote our names on your ass," he said.

None of them had paid attention to Jeff Deitrich.

Not until he came around the hood of the car and tore into them with both fists, hooking one deputy in the eye, knocking another to the ground with a bloody nose.

Hugo's deputies, joined by two highway patrolmen, wrestled him against the grille, kicked his ankles out from under him, and jerked his chin up with a baton.

"You spoiled fart, we're trying to help you. This woman damned near killed people," Hugo said.

"That's my wife. One of you put your hand on her again and my old man will have you cleaning litter boxes at the animal shelter," Jeff said.

"Your wife?" Hugo said.

"We got married in Mexico."

Hugo Roberts laughed and lit a cigarette. He removed a piece of tobacco from his tongue and looked at it and started laughing again.

"Let him up and see if you can get his daddy on the radio. Tell me this job ain't a toe-curlin' sidesplitter," he said.

10

JUST BEFORE NOON ON MONDAY MORNING RONNIE Cruise and Cholo Ramirez came through my office door. Ronnie threw a white envelope wrapped with a rubber band on my desk.

"What's that?" I said.

"A down payment, a retainer. Whatever it's called. A thousand dollars. We want you to represent Esmeralda," Ronnie said.

"Yesterday you were threatening me in front of a church," I said, and threw the envelope into his chest.

"This ain't about me. Jeff Deitrich got her wired on leapers and married her in a chicken yard down in Piedras Negras," Ronnie said.

"That's not how she told it to me," I said.

The skin on Ronnie's face flexed against the bone. "You already talked to her? She says she wanted to marry Jeff?" he asked, his mouth slack.

"I went to see her because I think she's getting a bad deal, Ronnie. Here's the card of a bondsman across the square. I'll be at her arraignment this afternoon. Use that money to work out something on the bail," I said.

"Why you looking out for Esmeralda?" Cholo asked.

"Because she's stand-up," I said.

His eyes narrowed, as though there were a trick in my words. He wore a white undershirt and his shoulders and upper arms had the swollen proportions of a steroid addict. He stood in front of the glass wall case that contained the revolvers and Winchester rifle of my great-grandfather without seeming to have ever noticed it. His reflection wobbled between the glass and blue felt background like a man trapped under lake ice.

I waited for him to speak but he didn't.

"A pilot named Bubba Grimes told me Earl Deitrich has a weakness for gambling. I hear you told Temple Carrol a story about turning over card games. Is there a connection there, Cholo?" I said.

"No."

But Ronnie was looking at the side of Cholo's face now.

"I said no," Cholo repeated.

"You two guys build cars that belong on magazine covers. Why do you waste your energies with gangbangers?" I said.

Ronnie Cruise pointed the index and little fingers of his right hand at me, like devil's horns. "Man, you're a Heart only once. You got a tattoo on your throat like Cholo's, you got shit in your blood and everybody on the street knows it. You were a Texas Ranger?" he said.

"That's right."

"Then you should understand."

• • •

AFTER THEY LEFT I called Temple and asked her to visit the woman's section of the jail to ensure that nothing untoward was happening to Esmeralda Ramirez.

"I thought you already went over there," she said.

"It doesn't hurt to err on the side of caution," I said.

"Is that the reason you called?"

"No. Have dinner with me."

"I'll think about it," she said, and hung up.

I walked to the window and looked out on the square, at the blinding white reflection of sunlight on the cement and the deep green of the oaks moving in a hot wind. I tried to keep my thoughts straight in my head but I couldn't. I kept thinking of both Temple and Peggy Jean Deitrich and wondered at how it was possible to feel trepidation, guilt, and attraction whenever the name of either one came into my mind. I heard the secretary's voice, then the door of my office ease open on the rug.

Ronnie Cruise stood in the doorway, the envelope full of money stuck down in his belt.

"She told you she got married 'cause she wanted to? She wasn't fried when she done it?" he said.

"I'm not her priest, Ronnie."

"I was just clearing it up, that's all. I'll be at the arraignment. I got no beef," he said.

I bet, I thought.

• • •

ESMERALDA was released on bail at four that afternoon. Her brother, Cholo, and Temple Carrol and I walked with her toward Cholo's car, which was webbed with dried mud from the tomato field she had plowed through. The late sun was like a yellow flame in the trees and she shielded her eyes and kept looking at the row of cars parked up and down the street.

"Ronnie's waiting in the car. He wasn't sure you wanted him inside," Cholo said.

"Why'd you bring him? It's not his business. Stay out of my life, Cholo," she said.

"Don't treat us like that, Esmeralda. We're your people. It's you who don't have no business up here," Cholo said. Then his face clouded and his metabolism seemed to kick into a higher register. "I don't understand nothing that's going on here."

But she wasn't listening to him. Her eyes swept the street once more. She pirouetted on the sidewalk and stared into my face.

"Is Jeff in jail? Because of the gay guy at Shorty's?" she said.

"The guy Jeff beat up had a change of heart. He dropped the charges and decided to vacation in Cancun," I said.

But the inference about the way Jeff's father handled business did not show in her face. "Then where's Jeff?" she said.

A steel-gray limo with tinted windows pulled into a yellow zone next to Cholo's car and Earl Deitrich got out of the back door, dressed in dark blue jeans and soft boots and a snap-button shirt. Peggy Jean stayed far back in the interior of the limo, her face veiled with shadow, her white dress glowing in a ray of sunlight. The chauffeur, a peculiar man named Fletcher, who seemed to have no past or origins, stood on the opposite side of the limo, his arms propped on the roof, a fixed smile on his mouth.

Earl's face was warm with sympathy, his hands open, as though he were about to console a survivor at a funeral.

"Thank the Lord I caught you," he said to Esmeralda. "My attorney is going to contact you tomorrow. We'll get everything worked out. Believe me, Jeff wants to do the right thing. In the meantime, you call me with any problem you have."

"What are you talking about?" she said.

"Young people act hastily sometimes. That doesn't mean they have to ruin their lives over it. We're here to help. We're in this thing together," he said.

"Where's Jeff?" she asked.

"He's got some things to work out. But he's going to have to do it by himself. It's important for us to understand that, Esmeralda," Earl said.

"He marries my sister but he's got things to do by himself? She don't have no more to say. You send the lawyer around, he talks to me first," Cholo said.

Earl's chauffeur walked around the grille of the limo and stood inches from Cholo's back, smiling at nothing, the black hair that was combed on the sides of his bald pate ruffling slightly in the breeze. He wore black slacks and shined shoes and an open-necked long-sleeve white shirt with cuff links that had red stones in them.

Earl's eyes looked directly into the chauffeur's. The chauffeur's gaze shifted to a spot across the street and he stepped backwards as though an invisible hand had touched his chest.

"You're right, Cholo," Earl said. "Everybody needs to be included in on this, informed about everything that's happening. Absolutely."

"You think I married your son so I can take your money? You're pitiful, Mr. Deitrich," Esmeralda said.

"I don't blame you for having bad feelings. I just want to—" Earl began.

Ronnie Cruise, who sat behind the Mercury's steering wheel, lifted his eyes into Earl's face. Ronnie's eyes were absolutely black, without luster, dead, devoid of all moral sense.

"Like Cholo says, we got nothing else to talk about here. No disrespect, but tell your man there, what's his face, Fletcher, to get his fucking hand off Cholo's paint job," Ronnie said.

A FEW MINUTES LATER Temple Carrol and I watched the limo and the customized Mercury drive in different directions through the cooling streets of Deaf Smith. Peggy Jean had never spoken. Not to me, not on behalf of decency or fairness or in some token way to show a bit of kindness toward a Mexican girl who was about to discover you didn't leave the rural slums of San Antonio because a drunk white boy married you in Piedras Negras.

"How do you read all that?" Temple asked, lifting her shirt off her moist skin and shaking the cloth.

I couldn't answer. I kept thinking about Peggy Jean and the net of shadow and light on her skin and white dress and her silent participation in her husband's evil.

"You still on the planet?" Temple said.

"What do I think?" I said. "I think Jeff Deitrich is a sexual nightmare. I think he's violent and dangerous and has racist instincts. I hope Esmeralda gets as far from the Deitrich family as possible."

"Who lit your fuse?" Temple said.

THAT NIGHT THE SKY was blue-black, veined with dry lightning, and brushfires burned in the hills west of Wilbur Pickett's place out on the hardpan. Deer broke down the wire fence on the back of Wilbur's pasture, and his Appaloosa and two palominos wandered out into the darkness.

Kippy Jo stood at the kitchen window, the breeze in her face, and listened to Wilbur hitch the horse trailer on his pickup truck and rattle past the barn out into the fields. Then she fixed coffee for herself and drank it at the kitchen table. When he didn't return in

an hour, as he had promised, she went into the backyard and looked in the direction of the hills and listened to the wind, her black hair whirling on her
neck.

She heard horses nickering in an arroyo, the
locked windmill blades buffeting against the wind,
the water from the horse tank leaking over the rim
into the dirt. Inside her mind, she saw an alfalfa field
that bloomed with a fecund, green odor when lightning leaped in the sky; a train crossing a trestle in the
hills, and in its aftermath pieces of flame coiling like
snakes around the greasewood. She could hear the
clicking of the train wheels on the sides of the hills,
then the echo of the whistle blowing back over the
tops of the cars.

When the train was gone she should have heard
only wind again, and the wet, coursing sound it
made across the alfalfa when Wilbur had opened the
irrigation locks and flooded the pasture. But she
heard a different sound now, first an engine, then
wind flapping across a moving surface, and she
knew the winged man had arrived.

She turned out all the lights in the house and
walked out to the barn and felt the lightbulb inside
the door for heat. She pulled the beaded chain on it
and heard it click off and stood with one hand on the
edge of a stall, listening. A washtub Wilbur shelled
corn in oscillated in the wind on a wood peg against
a post. She walked to the opposite end of the barn
and looked out at the darkness and the sky that flared

with dry lightning and heard the thunder rolling across the hardpan like apples tumbling down a wood chute into a cider press.

Horses labored out of the arroyo, their chests heaving, their hooves thudding on the sod, spooking walleyed from a presence that moved out of the darkness toward the house.

Kippy Jo retreated backwards, touching the screen with her hand, pulling it open, and stepping inside the kitchen, her blind eyes lighted by the sky. She latched the screen, bumped against the table, and felt her heart seize in her chest at the squeak the wood legs made against the linoleum.

She heard the winged man unchain the lock on the windmill and the blades clatter with life and the well water sluice cold and bright out of the pipe that extended over the horse tank. His hair flowed off his head like feathers, and he cupped his hand under the pipe and rubbed water on his face and through his hair, then wiped his skin and hair dry with his coat sleeve and drank from a heavy bottle that he carried in one hand.

When he stepped away from the tank his feet made cleft-shaped tracks in the mud.

Kippy Jo breathed hard through her mouth. The landscape in her mind had changed, and she saw the winged man in a foreign place, one of rain and heat where fish heads were strewn on a dirt road that wound between cinder-block huts with tin roofs, and the winged man and soldiers in uniform with steel helmets were pushing Indians backwards into a ditch.

The winged man was right outside the screen door now, one foot poised on the bottom step. The wind straightened the curtains, flapping the tips, and puffed open the front door. Kippy Jo felt her way along the wall to the bedroom and touched one prong of the antler gun rack that Wilbur had nailed above the dresser.

What had he said about the gun? She couldn't remember clearly. *There ain't no such thing as an unloaded firearm in this house, Kippy Jo. A person remembers that, he don't ever have an accident.*

Was that it?

She wasn't sure.

She lifted the .308 Savage lever-action off the antler prongs, then opened the drawer of the nightstand and removed a .22 Magnum revolver that was inserted in a holster that had no cartridge belt. She sat on the bed and waited, the lever-action rifle across her lap.

The winged man sliced the screen with a knife blade and popped the latch free with one finger and stepped inside the kitchen. He hesitated, listening to the darkness, touching the warmth of the coffeepot on the stove.

Then he pushed open the screen door and let it fall back against the jamb, but she knew he was still inside the house. She fitted her hand inside the lever that would feed a round into the rifle's chamber, but she didn't know if there were bullets in the magazine or if in fact a round wasn't already seated in the chamber.

There ain't no such thing as an unloaded firearm in this house.

What had he meant?

She remained motionless on the bed and left the lever in place. Then she felt the safety and clicked it off and hooked her index finger around the trigger.

The winged man's eyes had adjusted to the darkness now and he didn't need to turn on the light when he entered the bedroom. In her mind the room was filled with moonglow and the winged man stood above her, his eyes fixed on the rifle, unsure whether the next sound his feet made would offer her a target.

She raised the rifle toward his chest and pulled the trigger.

Nothing.

The winged man exhaled his breath in a fetid plume of alcoholic air that touched her skin like damp wool.

"Darlin'," you aged me ten years," he said, and gently pulled the rifle from her hands and sat next to her on the bed. He set his bottle on the floor by his feet and pulled the lever loose from the stock of the rifle.

"Magazine's full. You could have boiled my cabbage," he said. When she didn't reply, he moved closer to her and fitted his arm around her waist. "Wilbur due back directly?"

She looked straight ahead, her right hand resting under a pillow.

"I ain't a bad man, darlin'. I always go the extra mile to work things out. Anybody knows me will tell you that. I ain't that fond of Earl Deitrich myself," he said.

He leaned toward her, his eyes shut, and pressed his lips against her cheek, his forearm gathering her waist closer against him, his tongue quivering slightly against her skin.

Her fingers closed on the wood grips of the revolver. She slipped it from the holster under the pillow, cocking the hammer back with her thumb, locking the cylinder into place. When she pulled the trigger, the barrel was two inches from the winged man's right eye.

His weight tumbled to the floor. But he was still alive, one hand cupped on the angular wound that had torn away the edge of the socket. His metal-sheathed, pointed boots kicked at the bed frame and his other hand tried to lock around her ankle.

She stood above him and cocked the revolver and fired a second time. She heard his weight flatten into the floor and one boot vibrate briefly like a woodpecker's beak against the wall.

Then she sat down on the bed again and waited.

An hour later, when Wilbur burst into the house,

turning on lights in every room, shouting, "Kippy Jo, what's going on? There's a plane out in the field . . . Oh Lord, what's happened here? What'd this guy try to do?," she was still sitting on the bed, the revolver on top of the pillow, her white cloth slippers patinated with blood.

Wilbur sat beside her and held her against his chest. It seemed a long time before he spoke.

"He hurt you?" Wilbur said.

"No."

"It's that guy Bubba Grimes," he said.

"I know," she said.

Wilbur took a deep breath, like a man who accepts the fact that the world is indeed beyond him.

"His coat's got buckskin fringe on the arms. His teeth look like they was soaked in Cold Duck. He's the guy with wings, ain't he?" Wilbur said.

"Yes."

"You shot both his eyes out, Kippy Jo. That's what Indians do when they don't want somebody's spirit to find the Ghost Trail. They're gonna say you murdered him."

She put one hand in his, then drew her bare feet under her so they would not have to touch the floor.

11

THE NEXT MORNING I SAT IN MARVIN POMROY'S office. He was reading the homicide report filed by one of Hugo Roberts's crime scene investigators. He was reading it for the third time, his elbows propped on his desk blotter, his forehead resting on his fingers.

He blew out his breath and tapped a pencil on the blotter.

"Hugo's calling it homicide, Billy Bob. His work's sloppy, but I can't argue with him on this one," Marvin said.

"She's blind. He broke in her house. He had a .38 on him. He was probably going to rape her, then kill both her and her husband."

"Why would Grimes want to kill them?"

"Because Wilbur won't cop a plea and let Earl Deitrich collect from his insurance company," I said.

"Kippy Jo blew out both the victim's eyes. You think that might show deliberation?" Marvin said.

"I'll say it again. She's blind. From birth."

"You told me she sees things inside her head," he said.

"You're going to tell a jury that?" I said.

"When they shoot once, maybe it's self-defense. A

second shot, point-blank in the head, is an execution."

"How'd you like to have Grimes in your wife's bedroom with a .38 revolver?" I asked.

"Just get out of here, will you?" he said.

I walked down the corridor to the concession stand by the stairs, drank a root beer, and used the pay phone, then went back into Marvin's office. He was talking angrily on the phone, the overhead light shining on his close-cropped scalp, his face bright with a pink glaze.

"Who was that on the phone?" I asked after he hung up.

"Hugo Roberts, who else? What do you want?" he said.

"I called the FBI and a homicide cop in Houston. I thought they ought to know another associate of Earl Deitrich has shown up dead, this time while breaking into the house of a man Earl accuses of stealing from him."

"You did that?"

"Sure."

"Those dope transporters y'all went up against down in Coahuila? You ever take any of them prisoner?"

"Everybody kept the lines simple, Marvin. The winners got to see the sunrise."

I thought he was going to make a point, but he didn't. Instead, he leaned back in his chair, his chin propped on his fingers, and looked at me reflectively.

"We're cutting a warrant for Kippy Jo Pickett's arrest," he said.

"What was that blowup with Hugo Roberts about?" I said.

"None of your business. But I'll tell you this much. Kippy Jo had traces of Grimes's blood on the tips of her left hand. I think she felt his face before she parked the second round in his other eye. Forget the blind-girl defense, Billy Bob."

"You're hiding something," I said.

T HAT EVENING my little friend Pete walked from his house through the back of my property to my back screen porch. He carried a huge straw basket that was loaded with fruit, chocolate wrapped in gold foil, and cellophane bags of cactus candy and Mexican pralines. The strap of a brand-new black fielder's glove, with white leather thongs through the webbing, was buttoned around the basket's handle.

"What you got there, bud?" I said, opening the screen door for him.

"Ms. Deitrich brung it by the house this afternoon. My mother told me to bring it over here and leave it. She says she ain't letting no rich people look down on us."

"I'm not following you."

"She says Ms. Deitrich don't care two cents about me. This has got something to do with y'all." He hefted the basket onto the plank table and sat down on a bench and looked at his tennis shoes. The yellow cellophane and red ribbon that enclosed the basket were undisturbed. A greeting card hung halfway out of an envelope taped to the basket's handle. It read:

Dear Pete, I don't know if you remember me from church or not. But I know you're a friend of Billy Bob's and that he is very proud of you. Please accept this gift as a congratulations for your hard work at school and your fine performance with your baseball team.

Your friend,
Peggy Jean Deitrich

I believe Ms. Deitrich has high regard for you, Pete," I said.

"It don't matter. I cain't take none of this back home. My mother'll throw it in the garbage." His eyes lingered on the fielder's glove, then he twisted his mouth into a button and looked into space, as though the glove meant nothing to him.

"You want to saddle up Beau?" I asked.

"No. I got to weed the garden. Things ain't too good at the house right now."

I nodded, then watched him walk past the chicken run and along the edge of the irrigation ditch, stopping to throw dirt clods at the water. Then he crossed the small wood bridge that spanned the ditch and climbed up the hill into the pine trees that concealed the dirt yard and clapboard house where he lived.

PEGGY JEAN SOMETIMES did volunteer work in the evenings at the library. The sky was piled with rain clouds and the sun was a dying orange fire between two hills when I drove into town. The library was a one-story, peaked-roof building with the tall, domed windows that were characteristic of public buildings at the turn of the century. The lights were on inside the windows and the oak trees on the lawn were black-green with shadow.

Peggy Jean was behind the circulation desk, wearing a flower-print dress and horn-rimmed glasses. I set the candy and fruit basket on top of the desk. The library was almost deserted.

"Pete's mom won't accept this. He can't keep the glove, either," I said.

"Is she angry at the boy?"

"She's a drunk. She's angry all the time."

"I'm sorry. After that situation at the courthouse, I mean, the way the Mexican girl was treated, I wanted to apologize in some way."

"You don't owe me one."

"I didn't say I did. How do you think I felt, watching that girl patronized and dismissed like that? But I couldn't do anything about it, not without starting a fight right there on the street," she replied. She took off her glasses and let them hang from a velvet cord around her neck. "I'm thinking of leaving Earl."

I felt my hand close and open at my side and a tingling sensation in my throat that I didn't understand.

"You'll do the right thing," I said.

"I haven't done the right thing in twenty years, Billy Bob."

Then I realized who was sitting at one of the reading tables against the far wall, his hands clasped like paws on edges of a huge *Life* pictorial history, the top of the book obscuring the lower half of his face, so that he resembled the World War II cartoon drawing of Kilroy.

"That's Skyler Doolittle," I said.

"The man who claims Earl cheated him out of his watch?"

"Does Skyler know who you are?" I asked.

"No, he comes in here all the time. Poor soul, I feel sorry for him."

The overhead lights blinked to indicate the library would close in five minutes.

"I guess you have a ride home," I said.

"Earl's picking me up," she said.

"I see. Well, good night, Peggy Jean," I said.

"Good night," she said.

Outside, a moment later, as the rain clouds pulsed with veins of lightning, I witnessed one of those improbable incidents that you know will result in grave harm to an innocent party, one whose life seems destined to be governed by the laws of misfortune.

Skyler Doolittle, in his wilted seersucker, walked down the library steps behind Peggy Jean just as Earl Deitrich's maroon Lincoln pulled to the curb and Earl popped open the passenger door for his wife.

Earl's face was rainbowed with color in the glow of his dash.

"I don't believe it. You're stalking my wife," he said.

"I haven't did no such thing," Skyler said.

Peggy Jean got in the car and closed the door. But Earl did not drive away. He made a U-turn and slowed by the curb, rolling his window down on its electric motor so he could look directly into Skyler's face.

"You malignant deformity, you just made the worst mistake of your life," he said.

I was standing in the shadows on the corner and Earl did not see me. For some reason I could not explain, I felt obscene.

EARLY THE NEXT MORNING, before I went to the office, I drove to a sporting goods store in the strip mall on the four-lane, then returned to the west end of the county and headed down the dirt street that fronted Pete's house. When no one answered the door, I walked around back. He stood barefoot in the tomato plants, hoeing weeds out of the row, the straps of his striped overalls notched into his Astros T-shirt.

"Give it a break, bud," I said, and sat down on a folding metal chair. I put my Stetson on his head and popped loose the staples on the shopping bag in my hand, then reached inside it.

"Where'd you get the glove?" he asked.

"A client gave me this two or three years back. I put it up in the closet and forgot all about it."

His gaze shifted to the back door and windows of his house.

"That's why it's still in the shopping bag?" he said.

"Right, because I don't have occasion to use it. But you're missing the point. Anybody can own a fielder's glove. The art comes in molding the pocket." I opened a cardboard box and rolled an immaculate white, red-stitched baseball out of it. "See, you rub oil into the pocket, then mold the ball into it and tie the fingers down on top of it with leather cord. Watch."

I heard his mother open the screen behind us and smelled the cigarette smoke that curled away from her hand into the clean vibrancy of the morning air.

"What ch'all doin'?" she said.

"I had this old glove lying around. I thought Pete might get some use out of it," I said.

"He ain't eat his breakfast yet," she said.

"He'll be right in. How you been doing, Wilma?"

But she closed the door without answering. I winked at Pete and handed him the glove and removed my Stetson from his head.

"Are lawyers supposed to lie, Billy Bob?" Pete asked.

"Not a chance."

"You're mighty good at it."

"Yeah, but don't tell anyone," I said.

"I ain't." His eyes squinted shut with his grin.

TWO DAYS LATER Kippy Jo Pickett's bail was set at seventy-five thousand dollars. After she was taken back up to the women's section of the jail, I caught Marvin Pomroy in the corridor outside the courtroom.

"They're mortgaging their place to make the bail," I said.

His eyes clicked sideways behind his glasses and looked somewhere else. "I'm sorry," he said.

"This is all over one man's pride and avarice," I said.

"Sure it is," he said. He set his briefcase on the arm of a wood bench and unsnapped the locks on it. He removed an eight-by-ten crime scene photo and put it into my hands without bothering to look at me. Bubba Grimes's mutilated eyes were sealed with the coagulated blood that had welled out of the entry wounds. "Keep it. I have a dozen color slides or so for the jury," he said.

THAT EVENING PETE and I bought a bucket of fried chicken and cane-fished for shovelmouth under a weeping willow on the bank of the river. The sun was a dull red on the western horizon, as though it were surrendering its heat to the darkness that lay beyond the earth's rim, and when the wind blew from the river, the grass in the fields turned pale in the light slanting out of the clouds and the wildflowers seemed to take on a new color.

"Are Wilbur Pickett and his wife going to the pen?" Pete asked.

"Not if I can help it."

Pete's face was pensive, the way it became when he put the adult world under scrutiny.

"People are saying Wilbur's wife shot that fellow 'cause they were all stealing from Mr. Deitrich," he said.

"They're wrong."

His brow furrowed as another question swam in front of his eyes, like a butterfly that wouldn't come into focus.

"If Mr. Deitrich is trying to put your clients in jail, how come you and Ms. Deitrich are such good friends?" he asked.

"Something just pulled your cork under."

He jerked on his pole. The cork and weight and hook came flying out of the water into the grass.

"He must have taken off," I said.

"Durn, I knew you was gonna say that."

Then Pete looked past my shoulder at a low-slung, chopped-down Mercury coming through the field. In the muted light its tangled colors took on the deep reddish-purple hue of a stone bruise.

"I'm heading back home," Pete said.

"No, you stay here. This is your place. You never have to leave it, not for any reason."

"Them gangbangers are no good, Billy Bob. You don't see what they do when people like you ain't around."

I set down my cane pole and walked toward the Mercury before it reached the riverbank. Cholo Ramirez pulled to a stop and got out, his baggy khaki trousers hanging loosely from his hips, his ribbed, white undershirt molded to his physique. His tan shoulders seemed to glow with the sun's fire.

"How much can I tell you and be protected?" he said.

"You mean by client-lawyer privilege?"

"Whatever."

"You're not my client. I'm not taking on any new ones, either."

He gazed at the river, his hands opening and closing at his sides.

"Esmeralda married a *maricón,* man. He beats up queers 'cause that's what he is. She told me how they made love on an air mattress on the Comal River. I was getting sick," he said.

"I don't know if you've come to the right place, Cholo," I said.

"Me and Earl Deitrich got a history. I can jam him up real bad, man. But I got to have guarantees."

"What's he done to you?"

"It's what he's doing to Esmeralda. She ain't no

gangbanger, man. She makes As in college. He sent a lawyer to the house. Five thousand dollars for her to get lost."

"You want more?" I said.

Cholo stepped closer to me. I could smell the heat in his skin. For the first time in months I saw the silhouette of L.Q. Navarro on the edge of my vision, his ash-gray hat shadowing his face, his white shirt glowing against his dark suit, his index finger wagging cautiously.

"Esmeralda ain't somebody's pork chops you pay for by the pound. She thinks Jeff loves her. If he loves her, how come he lets his old man treat her like she's the town pump?" Cholo said.

"How did you know I was back here?" I asked.

"I walked around back. I looked in your barn. I seen you and the little boy riding your horse out here."

"You walked around back?"

"You got a hearing problem? I'm talking about my sister. *What,* I didn't have permission to walk behind your fucking house?"

"Come to the office, Cholo. We'll talk this stuff over. Maybe I can help," I said.

His brow was creased into rolls of grizzle, his eyes pulled close together like BBs.

"I'm all mixed up. I can't think. It makes my head hurt," he said.

I walked away from him and picked up my cane pole and swung the bobber out into the current. I kept my back turned until I heard the Mercury engine roar to life and the weeds in the field clatter under the front bumper.

L.Q. Navarro leaned with one shoulder against the willow tree, rolling a cigarette. He popped a lucifer match on his thumbnail and cupped it to the cigarette, and I saw the flame flare on his mustache and dark eyes and grained skin.

"That boy will cook your liver on a stick," he said.

ONCE IN A WHILE you hear about truly wicked abuses inside the system: In California, rival Hispanic and black gang members forced into a concrete-enclosed recreation area while a gunbull waits to blow away a particularly troublesome inmate as soon as the fighting starts; over in Louisiana, an inmate kept for years in solitary confinement, until he permanently damages his brain by beating his head against an iron wall; a Haitian immigrant sexually tortured with a plumber's helper in the rest room of a New York City police station.

You hope it's only a story. Or that, if true, the culpable parties have been fired or jailed themselves.

That's what you hope.

Sunday morning Skyler Doolittle went to a fundamentalist, Holy Roller church in the West End, one that had trailed its legends of snake handling, drinking poisons, and talking in tongues all the way across the chain of southern mountains into the hill country of rural Texas.

When he left the church he ate lunch at a truck stop and returned to his room in a backstreet sandstone hotel that had no air-conditioning and where the dust from a feeder lot blew through the windows above the old wood colonnade.

He turned the key in the lock and stepped inside the door. On his bed and floor and nightstand were photographs of children. The draft through the door blew the photographs into a vortex, one filled with images that made his eyes water.

Two uniformed deputies in shades stepped through the door behind him. The taller of the two was named Kyle Rose; a pale, shaved area still showed in the back of his scalp where I had driven his head into the log wall of Hugo Roberts's office. He removed the sunglasses from his face and pinched the red marks on the bridge of his nose. His mouth was a stitched line, hooked downward on the corners. He pulled the shades on the windows.

"Ain't nobody here but us chickens now," he said.

THE CALL CAME TO MY HOUSE Sunday night, not from Skyler Doolittle but from a janitor in the jail section of the county hospital.

"It happened out in the parking lot. I seen it from

the upstairs window. They had him between two
cars. This cop had some kind of electric gun in his
hand," he said.

"Skyler told you to call me?"

"Yes, sir."

"What's your name?" I asked.

He started to speak, then hung up.

A half hour later an orderly at the hospital unlocked a plain metal door on an isolation room
whose floor and walls were overlaid with mattresses.
Skyler Doolittle stood in a corner, wearing nothing
but boxer undershorts that were printed with smiling
blue moons. His body was streaked with red abra-
sions, like rope burns.

"They beat you?" I said.

"At my hotel, 'fore they took me out to the car. In
the parking lot a man put a stinger on me. His name's
Kyle Rose. He done it all over my back."

"I'm going to get you transferred to a bed, Mr.
Doolittle. My investigator will check on you later
tonight, and I'll be back to visit you in the morning."

Then I noticed a change in his eyes; they had
taken on a color they hadn't possessed before, like
lead that's been scorched in a fire. His posture, even
his muscular tone, seemed different, the tendons in
his fused neck like braided rope, his chest flat-
plated, the upper arms swollen with glandular fluids.

"This fellow Deitrich and the man with that
stinger?" he said.

"Yes?"

"My thoughts don't seem like my own no more. I ain't never hurt nobody on purpose. I'm a river-baptized man. I fear a great evil is fixing to draw me inside it. I got no place to turn with it."

12

I WAS TO BE OF LITTLE HELP TO SKYLER Doolittle. Five days later, I watched him leave Deaf Smith in a blue state bus with grilles on the windows for a state mental hospital in Austin. At the time I even thought he would be better off, safe from the torment visited upon him by Hugo Roberts's deputies.

I paid little attention to the man with fan-shaped sideburns chained hand and foot next to him.

THAT EVENING LUCAS asked me to come out and see the farmhouse he had rented forty miles west of town. He said he had rented it in order to be closer to his job on an oil rig. But his pride in living on his own and paying his own way was obvious.

We stood in the front yard, surveying the bullet-pocked window glass, the scaled white paint, the gutters clogged with pine needles, the collapsed privy and the windmill wrapped with tumble brush in back. In the side yard the branches of a dead pecan tree were silhouetted like gnarled fingers against the sun.

"I got an option to buy. With a little fixing up, it'd be a right nice place," he said.

"Yeah, it looks like it's got a lot of promise," I said, trying to keep my face empty. From inside I could hear Elmore James singing "My Time Ain't Long" on a CD. "Who lives in the trailer out back?"

"Nobody reg'lar." He looked about the yard, his expression blank.

"Nobody regular?"

"Yeah, I mean a friend or two might stay over. Come on inside. I'll show you my new electric bass."

He had scrubbed out the interior of the house with lye water and set coffee cans planted with petunias in the windowsills and hung his twelve-string and slide guitars, mandolin, banjo, and fiddle from felt-covered hooks on the living room walls. His musical talent was enormous. He referred to country and blues and rock musicians, both living and dead, by their first or nicknames, as though he and his listener knew them intimately: Hank and Lefty, Melissa, Lester and Earl, Janice, Kitty, Emmylou, Stevie Ray, Woody and Cisco. The irony was that in his humble reverence he was unaware he was as good as or better than most of them.

I heard a car turn off the county road into the yard.

"Check out this next cut on the CD. It's 'Rocket '88,' Jackie Brenston. The first real R&B record ever made," Lucas said.

Through the side window I saw a yellow convertible park in front of the dented and sagging silver trailer that was set up on cinder blocks. The driver wore a hard hat and a denim shirt that was spotted with drilling mud. The Mexican girl next to him pushed her hair back on her head with one hand. Her hair was long and dark and looked as though it had been stained with iodine.

"Jeff Deitrich and Esmeralda Ramirez are living here?" I said.

"I got him a job on my rig. The guy's trying to straighten out his life. It ain't gonna be easy for them two."

"He's putting you in harm's way."

"What if you'd taken that attitude when I was in trouble? I'd be chopping cotton in Huntsville Pen."

Through the window I watched Jeff walk inside the trailer with his arm around Esmeralda's shoulders, a lunch bucket in his left hand. I let out my breath and sought words that would seem reasonable and hide the fear that gripped my heart. The wind slapped the door of the trailer into the frame like a pistol shot.

THE MAN CHAINED HAND AND FOOT next to Skyler Doolittle was named Jessie Stump, an armed robber, speed addict, and psychopath who shot a Mexican judge in a courtroom, jumped through a second-story glass window, and escaped into the heart of Mexico City. He was also one of my ex-clients. When I got him off on a forgery charge, he paid my fees with a bad check.

There were five inmates in jailhouse orange jumpsuits sitting on the passenger seats in the rear of the bus, and two uniformed deputy sheriffs in front, their backs protected by a wire-mesh partition. Jessie was the only inmate who had been locked in both wrist and leg manacles. He leaned forward, his chains tinkling, and removed a leather-craft tool from his shoe, one with a thin, needle-sharp steel hook on the end. Then he inserted the tip into the lock on his right wrist and twisted gingerly, as though he were correcting the mechanism in the back of a clock.

When the serrated steel tongue of the manacle popped loose, Jessie slipped a small bar of soap into his mouth and started to work on his leg chains. Skyler Doolittle's hand closed around his like a large ball of bread dough.

"You go, I go," Skyler whispered.

Jessie's hair was coal black, his narrow face cratered with acne scars, his dark eyes wired. His lips were pinched together to hold the soap that was melting inside his mouth. A thought, a moment's resentment, the consideration of alternatives, perhaps, seemed to hover in front of his eyes, then disappear. He inserted the tool in the manacle on Skyler's left wrist. His fingertips were black with grime, his nails as thick as tortoiseshell, but he rotated the shaft of the leather-craft tool as delicately as a surgeon.

A minute later Jessie rolled a topless container of Liquid-plumr down the aisle and collapsed on the floor, writhing, his feet thrashing, his mouth white with foam.

The deputy riding shotgun stared back through the wire mesh.

"Pull it over. Stump's done swallowed drain cleaner," he said to the driver.

The bus stopped on the swale. The guard by the front door got up out of his seat, unholstered his revolver and set it on the dashboard. He unlocked the wire-mesh door that gave onto the aisle.

The guard was near retirement, his face ruddy with emphysema, his stomach hanging over his belt like a sack of grain. His hand touched Stump's shoulder.

"Hold on, son. We'll get the medics here. They'll pump you out," he said.

Then Jessie was on his feet, the tape-wrapped shank pressed against the guard's jugular.

"You key that radio and I'll slice his pipe," he said to the driver, who was young, only two years on the job, and had suddenly realized the cost of underestimating the potential of the men he ferried back and forth daily from a half dozen service institutions.

Jessie pushed the older guard down the aisle, through the wire-mesh door, and picked up the revolver off the dashboard. He pointed it at the side of the driver's head and pulled the driver's gun from its holster.

"Drive the bus down that side road into them pines," he said.

The bus bounced down a dirt road into deep shade, past a pond that was green with lichen and dimpled with the tracings of insects and dragonflies. Jessie reached past the steering wheel and turned off the ignition.

"Y'all get out," he said.

"What you gonna do, Jessie?" the driver said.

"Some days a guy just gets up and brushes his teeth in the commode," he replied.

"Them state hospital people are gonna certify you. You won't never do time," the older guard said.

"They give me electroshock, bossman. I bit right through that rubber hose they put in my mouth. Lordie, I cain't go through that un again," Jessie said.

He herded the two guards out the door, pushing them in the back toward the pond that rang with a greenish-yellow light. The other inmates stared from the bus windows, some already starting to turn their faces away, as though they were being forced to watch the showing of a film they didn't want to see.

"Just look the other way and kneel down. Look at the water. It's full of frogs. They're jumping all over the place. See?" Jessie said to the guards.

"My salary is all my old woman's got. You must have gone to a church at one time, son. Ain't none of you boys all bad," the older guard said. Then his words broke in his throat and died and his lungs heaved in his chest for breath.

"I didn't just go to church. My daddy was a

preacher. He burned me with cigarettes and choked to death on a woman's glass eye in a motel room. You look at them frogs. There's one yonder fat as a football," Jessie said. He stepped back from the two guards, his hand tightening and untightening on the grips of the pistol, his palm making a popping sound, as though there were adhesive on his skin.

Then Skyler Doolittle was standing behind him, a clutch of chains and manacles dripping from one hand.

"Have they did something bad to you?" Skyler asked.

"*They* ain't. Back at the jail, a couple of them others took me down for midnight Bible study. Magpies all set on the same bush," Jessie said.

"You aiming to walk through a woods in these orange suits?" Skyler asked.

"What?" Jessie said.

"Get their uniforms off and chain them up. Don't you hurt them, either," Skyler said.

"Who put you in charge? Don't you walk off like that. You listening to me?" Then Jessie stared at Skyler's bare skin. "Man, they done the same thing to you, ain't they?"

Skyler had unzipped and stepped out of his orange jumpsuit and mounted the bus's steps. His body was striped with bruises, like the color in rotten fruit. He reached under the dashboard with both hands and tore the radio out of its fastenings and threw it out on the ground like a dead animal.

"What's the name of them two give you midnight Bible study?" he said.

AT FALSE DAWN the next morning I drove out to Wilbur Pickett's place. The sun was still below the horizon, and the air was a dense blue and the shapes inside it not quite formed. When I got out of the car I could smell the heavy, cold odor of well water and coffee boiling and pork frying in the kitchen. Then I saw Wilbur riding his Appaloosa through the grass from the west, his face covered with shadow under his hat, a lamb gathered against his stomach with one arm. He dismounted by the barn and set the lamb on a worktable inside the door and stroked its head.

"Reach me that first-aid kit, will you?" he said.

"What happened?" I asked.

"Some dumb bastard left a steel trap out there in the hills. I'd like to slam his hand in a car door and see how he likes it."

There was a bright red bracelet incised around the lamb's right leg. Wilbur poured disinfectant on the wound and washed and applied salve to it, then began cutting strips of gauze and tape with a pair of scissors while I held the lamb.

"You left a message on my machine. Something about this fellow Fletcher who works for Earl Deitrich?" I said.

Wilbur twisted his head and looked back at his

house. The curtains were flapping whitely in the kitchen window.

"I come home yesterday and this guy Fletcher was parked in the drive, leaning against his limo, watching Kippy Jo hang wash in back," Wilbur said.

"What'd he want?"

"Wait a minute," Wilbur said, and bandaged the lamb's wound and set the lamb down on a bed of straw in a stall. He removed a sealed gallon jar from a plank shelf. It was filled to the top with loamy, reddish-brown dirt that was marbled with black streaks against the glass. He unscrewed the top of the jar and handed it to me.

"Smell it," he said. Then he waited, and said, "Just like salt water and humus and rotten eggs, ain't it?"

"Oil?"

"Sweet crude, as black and pure as it gets. You can eat it on ice cream. Kippy Jo inherited two hundred acres in Wyoming her grandfather owned. That's the core sample on what's gonna be the Kippy Jo Number One. Don't nobody know about it. At least that's what I thought till this guy Fletcher showed up.

"I asked him what he was doing in my damn driveway. He goes, 'We hear you got a drill site located in Wyoming. If you want to unload it, we can introduce you to the right people.'

"I say, 'Even if I knew what you was talking about, why would I want to deal with anybody mixed up with Earl Deitrich?'

"He goes, 'To make your troubles go away, Mr. Pickett.'

"I say, 'My wife's charged with murder. You gonna make that go away?'

"He says, 'With one phone call, my friend.' Then he looked at Kippy Jo in the backyard, smiling, like he was thinking of a private joke."

Wilbur watched the lamb trying to get to its feet in the stall. The interior of the barn was dissected with beams of bluish light.

"How would Earl Deitrich know about your land?" I asked.

"He's a big man in extractive industries. I had the core tested at a lab in Denver. They all know each other," Wilbur said. "That pipeline deal in Venezuela? Every dollar we make is going into our own drilling company. Billy Bob, I'm talking about an oil and natural gas dome big as that Tuscaloosa strike back in the seventies."

"That's what all this has been about, hasn't it? He wants your oil property," I said. "What'd you tell Fletcher?"

"To keep his eyes off my wife. To get his damn car out of my driveway."

"That's the ticket."

He pulled the saddle off the Appaloosa and flung it across a sawhorse.

"It's all bluff. If I got to give it up to get Kippy Jo off, that's what we'll do." He replaced the jar of oil sand on the shelf. "It's funny what can happen just from setting down at the wrong man's table, ain't it?"

He took off his hat and wiped his forehead with his sleeve, then grinned, blade-faced, in the sun's first pink light.

Then something happened that I would not quite be able to get out of my memory. His innocent nature, his devotion to his wife, his concern for an injured animal, seemed exquisitely caught in the moment, until I smiled back at him and looked directly into his eyes. When I did, he dropped his head and buttoned a shirt pocket, as though he did not want me to see beyond an exterior that I obviously admired.

13

TEMPLE CARROL CAME INTO MY OFFICE MONDAY afternoon and sat down in front of an air-conditioning duct and let the wind stream blow across her body. Her blouse was peppered with perspiration.

"Pretty hot out there?" I said.

"I just spent two hours in the basement of the courthouse looking for the list of possessions on Bubba Grimes's body. It was buried in a box on a shelf right next to the ceiling."

She handed a manila folder to me with several departmental forms and penciled sheets from a yellow legal tablet inside. When he died Bubba Grimes's pockets had contained car keys, a roll of breath mints, a wallet with fifty-three dollars inside, a comb, fingernail clippers, a wine cork, a Mexico peso, and three dimes.

"You checked the possessions bag?" I asked.

"Yeah, it's just like it says there." She held her eyes on my face.

The possessions sheet was marked up, words smeared or scratched out. I picked up the phone and punched in Marvin Pomroy's number.

"I'm looking at some of the expert paperwork done by Hugo Roberts's deputies. For some reason it was filed in the basement with documents that are a hundred years old," I said.

"Talk to Hugo," he said.

"You know what's not on the possessions list?"

"No."

"A pocketknife. But at the bottom of the form a word is scratched out. It's scratched out so thoroughly there's no paper left," I said.

Marvin was quiet a moment. "So Hugo's boys get an F for penmanship and neatness. The scene investigator said Grimes was carrying only what's on that list."

"Grimes cut the back screen. He had to have a knife to do it. Forensics would have given us exculpatory evidence. That knife probably had strands of wire on it. I think that's why you had a blowup with Hugo over the phone. You know he's destroyed evidence."

"No, I don't know that."

"This stinks, Marvin. Don't let them drag you down with them."

"You quit the U.S. Justice Department and went to work for the dirtbags, Billy Bob. Maybe I don't always like the system I serve, but this county is a better place because of the work I do. Nothing derogatory meant. Maybe you like watching sociopaths prop their feet on your desk," he said, and hung up.

LUCAS SAID THE FIGHT between Jeff and Esmeralda actually started at the rig, on the night tower, when Jeff showed up late for work, then sassed the driller and later got careless and almost cost another floorman his life.

Imagine an environment filled with the roar of a drill motor, the singing of cables, chains whipping off pipe, hoists and huge steel tongs swinging in the air, drilling mud welling out of the hole over your steel-toed boots, the heat of flood lamps burning your skin. The night sky blooms with dry lightning, and the constant, deafening noise eats at your senses. It's a dangerous environment. But it's also one that's monotonous and mind-deadening. For just a moment, you daydream.

The tongs swung into the man next to Jeff and knocked him all the way across the platform. His bright orange hard hat rolled into the darkness like a tiddlywink. The driller shut off the engine. When the injured man sat up, his arm hung loosely from his shoulder, and the back of his wrist quivered uncontrollably on the floor. He looked stupidly at the others as though he didn't know who he was. A piece of canvas flapped in the silence.

After the injured floorman was driven to the hospital, Jeff put his bradded gloves back on and waited for the derrick man, high up on the monkey board, to unrack a section of pipe and send it down with the hoist. Then he realized the driller and the rest of the crew were looking at him, waiting for something.

"You made three mistakes in one night, Jeff. See

the timekeeper for your drag-up check," the driller said.

"I apologize for messing up. I just haven't been feeling too good," Jeff said.

"Ain't everybody cut out for it. Heck, if I had your looks, I'd go out to Hollywood. Anyway, take it easy, kid," the driller said.

A moment later Jeff was standing out in the darkness, beyond the circle of light and noise that oil field people called the night tower, watching what were now his ex-co-workers wrestle the drill bit, hose the drilling mud off the platform floor, and go about their routine as though he had never been there.

AT BREAKFAST with Lucas and Esmeralda in Lucas's kitchen, Jeff went over the incident on the platform floor again and again, analyzing what went wrong, rethinking what he should have told the driller, wondering if in fact the accident was his fault or if he had simply been made a scapegoat because he had sassed the driller earlier.

"Roughnecks get run off all the time. That's part of the life out there, Jeffro. It ain't no big deal," Lucas said.

"That's right, Jeff. There's a lot of work in San Antone now," Esmeralda said.

"Like doing what?" he asked.

"The restaurant where I work. They need an assistant manager," she answered.

His face was dull with fatigue, but a residual sense of annoyance, like a black insect feeding, seemed to glimmer in his eye.

"We can drive down there this morning. I need to stop at the washateria and go to the Wal-Mart, anyway. Cholo needs me to buy him some underwear," she said.

"You think I'm going to spend my morning shopping for your brother's underwear?" Jeff said.

"Hon, you had a bad night. Now lighten up," she said, and rested her palm on his arm.

He turned his face away from both Esmeralda and Lucas and stared out the rusted screen at a piece of guttering swinging in the wind and the yard that was matted with dandelions.

LATER IN THE MORNING Lucas turned on the electric fan in the back bedroom and went to sleep. He was awakened in the thick, yellow heat of the afternoon by quarrelsome voices out in the trailer, insults hurled like a slap, a table knocked over, perhaps, dishes clattering to the floor.

"The problem is not a stupid job on an oil derrick. You take me to lounges where it's dark. We go to restaurants where nobody knows you. You don't like being with me in the daylight," Esmeralda shouted.

Jeff burst through the door into the yard, with no shirt or shoes on, and got behind the wheel of his convertible. Then realized he had left his keys inside. He put his head down on his arms and started to weep. Esmeralda walked outside in a pair of blue-jean cutoffs and a halter, her face suddenly filled with pity, and stroked his hair and the back of his neck. Then the two of them went back into the trailer, their arms around each other's waist, and stayed there until sunset.

LUCAS WAS OFF THAT NIGHT and had planned to go into town. But Jeff and Esmeralda came to his door, their faces glowing with the promise of the summer evening, as though none of the day's events held claim on their lives. Jeff took the last toke off a roach, held the hit in his lungs, then let the smoke drift lazily off his lips into the wind. He was dressed in a tailored beige sports coat and dark blue slacks. She was wearing a pink organdy dress, hoop ear-rings, lavender pumps, and cherry-red lipstick. Jeff's necktie dangled from his coat pocket, almost as though he wished to demonstrate his indifference to decorum.

"You're going to dinner with us at Post Oaks Country Club," Jeff said.

"I appreciate it, but that's a little rich for my blood. Say, if y'all are holding, I got to ask you not to bring it on my property. I don't mean no offense," Lucas said.

"That was the last of my stash, Lucas, my boy. Hey, you're not going to hurt our feelings, are you?" Jeff said.

To its members Deaf Smith's country club wasn't simply an oasis of wealth in the middle of south-central Texas; it was the architectural expression of a cultural ideal in an era given over to vulgarity, urban ruin, and eastern liberals who destroyed standards and enfranchised an underclass made up of modern Visigoths.

The gardens and circular drive planted with oaks, the blinding-white columned entrance, the sun-bladed, turquoise pool shaped like a huge shamrock, the flagstone terrace dotted with potted palms, these were all lovely to look at but were only symbols of the club's luxury and exclusivity; its uniqueness lay in its tradition, one that went back to the early 1940s, when dance orchestras played Glen Miller's compositions on the terrace and worries over ration stamps and the war in Europe and the South Pacific were as unthreatening as the distant drone of a Flying Fortress on a training flight in a magenta sky.

The late fall might fill the trees with the smells of autumnal gases, and the shamrock-shaped pool might be drained and scrubbed with bleach and covered with canvas in winter, but mutability and death seemed to hold no sway once one entered the geographical confines of the club, which extended from the impenetrable hedges by the road, across the fairways sprayed weekly with liquid nitrogen, to the bluffs that overlooked the lazy, green bend of the river. The balls, the graduation parties, the conviviality of the bar and card room on the ninth tee, the candlelight dinners on the terrace, were part of the world's grandeur, given to those who had worked for and deserved them, and did not have to be defended. The red leaves blowing out of a hardwood tree in November were no more an indication of one's mortality than the aging and transient nature of the staff who, when they disappeared, were quickly replaced by others whose similarity to their predecessors hardly signaled a transition had taken place.

Lucas and Jeff and Esmeralda sat in the front seat of Jeff's convertible, their hair blowing in the wind as they drove out of the western end of the county into green, sloping hills and evening shadows breaking across the road. But Jeff did not want to go straight to Post Oaks Country Club. He pulled into a blue-collar bar above the river, one with takeout windows and an open-air dance pavilion and a jukebox in back.

"I don't want to go here, Jeff," Esmeralda said.

"Why not?" he said.

"We dressed up to go to a beer joint? I'm hungry. I don't want to drink on an empty stomach," she said.

"You're not dressed up," he said.

She looked at the side of his face. She placed one hand on top of his.

"What's wrong, hon?" she said.

"Nothing. Will you stop pawing me while I'm driving?" Then he forced a grin on his mouth. "I just want to get a drink. I got fired from my job last night. The tables at the club are crowded till eight o'clock. We can get some nachos. Right, Lucas?"

But Lucas didn't answer.

They drank two rounds of vodka collins, gazing at the river, the smoke from a barbecue pit attended by bikers and their girlfriends drifting across the table. Jeff kept pulling on his earlobe, biting his lip, glancing irritably at the bikers and their girls, almost as though he wanted to provoke them.

"Okay, okay, we're going. Give it a rest," he said to Esmeralda, even though she had said nothing to him.

When they pulled into the country club's driveway and stopped in front of the columned porch, Jeff got out of the car and took the parking ticket from the valet as though he were in a trance. He walked through the glass doors ahead of Esmeralda and Lucas, letting the edge of the door slide off his fingertips behind him. It was almost nine o'clock and the dining room should have been empty, the waiters gathering up silverware and soiled tablecloths and dropping wilted flowers into plastic bags. But instead the chandeliers filled the room with gold fire; carnations and roses floated in crystal bowls on the tables; and a throng of forty people was in the midst of a wedding rehearsal dinner.

One of the guests at the rehearsal dinner was Rita Summers, Jeff's ex-girlfriend. Her hair was as gold as the chandelier above her head, her blue eyes as intense as a hawk's. She took a cigarette without asking from an older woman's case and lighted it and blew smoke at an upward angle out of the side of her mouth. Jeff led Esmeralda and Lucas to a table in the corner and seated himself so his back was to the wedding party.

"This is a right nice place," Lucas said.

"Right nice? Yeah, that says it. That really says it. Right nice," Jeff said, as if his statement held a cryptic profundity that no one else understood.

"That girl over there, the one staring at us. She's the one who told me her food tasted like dog turds," Esmeralda said.

"She's nearsighted. She's got a bug up her ass. Who cares what her problem is? Just don't look at her," Jeff said. "Did you hear me? Look at the menu."

"Jeff, this ain't turning out too cool," Lucas said.

"Tell me about it," Jeff said, and snapped his fingers at a waiter. "Andre, bring three T-bones out here, three schooners, three tossed salads. Shrimp cocktails for them, none for me. I'll take a Jack and Coke now."

"Very good, Mr. Deitrich," the waiter said, and bowed slightly without ever looking at Lucas or Esmeralda. Jeff pulled the menu out of Esmeralda's hands and gave it to the waiter.

"Wow, what a take-charge guy," Esmeralda said.

"At this time of night, in this particular club, you either order steak or you eat warmed-up leftovers. I know that, you don't. So I was saving everybody time," Jeff said.

"I think I need to find the ladies' room. You know, in case I have to throw up later," Esmeralda said.

"You want to explore? It's a club. Can't you just . . ."

"What?" she said.

"Quit turning everything into a problem. Let's just eat dinner and get out of here. Oh, forget it," Jeff said, and flipped a tiny silver spoon in the air and let it bounce on the tablecloth.

But before Esmeralda could get up from her chair, Rita Summers walked across the carpet and stood by their table, smoking her cigarette.

"Congratulations on your marriage, Jeff. I wish I'd had some preparation. I would have sent a gift. I really would," she said. She had a peach complexion and shadows pooled in the folds of her blue satin dress and there was a shine on the tops of her breasts.

"Yeah, thanks for dropping by," Jeff said, one arm hooked over the back of his chair, his eyes gazing out the French doors at the underwater lights glowing off the swimming pool's surface.

Rita took a puff off her cigarette and left lipstick on the tip. "I guess you've worked out all your little sexual problems. I'm so happy when the right people meet," she said.

The waiter brought Jeff's Coke and Jack Daniel's on a tray, and Jeff drank the glass half empty, his eyes deepening in color, then swung a cherry back and forth by its stem and stared at it.

"You want to clarify that last remark?" Esmeralda said.

Rita smiled at Jeff, then bent down and whispered in Esmeralda's ear, her eyes uplifted maliciously into Jeff's. Esmeralda's face grew pinched, puckering like an apple exposed to intense heat.

Rita straightened up and looked down at Esmeralda. "He used to go to Mexican cathouses for it. But finally the only place that would let him in was run by a black woman down in the Valley," she said.

Esmeralda picked up her purse, one with spangles and pink fringe, and walked past the wedding party to the rest rooms, her chin tilted upward, the movement of her hips accentuated. But she could not hide the look in her eyes.

"If we weren't in this dining room, I'd kick your ass around the block," Jeff said to Rita.

"Oh, I know you would. You're just so . . . *studly*," Rita said, and made a feigned passionate noise and kissing motion with her mouth and rejoined her party. She leaned forward confidentially, telling a story to a half dozen others, all of whom were grinning.

"Get Esmeralda out of the can. We're going," Jeff said.

"Me?" Lucas said.

"You're not a member here. Nobody cares what you do. Go get her."

"Tell you what. I'll just walk out to the highway and hitch a ride. In the meantime, why don't you quit acting like your shit don't flush?"

"All right, I'm sorry. Sit down. I'll take care of it. God, why do I get myself into this stuff?" Jeff said. He finished his drink, then stood up, his face blanching slightly as the combination of whiskey and vodka on an empty stomach suddenly took effect.

He walked down the hallway to the ladies' room and went in without knocking. A moment later he and Esmeralda emerged in the hallway, his hand spread across the small of her back. Her cheeks were wet, her purse held tightly in both hands.

"She's a liar. She gave blow jobs to the whole backfield at SMU. She's treating you like a dumb peon," he said to her.

The waiter had wheeled their dinner to their table and was placing schooners of draft beer to the right of each steak platter.

"Bag it up for the dishwashers, Andre. We're gonna boogie on over to the Dog 'n' Shake. That's where it's happening," Jeff said, and signed the ticket on the serving cart.

Then he realized that Rita Summers and her friends were laughing, not abruptly, as they would have at a joke, but in a sustained, collective giggle that seemed to spread like a crinkling of cellophane at their table. He turned and saw their eyes fixed on Esmeralda's shoe and the long strand of wet toilet paper that was attached to the sole.

He gripped her upper arm, squeezing hard, and stepped with one foot on the toilet paper and tried to push her free of it. Instead, he only shredded the paper and matted it on his loafer. His rage boiled into his face and he stooped and tore Esmeralda's shoe off her foot and flung it under a table, then pulled her out the front door.

"All you had to do was just eat dinner. It was that simple. You people are a walking ad for the Ku Klux Klan. Stop making that sound," he said, while she rested her forehead against one of the white columns on the porch and hid her face in her hands.

14

I KNEW IT WAS WRONG.

In the same way a reformed drunkard places himself on an innocuous mission to a saloon or an unrewarded hunter at twilight fires a round through the window of a deserted stone house and turns his back on the crashing sounds inside.

Peggy Jean said the picnic at the cottage on the Comal River was for children from an orphans home, that Pete would probably love shooting the rapids with the others in an inner tube.

She wasn't wrong about that part. As soon as I parked the Avalon among a stand of pine trees above the river, he wrestled his inner tube from the car trunk and ran down a clay path between boulders to a sandy beach that paralleled a long, undulating riffle created by a wood dam built halfway across the current. His ribs and the bones in his back were as taut as sticks against his skin. Through the trees I saw him wade into the thick green coldness of the water.

"Don't worry about him. I hired two lifeguards to watch after them," Peggy Jean said.

She stood next to the cottage in a flagstone, trellised arbor overgrown with climbing roses. The cottage was the color of chalk against the trees, the windows hung with ventilated blue shutters, the wind chimes on the porch twirling in the breeze. She flipped a checkered tablecloth over a plank table and began setting it with plastic forks and spoons and cups that were painted with the pink faces of smiling pigs. She had flown in from Padre Island that morning, and there was fresh sunburn on her forehead and neck.

"We can't stay too long. His mom wants him back by dark," I said.

"Did you bring your trunks?" she asked.

"Sure."

"I'm going to take a swim. You can change inside. I'll use the bathhouse in back," she said. She watched my face. "Is something wrong?"

"No."

"You don't feel you should be here?"

"I don't study a lot on right and wrong these days," I said.

She fixed a strand of hair on her forehead. "Ernest Hemingway said if you feel bad about something the next morning, it's wrong and you should avoid doing it again. If you don't feel bad about it, you should take joy in the memory."

When I didn't reply, she turned and walked to the small bathhouse in back with a rolled towel under her arm. She'd had her hair cut and it was thick and burnished with gold light on the back of her neck.

The sun went behind a bank of rain clouds and suddenly the wind seemed cold and tannic through the pines. I looked at the firmness of her calves and the way her hips moved under her dress. An old iron water pump by the bathhouse was beaded with moisture that dripped off the pump handle into the dirt. I remained staring at the bathhouse door after she had closed it, my mouth dry, my face moist in the wind as though I had a fever.

I changed inside the cottage. Moments later she came back out of the bathhouse in straw sandals and a one-piece dark blue bathing suit.

"You still have your shirt on," she said.

"It's turned right cool," I replied.

"I'll fix you a drink."

"You know me. I'm still nine-tenths Baptist."

"Oh stop it," she said, and circled my wrist with her forefinger and thumb and tugged me gently inside the back door of the cottage.

She fixed two vodka collins at the bar that divided the kitchen and the living room. The door to the bedroom was open, and the bed was made up with a tight white bedspread and fat, frilled pillows and a folded navy-blue blanket at the bed's foot. She put the collins glass in my palm, then drank from hers, her face only inches from mine.

"I never thought you were much of a drinker," I said.

"With time, you learn to do all kinds of things,"

she replied. Her breath smelled like ice and mint leaves and was warm against my skin at the same time. "Do you want to sit outside?"

I didn't answer. Her hand lay on top of the bar and the ends of her fingers touched mine. She moved her fingers on top of my hand, then set down her glass and tilted her face up and held her eyes on mine. I kissed her on the mouth, then felt her body press against me, her weight rise on one foot, the muscles of her back flex under my hands.

Her hair smelled like salt wind and sunlight and I could feel her breath like a feather against my neck. Through the half-opened bedroom door the taut whiteness of the bedspread and the bloom of pillows at the headboard seemed the most lovely rectangle of light and symmetry and comfort in the world. She rubbed the top of her head against my mouth and pressed her stomach tightly against me, one hand slipping down the small of my back. In my mind's eye I felt already drawn inside the cradle of her thighs, inside the absolute glory and heat of her body, her mouth a throaty whisper against my ear.

Then I looked through the window and saw L.Q. Navarro in the front yard, leaning against a pine trunk, his arms folded, one boot cocked toe-down across the other, his face obscured by his hat.

"What the hell you doin', son?" his voice said.

I felt myself step away from Peggy Jean and the fullness of her breasts and the mystery of her eyes.

"Why are you staring out the window?" she asked.

"Because there's no sound," I replied.

"There's no—" she began.

"The children were yelling in the rapids. Now it's quiet. Why did they stop yelling?" I said.

"What's the matter with you, Billy Bob? Sometimes you act like you're crazy," she said.

But I wasn't listening now. I went into the front yard, into the wind that was colder than it should have been, into a smell that was like autumn woods and pine needles in shadow and the gases from dead flowers. From the edge of the promontory I could see the thick green surface of the river, the current bunching at the rapids, the braided foam that twisted and swelled in a long riffle over gray boulders, the evening shadows that seemed to transfix the bottom of the ravine with silence.

The two hired lifeguards, their torsos swollen with the contours of weight lifters, stood on the bank, surrounded by children, scanning the water in both directions. One lifeguard began pushing nervously at his forehead with his fingers; the other walked up and down the bank, questioning the children, his face reddening with exasperation, as though they were deliberately denying him the solution to his problem.

Then I saw Pete through the pines on the slope, forty yards down from the rapids, struggling in a whirlpool that had formed on the lee side of a huge boulder. His inner tube was on the outside of the vortex, only three or four feet from his grasp, but it might as well have been an ocean away.

He flailed at the water, kicking hard for the bank, then his thin shoulders spun in the center of the whirlpool and he went under.

I skidded barefoot down the slope over rocks and exposed tree roots and crashed through a nest of blackberry bushes onto the beach. On the far side of the stream I could see his face just under the surface, his eyes squinted shut, his hair floating from his scalp, his mouth pinched tight against the breath he wanted to draw from the water. I ran across a flat rock and dove headlong into the current, felt the cold strike like an anvil against the bone, then took two hard strokes and went under and grabbed him around the waist and brought him to the surface with me, throwing him as far as I could toward the bank.

Then my feet touched the soap-rock bottom and I gathered Pete in my arms and lifted him against my chest and waded onto gravel and sand and the tall clumps of grass growing along the bank.

I lay him down and stroked his head and rubbed his back and felt the warmth of his breath against my skin.

His face was white from exhaustion, beaded with water, when he looked up at me.

"I knew you was coming," he said.

"Almost didn't make it, bud," I replied.

"Cain't fool me, Billy Bob. I wasn't never afraid," he said.

I gathered him up on my shoulder and climbed up the path to the top of the promontory. Peggy Jean stood openmouthed in the front yard of the cottage, her skin prickled in the wind.

"The lifeguards were supposed to be watching. I gave them the exact number of children who'd be here. They could have no doubt about that," she said.

"I'll get my things out of the cottage," I said.

"I paid them to watch every one of those children, Billy Bob."

"I know. The problem's not yours."

"Then get that expression off your face."

I went inside with Pete still on my shoulder, then came back out with my clothes and boots bunched under my left arm.

"Ernest Hemingway is my favorite writer. I admired his great courage. But in the end he blew his head off with a shotgun. Goodbye, Peggy Jean," I said.

KYLE ROSE HAD A PROBLEM. All his life he had loved uniforms—the National Guard fatigues he wore to monthly meetings, the pressed, deputy sheriff's greenish-brown short-sleeve shirts and lead-striped trousers that looked like Marine Corps tropicals, even the bleached-white straw hat and shades and starched khaki pants he wore when he had been a migrant crew leader supervising stoop labor in bean fields.

The buzzed haircut, the flex of cartilage in the jaw, the eyes that could make county inmates and street people look at their shoes, this was only part of the appearance he cultivated, that told people who and what he was. You also had to be squared away, booted and hatted, the tendons in your body forming a geometrically perfect network of power inside a tight-fitting uniform. The opaqueness of your face and the tight seam of your mouth had to make them swallow.

But all of it had failed him, and he didn't know why or how to explain his feelings to anyone else.

Jessie Stump and Skyler Doolittle were out on the ground, somewhere in the hills across the river from where they had broken out of the jail bus. But why should that bother him? Stump was white trash and a crankhead; electroshock had turned his brains into scorched grits. Doolittle was a killer of children, a deformed pervert who looked like a dildo and belonged inside a circus wagon. Kyle Rose had pulled blacks by their hair out of Nigger Town clubs while their friends did nothing. Once he climbed a water tower and clubbed a sniper unconscious with the butt of his shotgun. A mainline recidivist who had been brought in from Huntsville as a witness in a trial threw his food tray against the drunk tank wall and sent the trusties scurrying down the corridor. Kyle Rose made him clean it up with his shirt, then crawl under the deadline that was painted on the cement floor.

Why did the thought of Skyler Doolittle and Jessie Stump out on the ground make words stick in his throat and cause him to unconsciously wipe his palms on his trousers?

Because they were not afraid of him. Stump was too crazy and Doolittle . . . Kyle Rose couldn't describe what it was that made Doolittle different. It wasn't just the fused neck. Doolittle's eyes seemed to accept pain as though that were the only condition he had ever known, like a naked man who has spent a lifetime on a trail that wanders endlessly through thornbushes. There was no handle on a man like that.

Kyle Rose bought a second handgun, a .25-caliber hideaway that strapped comfortably on the ankle. But a wire was trembling inside him, and neither the hideaway nor the shots of tequila he drank at lunch nor his belligerent rhetoric in the deputies' bullpen gave him relief.

"I think we ought to scour them cliffs above the river," he said to Hugo Roberts.

"What for? They ain't hurt the guards on the bus. I don't see no great danger out there," Hugo said. He sat in the gloom behind his desk, the smoke from his cupped cigarette climbing into his face.

"They're escaped prisoners. That's what for. One ought to be gelded, the other un stuffed back in his mother's womb," Kyle said.

Hugo propped his elbows on the desk blotter and

puffed on his cigarette and breathed the smoke out on his hands. He looked disinterestedly out the window.

"Provided they ain't already in Mexico, they'll come out when they're hungry. In the meantime, find yourself a woman, Kyle. Or take up paddleball. Why'd you stoke up them boys with a stun gun, anyway? All we need is the Justice Department sending undercover agents in here again," Hugo said.

Kyle Rose walked out of the sandstone blockhouse and slammed the door behind him with his foot. Hugo's other deputies kept their eyes fixed in a neutral space, the refrigerated odor of smoke and testosterone and expectorated Red Man wrapped on their bodies like cellophane on produce.

"We got to start using civil service exams, establish better screening. I think the boy's got a serious nervous disorder. I do," Hugo said. He puffed on his cigarette, breathing the smoke philosophically over his hands.

KYLE ROSE TOOK THREE DAYS OFF without pay and went to the trailer he owned on the river. The lawn was neat, nubbed down by goats, the pine trees widely spaced so Kyle had full view of all his surroundings. But he took no chances. The first night there he ran trip wire strung with tin cans around the tree trunks in the yard and loaded his scoped deer rifle and leaned it inside the front door. Then he sat in a deck chair on the screen porch with a cold bottle of Carta Blanca and watched the boat lights on the river, the fire in his neighbor's barbecue pit flaring under a piece of meat, the evening star rising above the hills into a mauve-colored sky.

He slept late and rose refreshed and had coffee with his neighbor, a retired enlisted man, then split firewood on a stump by the river's edge even though he would not need it until the fall.

It was amazing what a good night's sleep could do. His worries about Skyler Doolittle and Jessie Stump now seemed childish and inconsequential. Besides, they had invited whatever troubles befell them. Sometimes you had to shave the dice a little bit or nobody went down. That's what Hugo said. Skyler Doolittle had killed children while DWI, then had been picked up next to a school yard. How many free passes does a guy like that get? So they put some child porn in his room. Big deal. Rather that than this guy wipe out another busload of kids. Right?

Stump was another one who should have been fed into a tree shredder. The whole family had lived on a muddy, brush-tangled oxbow of the river for generations, inbreeding, shining deer, tapping into the county power line, stringing forest fires when the lumber mill wouldn't hire them, shooting holes in a Job Corps water tower.

No, a tree shredder wouldn't do it, Kyle thought. It would take napalm. Bring in fighter jets and nape the entire sinkhole, sterilize the earth they had walked on so the virus couldn't infect the gene pool worse than it already had.

In fact, as the day wore on, Kyle wished Doolittle or Stump would have a go at him. They all made noise about getting even once they were on the street. How they'd like to eat a toppling soft-nosed round from his scoped deer rifle? Whap. Just like blowing the back out of a watermelon.

That evening he went outside with his bow and quiver of arrows and pinned a fresh paper target on the hay bales he had stacked against his toolshed. The paper was shiny and soft, like oilcloth, when Kyle rolled it out and flattened it against the bale, and the image of the white-tailed deer seemed to shimmer with life in the fading light. From thirty-five yards Kyle drove a half dozen arrows into the deer's neck and sides, the fletched shafts quivering solidly upon impact.

It was a beautiful evening. The sky was purple above the hills, and the shadows seemed to drape the trees with a mosslike softness, like fir trees in a rain forest. He took a bottle of tequila out of an ice bucket on his shooting table and drank two fingers neat from a shot glass and chased it with Carta Blanca. This was the good life. It might even get a lot better after Hugo Roberts destroyed his remaining lung with cigarettes. Who was a better candidate for Hugo's replacement than Kyle Rose?

He lay his bow on the shooting table and walked

to the perforated paper target and began pulling the arrow shafts from the bales of hay. Rain was moving out of the south, dimming the fields in the distance, clicking now on the asphalt county road at the foot of his property. The air was dense and cool, like air from a cave, and the pine trees shook in the wind and scattered pine needles across the top of Kyle's trailer. For just a moment he thought he heard a tin can tinkle on a wire.

A bolt of lightning crashed in a field across the road and illuminated the trees, burning all the shadows from the clearing, and Kyle saw the tinkling sound was only the wind playing tricks on him. A solitary drop of water struck his head, hard, like a marble, and he finished gathering the arrow shafts from the hay bale.

When he turned around he saw a man in a yellow raincoat and shapeless fedora by the shooting table. The man's face was dark with shadow, but there was no doubt about what he was doing. He had notched an arrow, one with a filed and barbed point, on the bowstring and was pulling back the bow with the power of a man whose strength seemed more than human.

He heard the arrow whiz toward him, a sound like the air being scissored apart. He threw his hands in front of his face and tried to whirl away from the arrow's impact but instead took the point high up under his armpit. He felt the shaft traverse his lungs, felt the gift of breath and oxygen taken from him as quickly as the ruptured bladder of a football collapsing against the toe of a cleated shoe.

He felt blood rising into his throat now, his chest breaking into flame, the arrow's shaft catching under his right arm each time he tried to reach for the .25-caliber hideaway that was strapped to his ankle.

The man in the yellow raincoat and fedora walked toward him in the rain, notching another arrow on the bowstring. Kyle's fingers fluttered on the grips of the .25 automatic, then he freed it from its holster and tried to raise it in front of him. The hatted man kicked it from his hand as though it were a toadstool.

The second arrow pierced Kyle's jaws and embedded in the soft earth under the side of his face. In his mind's eye he saw himself as a fish cast upon land, red flowers issuing from his mouth, the pollen blowing across a pair of prison work boots.

He breathed hard through his pinioned cheeks, his eyes trying to absorb a last glimmer of gold light on the river's surface.

15

THE FOLLOWING MONDAY I STOOD AT MY OFFICE window and watched Marvin Pomroy cross the street, his starched white shirt crinkling in the sunlight. He disappeared into the alcove on the first floor of my building, and although I couldn't see him now, I knew he was mounting the stairs three at a time, as he always did. Moments later he sat down in front of my desk and wiped his glasses with a Kleenex. His face was egg-shaped, pink with heat, but not a hair was out of place.

"Boiling out there, huh?" I said.

He touched at his forehead with his shirtsleeve and ignored the question.

"The casts from the crime scene are of prison work shoes, the same kind we issue at the jail. Doolittle and Stump were both wearing them when they broke loose from the bus. They both wear size eleven, same size as the casts," he said.

"Doolittle's not a killer, Marvin," I said.

"That was an eighty-pound bow. Doolittle has the strength to pull it. Stump doesn't."

"Stump's a meth-brain. He destroyed his brother-in-law's house by running back and forth through the walls. He stuffed a Mexican's head in a drainpipe at Snooker's Big Eight."

But I could see Marvin's attention already starting to wander.

"A paramedic over at County says you brought a little half-breed boy into emergency receiving. You wanted his lungs checked out so he didn't develop pneumonia from a near drowning," Marvin said.

"That's right."

He got up from his chair and stood at the window and looked down at the street. "It happened around New Braunfels? At a swimming party for an orphans group or something?" he asked.

"This is why you came over here?"

"Peggy Jean and Earl Deitrich have a cottage down there. They sponsor a swim party for orphans once or twice a year."

"What's your point, Marvin?"

"You have three clients—Wilbur and Kippy Jo Pickett and Skyler Doolittle—involved in an adversarial relationship with Earl Deitrich. You're getting in his wife's bread and you ask me what's the point?"

"I don't care for your language," I said.

Marvin turned from the window and bunched my sleeve in his fist, his eyes full of pity and disappointment.

"You could be disbarred for stuff like this. You're a pain in the ass, but you're an honest man. If you let me down, Billy Bob, I'm going to bust your jaw," he said.

THAT EVENING KIPPY JO PICKETT hauled five buckets of water from the horse tank and started a fire of slat wood under an iron pot set on stones in the lee of the barn. She sat in the shade, upwind of the fire, and felt the heat begin to crawl through the iron and rise from the water's surface. The ground was littered with the chickens Wilbur had butchered on the stump before driving off to a temporary job at a rig out in the hills, their headless bodies flopping in the dirt, their feathers powdering with dust. When the first steam bubbles chained to the pot's surface, she lifted two chickens by the feet and dipped them into the water, then sat back down in her chair and began ripping sheaths of wet feathers from their skins and dropping them into a paper bag. That's when she heard the car turn into the drive and stop, the twin exhausts echoing off the side of the house.

She wiped her hands on a cloth and wrapped her fingers around the handle of the hatchet Wilbur had used to butcher the chickens and listened to a man's footsteps come up the drive and into the backyard.

She looked into the purple haze and the dust blowing from the hoof-smoothed area around the horse tank, and inside her mind saw a squat, brow-furrowed man with the thick neck of a hog watching her. The wind blew out of the north and swept her hair back over her shoulders and lifted her dress around her knees. The man approached her, guardedly, his feet splayed, his gaze sweeping the yard, the pasture where the horses nickered, the sun's fire on the western hills, his nostrils dilating like an animal emerging from a cave.

He paused when he saw the hatchet behind the calf of her leg. Her sightless eyes seemed to burrow into his face and probe thoughts and feelings that he himself did not understand. He swallowed and felt foolish and cowardly and wiped his mouth with his hand. Then she did something he didn't expect. She rested the head of the hatchet by her foot and released the handle and let it fall sideways into the dust.

"I'm looking for Wilbur Pickett," he said.

"He's at work. On the oil rig. He won't be home till morning," she answered.

He waved one hand back and forth in front of her eyes, his soiled palm only ten inches from her face.

"Don't do that," she said.

He stepped back, frightened again. He tried to think clearly before he spoke again. His tongue made a clicking sound inside his mouth. "How you know I did anything? How come a blind woman will tell a stranger she's all alone? That ain't smart," he said.

"You might be a violent man. But it's because others have hurt you," she said.

His face flinched as though flies were buzzing in

it. He opened and closed his palms at his sides and could hear himself breathing. He studied the flecks of whiteness in her blue eyes, the redness of her mouth, the way her black hair whipped around her cheeks in the wind. She pressed her dress down over her knees and waited for him to speak.

"I know stuff about Earl Deitrich don't nobody else know. I can bring him down," he said.

"We don't care what you can do," she replied.

"Don't talk to me like that. I'm here to help. We got a, what do you call it, we got a mutual interest."

"No," she said.

"Listen, lady, y'all got something he wants or he wouldn't be trying to send your old man to the pen. Your husband wildcatted in Mexico. It's got something to do with oil, ain't it?"

"It's not your business. There's fried rabbit and potato salad on the kitchen table. Bring it out," she said.

"Bring food out? I didn't come out here to eat. Look, lady"

"You hate Earl Deitrich because he treats you and someone close to you with disrespect. He's obligated to you but makes you feel worthless. You fight with him in your mind and he always wins."

He stepped back from her, his mouth opening to speak. Her words were like cobweb that he wanted to wipe out of his face. She rose from her chair and spread newspaper on the stump that was grained with dried blood and bits of chicken feathers. She set a stone on each side of the newspaper so the wind wouldn't blow it away.

"What's your name?" she asked.

"Cholo Ramirez."

"You're part Indian, Cholo. The spirits of all your people watch over you. Don't be frightened. Go get the food," she said.

He walked away from her toward the house, his head twisted back toward her, his close-set eyes like those of a wolf circling a steel trap. He stepped inside the kitchen door and pressed the heel of each hand hard into his temples, opening and closing his mouth until the whirring of blood ceased in his ears. The interior of the kitchen was painted with fire from the glow of sun through the west windows. He struck the heels of his hands repeatedly against the sides of his skull but his head would not clear. For a moment he felt he was deep under the earth, inside a box of flame that had been created especially for him and that he would never escape.

RAIN WAS FALLING across the sunset when Pete and I entered the stucco Catholic church where he and I attended Mass. It was cool from the electric fans that oscillated on the walls and the air smelled of stone and the water in the rain ditch outside. I lighted a candle for L.Q. Navarro in the rack of burning candle vases in front of a statue of Jesus' mother, then entered the confessional.

The priest was ten years younger than I, a thin, Mexican Franciscan named Father Paul who had once been a labor organizer for the United Farm Workers. He listened while I told him of my behavior at Peggy Jean Deitrich's cottage, the self-delusion that had put me there, the possible compromise of my clients' interest.

Then I relived the moment that had burned inside me like a hot coal. "A little boy I should have been watching almost drowned. In another minute he would have been gone," I said.

"I see," the priest said. Through the screen I could see his profile, his jaw propped on two fingers, his eyes staring into the gloom. "Is there more?"

"No."

"I have the sense there's something you haven't mentioned. I think it has to do with anger."

"I don't see the connection, Father."

"You don't have to answer this question if you don't want to. But do you regret the injury done the third party, the husband?"

I could hear the rain running off the tile roof outside the confessional, the sound of someone kneeling in a pew, a car passing on the wetness of the street.

"He's an evil man," I said.

Father Paul's profile turned toward me for just a moment, then he looked straight ahead again, as though resigning himself to an old knowledge about human behavior.

"By whatever power is vested in me, I absolve you of your sins. The peace of the Lord be with you, Billy Bob," he said.

THE LIGHT IN THE SKY was green when Pete and I walked outside and the rain was dripping into the shadows under the pines on the lawn. Pete wore his straw hat low over his eyes and breathed in the dampness of the air as though he were taking the world's measure.

"We still gonna get them buffalo burger steaks?" he asked.

"You bet," I said.

"That's Temple Carrol's car in front of the cafe," he said.

"It sure is."

"Why you stopping?"

"No reason."

"You sure tell a mess of fibs, Billy Bob. Soon as I figure out one angle of yours, you come up with another."

"Do me a favor, Pete."

"What's that?"

"Stay out of my head."

"I knew you was gonna say that."

The inside of the cafe was brightly lit, the front window beaded with rainwater, the fans ruffling the oilcloths on the tables. I hadn't seen Temple since the incident at Peggy Jean's cottage on the Comal and my voice felt thick in my throat when we sat down at her table. The side of her face was pink from the sunset and rippled with the shadows of raindrops running down the window. She kept looking inquisitively into my eyes.

"Y'all go to church on weeknights?" she said.

"Billy Bob went to confession," Pete said.

"Oh? Did we do something we shouldn't?" she said, looking at me strangely.

"I got pulled in a whirlpool. Billy Bob saved my life. But he blames himself 'cause I was in the whirlpool. That ain't no reason to go to confession," Pete said, and began chewing on a breadstick.

"You were in the river? It's pretty high this time of year for swimming, Pete," she said.

"We was at Ms. Deitrich's place in New Braunfels. That's what I was saying. Billy Bob and Ms. Deitrich was up changing at the cottage when I got pulled into the whirlpool," Pete said.

"Oh, at Ms. Deitrich's. South Texas's angel of charity. I should have known. Did you have a good time, Billy Bob?" Temple said, her eyes peeling the skin off my face.

"It wasn't a good day. It was also the last one I'll have like it," I said.

"Why is it I don't believe you? Why is that, please tell me?" she said. She set down her coffee cup in the saucer, picked up her check, and rose from the table.

"What ch'all talking about?" Pete asked, his face filled with confusion.

• • •

EARLY WEDNESDAY MORNING I got the milk delivery off the porch and picked up a half dozen eggs around the chicken run and under the tractor and put them in an apple basket and began beating an omelette in the kitchen. Beau was drinking out of an aluminum tank just inside the rails of the horse lot and I saw his head lift at the sound of a car in my drive.

Marvin Pomroy came around back and tapped on the screen door to the porch. He wore a seersucker suit and narrow brown suspenders with his white shirt. I thought he had come to the house to apologize for threatening to break my jaw. Wrong. He sat down at the kitchen table without being invited and began smacking one fist erratically into his palm.

"Yes?" I said.

"I think Wilbur and Kippy Jo Pickett and Skyler Doolittle are all guilty of various crimes. I think guilty people come to you as a matter of course, primarily because you're a sucker for daytime TV watchers who model their lives on soap operas. So my being here has nothing to do with a change of attitude about your clients," he said.

"Thanks for the feedback on that, Marvin."

"But because your clients are dirty doesn't mean that Earl Deitrich isn't."

"You've got a problem of conscience?" I asked.

"No. What I've got is this character Fletcher Grinnel, Deitrich's chauffeur. A week ago he was staring at me in the courthouse with this smirk on his face. I said, 'Can I help you with something?'

"He says, 'I was just admiring your suspenders. I served with a man, an ex-banker, actually, who always wore suspenders like that when we were on leave. He was a ferocious fighter. You'd never believe it from his appearance.'

"So I said, 'You were in the military?'

"He goes, 'Here and there. Mostly with a private group. Ex-Legionnaires, South African mercs, guys who were drummed out of the British army, that sort of thing. But we saved a lot of Europeans from the wogs and the bush bunnies.'"

Marvin paused, his eyes blinking.

"What does this have to do with my clients?" I asked.

"Several political pissants in Austin keep calling me up about Wilbur and Kippy Jo Pickett, like somehow I'm not fully committed to the situation. Then I have this encounter with Fletcher Grinnel, who seems to think he can use racist language with me as though we're in the same white brotherhood. So I called in a favor from a federal agent in Washington and had him run this guy.

"Grinnel is a naturalized U.S. citizen from New Zealand. He's also worked for some very nasty people in South Africa and the Belgian Congo. He thinks cutting off body parts is quite a joke."

"That's on his sheet?"

"No. Grinnel told me his friend, the ex-banker

who wore suspenders like mine, made necklaces of human ears and fingers that he traded for ivory and rhino horn. Grinnel said his friend put a burning tire around a man and made his family watch."

Marvin sat very still in the chair, his face bemused at the strangeness of his own words, one strand of hair hanging in the middle of his glasses.

"I think once in a while we're allowed to look into someone's eyes, somebody who a moment earlier seemed perfectly normal, and see right to the bottom of the abyss," he said. "But maybe that's just my fundamentalist upbringing."

His eyes lifted earnestly into mine, as though waiting for an opinion.

THAT EVENING Wilbur Pickett drove a flatbed pipe truck into my backyard and stepped down from the cab with a half pint of whiskey in his hand. His skin was filmed with dust, his washed-out denim shirt unbuttoned on his chest, his battered hat streaked with grease.

"You're listing hard to port, bud," I said.

"I got run off two jobs in one day. The driller cut me loose at the rig and the water well boss said he felt ashamed at hiring a rodeo man to do nigra work. Told me he was firing me out of respect. How about them pineapples?" he said.

"Were you drunk?"

"No. But I'm working on it."

"Why'd they run you off?"

He tipped the half-pint bottle to his lips and drank gingerly, perhaps no more than a capful, the whiskey lighting in the glass against the sun.

"Somebody got to them. Somebody with the name Earl Deitrich, I expect," he said.

"We can do something about that," I said.

"No, you cain't. He's the man with the money and the power. I thought folks here'bouts would stand behind one of their own. That's the thinking of a fool, son."

"Come inside."

"Nope. I'm throwing it in. Cut a deal with that fellow Pomroy."

"What?"

"I'm letting Earl Deitrich in on our drill site up in Wyoming. Neither me or Kippy Jo is going to jail."

He tried to hold his eyes on mine, then his stare broke and he drank from the bottle again.

"I don't care what Deitrich or his people have told you. Marvin Pomroy won't have anything to do with something like this. Frankly I won't, either," I said.

"Then I'll get me another lawyer."

"That's your choice, sir."

"I ain't no 'sir.' I ain't nothing. But at least I ain't been sleeping with the wife of the man trying to put my friends in jail."

His face was sullen, embarrassed, and accusatory, like a child's, all at the same time. I turned and walked back inside the house. I heard him fling his uncapped whiskey bottle whistling into the twilight, then start his truck and back out into the street, tearing a swatch out of a poplar tree.

WHAT COULD I DO about Wilbur? The answer was nothing. I drove out to his house on the hardpan in the morning. As I approached the house a '49 Mercury roared past me in the opposite direction.

Kippy Jo Pickett was on the front steps, in the shade, snapping beans in a pan, when I walked into the yard.

"That was Cholo Ramirez's car," I said.

"Yes, he just left."

"What's he doing here?"

"Visiting. Telling me about his life, his cars, things he worries about."

"That kid has brain damage. If I were you, I'd leave him alone."

"His mother's boyfriend broke his skull when he was a baby. Do we also throw away the part of him that wasn't damaged? Is that what you mean?"

I looked off in the distance, across the hot shimmer of the fields, and watched Cholo run a STOP sign, then swerve full-bore around an oil truck.

"Where's Wilbur?" I asked.

"He went down to the state employment office."

"Earl Deitrich's trying to jerk y'all around. If you're jammed up for money, I can lend you some. Don't give in to this man."

Her eyes fixed on my face and stayed there. A brown and white beagle lay in a shallow depression by the side of the gallery, its tail flopping in the silence.

"You'd do that?" she asked.

"Pay me back when y'all punch into your first oil sand."

"Wilbur's scared. He sits by himself in the kitchen in the middle of the night. He thinks I'm going to prison."

"Listen, Kippy Jo, men like Earl Deitrich steal people's dreams. They have no creative vision of their own, no love, and no courage. They envy people like you and Wilbur. That's why they have to destroy you."

She was quiet a long time. The sun was hot and bright in the sky, and the pools of rainwater in the alfalfa glimmered like quicksilver. Kippy Jo set down the tin pan of snapbeans and kneaded the thick folds of skin on top of the beagle's neck. The wind blew her hair in a black skein across her eyes.

"He won't listen," she said.

EARL DEITRICH WAS ONE of those who believed that when force, control, and arrogance did not get you your way, you simply applied more of the same.

That night the moon was down, and rain clouds sealed the sky and heat lightning flickered over the hills in the west. Wilbur and Kippy Jo slept under an

electric fan, the drone of the motor and the tinny vi-
bration of the wire basket over the blades threading
in and out of their sleep as the fan head oscillated on
its axis. At 2 A.M. Wilbur heard a crunching sound,
like car tires rolling slowly across pea gravel. He
rose from the bed in his underwear and lifted the
.308 Savage lever-action from the rack and walked
barefoot into the living room. He looked out into the
drive and at the road in front and saw nothing. He
leaned down on the windowsill, the curtains blowing
against his skin. He stared into the darkness until his
eyes burned and he imagined shapes that he knew
were not there.

He walked into the kitchen and took a quart of
milk from the icebox and drank from it. Then he
heard car tires crunching on the gravel again, rolling
faster this time, and he realized the sounds had come
from the back of the house, not the front.

He opened the screen door and stepped into the
yard just as three men pushed his pickup truck out
onto the road, turned over the engine, and jumped inside. He ran to the side of the house, threw his rifle
to his shoulder, and levered a round into the chamber.

He moved the iron sights just ahead of the driver's
window, saw the man silhouetted against a light on a
neighbor's barn, and felt his finger tighten on the
trigger. Then he blew out his breath and lifted the
barrel into the air, resting the stock in the cradle of

his left arm. He watched the truck disappear down the road toward the hills in the west.

He heard Kippy Jo behind him.

"I'll call 911," she said.

"It won't do no good. It'll just bring Hugo Roberts and them thugs of his back out here."

"Come back in the house," she said, tugging at his arm.

"No. They turned off the road into the hills. They're stopping for something. I'm going after them sons of bucks."

"That's what they want you to do."

"Then they should have thought twicet about what they prayed for. That's a Wilbur T. Pickett guarantee."

Wilbur put on a cotton shirt and jeans and a pair of boots and hung a flashlight on a lanyard around his neck and bridled one of his palominos and rode it bareback out to the hills, the lever-action Savage propped across the horse's withers. He rode through arroyos and a sandy wash dimpled with pools of red water. He rode up a steep incline into mesquite and blackjack that had been scorched black from brush-fires, into stands of green trees, across rocky ground, and onto a plateau that looked out on the railroad trestle.

Heat lightning leaped between the clouds and he saw his truck parked down below, under the stanchions of the trestle.

He brought his boot heels into the ribs of the palomino, leaning his weight back toward the rump, his rifle held vertically in his right arm, and rode down the slope into the ravine.

The wind shifted and an odor struck his face that was like a green chemical, like the smell of a river that has receded from flood stage and exposed the remains of drowned livestock.

Both of the truck doors were open and Wilbur could hear blowflies droning in the darkness. He unhooped the flashlight from his neck and slipped from the horse's back and walked around to the front of the truck.

A figure sat stiffly behind the steering wheel, the hands resting motionlessly on each side of the horn button. Strands of gray hair lifted in the hot wind around a face that seemed to have no features, that was as black as leather that had molded in the ground.

When he flicked on the flashlight he saw his mother in her burial clothes, now stained by groundwater, her chin and the corners of her mouth puckered tightly against the bone in an eternal scold, her slitted eyes staring at him as brightly as fish scale.

THE FOLLOWING MORNING Wilbur recounted all the above in my office, spinning his hat on his index finger.

"They dug up your mother's grave?" I said incredulously.

"They sure did. My bet would be on that Fletcher fellow. Anyway, I already called Earl Deitrich," he replied.

"You going to let him get away with—"

He flipped his hat by the brim up on his head. "My mother was a long-suffering, Christian woman. I know that 'cause not a day passed without her telling me. She told my daddy that so often he used to walk around the house with wads of newspaper screwed in his ears. He even said she'd get up out of the grave to tell the rest of us how worthless we was.

"So that's what I told Earl Deitrich. That woman has been a lifetime motivator. The best part of Earl Deitrich run down his daddy's leg and there won't be a beer joint left in Texas the day Kippy Jo and me cut him in on our oil site. Durn, if that boy didn't slam down the phone, then pick it up and slam it down again."

16

IT SEEMED LIKE NOTHING WENT EASY FOR JEFF Deitrich. Or at least that's what he told Lucas Smothers after he came back from seeing his father and being told he had one of two choices: lose Esmeralda Ramirez and her beaner relatives or get used to the lifestyle of oil field trash.

"He had my name taken off the membership list at the club. He canceled all my credit cards," Jeff said.

"So flush the club," Lucas said.

"Luke, my boy, black basketball players with orange hair and collard greens for brains make twenty million dollars in a season. Think about where you're going to be on your current salary in ten years."

Jeff had sailed yachts and deep-sea-fished since he was a child. He drove to Aransas Pass and tried to get on as a boat pilot ferrying supplies to offshore oil rigs. The owner of the boatyard listened attentively, chewing on a matchstick, and told Jeff to come back in the morning, that maybe they could work something out. Jeff and Esmeralda took a twenty-dollar room at a motel behind a truck stop, then Jeff went down to the boatyard at 5 A.M. The owner had left word with the foreman that Jeff could start his trial period right away, cleaning the grease trap behind the office and shoveling out the hold of a shrimper.

The foreman had to lock himself in a bathroom.

On the way back home Jeff stopped in San Antonio and scored four fat bags of rainbows and blues and a bag of Afghan skunk.

"Why you need all that dope?" Esmeralda said.

"Try to concentrate on what I'm saying. We don't have any money," he said, enunciating each of his words. "The way to get money is to buy something cheap, then sell it to dumb people for a lot more than it's worth. It's why Mexicans never get out of the barrio."

But that night two Jamaican dealers from Dallas met Jeff in an abandoned picnic ground down the road from Shorty's and, instead of handing him an envelope full of cash, pointed a .357 Magnum in his face and picked up the four Ziplocs of rainbows and blues from the car hood and dropped them in a shopping bag.

"I know where you guys live. Y'all are going to have some visitors," Jeff said.

"Say, mon, why don't we do it dis way? We just take your thumbs wit' us and save you de gas money," the man with the gun said.

Jeff watched the taillights of their car move away into the darkness, the dust from the tires drifting as palpably as grit into his hair.

• • •

THE TIN TRAILER was boiling with heat when Jeff woke in the morning, his face netted with hangover and inchoate rage at being ripped off by two calypso mop-heads his father wouldn't allow to drink out of the garden hose. He came through the back door of Lucas's house and made toll calls without permission, pacing up and down, barefoot, his breath bouncing sourly off the receiver.

"I'm going to stick their flippers in a vise," he said. "Just pick up Hammie and two or three other guys and cover my back . . . No, I'm serious. I'm going to break their fingers, then their wrists. You want the word on the street we're anybody's fuck? They're going to eat their next meal out of a dog bowl . . . We having a memory lapse, Warren? You remember that hit-and-run in Austin?"

Ten minutes later Lucas heard Jeff and Esmeralda fighting inside the trailer.

"Because I need it. Because I couldn't sleep all night. Because you snore. Because I got barbed wire in my head. You tell me where it is!" Jeff said.

"You know how much you smoked already? Look at your eyes. They're full of blood clots. You stink like a street person."

"I'll say it one more time, Esmeralda. Where's my stash?"

"I burned it."

"Sure you did. That's why birds are dropping out of the sky."

He began tearing her clothes off the hangers in

a closet and throwing them through the front door. Then he walked out onto the steps with her storage trunk over his head and heaved it end over end into the yard. The top burst open, and he rooted in it like a badger digging in a hole, flinging her jewelry and shoes and scrapbooks and red and purple rayon undergarments into the air. His face was white and sweating, his jaws flecked with stubble.

"You need to go to detox, Jeff. You're sick," she said.

"What I'm sick of is salsa and onion breath and your brother Cholo's stupid face and the thought I've been coming in the same box as Ronnie Cruise. I want to scrub you off me with peroxide."

"Maricón," she said.

He straightened up slowly. "You called me a queer? That's what you just said? A queer? Say it again and see what happens."

"Maricón!" she said. *"Cabrón! Cobarde! Maricón! Maricón! Maricón!"*

"Your face looks funny like that. All out of shape. Funny and stupid," he said, smiling strangely. "I know a truck stop where I can get you on, doing hand jobs. I'll take a shower and drive you there. You can tell them about your credits at the Juco. They'll be impressed. For some reason, Esmeralda, I feel just great."

• • •

LUCAS TOLD ME THIS STORY early Saturday morning while I curried out Beau in the lot. We were in the shade of the barn and the morning was still cool and the wind off the river smelled of wet trees and wildflowers and the livestock in my neighbor's pasture.

"Jeff's gone?" I said.

"He burned rubber for thirty feet. He shot me the bone when he went by. What a guy," he said.

"Where's Esmeralda?"

"Staying at the trailer," he said.

I straightened up and paused in my work, my arms resting on the warm indentation of Beau's back. Lucas looked down at his foot and kicked at the dust. The brim of his straw hat was curled into a point on the front.

"She lost her restaurant job. She don't have no place to go," he said.

"She has a family."

"Just Cholo. He's crazy."

"That's the point. Stay away from those people."

"Which people is that?"

"Don't make a racial deal out of this. You know what I'm talking about," I said.

"You want me to run her off? Treat her like Jeff done?"

I opened the gate in the lot and turned Beau out into the pasture.

"I guess life was a lot simpler when I was y'all's age," I said.

"Yeah, I reckon that's how I got here," he replied.

• • •

SUNDAY MORNING I GOT A CALL from the county jail. My harelip, flat-nosed, meltdown client, Wesley Rhodes, had been out of the bag three days, then had gotten busted at four o'clock that morning for possession, driving without a license, and indecent exposure.

I waited for the jailer, a sweating fat man whose khaki trousers hung below his crack, to open up Wesley's isolation cell in the top of the courthouse.

"Why isn't he in the tank, L.J.?" I asked.

"It's full up on Saturday nights. Federal judge is always on our ass about it," he replied.

I sat down on a chain-hung iron bunk opposite Wesley. The sun had risen into the trees outside, and the light through the bars made lacy shadows on Wesley's face. He wore a dark blue see-through shirt and a studded dog collar around his neck and Cloroxed jeans belted tightly below his belly button. His wide-set green eyes stared at me with the angular concentration of a lizard's.

"What were you holding, Wesley?" I said.

"Blues. They been on the street a couple of days."

"Dilaudid?"

"They wasn't for me. There's a man I get together with sometimes. He cooks them. They're safer than the tar that's coming up from the Valley."

"What's the indecent-exposure charge?"

"I was taking a leak in the park."

"You selling yourself, Wes?"

He dropped his eyes and gripped his bunk and rocked on his arms.

"He takes me out to dinner and buys me clothes sometimes, that's all. I got to get out of jail. They're scaring me."

"In what way?"

"A couple of mop-heads, you know, dreadlocks, Jamaican guys, been unloading a lot of blues and rainbows. The word is they ripped them off Jeff Deitrich."

"So?"

"I was cuffed in the cruiser with a friend while the deputy was tearing up my daddy's car. I was telling my friend about Jeff getting stiffed by these two guys. Then the deputy comes back to the cruiser and picks up a tape recorder off the front seat. He plays it back, listening to everything I said, all the time staring at me like I done something really bad.

"I go, 'That's an illegal wiretap.'

"He goes, 'You better stick to being some rich junky's hump, sperm-breath.' Then he wouldn't put me in the tank. Why they pissed off, Mr. Holland? Is it 'cause I told them they cain't use that tape?"

"You don't have expectation of privacy in the back of a police cruiser, Wesley. But that's not the problem. While you're in here, you don't talk about Jamaicans taking off Jeff Deitrich. You hearing me on this?"

Wesley stood up from his bunk and looked at the

barred window above his head. An uneaten breakfast of powdered eggs and white bread and packaged jam lay on top of the toilet tank.

"My stomach's been sick. I ain't ever pissed them off before. Nothing don't feel right," he said.

"Give me your belt and that dog collar," I said.

"What?" he said.

Downstairs I dropped the collar and Wesley's wide leather belt and heavy metal buckle on the jailer's desk.

"Don't ever try to get away with something like this, L.J.," I said.

He dipped his fingers in a leather pouch and loaded his jaw with chewing tobacco, his lidless eyes never leaving mine.

LATER, AFTER CHURCH, I stopped by a supermarket in town, then drove to Temple Carrol's house, which was just down the road from mine. I could hear her working out on the heavy bag in the backyard, thudding her gloves into it, spinning it on the chain that was hooked into a beam on her father's open-air welding shed.

She didn't see me behind her. She wore gray sweatpants and a workout halter and red tennis shoes, and she was leading into the bag with her left, hooking with her right, and following with a karate kick. Her skin was flushed, her shoulders and the baby fat on her sides slick with perspiration.

"Have a picnic with me," I said.

She turned and lowered her gloves, chewing gum, her face without expression, the bag creaking on the chain behind her.

"You need a favor?" she asked.

"It's a nice day. I didn't want to spend it alone."

She pulled off her gloves one at a time. They were dull red, thin-padded, with metal dowels inside that fitted across the palms.

"I don't like being somebody's safety pin, Billy Bob," she said.

"I had to try. No hard feelings. I'll probably see you tomorrow."

"Were you in the sack with Peggy Jean?" she asked.

"No." I picked up a bottle cap off a spool table and flipped it with my thumbnail against the trunk of a pecan tree. "That doesn't mean my behavior was acceptable."

She looked at me for a long moment, her chestnut hair damp on her cheeks. Then she tossed one of her gloves at my face.

"I'll take a shower. Wait out here," she said.

WE DROVE THROUGH THE FIELD behind my house to the grove of cottonwoods that overlooked the river. The sky was gray with rain clouds, and leaves were blowing out of the grove onto the river's surface. The grass was tall and green in the shade, and I spread a tablecloth on the ground and lay out the containers of cold chicken and pinto beans and fruit salad.

"I saw you go past the house early this morning," she said.

"Wesley Rhodes implicated Jeff Deitrich in a drug deal on tape. The jailer put him in an isolation cell with his belt and a dog collar."

She rubbed at the back of her neck while I spoke, her hair blowing in the wind.

"You think they might try to hang him from a pipe?" she said.

"Could be."

"I'm supposed to check on him?"

"Nope. I'm going back up there this afternoon. I'll have him out on bond in the morning."

She nodded, her eyes moving curiously over my face. Then she squatted by the tablecloth and filled a paper plate with food and ate it standing up, looking out over the river.

I cupped her elbow in one palm.

"Sit down with me, Temple," I said.

"All right," she said.

I sat next to her and we ate in silence. Her hair kept getting in her eyes and I lifted one strand off her eyebrow and smoothed it back on her head. Her eyes settled on mine, then her face colored and she set her plate down and walked to the car and leaned against it, her expression hidden.

When I placed my fingers on her arm she moved

away from me as though she had been touched with ice. "I have to go back now. Thank you for the lunch. No, don't say anything else, Billy Bob. You think I'm tough. You're wrong. I can't cut this shit," she said.

It stormed that night. I developed a fever and a light-headedness that seemed to have no origin, and I fixed hot tea and lemon and drank it at my desk in the library while the rain swirled in the glow of the upstairs windows.

The rain slackened and my eyes burned with fatigue and I felt myself slipping off to sleep. I woke at midnight to mariachi music that made no sense, the voice of my son, Lucas, singing, L.Q. Navarro speaking in words that I could see move like moths on his lips but could not hear, the sound of water dipping into a vortex that was about to close on a little boy's head.

Lightning flared in the clouds beyond the barn and I saw a figure run from the fields, through the horse lot, into the barn, and I was sure L.Q. Navarro had taken up residence in my dreams for the night.

Then I saw the electric light go on by Beau's stall.

I took a flashlight out of a kitchen drawer and walked through the pools of rainwater in the back-yard and pulled open the barn door. Suddenly I was staring into the face of Skyler Doolittle, his bald head crisscrossed with rivulets of sweat. He was dressed in a cheap, pale blue suit that was far too small for him, a candy-striped shirt with popped buttons, a twisted necktie, white athletic socks, and jail-issue shoes. His body exuded a raw odor like night damp and moist clay and ozone.

"I got blood on my hands, Mr. Holland," he said.

"You killed Kyle Rose?" I said.

"That deputy with the stinger? Somebody kilt him?"

"With Rose's bow and arrow."

Skyler's face went out of shape, like white rubber, his eyes hot with thought.

"You didn't do it?" I said.

"No, sir."

"Then it was Jessie Stump," I said.

"I been working with him. The boy can be saved. He's had a terrible life."

"Why'd you come here, Mr. Doolittle?"

"I've got to have hep. I just don't know what kind. Now I got blood on my hands."

"Sir, you're not making sense."

He wiped his palms on the front of his suit and I saw the dark streaks on the cloth.

"A deputy sheriff tried to stop me at a crossroads. He was taking his gun out. I hit him till he didn't get up no more."

I sat down on a spool table and felt my eyes go out of focus and my energies drain. My field of vision swam with weevil worms.

"I can get you into federal custody," I said.

"Earl Deitrich come out of the Pit. I can smell

Satan on a man the way you smell sulfur in a storm. You was made different the day the preacher laid you back in the river and let the water fill your eyes with sky and trees. I ain't gonna be here to stop Deitrich. You got to do it."

"Mr. Doolittle, I'm not a theologian. I'm probably not even a very good attorney. But baptism was a simple ritual of the Essenes. It was just a way of welcoming a new person into the Christian community."

He rubbed the blood from his hands on his coat sleeves, his eyes as round as coins pushed into his face. Then, from a long way off, I could hear dogs barking, in a pack, the sound rising louder and louder on the wind.

"Come back in the house with me. I won't let them hurt you," I said.

"They'll kill Jessie Stump for sure. You ain't seen them at work."

I removed all the bills from my wallet, two hundred dollars, and put them in his hand.

"Goodbye, Mr. Doolittle," I said.

"Goodbye, sir," he replied.

17

THE NEXT DAY I ROSE EARLY AND SHOWERED and went out into the cool of the morning and put oats in Beau's trough and picked up litter from the storm in the yard. The fever of the previous night seemed to have flowed out of my body like water. I started to call Marvin Pomroy and tell him about the visit of Skyler Doolittle and to ask about the fate of the deputy sheriff whom Skyler had beaten; but the day was just too nice to contend with the irrationalities of a legal system that was never intended to be anything other than a cosmetic one.

Instead I drove to Lucas's rented house forty miles west of town and got to watch another form of irrationality at work—my son's.

He and I were talking in the front yard when Ronnie Cruise's 1961 sunburst T-Bird, with Ronnie behind the wheel and Cholo in the passenger seat, turned into the drive.

"My sister back there?" Cholo said from the window.

"What do y'all want?" Lucas said.

"Figure it out. To see my sister, man," Cholo said.

The car drove past the side of the house and stopped in front of the trailer.

I looked into Lucas's face.

"You keep your hand out of it," I said.

"It's my damn house. What's Ronnie Cross doing here? She eighty-sixed him a long time ago," he replied.

"Lucas—"

He walked to the side of the house and stared at the trailer, his hands on both hips, his coned straw hat pulled down on his face. Esmeralda and Cholo and Ronnie were now out in the dirt yard.

"I got a job in a restaurant here. I'm not going back to San Antone, Cholo," Esmeralda said.

"I'm your brother. You're gonna do what I say," Cholo said.

"These ain't our people up here. My mother says you can stay at her house. I ain't gonna bother you, Essie," Ronnie said. He wore a red bandanna on his hair and the points lifted in the wind.

"Then respect what I tell you, Ronnie," she said.

"You got something going with Smothers over there?" he asked.

"He was good to me. Leave him alone," she said.

"What we got here is all kinds of people dumping on us," Cholo said. "Jeff's old man just got your marriage annulled. It don't exist. That means Jeff used you to glom his big-boy and threw you away like toilet paper," Cholo said.

Lucas stepped farther out into the drive and said, "You guys got the message. She don't want y'all here." His hands were inserted flatly in his back pockets and the skin of his face was tight against the bone.

"I'll say this once. This is a private conversation," Ronnie said.

"Fuck you, Ronnie. You're on my property," Lucas said.

Ronnie breathed slowly through his nose and picked at his nails. He cut his head at Lucas, then at me.

"We came here to work something out that don't got nothing to do with you two. But you treat us like we're spit on the bottom of your shoe. No different than Mr. Deitrich. You think you can bing with us, man? You really think that?" he said.

"We're not part of your problem. You need to understand that," I said.

Ronnie wiped at his nose, looking at nothing.

"Call me, Essie," he said to Esmeralda.

"It's over, Ronnie," she said.

He rubbed his thumb back and forth across his forehead and walked toward his car, his face lost in thought, suddenly oblivious to our presence.

Lucas and I watched the T-Bird disappear down the road.

"How do you read that?" Lucas asked.

"Don't ever humiliate a guy like Ronnie Cruise in front of his peers," I said.

"Well, he ain't coming on my property and wiping his feet on people," he said.

I looked at his profile against the early sun, the

heat in his cheeks, the manly energy in his eyes, and felt my heart sink like a stone in a well.

IT'S STRANGE HOW PEOPLE BLOOM, even in poisonous soil, once they allow themselves to become what they've always been.

Jeff Deitrich had rebelled against his father and married a Mexican girl and had tried to cut it on the floor of a drilling rig. But he quickly learned that yielding to the seduction of his father's world brought no penalty, instead only celebration of the returned prodigal, and that he had been foolish to compete with people who secretly coveted the opulence that was his by right.

At the end of the week I had to go out to Post Oaks Country Club and meet a client, an obese, self-deluded, thoroughly corrupt oilman who was about to enter Huntsville Penitentiary.

We sat in the cooling shadows on the terrace while, not far away, golfers on the driving range were hitting into an enormous white net. My client's face went soft and then nakedly lustful as he gazed over my shoulder.

"I'm born again, but an elegant woman like that can sure give a man thoughts," he said.

I turned in my chair and saw Peggy Jean and Jeff Deitrich, side by side, dressed in tennis whites, hitting off the rubber tee into the net. Jeff's form was perfect, his skin tanned as dark as the polished wood in his club. Peggy Jean rested one hand on his shoulder, her head bending down with laughter as both of them shared a joke, more like confidants or even sweethearts than child and stepmother.

"It's too bad Earl don't spend more time at the fireside and not at the poker table. For a while I thought he was going to be selling his furniture out on the lawn. He must have hit a gusher," my client said.

"Excuse me?" I said.

"Don't pay me no mind. If I was single, I'd probably drool a bucket full."

"I was thinking about Jeff," I said.

"Jeff? His mother should have thrown him back and raised the afterbirth. You mixed up with that little pisspot? I thought you had some smarts. No wonder I'm headed for the pen."

I said goodbye to my client and walked past Jeff and Peggy Jean toward my car. Then I stopped and looked at their backs until they both felt my eyes on them.

"Why, Billy Bob. Come have a drink with us," Peggy Jean said. And she seemed to say it with genuine warmth.

"I'd like a word with Jeff," I said.

The smile went out of her face. "I beg your pardon?" she said.

"Would you step over here, please, Jeff?" I said.

He grinned good-naturedly, as though tolerating a harmless aberration, then came toward me, resting his club on his shoulder.

"What's up, Billy Bob?" he said.

"You exploited my son's friendship. You used his home, then dumped your wife there. Now Lucas is taking your weight with Ronnie Cruise," I said.

"I can't control what others do. You sure you don't want to hit some balls or have a drink?"

"You're quite a guy," I said.

He winked at me, his eyes full of ridicule, and went back to the tee. Peggy Jean had never moved, her face stamped with the insult of being rebuffed publicly in her own club.

She waited for me to speak or say goodbye. But I didn't. Behind me, I heard a suck of air as Jeff cut his club viciously into a golf ball.

ON THE WAY HOME I felt my stomach suddenly seize and constrict, as though the lining were being stapled by a machine. My breath went out of my mouth, and my chest hit the steering wheel. Up ahead, I saw Temple Carrol working in her yard, pulling weeds on her hands and knees out of a hydrangea bed and throwing them behind her on the grass. I turned into her drive and sat very still behind the wheel, my face sweating.

She glanced over her shoulder, then continued her work. I wiped my face on my sleeve and opened the door and got out. Then I had to sit down again.

Temple walked toward me, wiping her hands on her shorts, blowing her breath up into her face to remove a strand of hair from her eyes.

"You all right?" she said.

"I must have eaten the wrong thing."

She cupped her hand on my forehead.

"You're burning up. I'll drive you home," she said.

"I'm fine." I tried to smile. "Saw Jeff Deitrich at the country club. He was born to it."

"Earthshaking news."

"You hear anything about Earl Deitrich having a big infusion of cash in his business?"

"Move over and quit worrying about the Deitrichs," she said, and nudged me sideways into the passenger seat.

A few minutes later she walked me to my front door, one hand under my arm.

"Get in bed and I'll check on you in a couple of hours," she said.

"What about my car?"

"I'll bring it back. Do what I say."

I went up to my bedroom on the third floor and switched on the floor and ceiling fans and opened the windows wide and lay down on top of the sheets in my underwear. In minutes my pillow was soaked. Outside the window, in the setting of the sun, I could see the vast green rolling landscape to the west, as though I were looking into the vastness of the world itself, with all its shadows and mysteries and its alluring red-tinged precipices that fell away into darkness.

I went into the bath and showered and lay down again but found no relief. It was dark now, and in my mind I saw the flashes of gunfire in the arroyo where L.Q. Navarro died, relived the moments when bullets pierced my own body like hot pokers, floated once again in the warm water that Morpheus prepared for his friends.

Kippy Jo Pickett had called me a giver of death. Her words were like spittle in the face, and I could not dismiss or forget them. L.Q. and I killed Mexican drug mules on the pretext they would otherwise never be made accountable for their crimes; but the truth was we killed them because we personally loathed what they were and what they did and we took enormous satisfaction in leaving them where they fell, a card twisted in the mouth, for their friends to find.

Then I saw L.Q. standing at the foot of my tester bed, his hat and pinstripe suit streaked with dust, his white shirt glowing radiantly in the dark. He inserted a gold toothpick in the corner of his mouth.

"Get rid of them thoughts. It was me got us down there, bud," he said.

"I got something bad in me, L.Q. It's just like the time I caught one in the chest."

"The trip across ain't bad. It's just like you and me splashing hell for breakfast through the Rio Grande. You blink and there's ole red-eye coming up in the east."

"I'm afraid."

"You ain't got to be. It'll happen for you. It's the one moment you ain't got to plan," he said, then

turned, as though distracted by something behind him, a gleam of light reflecting on his gold toothpick.

Temple Carrol came through the door and walked right through him and out the other side, so that his presence was now a black-purple silhouette around her body.

She sat on the edge of the bed and took both my hands in hers and looked into my face.

"I shouldn't have left you," she said.

I wanted to answer but I couldn't. I could hear my teeth rattling in my jaws. She wiped my brow with her hand and touched my cheek with the back of her wrist.

"I'm going to get some water and some damp towels," she said, and started to rise from the bed.

But I held both of her hands tightly in mine, and like a child I pulled her toward me, put my face in her breasts, slipped my arms around her sides, felt her hesitate momentarily, then lie down against me and place her hands on the back of my head and neck, one knee pointed across my thigh.

I could hear a cacophony of huge, thick-bodied birds outside the window and the flapping of wings that spread as wide as a man's arms.

The whirring sounds in Temple's chest were like those inside a seashell, like wind and salt tide blowing onto a beach. I held her against me while carrion birds drifted in a red sky behind my eyelids.

18

I AWOKE IN THE HOSPITAL THE NEXT AFTERNOON. A hard yellow light filled the room and seemed to enamel the walls and furniture with a severity and coldness that was unrelated to the season. The inside of my throat was raw, as though it had been scraped by a metal tool, and my head reeled when I went into the bathroom.

I got back into bed and held a pillow across my eyes and tried to sleep but couldn't. A half hour later a tall physician in greens by the name of Tobin Voss came in and sat on the foot of my bed. His jaws were unshaved, his thick graying hair uncombed. He had been a helicopter pilot in Vietnam but never spoke except in an oblique way of his experience there.

"You feel like somebody hit all over you with an ice mallet?" he asked.

"What's wrong with me?"

"Tainted food maybe. We pumped your stomach out. You don't remember it?"

"No."

"We were a little worried about you for a while. Your girlfriend, the one who brought you in? She's quite a gal."

"She's a private investigator who works for me."

"I've got it. At two in the morning your P.I. is at your house. Sorry I had things confused," he said. "Is anybody mad at you?"

"What are you telling me, Doc?"

"I've seen Third World peasants eat rice from storage dumps we poisoned. You brought back some memories."

He stood up from the bed and looked out the window at the trees below. The backs of his arms were covered with salt-and-pepper hair. When he turned back from the window he was smiling.

"Your private investigator? She pushed your gurney into the E.R. and put the fear of God in a couple of people. She's not looking for a job in midlevel management, is she?" he said.

I GOT HOME LATE that evening, light-headed and dehydrated, the inside of my eyelids like sandpaper. I went out to the barn and removed two vinyl sacks of garbage from the garbage cans and emptied them on a large piece of plywood and used a garden rake to separate out packaged and canned food from any that might have been tampered with.

Mixed in with the takeout food from a half dozen restaurants and stores were the remains of watermelon, cantaloupes, strawberries, and bananas I had bought at roadside stands. But local merchants and tailgate fruit vendors didn't lie in wait to poison their customers. Maybe Doc Voss just had too many shadows left in his mind from Vietnam, I thought.

Temple Carrol's car came up the drive and stopped. I raked all the decaying food I had bought in supermarkets into a pile and rebagged it, then leaned over and picked up an empty half-gallon milk carton.

"I went to the hospital this afternoon and you were asleep. When I came back you were checked out," Temple said.

"I hear you shook them up in the E.R.," I said, and sat down on the scrolled-iron, white-painted bench under the chinaberry tree, my head dizzy from bending over.

She wore a pair of soft boots and rust-colored jeans and a checkered tan shirt. Her eyes fixed on mine while she slipped a stick of gum in her mouth.

"You remember a lot?" she asked.

"Big blank."

She nodded, her jaws chewing slowly.

"The doc says maybe you saved my life," I said.

"Dull night. A girl has to do something for kicks."

The sky was lavender and streaked with fire behind her head. She put her hands in her back pockets and lifted her chin slightly.

"I guess I remember pieces of things," I said.

"Pieces? Wonderful choice," she said.

I looked away from her stare. My face was cold and moist in the breeze. I could feel blood veins tightening in my head, my vision slip in and out of focus. "You were there for me. That's what I re-member, Temple," I said.

"There for you? Wow," she said, her face heating.

I couldn't think of an adequate response. I ran one hand through my hair and stared at the tops of my boots.

"What are you doing with that milk carton?" she said irritably.

I rubbed my thumb over a tiny burr on the side, then splayed open the top for Temple to look inside.

"I have the milk delivered. There's a puncture in it. Like the kind a hypodermic needle would make," I said.

ON MONDAY MORNING I met Tobin Voss in his of-fice out by the four-lane. A half dozen books were opened on his desktop. On a glass-covered bookcase behind his chair was a framed color photograph of him and his flight crew in front of a Huey helicopter.

"Here's a copy of the paperwork from the lab. You ever hear of a World War II Japanese group called Unit 731?" he said.

"No."

"They conducted experiments on Chinese prison-ers in Manchuria. The subject probably doesn't come up often in our trade negotiations with Tokyo. Traces from your specimens show similarities to a couple of toxins they developed."

"Are you sure?" I asked.

"Put it this way. I can't tell you with certainty the toxic element that was in your system. But I can tell what it's not. So that creates an area of speculation. The best I can come up with is this historical stuff." Then he smiled and asked, "You haven't been to Africa lately, have you?"

"Why?"

"According to my nifty book here on political intrigue and assassination, Unit 731's gift to biological warfare has been used to murder several democratic leaders in Africa, primarily because its symptoms are like a number of fatal viruses carried by diseased animals."

"How about Central Africa, the old Belgian Congo?"

His eyes dropped to an open page in his book, then looked at me again.

His humorous cynicism was gone. "How'd you know?" he said.

TUESDAY WESLEY RHODES was in my office, wired, shaking, and wrapped so tight his eyes were bulging out of his head. In spite of the temperature outside, he wore two long-sleeve shirts to give his body dimension, and motorcycle boots with two inches of platform glued on the bottoms.

"You're speeding, Wes," I said.

"Coke won't hammer out the kinks no more," he

said, grabbing one wrist, then the other, raking his cupped palm over the back of the opposite hand as though he were trying to wipe rainwater off it. "Everything's coming apart. I boosted a few places. I peddled my ass. I creeped a funeral home. I never done no real harm."

"You always took your own fall, too. That's stand-up, bud. How about kicking it into neutral?"

So he told me about his weekend with the East Enders.

Hammie Wocheck, Jeff Deitrich's buddy from the University of Texas, cruised by Wesley's paint-peeling, termite-eaten house and sat in his pickup truck with the engine idling until Wesley got up off the porch and walked out to the swale. Hammie's blond hair was wet with gel, his face sunburned, the side of his thick neck still scabbed with the purple and burnt-orange tattoo of a butterfly. His huge upper body seemed to fill up the window of the truck, the way an elephant might look inside a phone booth.

"Wes, my man, we need you to go with us to Big Dee, call up a couple of mop-heads on their beeper. I'm talking about the Jamaicans who took down Jeff Deitrich. This your house, huh?" Hammie said.

"I ain't lost nothing in Dallas."

"Point of honor, Wes. We got spear chuckers tracking monkey shit into our town, selling bad dope to people, messing up little kids. Problem two is you dropped Jeff's name into the bowl. Believe me, that did not float. You need to square it, little buddy. Give your old man this six-pack. Tell him you're doing a righteous deed for the town. He'll relate to it."

They drove to Val's and met Jeff Deitrich and Warren Costen and two others, one of whom was a fat guy named Chug Rollins, who must have gotten his signals wrong because he was dressed up like queer bait. Then they convoyed in three cars to a little town south of Fort Worth. Wesley had never liked Chug; he was like most big, fat guys—he had a mean dude hiding inside all that blubber, one that liked to push around little guys. But Warren was another matter. Except for his long torso, he looked like a surfer or a movie star, with his big arms and flat-plated chest and sandy hair. Warren kept cracking open Budweisers from the cooler and passing them to Wes, offering him a smoke, even telling him they should shitcan this mop-head gig. But what are you going to tell a guy like Jeff when he's got a telephone pole up his ass?

"I thought we was going to Dallas," Wesley said.

"Jeff's got a special place he wants to 'front these dudes. When you get them on the line, read them the directions on this piece of paper," Warren said.

"To a rock quarry? They ain't gonna come," Wesley said.

"Hope they do, Wes. Jeff is in a bad mood. I hate to get in his way when he's like that," Warren said. He shook his head profoundly.

Wesley took two hits of speed and washed them down with his beer.

He used the pay phone on the side of a shut-down filling station while the others watched him from the heated darkness. Insects thudded against the interior light overhead. His skin felt as though it were wrapped with damp wool.

The mop-head answered the beeper page but acted like somebody threw easy money in his face every day.

"Where you get four grand, mon?"

"It belongs to a fudge packer, the guy I been buying blues for."

"We give it some thought. We meet you on the highway. You better change your life, mon. Stop hanging with dem AIDS people."

The mop-head gave Wesley directions to a Dairy Queen and hung up before Wesley could argue. Wesley was terrified when he stared out of the lighted phone booth into Jeff's face.

"I told y'all they wouldn't go to the quarry. It ain't my fault," he said.

"You did great. They're gonna take you down, little buddy," Hammie said.

It didn't make sense. What were they talking about? Wesley's head throbbed.

All of them were grinning at him now, but in a tolerant, avuncular way, as though they had accepted him as one of their own.

"You got another beer?" he said.

A half hour later Wesley sat behind the wheel of Chug's car, with Chug eating a banana split in the passenger seat, ice cream and strawberry juice and chocolate smeared on his mouth. Wesley started to ask him why he was dressed up like a fruit, but he remembered the damage Chug used to do to his opponents when he was a high school varsity lineman.

So instead he said, "Jeff just wants his stash back? Ain't nothing real bad going down, huh, Chug?"

Chug adjusted the tweed hat on his head and winked. "You know Jerry Lee Lewis got kicked out of divinity school here?" he said.

The two mop-heads pulled into the Dairy Queen in a black Mercedes and got out and leaned down on the windowsills on both sides of Chug's car. They smelled of funk and onions and fish and unwashed hair that had been plaited with aloe.

"We don't go nowhere till we see some money, mon," the one at Chug's window said.

Chug lifted up a napkin from his lap and exposed a roll of one-hundred-dollar bills crimped together with a rubber band. He smiled, his tongue lolling on his teeth. A tiny green stone gleamed in his earlobe.

"There it is, hard as a cucumber. You want to touch it?" he said.

"You can follow us. We got a place to do business. But don't be talking that way to me, mon. We don't got dose kinds of problems in the Islands," the man at Chug's window said, his dreadlocks swinging like dusty snakes on his cheeks.

"How we know y'all won't beat us up?" Chug said, his face suddenly soft and vulnerable.

"You too sweet and de little man there too rough," the man at the window said.

So the mop-heads were smart-asses as well as take-down artists, Wesley thought as he followed the Mercedes down the highway. Just like everybody else, making fun of him because he was short and didn't think fast and his meal ticket was with a fudge packer or two. Well, maybe they needed to get their paint scratched up a little bit. Like Hammie said, point of honor. It made Wesley feel good to know he was on the same wavelength as guys like Hammie and Warren.

The Mercedes turned off on a dead-end gravel road and drove between rolling pasture, then stopped by the desiccated and paintless shell of a farmhouse that was squeezed to breaking inside a stand of blackjack.

The mop-heads cut their lights and walked back toward Chug's car. One of them opened Chug's door.

"Step out here in de road, mon. We need to count your money," he said.

"Really?" Chug said, standing erect now, the mop-head finally realizing how big Chug actually was.

"Yeah, 'cause dat's too much money for you. We think maybe you just give it to us," the mop-head said, his hand reaching for the .25-caliber automatic pushed down in the back of his beltless slacks.

That's when Chug hit him in the stomach, harder than Wesley had ever seen anyone hit. That was also when Wesley pulled the remote latch on the trunk and heard Hammie climb out on the gravel and saw Warren and Jeff each coming fast down the road in separate vehicles, their headlights so bright they made his eyes water.

He turned away from what happened next. The blows from fists and knees and feet finally stopped and the dust drifted into the trees and broke apart in the wind, and he thought it was over, that they would be on their way back to Deaf Smith in a few minutes and he would be in his father's house by dawn.

But Hammie looked down at the mop-heads and said, "Hey, you guys got to check out that rock quarry. It's a pretty spot. You'll dig it."

THE QUARRY looked like a large meteor hole filled with green water, the shale sides tapering down to the surface under a sky that was bursting with stars. The mop-heads were belted into the backseat of their Mercedes, both doors open, their wrists fastened behind them with plastic flex-cuffs. In the darkness their faces were the color of eggplant, welted and glistening with blood.

But they weren't afraid, Wesley thought. They had proved that when they took their beating without asking for mercy. One of them had even told Chug he'd give him a discount on diet pills.

But now Jeff was taking a gas can and an emergency flare out of his car. Oh man, this wasn't happening, Wesley thought.

Hammie, Warren, Chug, and the other guy were sitting on a grass-tufted mound of dirt, eating fried chicken from a plastic bucket and drinking more beer. How could you eat after you pounded the shit out of two guys? Wesley thought. These East End guys were meaner, more unpredictable and dangerous than anyone he'd known inside. Jeff had a crazy light in his eyes, like he'd loaded up on screamers or whites on the half shell melted down in booze. He was squatted down on his haunches now, eating a drumstick not five feet from the Mercedes, with the gas can resting by his foot. He finished chewing and threw the chicken bone at the mop-head who was closer to him.

"What do you think is about to happen in that insignificant life of yours?" Jeff said.

"My mother give me over to de spirits when I was born, mon. I don't argue wit' what they do," the mop-head answered.

Jeff stood up and unscrewed the plastic cap on the flexible hose that was screwed into the top of the gas can. He held the emergency flare under the mop-head's nose like a police baton and pushed his head back on his neck.

"You ever read about Nero? He used Christians for candles. You guys Christians?" Jeff said.

When the mop-head didn't reply, Jeff popped him across the nose with the flare, then swung the can idly back and forth, letting the gas slosh against the tin sides.

Warren and the others had stopped talking now, their faces suddenly tuned in to what Jeff was saying. Warren rose casually to his feet, wiping the grease off his hands on the back of his jeans. He picked up a jack handle that was stuck sharp-end-down in the sand.

"We already got their stash, Jeff. Maybe we should just remodel their car a little bit. Let them take a visual lesson back home," he said.

Warren walked in a circle around the Mercedes, breaking head- and taillights as though he were cracking hard-boiled eggs with a spoon.

"What'd you think I was going to do?" Jeff asked him.

"What do I know?" Warren said.

"You guys are too much," Jeff said, and walked to his yellow convertible and unscrewed the cap on his fuel tank and inserted the gas can hose inside.

A wind smelling of distant rain and watermelon fields seemed to blow out of nowhere. Hammie, Warren, Chug, and the other guy started talking and laughing at once, dipping their hands down into the cooler's melted ice for another Budweiser.

The mop-head behind the wheel of the Mercedes said something to his friend, then both of them grinned, their teeth pink with blood in the starlight.

"Say again?" Jeff asked. He tilted the can upward, draining it, and set it on the ground.

"Hey, mon, you had a nice Mexican wife. Cholo's sister, right? She just don't like white bread."

"So repeat what you said."

"You got a thing for wearing her underwear. Dat's what Cholo say. Not me, mon."

Jeff stuck his hands in his back pockets and studied the ground for a long moment, brushing pebbles and dirt under the sole of one loafer. He combed his hair. He huffed an obstruction out of his nose. He sucked the saliva out of his cheeks and spit it into the darkness.

The mop-heads stared indifferently into space, occasionally shaking a mosquito out of their faces.

Jeff walked around the far side of the Mercedes and closed the back door, then returned to the driver's side and closed that door, too.

"Jeff?" Hammie said.

But Jeff didn't answer. The Mercedes was pointed downward on a slope that twisted between huge, grass-grown mounds of dirt and stone. Jeff used a beach towel to wipe down the Mercedes's door handles, the steering wheel, and dashboard, then the ignition keys when he started the engine.

"Hey, we got a pair of big eyes here," Warren said, nodding at Wesley. "Listen to me, man. I got a future. I don't want to leave it here tonight."

"Don't put your hand on me again, Warren," Jeff said, and dropped the Mercedes into gear.

The mop-heads craned their necks frantically, their bodies straining against the seat belts, like people involuntarily riding in the back of a taxi that had no destination. The Mercedes rolled down the slope toward the water, gathering speed, the front end suspension adjusting for the undulations in the slope. For a moment Wesley thought the car was about to high-center on a pile of rock and swerve into a small hill and stall out but it didn't.

The mop-heads twisted their heads and looked at him through the back window just as the car bounced hard over a rise in the slope, springing the trunk in the air, and disappeared between two mounds of dirt and sand.

Then Wesley heard the engine hiss like a molten horseshoe dipped in a trough when the car's front end dropped over the embankment into the water.

Jeff popped the emergency flare alight and walked up on a rise and held the flare aloft, bathing the crater and its yellow banks and the reeds in the shallows with a red glow. Thirty feet out, water was flowing and channeling like the currents in a river through the opened windows of the car, sliding over the roof now, the green silt obscuring the shapes that fought desperately inside the rear glass.

Then the car was gone from view and Wesley was running in the darkness, alone, away from the crater and the air ballooning to the water's surface, filled, he was absolutely sure, with the voices of men who called out his name.

19

"WHAT DID YOU DO NEXT?" I ASKED WESLEY.

"I run all the way back to the highway. Jeff Deitrich picked me up hitchhiking," he answered. His face was gray, his hair soaked, like a man in mortal terror.

"We can do the right thing, Wes."

"Like go across the street and tell your buddy Marvin Pomroy what I just told you?"

"We get the jump on it. Let the others fall in their own shit."

"You're old. You ain't got to worry about guys like Jeff Deitrich and Chug Rollins. I hate this town. I hate being dumb and not having no money and not knowing when other people are making fun of me. I'm Jonesing real bad. I got to cop," he said.

"No dope. Just for today. We'll get you into detox."

But he went out the door. The back of his shirt looked like someone had pressed a rolled, wet towel from his shoulder blades down to his wide leather belt.

THAT AFTERNOON I sat in Marvin Pomroy's office and gazed out the window at the courthouse lawn.

"You want to tell me why you're here?" he asked.

"It's been a slow day."

"With your clients? I take that back. You don't have clients. You supervise a crime wave."

But it was obvious I saw no humor in his remark. He took off his rimless glasses and sighted through the lenses as though he were looking for blemishes.

"Earlier I saw you go into the drugstore and buy four different newspapers," he said. "I wonder why a defense attorney would do that."

"Beats me," I said.

"One of your clients has confessed a particularly atrocious crime or told you something else that really bothers you. Since most of your clients are mentally impaired, you want to believe he's just hallucinating. Tell me I'm wrong," he said.

I cut my head noncommittally.

"Jerk yourself around all you want. You hate these sleazebags worse than I do," he said.

"You have a Little League schedule handy?" I asked.

"Clever," he said.

But my day with Marvin Pomroy wasn't over. Just before 5 P.M. I looked down from my office window into the burned-out end of another ninety-nine-degree afternoon and saw two sheriff's department cruisers and a van loaded with rifle-armed deputies park in the shade on the north side of the courthouse. The deputies got out on the sidewalk, looking hot and weary, their uniforms and campaign hats powdered with dust.

I called Marvin.

"What's going on with Hugo's goon squad?"

"Glad you asked. Your clients, Skyler Doolittle and Jessie Stump? They're up in the hills above Earl Deitrich's place. How do we know that? Because Jessie Stump put a steel-barbed arrow two inches from Earl's head this afternoon."

"Why would Jessie want to hurt Earl?"

"Could it have something to do with the fact Doolittle thinks Earl is the Antichrist? Could Doolittle possibly be behind it? Search me."

"Maybe Earl and Jessie have found each other."

"Which church do you attend, Billy Bob? The only reason I ask is that I'd like to avoid it."

TUESDAY EVENING Wilbur Pickett made a mistake. He stopped at Shorty's for barbecue, then left Kippy Jo there while he went down the road to sell a man a welding machine.

She sat at a plank table on the screen porch and felt the breeze come up and the shadows lengthen on the river and the sun cut the tops of the cliffs with a yellow glare before it settled into an indistinct purple haze beyond the pasturage to the west.

The sounds around her were those of young people who spoke too loudly, who gave the waitress their orders as they would to a post, who were casually profane, as though the validation of their own power could be achieved only by their assault on the sensibilities of others.

But inside her mind she saw Wilbur's pickup truck turning into the welding shop down the road and she knew he would be back in fifteen minutes, just as he said he would, and she ate her food and listened to the sounds of the wind and the river threading around the boulders in the current and paid no attention to the voices from the next table.

Then she heard a car engine that was too powerful for the frame it was mounted on, the driver double-clutching as he shifted down and turned into the parking lot, the throaty rumble of his dual Hollywood mufflers bouncing off the front of the building like a glove in the face.

The voices at the next table died when the driver came through the screen door.

He saw her but he didn't speak. He seemed to study the people at the next table, his body swaying, the boards bending under his hobnailed boots, an odor like smoke, alcohol, and body grease emanating from his clothes.

He walked to the bar and came back out with an iced mug of draft beer in his fist. His shoulder struck the doorjamb and the beer splashed over the mug's rim onto the floor.

He was standing behind her chair now, the wall fan wafting across his body, blowing the rawness of his odor on her skin. He steadied himself with one hand on the back of her chair, the muscles of his upper arm swelling with blood, his knuckles touching her shoulder blade.

"Where's your husband at?" he asked.

"This is a bad place for you. You shouldn't come here," she replied.

"Anybody hurt me, Purple Hearts will take people out of here one by one. They'll cut phone lines. Won't nobody be able to help them."

"You're empowering your enemies."

"I'm gonna bring Deitrich down. I'm gonna hurt him for what he done to you."

"Sit down with me. Put your hands in mine."

But he wasn't listening to her now. He turned at a snigger, a remark about Mexicans, his elbow striking the back of someone's head. Then he shoved a tray stacked with barbecue ribs onto the floor and flung his beer into a man's face and spit in a woman's hair.

He had no chance. The men from the table he had violated were joined by others, men with redneck accents and drilling mud on their clothes, and they swarmed over him and pushed him outside, trundling him in their midst down a leaf-strewn embankment to the riverside.

In her mind the trees along the bank and the cliffs above the water were no longer a repository of shadow but were now lighted with a kinetic yellow and black brilliance, as though the sun were shining at midnight.

Kippy Jo stood at the porch screen, listening to the sounds that rose from the riverbank. The crowd had formed a circle, but all their physiological differences had disappeared. They had only one face, and it and their bodies looked made of baked clay, and they used the sharp points of sticks to prod the man in the center back and forth, as they would a bear in a pit.

Angular tubes of red light burst from the wounds in his skin. His throat roared, his hands thrashed at the air like paws. Then his face lifted toward her, one eye squeezed shut like a lump of cauliflower. She could feel the pointed sticks cut into her own ribs and chest, just as they did his. She felt her way between the tables and out the door and down the path to the riverbank, touching the bushes on each side of her, cobweb clinging to her hair.

She smelled the hot stench of the crowd and stopped. She sensed the presence of a shape in front of her and reached out and touched the hardened muscles in a man's back and felt him jump as though the tips of her fingers had burned his skin.

The faces of everyone in the circle turned slowly upon her.

"Lady, you don't have any business down here," a man said. But the confidence in his voice drained before he had finished the sentence.

She stepped inside the circle and touched the face of the man in the center, the wetness running out of his hair, the eye that trembled under her fingertips.

She ran her hand down his shoulder and fitted it inside his upper arm.

"You have to take me out to the road and stay with me until Wilbur comes back," she said.

She thought he would argue but he didn't. They walked together toward the path, the crowd parting in front of her, looking into her sightless eyes as though the power they had feared all their lives lay hidden there. The wind gusted off the river, scattering pine needles across the clearing, then the sun that had blazed at the top of the sky died and the riverside went dark again and the only heat she felt was the brilliance of high-beam headlights that someone had shined across the water onto the cliffs.

Kippy Jo and Cholo Ramirez stood by the front of the parking lot like two bronze statues welded at the seam until Wilbur's pickup truck came skidding to a stop in a rooster tail of dust behind them. His eyes went past them to the crowd that was still standing in front of the screen porch.

"What in the hell you doin' with my wife, boy?" he said.

"SHE SAYS I AIN'T FAIR TO HIM. I say he could have gotten her killed," Wilbur said to me the next day in my office.

"You don't like him?"

"I don't like him coming around Kippy Jo. That boy's a criminal, pure and simple. Besides, he looks like a toad frog somebody kept mashed down inside a Vaseline jar."

"Why are you telling me all this?" I asked.

"Earl Deitrich ain't the only one on his shit list. Is your son getting it on with a Mexican gal named Esmeralda?"

THAT EVENING I SAT on a wooden stool behind Lucas's rented house and watched him can-water the tomato plants in the rocky plot of ground he called a vegetable garden. The air was hot and still and thick with birds, and out on the state road I heard a semi-trailer roar by and saw a turkey buzzard rise from a piece of roadkill on the edge of the asphalt. While he sprinkled and dusted his plants, Lucas kept glancing up at the trailer where Esmeralda was living, as though she could hear his words.

"I ain't afraid of Cholo. I ain't afraid of Ronnie Cross, either," he said.

"Foolish words, in my view," I said.

"Well, you ain't me."

"L.Q. Navarro used to tell me there're two kinds of friends you can have by the tote sack—the kind that find you when you're in tall cotton and the kind that find you when they're in trouble."

"Boy, I wish I was smart and had all them things figured out."

"You know what heartwood is?"

"Sure . . . What is it?"

"Some trees add a layer of new wood under their bark each year. The core of the tree grows stronger and stronger, until it's almost like iron. Old-timers say they used to bust their axes on it."

"Yeah?" Lucas said, his eyes wandering away from me now. Esmeralda was hanging her wash on the clothesline, her hair wrapped in a towel. "What's that have to do with what we're talking about?"

"I'm not sure. I'll study on it and let you know," I said.

"You're a mysterious man, Billy Bob."

I walked back to my car and did not reply.

MY FATHER WAS a tack and hot-pass welder on pipelines all over Texas, and when I was nine years old he took my mother and me with him on the line into the Winding Stair Mountains of eastern Oklahoma. It was early fall and the canopy of the hardwood trees had already started to ruffle with red and gold all the way to the massive outlines of the Ozarks. My father wasn't an overly religious man, but he made an effort to tithe and he wouldn't normally drink except on Christmas and July 4. By chance the pipeline was shut down our last Sunday in the Winding Stairs and he took me with him to a camp meeting on the banks of a pebble-bottomed stream whose water was the color of light green Jell-O.

The choir was a string band, the preacher a rail of a man who opened his Bible as though to read, then looked heavenward with his eyes squeezed tightly shut yet never misspoke a line. The congregation shook and trembled and spoke in tongues and in the next breath ate dinner on the ground and off the tailgates of farm trucks. But those were not the images that defined for me that seminal afternoon of my childhood.

The banks of the stream had eroded sharply during a spring torrent, and the root systems of the overhanging trees trailed in the current like brown spiderweb. The trunk of each tree looked swollen and hard, the bark glistening and serrated, as though the root system had drawn the coldness of the water into the wood and filled it with a hardness that would blunt nails.

The preacher stood waist-deep in the current and dipped a fat woman backwards, the current sliding across her closed eyes, her white dress tied around the knees with a blue slash so it wouldn't float up from her thighs.

"You up to it?" my father asked.

"I ain't afraid," I said.

"Don't let your mother hear you using 'ain't.' That water's like ice, bud."

"I been in a lot worse."

I felt his large hand cup on the top of my head.

A few minutes later I stood barefoot on the pebbles, the coldness of the water sucking around my thighs and genitals, my palm clutched in the preacher's. He leaned me back in the water and a vast green light seemed to cover my face and steal the breath from my lungs and invade my clothes and burn my skin.

Then, just as the preacher raised my face from the water, I opened my eyes and saw the trees arching overhead and the leafy green and yellow design they formed against the sky, and without knowing the words to circumscribe the idea, I knew I had entered a special and inviolate place, a private cathedral suffused with stained light that I would always return to in memory when I felt I was unworthy of the world.

While my father dried me off by a fire and put his old army shirt on me, the one with the Indianhead Division patch and sergeant's stripes on the sleeve, I glanced back at the stream and it looked ordinary now, apart from me, dotted with half-immersed people whom I did not know.

"What kind of trees are those?" I asked.

"Heartwood," my father said. "They grow in layers, like the spirit does. That's what Grandpa Sam used to say, anyway. You just got to keep the roots in a clear stream and not let nobody taint the water for you."

His jaw was filled with a ham sandwich, and it seemed to swell into the size of a softball when he grinned.

20

ONE NIGHT EVERY SUMMER THE TOWN HELD A celebration for itself in our small amusement park and beer garden on the river. At sunset a brass band composed of musicians in straw boaters and candy-striped jackets struck up "San Antonio Rose" and someone switched on the Japanese lanterns in the trees, and the hedges and pea-gravel paths and concession stands and carnival booths took on the bucolic and softly focused qualities of a late-nineteenth-century painting. The social distinctions of the town were put in abeyance, and working people, college students, farmers, the business community, the mayor and his family, even Hugo Roberts and his deputies, all mingled together as though the following day held the same promise and opportunity for each of them.

Temple Carrol and Pete and I rode the Tilt-a-Whirl and the bumper cars and ate cotton candy and strolled out by the dance pavilion that overlooked the river. The three of us sat on a green-painted wood bench at the top of a slope that was terraced with cannas and hibiscus and rosebushes and a rock-bordered pond whose goldfish were molting into the albino discolorations of carp. It was Pete who first noticed Peggy

Jean Deitrich out on the dance floor with her husband, Earl, and when he did, he waved at her.

"There's Ms. Deitrich, Billy Bob," he said expectantly.

"Yeah, it sure is," I said, glancing over my shoulder.

"Ain't you gonna wave back?"

"She's busy right now," I said.

He frowned and squinted into space. Then he waved again, as though he could make up for our not doing so.

I turned on the bench and looked back at the dance pavilion. Peggy Jean was standing with her husband by the punch table now, but her gaze fell directly on my face. Her expression was disjointed, as though I had failed and wounded her without even having the grace to explain why. Her lips seemed to part in anticipation, forming words that she wished to draw from my mouth.

I turned back toward the river and looked out through the electric haze over the gardens and the goldfish rising in the pond for the bread crumbs a child was throwing at them.

"I think I'll take Pete for a cold drink," Temple said.

"I'll go with you," I said.

"That's all right. Why don't you just take care of business here," Temple said, and walked back up through the trees to the concession area.

"Temple?" I said. But she and Pete had already disappeared up the path into the shadows.

I pulled the last strand of cotton candy off the paper cone it was wrapped on and threw the cone into a trash barrel. I tried to scrub the stickiness off my hands with a paper napkin, then I gave it up and threw it in the trash, too.

I heard light footsteps on the gravel behind me, then smelled Peggy Jean's perfume.

"Do you know what it feels like to have someone stare at you, then turn away when you try to wave at them?" Peggy Jean said.

"How are you?" I said.

"What gives you the right to snub me in public? Can you tell me what it is I've done to you?"

"You're married. I didn't want to recognize that fact. The fault is mine."

"We shared a great deal when we were young." Her eyes held mine. "I'm not talking about just one afternoon. We were true friends. Are you just going to step across a line and pretend we don't know each other? That's sick, if you ask me."

I leaned forward on my elbows and turned my hat in my hands and bounced the brim on the tip of my boot. Then the words I should not have spoken had their way.

"What happened to you, Peggy Jean? You used to be one of us. Why'd you go off with a guy like Earl? Was it the money?" I said.

In the corner of my eye I could see her hand clenching and unclenching against her organdy dress, hear the fractured breathing that was about to crest into tears.

"I'm sorry I said that," I said.

But it was too late. She strode back toward the pavilion, her hair swinging on her shoulders. I don't know what her face looked like, whether it was tear-streaked or angry or bloodless with humiliation or numb and distraught with personal loss, but Earl and Jeff Deitrich had disengaged from their friends and were both staring at her, then at me, their eyes blazing, like men who had witnessed another man commit a cowardly and brutal act against a woman or child.

"You want to get Earl Deitrich before he gets you?" a voice next to me said.

Cholo Ramirez wore gray slacks and a shiny black dress shirt with a pomegranate-red print tie. His left eye was taped over with a square of white gauze. Ronnie Cruise stood behind him in the shadows, a Popsicle stick in the corner of his mouth.

"Ask him about killing himself in the Red Pine Lodge. Ask him what happened to his friends in that water-bed skeet club between Houston and Conroe," Cholo said.

"What's he talking about?" I said to Ronnie.

"You're a religious guy, right, worrying about stuff like people wearing rosaries around their necks? Listen to Cholo, maybe discover how we dress ain't the big problem in your town," Ronnie replied. His dark eyes that seemed impervious to whatever degree of joy the world could offer him wandered over the strollers on the gravel paths and the aerial fireworks popping in pink and white showers above the river. "Does this shithole ever get tired of itself?" he said.

CHOLO'S SKIN WAS GLAZED with sweat when he came into my office at noon the next day. He hooked a finger over the neck of his T-shirt and pulled it out from his chest and smelled himself.

"That sidewalk will burn through the bottom of your shoes," I said.

"I picked up a sheriff's tail south of town. The guy stayed with me all the way to your office," he said. He chewed on a hangnail.

"They don't see many cars like yours. I wouldn't worry about it."

"This guy had that Fletcher fuck in the car, that ex-mercenary guy or whatever who does scut work for Deitrich."

"Why do you want to dime Earl now, Cholo?"

"'Cause Kippy Jo Pickett says I got to own up. She says maybe I'm gonna be on the Ghost Trail." He hunched his shoulders forward and made a coughing sound, but his throat wouldn't clear.

"The what?" I asked.

"When Indian people die, they disappear down a trail. Light goes through their bodies, and they get pale and gray, like bad milk, and finally you can't see them no more. That's what Kippy Jo said."

"You think you're going to die?"

"You got something cold to drink? I need a beer. Maybe a shot of rum. You got that?"

"No."

He wiped his hair and his eyebrows with a handkerchief. Then he pressed both fists into the sides of his head and squeezed his eyes shut.

"I can't think good when it's hot," he said. "Ronnie's uncle is connected up with some peckerwoods out of Houston. Ronnie didn't have nothing to do with it, though. They was working a scam in Kerr County at a place called the Red Pine Lodge. A shill brought big oil guys in there to play 'Hold 'em.' We'd turn the game over, scare the shit out of the marks with shotguns, play like we was torturing and killing people down in the basement."

"This isn't new information, Cholo. You told this to Temple Carrol when she picked you up for jumping bail."

"Yeah? The shill brought Earl Deitrich into the game. We came through the door with nylon stockings over our heads, knocking people on the floor, breaking glasses and whiskey bottles, throwing poker chips and playing cards in people's faces, yelling at Deitrich, slapping his face, jamming the shotgun in his nuts.

"Then we led everybody one by one downstairs. The screams that come up them stairs was so real they scared me. We fired off a bunch of twelve-gauge rounds in a barrel and threw chicken blood all over everybody. It looked great. Then this woman, the dealer, lies down in the middle of all those bodies. She's got on a white blouse and skirt and it's got chicken blood on it, too. This broad was in porno movies and she was real good at acting. She knew how to twitch, with her eyes closed, just like she was gonna bleed to death unless somebody got her to a hospital.

"So we walk Earl Deitrich downstairs and we tell him, 'Look, man, one guy got out of control down here. We still don't know where the bank is at. You got a chance to live, man. What's it gonna be?'

"He thinks for a minute. Can you believe that? Bodies are all over the floor and he stands there thinking. Then he says, 'There's a safe under the duckboards behind the bar.'

"One of our guys goes upstairs and comes back with handfuls of money, like it's a big surprise. Then we tell Deitrich, 'Look, man, we got nothing against you. But you saw too much here. The broad is still alive. Pump one into her and that puts us all on the same side.'

"The guy saying this takes the magazine out of a Beretta nine-millimeter so Deitrich knows only one round's in it and hands it to him and waits for him to pop the broad. Deitrich just stands there with the piece in his hand, thinking, a smile on his mouth.

"Our guy goes, 'You got a hearing problem?'

"Deitrich says, 'You know, you guys have brought my year to a head. It's been a real pisser. How about all of you kiss my ass?' And he shoots himself in the side of the head.

"We can't believe it. Neither can he. Smoke is rising from his hair and he's smiling at us. He opens and closes his mouth like he's gonna be deaf a month and says, 'A blank, huh? I got to admit, it's a slick blackmail operation. But you're amateurs.' Then he pitches the piece back to the guy who give it to him and says, 'Clean yourselves up, then I want to have a talk with you all.'"

Cholo wiped the heat and grease from his eyes with the flats of his fingers and walked to the air conditioner and hit on it.

"Why don't you get some central air, man? This place is a kitchen," he said. He looked through the blinds, down onto the sidewalk.

"Go on with your story," I said.

"That deputy's still down there, the one with the ex-mercenary fuck. You told somebody I was coming here today?"

"Nope."

"Kippy Jo trusts you. But you ain't earned no points with me."

"That's too bad."

"Maybe you're setting me up. You was a Texas Ranger. That means you still got a badge up your hole."

I could feel the anger rise in my chest and seize in

my throat, but I kept my eyes focused on nothing. In the far corner of the room I thought I saw L.Q. Navarro leaning against the woodwork, his ash-gray Stetson tilted on the back of his head, his eyes filled with humor.

"Get out of here," I said to Cholo.

"Wha—"

"Go learn some respect for other people. I'm full up on bullshit and rudeness today."

"I don't believe you, man."

"It looks like that's an ongoing state with you, Cholo. Adios. No ethnic slur intended," I said.

After Cholo was gone, the door and glass still trembling from being flung back against the wall, L.Q. sat down in the deerhide swayback chair, took out his pack of playing cards, and began a game of solitaire on the bottom of an inverted leather wastebasket.

"You done the right thing. He wasn't going to give you the rest of it. That kid's been in and out of Juvie since he was knee-high to a fireplug," L.Q. said.

"You think he'll be back?"

"It don't matter. You got to make them wince inside. You know who said that? Wyatt Earp."

"I'm going to lunch."

"Eat a second helping for me," he said. He remained concentrated on his card game and didn't look up.

• • •

I RAN INTO TEMPLE on the courthouse walk the next morning and told her about Cholo's visit.

"You threw him out?" she said.

"He was confessing to stuff there's no record of. He wants me to bring down Earl Deitrich without implicating himself. I think Cholo burned that savings and loan for Earl and killed those firemen down in Houston. Maybe he was responsible for the accountant's heart attack, too."

"Earl Deitrich fired a gun into the side of his head?"

"You admire that?"

"I didn't think he had that kind of guts," she said.

I shook my head and walked into the courthouse. Two hours later Temple called me at the office.

"I just got a call from Cholo. He says you dissed him. He says he'll unload his whole story if I'll meet him at a gym in San Antone. He says he was at the fire in Houston."

"Make him come to you."

"I'm meeting him at ten in the morning," she said.

"Do you ever listen to me about anything?"

"Not really," she said.

"What's the name of the gym?" I asked.

IT WAS LOCATED in a dirty white two-story cinderblock building on the edge of a warehouse district. The rooms were air-conditioned, but the smell of sweat and testosterone and soiled jerseys and socks left to dry on floor fans was overpowering. Temple and I walked through a basketball court filled with slum kids, through a free-weight room, into an annex that contained speed- and heavy bags and a boxing ring. The noise of the speedbags thudding on the rebound boards was deafening.

Cholo was dressed out in black Everlast trunks and a sweatshirt cut off at the armpits, pounding both gloved fists into a heavy bag. The sweat whipped from his hair with each blow.

He saw us and held the bag stationary and looked past Temple at me. He had removed the dressing from his left eye, and the white of the eye was clotted with broken purple veins.

"What's he doing here?" he said.

"We're on a tight schedule, Cholo. You want to fling more bean dip around, we're gone," I said.

"I don't like you, man," he replied.

"Hold the bag for me," Temple said.

"Do what?" he said.

She spun and hit the bag dead-center with a karate kick.

"You can do that?" he said.

"What's the deal on Earl Deitrich and the skeet club?" she said.

"I'll take a shower and we'll go somewhere," he said. "But first there's this guy been pinning me. I gotta straighten him out."

"Which guy?" she said.

"Don't worry about it. Have a seat. This kind of guy is, what d'you call it, predictable," he said.

We watched from a bench against the wall while Cholo continued hitting the bag. It didn't take long to see the scenario at work. A blond man, with brilliantine in his hair, was skipping rope by the ring, crossing his wrists, slapping the floor hard under his flat-soled shoes, an indolent grin on his mouth as he stared straight into Cholo's face.

"You make that guy?" I said to Temple.

"Used to be a mule for Sammy Macc? Out of Houston, he did a vice snitch, I thought he was in Huntsville," Temple said.

"Johnny Krause."

"Yeah, that's it. He beat the homicide beef on appeal. What's he doing here?"

The man named Johnny Krause stopped skipping rope and picked up a pair of sixteen-ounce sky-blue sparring gloves from the apron of the ring and walked toward Cholo. He paused no more than a foot from Cholo, pulling on his gloves, his abdominal muscles protruding slightly over his elastic waistband, indifferent to the possibility of being hit by Cholo's elbows or the bag swinging back on its chain.

"Go three with me. I'll take it easy on you," he said.

"I want to go three, I'll ask. Go fuck your 'easy,' too," Cholo said.

Krause made a casual face and turned his head to the side and looked into space. His blue, white-striped trunks reached almost to his knees and clung like moist Kleenex to his skin. "Suit yourself. You been staring at me all morning. I thought you wanted to go," he said.

"Me staring at you?"

"Don't worry about it. Sorry I bothered you, Paco," Krause said, and rubbed the sweaty top of Cholo's head with the palm of his glove.

Cholo knocked his arm away.

"Who you calling Paco, man?" he said.

"That ain't your name?" Krause kept smiling and tapped Cholo on the ear, winking, raising his guard now, his head ducking down behind his gloves as though he were about to be hit. "I been hearing you're one badass mean motherfucker. Don't hurt me, mean motherfucker," he said.

Cholo stepped away from the bag and swung at Krause, his glove ripping into empty space, pulling him off balance.

"The wind almost knocked me down. I got to carry an anchor around. Get me out of here," Krause said.

Others had stopped their workout and were watching now, laughing, making remarks behind their gloves to one another.

"Get a timekeeper. We don't use no headgear, either," Cholo said.

Johnny Krause sprang into the ring, threw a combination left and right at the air, his lips pursed, his chin tucked into his chest. Then he leaned back into the turnbuckle, his arms spread on the ropes, and watched Cholo, down below, pulling on the other pair of blue gloves with his teeth.

I stepped between Cholo and the apron of the ring. "I don't know why, but he's setting you up. Don't do it," I said.

"Fuck you," he replied, and climbed up into the ring, the tattoos of a knife dripping blood and a death's head on his throat running with sweat.

An old man with white, puckered skin and hair like meringue clicked a stopwatch and clanged the bell. Johnny Krause had either fought professionally or in prison, because he took complete control of his environment as soon as he moved to the center of the ring.

He stepped sideways, bobbed, or jerked backwards so quickly that Cholo couldn't touch him, all the time feigning restraint, as if Cholo were the aggressor in what should have been a sparring match.

"Whoa! You trying to take my head off? This ain't Mexico City. Hey, we got no cut man here. Maybe I'm a bleeder. Help!" Krause said, dancing, his sky-blue gloves at his sides.

Cholo reminded me of old film clips of Two-Ton Tony Galento, wading forward with the plodding solidity of a hod carrier, throwing one wild overhand punch after another.

Except Cholo's fists could not find his opponent or the smile that mocked him.

Krause jabbed Cholo around the eyes with his left, pow, pow, pow, that fast. Cholo's face twitched, his eyes watering as though he had been Maced. Then Krause hooked him on the ear and caught him hard on the jaw with a right cross, knocking his mouth-piece through the ropes. When Cholo tried to clench him, Krause thumbed him in his bad eye and nailed him again, this time in the mouth.

The timekeeper was jerking the rope on the bail, waving one hand in the air for Krause to stop.

Krause set himself and drove his right fist straight into Cholo's unprotected face, bouncing him off the ropes, spiderwebbing his nose and chin with blood. Cholo rolled on the canvas, disoriented, and fell off the apron onto the cement, turning over the spit bucket.

"We don't have no dirty fights in here. What's wrong with you?" the timekeeper said.

"You got it turned around. He was trying to scramble my eggs," Krause said.

He climbed through the ropes and dropped to the cement, avoiding the wetness from the spit bucket.

"You all right, buddy? You were coming hard. You didn't give me no choice," Krause said.

Cholo got to his feet, his eyes crossing, and pulled his gloves off one at a time by trapping them between his arm and his chest. He tossed them to the floor and hitched up his genitalia.

"I got your lunch hanging," he said.

"What can I say?" Krause said.

Cholo walked unsteadily toward the dressing room, a towel crumpled against his mouth and nose.

"You got crazy people in here. What kind of dump is this?" Krause said.

Someone picked up Cholo's gloves off the floor and started to put them in an equipment box under the ring.

"Them are my gloves," Krause said, popping open a paper bag for the man to drop them in.

BUT IF CHOLO RAMIREZ was indeed intended to embark on the Ghost Trail of his Indian ancestors, its entrance was not marked by cottonwood trees along a riverbank on a windswept green plain. The Ghost Trail for Cholo lay inside the incessant scream of a shorted-out car horn and the heated smell of car metal and exhaust fumes and asphalt only a block from the Alamo. That's where the paramedics pried his hands off the steering wheel of his '49 Merc and tried to abate the convulsions in his body and the hemorrhage that was taking place in his brain.

While they strapped him down to a gurney, a frustrated policeman popped the Merc's hood and tore the wiring from the horn like a severed snake.

21

CHOLO'S FUNERAL WAS HELD THREE DAYS LATER in a white stucco church with a red tile roof and a small neat yard next to the elementary school he had once attended, the only well-maintained buildings in a neighborhood of dilapidated one-story, flat-roofed homes that could have been machine-gun bunkers. His fellow gangbangers tried to turn the funeral into a statement about themselves, dressing out in black cloaks with scarlet linings, posting somber-faced, narrowed-eyed lookouts in the church vestibule and parking lot. But basically it was a pathetic affair. The back pews were empty; the gangbangers sweated inside their cloaks and smelled themselves; obese women in black wept with such histrionics that the other mourners took deep breaths and raised their eyebrows wearily; and Cholo lay in a cheap wood casket, dressed in a shiny suit that looked like it had been rented for a graduation ceremony, a rose in the lapel, his hair stiff with grease against the rayon pillow, a rosary wrapped around fingers that still had dirt under the nails.

If there were two people there who seemed genuinely saddened, it was Ronnie Cruise and Esmeralda Ramirez. They sat on opposite sides of the church. Neither looked at the other, nor at anyone around them.

I caught Ronnie on the church steps after the service.

"You're the man," I said.

"You're always talking in code. I don't understand what you're saying. I think you got shit for brains being here," he replied.

He got in his car and drove away. I followed him to the graveside service, then to the rural slum neighborhood where he lived. He turned into his dirt driveway, staring in the rearview mirror when I turned in behind him. But he went inside as though I were not there.

The house had probably been built from a double-wide trailer and modified and added on to over the years. There was a picture window in front, a carport on the side, and the bottom portion of the walls was covered with a half-brick shell, to affect a suburban 1950s home. A solitary mimosa grew like a huge green fan in the dirt yard, and in back, beyond the carport, I could see banana trees bending in the wind along a drainage ditch.

A woman with breasts like watermelons and black hair wrapped in a bun on her head opened the front door and looked at me with a neutral expression, then closed it again. A moment later Ronnie came from around back, barefoot now, in a pair of beltless jeans and a T-shirt, a bird dog pup trailing behind him.

"Why'd you say I was the man?" he asked.

"Cholo's dead. That means you're going on the stand."

"For what?"

"To tell everyone about Earl Deitrich's dealings with Cholo."

"That's called hearsay. Even I know that much."

"It's called a subpoena. You'll be in court of your own accord or you'll be there in handcuffs, Ronnie."

"I've heard it before. I'm gonna be picking up the soap in the county bag. It don't flush."

"Cholo was murdered," I said.

"You mean the guy busted a vein in Cholo's head?"

"I've got a friend named Doc Voss. He's buds with the pathologist who did the postmortem on Cholo. The pathologist thinks a toxic substance of some kind was rubbed in Cholo's face. Something that acts like cyanide."

"Thinks?"

"This ex-con, Johnny Krause, the guy who got Cholo into the ring? He loaded up a vice snitch with angle iron and put him in the San Jacinto River for Sammy Mace."

Ronnie pulled on an earlobe, then picked up a soft cloth off a workbench under the carport and rubbed it on the hood of his T-Bird.

"Sammy Mace's dead. He got blown away by a cop a year or so back," he said.

"I think Johnny Krause found a new employer. I'd

like to ask him that, but nobody can find him. You have the same information on Earl Deitrich that Cholo did. Where's that leave you, Ronnie? You want Johnny Krause looking you up?"

He held up one palm and ticked at a callus with his thumb, staring at it as though it held special meaning for him. He hooked his thumbs inside the pockets of his jeans and looked at a spot six inches to the right of my head and sucked in his cheeks, then cleared his throat before he spoke.

"Your boy, the one sleeping with Esmeralda? He don't run scared. But you think I do. Is it 'cause I'm Mexican and you think I'm dumb or 'cause I got a sheet and I ain't as good as other people and you can work my stick? I think you better go, Mr. Holland. I don't want you coming around my mother's house no more."

LATER THAT AFTERNOON I looked out my back porch and saw Pete sitting on the top rail of Beau's fence. I picked up a glass of iced tea and took a can of Pepsi from the icebox and walked out to the lot. The breeze smelled of rain out in the hills and the windmill had turned north, its blades ginning furiously.

"What you doing out here by yourself, bud?" I asked.

"You said we was gonna look for arrowheads." He ignored the can of Pepsi I balanced on the rail.

"Sorry, I forgot. Let's hitch the trailer on the truck and get Beau in."

But his face remained preoccupied. He kept squeezing a half dollar in his palm and looking at the red lines it made in his skin.

"I seen Ms. Deitrich in town," he said.

"Oh yeah, Ms. Deitrich."

"She was coming out of the grocery. She had two big sacks in her arms. One was fixing to split. I tried to take it from her before the milk bottle broke on the cement."

He stopped and watched Beau walking from the pasture toward the lot.

"Go on," I said.

"She said I was gonna make her drop it. She said, 'You're in the way. Take your hands off the bag.'"

"She didn't mean anything by it."

"You weren't there. She was mad. The bag split all over her hood. She said, 'See what you made me do?'"

"I guess she was having a bad day, Pete."

"After she got her stuff in the car, she dug a half dollar out of her purse and said, 'Go buy yourself some ice cream or something. Go on, now. Next time just let big people work out their problems. You're a little too nosy sometimes.'"

He climbed down from the fence and looked at the late sun as though it contained an insult.

"I don't want her durn money. I stopped to hep 'cause she was having trouble," he said.

"I don't see her, Pete, so I don't know what to tell you."

He ringed the edge of the half dollar with his index finger and flung it toward the tank. He watched it arch out of the light into the grass. His face was hot and dusty and there were moist lines that had dried on his cheeks.

"Where you goin'?" I said.

"Home."

"Beau's going to be disappointed if we don't take him out."

"How come she acted like that? I thought she was nice. She ain't no different from the people my mother hangs with up at the beer joint. They're nice long as somebody is watching them."

The answer to his question was not one I wanted to think about.

IT WAS ALMOST SUNSET when Pete and I rode up a creekbed between two steep-sided hills that were deep in shadow and moist with springs that leached out of the rocks. Beau's hooves scraped on the flat plates of stone along the creekbank and I could feel Pete's weight swaying back and forth behind the saddle.

"You don't think these was Apaches living along here?" he said.

"Too far east," I replied.

"Maybe they was Comanches."

"Too far south."

"Then what was they?"

"Probably Tonkawas."

"The ones that let the Texans run them up into Oklahoma?"

"That's the bunch."

"They don't sound too interesting," he said.

We got down from Beau and I unhooked the strap of my rucksack from his pommel and we walked through heavy brush to a faint trail that angled up the hillside through pine trees and soft ground that was green from the moisture in the drainage. Scrub brush and redbud trees grew close into the cliff wall, and if you looked carefully you could see a ragged opening behind the foliage.

"I heard some people in town say Wilbur Pickett's wife is crazy," he said.

"You believe that?" I asked.

"No. I feel sorry for her."

"Because she's blind?"

"No. 'Cause they're scared of her. Scared people hurt you."

"You're a smart kid, Pete."

"I wish we could stay up here all the time. It's a perfect place. There ain't nobody around but just us."

The trail leveled out on a bench and we walked between the scrub brush and the cliff wall to an opening in the rock, close to the ground, no more than three feet in diameter, that looked like it had been gouged out of prehistoric clay by a huge thumb.

It was black inside and we could feel the coolness of the air puffing against our faces and smell the wetness of the stone and the odor of field mice that nested on the ledges where the cave's ceiling rose much higher than the entrance.

The sun's last rays were pink on the crests of the ravine and I could hear Beau blowing down below. I untied the rucksack and opened my pocketknife and began slicing a red onion and a roll of salami and a loaf of French bread on a rock. Pete pulled my flashlight out of the sack and played with the switch, clicking it off and on, then squatted down and shined the beam back into the cave.

"Somebody's living here, Billy Bob," he said.

I stooped down beside him and looked through the entrance. Vinyl garbage bags had been split open and spread on the silt floor of the cave and a large sheet of canvas flattened on top of them in what looked like a sleeping area. A firepit had been dug close to the entrance, and smoke had blackened one wall and part of the overhang. Venison bones protruded like teeth from the ash in the center of the pit and there was a glycerin shine from meat drippings on the firestones.

Cans of Spam and sardines and Vienna sausage and boxes of cookies and crackers were stacked along a board shelf someone had wedged into the wall. A shiny gallon molasses can filled with water was covered with a piece of cheesecloth to keep out dust. Two sleeping bags were rolled and snugged tightly with clothesline cord, as though the owners lived in preparation for leaving hurriedly. Propped upside down with sticks against the wall was a pair of scuffed work shoes with leather strings and hook eyelets at the top of the tongues.

"You reckon it's some bums come up from the train track?" Pete asked.

I picked up one of the work shoes and turned it over in my hands. "That's jailhouse-issue, Pete. Let's leave this be."

"You mean these guys might be escaped convicts?"

"Could be."

"We gonna call the sheriff's department?"

"I don't figure it's our business."

"They're in our cave. They're messing it up. They probably go to the bathroom anyplace they feel like. I bet they got B.O."

"Pete?"

"What?"

"Don't say any more. Let's get Beau and leave quietly. Forget what we saw here."

He looked at me quizzically, one eye squinted partly shut.

WE RODE BEAU up the ravine, out of the shadows into the sun's last yellow glow against the sky. Then we crossed a glade full of wildflowers and looked out on the valley owned by Peggy Jean and Earl

Deitrich and, directly down below, their white home couched like a giant gold-streaked molar in the hillside.

I heard the sound of an engine grinding down a two-track road from the pines above us. Then I saw the black roll-bar Jeep turn out of the road and head toward us through the glade, the grass and wildflowers pressing flat into the soil under the Jeep's cleated tires.

Four young men sat in the Jeep, wearing shades and T-shirts and camouflage pants, their arms and foreheads red with fresh sunburn, bolt-action scoped rifles propped next to them. I felt Pete's hands tighten involuntarily on my waist.

The driver, Jeff Deitrich, pulled the Jeep in front of us and put the transmission in neutral. He grinned lazily at me, his eyes hidden by his shades.

"How you doin', Billy Bob?" he said.

"Not bad. Y'all aren't hunting out of season, are you?" I said, smiling back at him.

"The cops haven't been able to find your friend Doolittle. We thought we'd help out," he said.

"Let's see if I have your friends' names right. You're Hammie, you're Warren, and you're Chug," I said, moving my finger from one to the next.

"Pretty good," Jeff said. "What are you doing on our property, Billy Bob?"

"This isn't yours. The state has an easement through here."

"Don't argue with a lawyer," he said.

"Skyler Doolittle is for the most part a harmless man," I said.

"He's gonna be a lot more harmless if we find him," Chug said. He drank out of a quart bottle of milk, his face round and flushed with heat, his throat working steadily.

I flipped the ends of Beau's reins idly on the back of my wrist.

"Jessie is another matter, though. He's half white trash and half Comanche Indian. He'll tie you down in your bed and put a sock in your mouth and skin you like a deer. Ask the sheriff, Chug," I said.

The three passengers in the Jeep looked at one another. The one named Warren stuck an unlit cigarette in his mouth, then pulled it out and rolled the barrel of the cigarette back and forth between his fingers.

"The people at the state mental hospital thought they'd blow out his aggressions with electroshock. He bit through the rubber gag, then got a hand free and chewed a technician's finger off," I said.

"My uncle used to hire Jessie Stump to clean gum off the seats at the Rialto. He got stuck in the chimney when he tried to rob the hardware store. The county jail in Llano wouldn't take him because he's not toilet trained. Good try, counselor," Jeff said, and laughed, then drove back on the two-track road. But his passengers were silent, their expressions dull with either fatigue or reconsideration about the wisdom of hunting Jessie Stump.

The wind dented the grass and flowers in the glade and a drop of rain stung me in the eye like a BB.

"The guys they're looking for are living in our cave, ain't they?" Pete said.

"That'd be my guess."

"Are those stories true about Jessie Stump?"

I wet my lips. "I kind of made those up," I said.

"I don't like to hear about stuff like that, Billy Bob. I don't want to come up here for a while. Don't lie to me about Jessie Stump, neither. It means you don't respect me."

I turned around in the saddle and looked at him. But his eyes stared at the ground as it moved past us, as though our shadows knew each other in ways we did not. He removed his hands from my waist and rested them on the cantle.

22

I WENT TO MARVIN POMROY'S HOUSE EARLY THE NEXT morning, before he left for work, and found him out on the patio behind his white gingerbread house, his newspaper propped against a glass of orange juice, a piece of toast held in his fingers while he read the box scores on the sports page.

His backyard was spacious and filled with trees and flowering bushes, and blue jays and mocking-birds flew in and out of the sunlight. His wife waved at me from the French doors that gave onto the dining room and held up a cup of coffee with a question in her face.

"No thanks, Gretchen," I said, and sat down at Marvin's table without being asked.

"Can't it wait till I get to the office?" he said.

"Did you talk to the pathologist in San Antone?"

"Yeah, I did. He said Cholo Ramirez was sniffing model airplane glue before he died. There was a sock loaded with it on the seat beside him."

"That's not what killed him."

"Maybe not. But the pathologist isn't sure what did. Boxing gloves with poison on them? Sounds like Elizabethan theater."

"Wake up, Marvin. Earl Deitrich is treating you like a bought-and-paid-for stooge."

He folded up his newspaper and set it to the side of his plate. His shirt looked as smooth and white as new porcelain.

"As a public official I have to accept all kinds of abuse at the courthouse. That doesn't apply in my home," he said.

"That Mexican kid had a chemical time bomb put in his head."

"Not in this county he didn't."

"There's nothing like seeing cartography used to compartmentalize evil," I said.

Marvin rose from his chair and picked up his newspaper and glass of orange juice and went inside the house and closed the French doors gingerly with one foot.

THE NEXT DAY WAS SATURDAY. Lucas Smothers woke before dawn and drank coffee on the back steps of his rented house and watched the sun break across the fields and light on the trailer where Esmeralda Ramirez was still living. She had hand-washed her undergarments the night before and hung them on the clothesline in back, and now they moved in the breeze and he felt vaguely ashamed when he realized he was looking at them.

He had convinced himself he had no romantic interest in her, that he could no more ask her to leave than he could refuse to help an injured person on the highway. But when she had cleaned his house for him and hung curtains in his windows, he'd found himself following her from room to room, telling her about the bands he had played in, listening to her talk about her classes at the Juco, all the time watching her eyes and her mouth, embarrassed at the level of arousal they caused in him.

He wanted an excuse to touch her. She tied her hair up on her head while she worked, and when she stood on a chair and lifted a curtain into place, her back looked strong and muscular, her exposed hips tapering outward just below her belt line, the backs of her thighs hard, as though she were wearing heels. When the chair legs wobbled, he started to grip her waist, but she steadied herself against the wall with one hand and said, "Don't worry. I'm not going to fall."

When Cholo died, Lucas thought Esmeralda would turn to him. But she didn't. She returned from the funeral dry-eyed and withdrawn, like a person who has been in a subfreezing wind and sits alone by a stove with the memory of cold burned deep into the face. That evening he tapped on her screen, and when she appeared in the doorway, the overhead light breaking over her shoulders and reddish-brown hair like gold needles, he said, "If you ain't eat yet, I'm fixing to put some food out on the table. Or I can bring some over. I mean, if you're hungry. Or maybe you just want to take a walk or something." Then he took a breath and said, "I ain't good at words. I'm sorry about your brother."

"That's nice of you, Lucas. But I have to go to work," she replied.

"Work? That tub of guts at the Dog 'n' Shake is making you come in the same day your brother was buried?"

"I'll see you later, Lucas," she said, and eased the inside door closed in his face.

She didn't even ask him for a ride. Instead, she put on her pink uniform and waited out on the road for the county bus to pick her up and carry her out to the small drive-in not far from the Post Oaks Country Club.

Now he sat on his back steps in the early morning coolness, looking at her undergarments on the clothesline, wondering if he was prurient or simply a fool. No sound at all came from inside the trailer. The sun rose above the house in a red ball and he flung the coffee from his cup into the dust and laced on his steel-toed boots and drove his pickup truck out to the drilling rig where he had an eight-hour one-hundred-degree shift waiting for him on the derrick floor.

THAT EVENING, when she got off from work at the Dog 'n' Shake, Ronnie Cruise was waiting for her in the parking lot. He was dressed in slacks, polished loafers, and a new sports shirt, clothes he normally didn't wear, and his hair had been freshly barbered and his jaws glowed with aftershave lotion.

He leaned down in the T-Bird's passenger window so she could see his face.

"I'll take you home, Essie," he said.

"I have a bus pass," she replied.

His car was parked in the shadow of an oak tree, and the engine ticked with road heat.

"Come on, you been on your feet all day," he said.

"Thanks, anyway, Ronnie. Really."

She walked out to the edge of the road and stood where the bus would stop. She twisted her mouth into a button and stared at the entrance to the country club and the fairways along the river and the sun that had descended into a red cloud of dust and rain blowing on the horizon.

Ronnie sat behind the steering wheel of his car, his head on his hands. He started the engine and drove in circles around the Dog 'n' Shake, his tires squealing softly on the pavement, while children eating at the outdoor tables watched him with wide grins on their faces.

The bus stopped for Esmeralda, then the doors closed with a rush of air and the bus heaved out into the road again with Ronnie's T-Bird behind it. Esmeralda sat behind the driver's seat and tried to ignore Ronnie's behavior, but when she glanced into the wide-angle mirror on the driver's window she saw three cars come out of the country club driveway and fall into line behind Ronnie's.

She walked to the back of the bus and looked out the rear window. Ronnie grinned up at her through his windshield, giving her the thumbs-up sign, like an idiot, oblivious to the automobiles behind him.

Who was driving the car immediately behind Ronnie's? she asked herself. It was one of Jeff's friends, what's his name, the one she disliked even more so than the others. He was big all over, layered with beer fat, his neck as thick as a pig's. He was like most fat men she had known—he affected humor and detachment from the world, but he used his irreverence to hide his cruelty, his vulgarity to disguise his fear and hatred of women.

Esmeralda waved her hand back and forth at Ronnie and pointed at the cars behind him. But he continued to grin mindlessly at her, pushing in his clutch and gunning his engine so his Hollywood mufflers rumbled off the asphalt.

She would have gotten off the bus and ridden with him, but he swung over the center line and roared past the bus and two other cars in front before he crossed back over the line and reentered his lane.

She returned to the front of the bus, swaying with her hand in a strap, and tried to see him through the front windshield. But instead of Ronnie's T-Bird, she saw Jeff's friend Chug Rollins, that was the name, pass the bus and cut back quickly into the flow of traffic, followed by the two other cars from the country club.

The bus headed into the dying sun, dipped down through road depressions filled with shadow, took on more passengers, mostly Hispanics and black people who worked as maids and janitorial help. Their muscles were flaccid with fatigue, their faces tired, lined, indifferent to what others might think of their slack jaws and the emptiness in their eyes.

She kept standing up in the aisle, searching the road for sign of Ronnie's T-Bird. But the sky was turning purple above the hills now and most drivers had switched on their headlights and she couldn't distinguish one car from the next. Maybe Ronnie had started back toward San Antone, she thought. Why was he so stubborn? Her brother was dead and one day Ronnie's luck would run out the same way. For what? So they could wear gang colors and have the respect of sociopaths in the prison yard at Huntsville or Sugarland? She had told him it was over. She had deserted him, slept with another man and done things with the other man she didn't even want to remember. Certain kinds of injuries don't heal, she thought, not when you do them with forethought to yourself and those closest to you. Why couldn't Ronnie understand that? He was as unteachable as Cholo.

He had come to the trailer behind Lucas's house, in khakis and a purple shirt open on his chest, the dry hint of reefer on his breath.

"I love you, Essie. I want you back. I don't care what you done," he had told her.

"Don't degrade yourself. It's embarrassing. When did you start smoking dope? God, I'm sick of this craziness," she replied.

Then she had seen something flicker and die in his face, and she bit down on her lip and watched him walk out of the trailer door and take his car keys from his pocket and look at them and put one wrong key after another into the ignition.

Now, on the bus, she felt tears welling up in her eyes and she looked down in her lap so no one would see her face.

Then she glanced out the window and saw Ronnie's car by the side of the road, empty, the left rear tire off, the bare wheel pressed into the dirt next to a crumpled jack.

She leaned close to the glass so she could see up the road. There he was, walking in the dusk toward a filling station and convenience store, the wind, now peppered with rain, blowing up clouds of dust around his legs.

The bus went past Ronnie. She went back to the rear window again, ignoring the irritation of the people around her, and saw the three cars from the country club turning around on a side road and heading back toward Ronnie, the drivers at first circumspect, looking in both directions, then leaning forward eagerly, as though they had just discovered a feared and wounded enemy caught in a steel trap and could not believe their luck.

Esmeralda walked hurriedly up the aisle and held onto the vertical pole behind the driver's chair.

"Let me out," she said.

"I cain't stop along here, lady. A truck will take the side of my bus off," the driver said.

"I have to get off."

"That's your stop up yonder, ain't it? Sit down before you fall and hurt yourself."

The bus pulled to the shoulder of the road a hundred yards from Lucas's house. She stepped down from the vestibule and began running along the gravel toward Lucas's house and the pickup truck that was parked in the front yard. The rocks were like flint through the bottoms of her slip-on shoes. The wind was full of grit that invaded her eyes and drops of rain as hard as marbles struck her face. A semitrailer roared past her, the backdraft blowing her sideways, filling her head with sound as though someone had clapped his hands on both her ears.

LUCAS HAD JUST SHOWERED and changed into a clean pair of Levi's and a soft shirt and was picking out "The Wild Side of Life" on his Dobro, dragging the slide up and down the neck, listening to the notes rise from the resonator and hover in the air like metallic butterflies. He saw the bus go by the front of the house, its windows lighted, and he wondered if Esmeralda had been on it. But he had decided not to bother her anymore, not to intrude upon either her grief or the strange relationships she had with both Ronnie Cross and Jeff Deitrich.

His skin still felt sunbaked from the hours on the drilling rig, the fat long since gone from his muscles, his big western belt bucket flat against the leanness of his stomach. By and large, roughnecks were a pretty interesting bunch, he thought. They rarely complained about the hard lives they'd led and were grateful to have whatever jobs came their way. Even though they worked together for years they usually didn't know one another's last names and didn't consider it an important element in a friendship. They talked constantly of their sexual conquests but in reality considered women a biological mystery and openly admitted they were physically dependent upon them. They were irresponsible, out of sync with the world, and often grinned snaggletoothed at the calamities they visited upon themselves. A guy could do worse than hang with a bunch like that, Lucas thought. It was probably like being in the Foreign Legion. Not a bad way to think of yourself.

He drew his steel picks across the Dobro's strings and slid the bar down the neck and started singing a song he had learned from a one-eyed ex-roustabout who used to pick beans for his stepfather:

"Ten days on, five days off,
I guess my blood is crude oil now.
Reckon I'm never gonna lose
Them mean ole roughneckin' blues."

Then Esmeralda burst through the front door, her pink uniform spotted with rain, her cheeks flushed as bright as apples.

"Ronnie had a flat. Some guys are about to jump him. You got to help," she said.

"Which guys?" Lucas said, rising slowly from the couch.

"Chug Rollins and two carloads of his friends."

"Chug?" he said, and closed and opened his eyes and blew out his breath. He felt a sickness in his stomach and a dampness on his palms that he didn't want to recognize.

"What's the matter?" she said.

"Nothing. I mean, what's between Chug and Ronnie? They got a history?"

"Are you serious? They hate Ronnie. They'll kill him."

He rubbed at his forehead and stared emptily into space. Only moments earlier he had felt surrounded by the imaginary company of his oil field friends. Now the room had become deserted. Even Esmeralda's presence hardly registered on the corner of his vision. The air was suddenly stale and bitter with a knowledge about himself that was as palpable as the odor that rose from his armpits.

"Yeah, Chug and them others ain't people to fool with. They ain't got no limits, Essie," he said, aware for the first time that he had used the pet name Ronnie had given her.

"Where are you going?" she said incredulously.

He went into the bedroom and returned with his boots and sat on the couch and slipped them on one at a time. His skin felt dead to the touch and he could not remember the question she had just asked him.

"I ain't never been seasick before. What's it supposed to feel like?" he said.

HE AND ESMERALDA drove back up the road and passed the filling station and convenience store, the neon tubing around the windows and the lights in the pump bays rain-streaked and glowing inside the dusk. In a wide turnout area on the left-hand side of the road they saw the three cars from the country club parked at odd angles, the silhouettes of ten or twelve people gathered in a circle on the far side, and birds rising noisily from the trees in a field.

Lucas shifted the truck down and flicked on the turn indicator and cut across the center stripe into the parking area. Lightning jumped between the clouds overhead and flickered whitely on the grass in the field. For just a moment an image caught in Lucas's eye that he would later associate with the event more than the event itself. A thin, blond kid with pipestem arms was drunk and had wandered out into the field

by himself and had pried a loose board from a collapsed shed. The board was flanged with rusty nails
on one end, and the boy was whipping it at the air,
his face oily and heated with booze, his eyes dull
with a resentment that had no source.

Lucas pulled past Chug's new lavender Cadillac,
the one his father allowed him to borrow from the father's dealership, and cut the headlights and the engine.

"Stay here, Essie," he said.

"I'm going with you."

"If this deal goes south, I want you to get to the
filling station and call Billy Bob Holland."

"What are you going to do?"

He listened to the engine cooling and looked in
the rearview mirror at the chrome grille and lavender
surfaces of Chug's Cadillac and the circle around
Ronnie Cruise and shook his head. "You got me," he
said, and got out and slammed the door behind him,
as though he could lock his fear inside the truck cab.

As he walked toward the group he heard
Esmeralda open her door and step down on the
gravel and follow him.

That woman is definitely not a listener, he
thought.

Chug Rollins was in the center of the circle with
Ronnie now, a white golf cap on his head, a blue silk
shirt with red flowers on it plastered wetly against
his skin. His white pants were hitched up like a sack
with a black leather belt below his belly button. His

back was an ax handle across, his upper arms swollen with the thick mass of pressurized fire hoses.

Lucas had seen Chug and his friends at work before. They targeted someone they didn't like and systematically quizzed and taunted him and made him admit behavior that was odious, that demonized him and made him unlike themselves. When it was established that he was deserving of no mercy, they tore him apart.

Homosexuals, Mexican and black gangbangers, an outside street dealer who tried to take over the local action, winos who wandered into the East End from the train tracks, they all got the same treatment. They didn't come back for seconds.

But Ronnie Cross was a different cut. He combed his hair while they insulted him, using both hands, his face composed, his cheeks sucked in. When he had finished and put his comb away, he leaned over and spit six inches from Chug's shoe.

"That's how greaseballs impress people? You show them you can spit?" Chug said.

"I don't see no greaseballs here," Ronnie said, lifting his eyes patiently toward the sky. "See, a greaseball is a guy who's mobbed-up. Now, if you're calling me a 'greaser,' like in 'spic,' I got to consider the source, which means it ain't worth worrying about. See, I don't think you got your shit together, or you wouldn't need a bunch of little fucks to follow you around and tell you, you don't got no weight problem. What I'm saying is, no offense meant, is a big guy like you shouldn't need to perform in front of windups, right?"

"That's cute," Chug said.

"No, man, 'cute' is when you put on golf drag and drive around in your old man's Caddy trying to score black cooze that wouldn't sleep with you if they was blind."

"Hey, Chug, how long you gonna take this?" somebody in the crowd said.

"You carry a shank, greaseball?" Chug said.

"You call it, man. Shanks, fist, feet, elbows, bottles, you want to go nines, that can happen, too."

"Chug, the guy just came up to give a girl a ride home from work," Lucas said from the rear of the circle. Suddenly he had become visible, and his voice stuck in his throat and his face felt tight and small and cold in the wind.

"What's with you, Smothers, you go off to A&M to major in dick-brain?" someone said.

But Chug raised his hand for the others to be silent.

"What are you doing with Jeff's ex, Lucas?" he asked.

"I just think it ain't right this many guys out here against one," Lucas said.

"You're not a bad kid. But that's still Jeff's punch. You want sloppy seconds, you check it out with Jeff first. Now, you take yourself and the jumping bean out of here. This doesn't concern you," Chug said.

Lucas scratched his eyebrow and looked at nothing. The headlights of a passing car swept over the group, seeming to light Ronnie's face as brightly as a candle. The afterglow of the sun had died on the horizon and the rain was falling softly out of a black sky. Lucas wiped his mouth with his hand and took Esmeralda by the arm and turned her toward his pickup truck with him.

"I thought Aggies only did it with sheep," someone said.

Esmeralda tried to pull away from Lucas, but his hand bit into her arm.

"You're going to leave Ronnie on his own? I can't believe you," she said.

"Get in the truck," he said.

"You turn my stomach," she said.

He didn't reply. He opened the passenger door and pushed her inside, then closed the door behind her and walked around the back toward the driver's side.

Lucas's stepfather had removed the factory bumper from the rear end of the truck and replaced it with two sections of six-inch steel pipe mounted and welded in a V-shape on a thick, cast-iron bib.

Esmeralda's face looked numb, beyond tears, freeze-dried with shame.

"Hitch up your seat belt," Lucas said.

"You worry about seat belts? You take me to the filling station. I'm going to call the police," she said.

"Same guys who molested you? Hang on!" he said.

He worked the transmission into reverse and floored the accelerator. The truck's tires spun gravel under the fenders and the rear end swayed back and forth as it raced toward the three parked cars. The V-shaped welded pipe, ragged on all the edges from the acetylene cut, tore first into the side of an Oldsmobile compact, peeling two long strips out of the paint and metal, then crashed into the rear fender of a Ford, blowing out the taillight and knocking the car's frame sideways. Then the pipe apex tore into the grille of Chug's Cadillac, gashing the radiator into a wet grin, crumpling the fenders up on the tires like broken ears.

Lucas dropped the transmission into low and spun away from the Cadillac, twisting the steering wheel to the right, heading straight for the circle of Ronnie's tormentors. At first they looked at him in disbelief, then scattered in front of his headlights, white-faced, running for either the road or the safety of the field and the trees. He hit the brakes long enough for Ronnie to jump into the cab beside Esmeralda, a cloud of tire dust and raindrops blowing across the dashboard. Then he floored the accelerator again and burned two long divots out of the dirt onto the asphalt, the rear end of the truck fishtailing on the wetness of the road.

Ronnie grabbed the windowsill of the passenger door with both hands and slammed it shut. His eyes were manic with energy, his skin shining with water.

He leaned past Esmeralda so he could see Lucas's face.

"We don't got no white bread in the Purple Hearts, but sometimes we make an exception," he said.

"Not in your dreams, Ronnie," Esmeralda said.

A highway patrol car passed them in the opposite direction, its siren screaming, the rain whipping in a red and blue and silver vortex off its light bar.

LUCAS WAITED FOR TWO HOURS at the house for the Texas Department of Public Safety or a group of Hugo Roberts's deputies to knock on his door. But no one did. He and Esmeralda drove Ronnie back to his T-Bird and helped him change his tire, passing the parking area that was now empty and pooled with rainwater and streaked with car tracks. Then he returned home and watched Esmeralda go inside the trailer and close the door and click on the lamp in her bedroom. He went into the house and tried to sleep, then gave it up and drank a cup of coffee in the kitchen by himself, the shadows and yellow light from the overhead bulb bladed on his bare shoulders, sure that he would be on his way to jail by midnight.

But no police came.

Were Chug and the others actually stand-up? he wondered.

No, they didn't want to admit they were taken down by a Mexican girl and a West Ender. They'd find a way to square it down the road. He had no doubt about that.

Why wasn't life simple? Why couldn't you simply go to work or attend college or play music in a band and be let alone? Why didn't time or age or the dues you paid buy you any wisdom?

How about Esmeralda? She hadn't even bothered to say thank you. In fact, after they dropped Ronnie off at his car, she had hardly spoken on the way back to the house. Go figure, he thought.

He went back into the bedroom and turned on the electric fan and lay on top of the bedspread with his jeans still on and rested his arm across his forehead. The rain had stopped entirely now and the moon had risen over the hills in the distance. Through the screen he could see the glow of Esmeralda's reading lamp against the orange curtain that hung in the trailer's bedroom window. She read books by Ernest Hemingway and Joyce Carol Oates. He'd seen the As she had made on her English papers. She was one smart woman but he'd be switched if he knew what went on in her head.

Then her shadow moved across the curtain and she opened the front door and walked out in the yard in a robe and disappeared behind his house. A moment later he heard her knock lightly on the back screen.

He turned on the kitchen light and looked at her through the screen. Her robe was tied tightly around the waist so that her hips were accentuated against the cloth and on her feet she wore fluffy slippers that looked like rabbits.

"Anything wrong?" he said.

"I keep hearing noises. I know it's just the wind, but I couldn't sleep," she replied.

"You want to come in?"

She made a face, as though she were arguing with herself. "If you're still up," she said.

"Sure. It's hot, ain't it? The rain don't cool things off that much this time of year," he said, holding the screen open for her, wondering if the banality of his remarks hid the desire that reared inside him when her body passed close to his.

"Ronnie wanted to come pick me up tomorrow. I told him not to," she said.

"It's better he don't have no more run-ins with Chug Rollins."

"You're in trouble because of Ronnie and me. I'm sorry for what I said earlier."

"I don't pay them East Enders no mind."

She seemed smaller now, somehow vulnerable, the light shining on the red streaks in her hair, hollowing one cheek with shadow.

"When it rains I see Cholo in the ground. His casket was made of plywood and cheesecloth. I keep seeing it over and over in my mind," she said.

"You all right, Essie?"

"No. I don't think I'll ever be all right. You didn't like Cholo. Not many people did. But he was brave in ways other people don't understand."

Lucas started to speak, then paused and unconsciously wet his lips, realizing, for the first time, that no words he spoke to her would have any application in her life. The light from the overhead bulb seemed to reveal every imperfection and blemish in her person and his own and make no difference. He couldn't translate the thought into words, but for just a moment he knew that intimacy and acceptance had nothing to do with language. The linoleum felt cool under his bare feet, the warm, green smell of summer puffing on the wind through the screens. He put his arms around her and felt her press against him as though she were stepping inside an envelope. He rubbed his face in her hair and kissed the corner of her eye and moved his hand down her back. Her breasts and abdomen touched against him and he swallowed and closed his eyes.

"Maybe you ain't seeing things real good right now. Maybe it ain't a time to make no decisions," he said.

Her hand left him for only a moment, brushing the wall switch downward, darkening the kitchen. Then she rose on the balls of her feet and kissed him hard on the mouth, squeezing herself tightly against him, her eyes wet on his chest for no reason that he understood.

Go figure, he thought.

23

LUCAS TOLD ME ALL THIS THE FOLLOWING morning, which was Sunday, while he swept the gallery and carried sacks of grass seed from the pickup bed into the shade. I sat on the railing with a glass of iced tea in my hand and watched him rake the dirt in the yard in preparation for seeding it.

"She told you Cholo was brave?" I said.

"He was her brother. What do you expect her to say?"

"His conscience was his bladder. He burned four firemen to death. The firemen were brave, not the guy who killed them."

Lucas worked the rake hard into the soil, the muscles in his arms knotting like rocks. He breathed through his nose.

"Why'd you come out here, anyway? To stick needles in me?" he said.

"Chug and those others will come after you."

"They ain't good at one-on-one."

"They don't have to be," I said.

He threw the rake down and split open a bag of seed with a banana knife and began scattering seed around the yard.

"You're down on Esmeralda 'cause of her race. It's bothered you from the get-go," he said.

"Criminality is a mind-set. It doesn't have anything to do with race. She's been around criminals most of her life and she instinctively defends them. Don't buy into it."

"I'm telling you to lay off her, Billy Bob."

"L.Q. Navarro was a Mexican. He was the best friend I ever had, bud."

He slung the rest of the seed around the yard, whipping the burlap empty, then stooped over to rip open another sack. When he did, he said something I couldn't hear, words that were lost in the shade and the muted echo off the house, words that I didn't want to ever recognize as having come from his throat.

"What did you say?" I asked.

He unhooked the knife from the split in the burlap and stood erect, his cheeks burning.

"I didn't mean it," he replied.

"Don't hide from it. Just say it so I can hear it."

"I said, 'Yeah, you killed him, too.'"

I emptied my iced tea into the flower bed, watching the frosted white round cubes of ice bounce on the black soil he had turned and worked with a pitchfork. I set the glass on the railing and walked to my Avalon, my eyes fixed on the long green level of the horizon.

I started my car engine and put the transmission in

reverse, then saw his face at the window. His eyes were shining.

"You don't ease up on me sometimes. You push me in a corner so's I cain't find the right words. I ain't got your brains," he said.

"Don't ever say that about yourself. You have ten times any gift I do," I said, and drove down the state road toward town.

I went five miles like that, past church buses loaded with kids and highway cafes that served Sunday dinners to farm families, all of it sweeping past me like one-dimensional images painted on cardboard that had no relation to my life. Then I turned around and floored the Avalon back to Lucas's. He had pulled a hose from behind the house and was watering down the seed in the front yard, spraying into the wind so that the drift blew back into his face.

"You going to the rodeo this afternoon?" I asked.

"I'm in the band. We open the show," he replied, gathering his T-shirt in his hand and wiping his face with it, unsure as to whether he should smile or not.

THE RODEO AND LIVESTOCK SHOW didn't begin that afternoon until the sun had crossed the sky and settled in an orange ball behind the shed over the grandstand at the old county fairgrounds, then Lucas's bluegrass band walked into the center of the arena, squinting up at the thousands who filled the seats, and launched into "Blue Moon of Kentucky."

Temple Carrol and Pete and I walked down the midway through the carnival and food concession stands that had been set up behind the bucking chutes, eating snow cones, watching the buckets on the Ferris wheel dip out of a sky that had turned to brass layered with strips of crimson and purple cloud.

The air smelled of hot dogs broiling in grease, candied apples, deep-fried Indian bread, the dust that lifted in a purple haze off the arena, popcorn cascading out of an electric pot, splayed saddles that reeked of horse sweat, cowboys with pomade in their hair and talcum coated on their palms, and watermelons that a black man hefted dripping and cold from a corrugated water tank and split open on a butcher block with a knife as big as a scimitar.

Then a bunch of 4-H kids on top of a bucking chute hollered down at a cowboy-hatted man in the crowd, their faces lit with smiles and admiration.

"Hey, Wilbur, we got one here can turn on a nickel and give you the change," a kid said.

"You ain't got to tell me. One bounce out of the chute and that one don't live on the ground no more," Wilbur Pickett replied, and all the boys grinned and spit Copenhagen and looked at each other pridefully in the knowledge that the bucking horse they might draw was esteemed by the man who had ridden Bodacious one second shy of the buzzer.

Wilbur and Kippy Jo walked past the plank tables

pooled with watermelon juice and seeds in the eating
area that had been set up under a striped awning that
ruffled and popped in the breeze. They stopped by
the corrugated water tank, and while Wilbur worked
three dollars out of his blue jeans to pay the black
man for two slices of melon, Kippy Jo cupped her
hands lightly on the edge of the tank and tilted her
head, her eyes hidden by sunglasses, staring at the
crowd on the midway as though faces were detach-
ing themselves from an indistinct black-and-white
photograph and floating toward her out of the gloom
and the electronic noise of the midway.

I followed her gaze into the crowd and saw Jeff
and Earl and Peggy Jean Deitrich by the merry-go-
round, the carved and painted horses mounted with
children undulating behind them. Chug Rollins came
back from the concession stand and joined them,
handing each of them a hot dog wrapped in a greasy
paper towel.

That's what I saw. Wilbur told me later what his
wife saw.

The sky was white, the sun ringed with fire above
an infinite, buff-colored plain, upon which columns
of barefoot Negroes in loincloths were yoked by the
neck on long poles. They trudged in the heat with no
expectation of water or shade, their eyes like glass,
their skins painted with dust and sweat, the inside of
their mouths as red as paint. Then she realized that
they were dead and their journey was not to a place
but toward a man in safari dress, his face concealed

from her, his head and body bathed in black light. Wherever he went, the Negroes followed, as though his back were the portal to his soul.

"Earl Deitrich," she said to Wilbur.

"Yeah. I seen him. He's early for the shithog contest," Wilbur said.

"No. The spirits of the Africans his ancestor killed are standing behind him. Their skulls were buried in anthills and eaten clean and used to line a flower bed."

"Let's go on up in the stands. I don't need that stuff in my afternoon. Cain't that fellow just find a grave to fall into?" Wilbur said.

She lowered her hand into the water tank, felt the melted ice slip over her wrist and the coldness climb into her elbow. The water seemed to stir, the corrugated sides ping with metallic stress or a change in temperature. Two muskmelons which had floated and bobbed on the bottom drifted like yellow air bubbles to the surface.

But the water she now looked down upon was green and viscous, and when the melons broke through the surface they were black and rough-edged, abrasive as coconuts, braided with hair that looked like dusty snakes.

"How'd you make them melons come up, lady?" the black vendor said, grinning, looking at his own reflection in her sunglasses.

She walked out on the midway toward Jeff Deitrich.

Jeff lowered his hot dog from his mouth as she approached, then Earl and Peggy Jean and Chug Rollins stopped talking, glancing peculiarly at Jeff, then turning as a group toward Kippy Jo.

"The black men you drowned . . . They'll float up from the car. They'll follow you just like the Africans do your father," she said.

"I think you got me mixed up with somebody else," Jeff said, his eyes shifting sideways.

"They were alive a long time after the car sank. They breathed the air that was trapped against the roof. Touch my hands and you'll see them. They're unfastening the safety belts that hold them in the seats of the car."

Jeff grinned stupidly, his mouth opening and closing without sound. He stepped back from her, as though he could pull an envelope of invisibility around himself, his face unable to find an acceptable expression, like a naked man on a public sidewalk.

IT MADE GOOD THEATER. But I suspected somebody would pay a price for it. I drove out to Wilbur's that night and tried to convince him of that in his front yard.

"Jeff Deitrich doesn't believe in your wife's psychic powers. He probably believes somebody informed on him," I said.

"You're telling me he done it, he drowned a couple of black guys?"

"I'm telling you he's a dangerous kid. He takes out his grief on others. Usually innocent people."

The windows in Wilbur's house were lighted behind him, his horses blowing and nickering out beyond the windmill.

"I ain't got no doubts about Earl Deitrich's family. You want to come in for a piece of pie?" he asked.

"I must speak a different language. You just don't hear me, do you?"

"I'm cutting you in for ten percent of my oil company."

"No, you're not."

"Son, anybody can be a lawyer or a rodeo bum. You ever see well pipe sweat moisture big as silver dollars? That's what happens when you punch into an oil sand. The air turns sour with gas and everything you put your hand on is dripping with money."

"Leave me out of your oil dealings, Wilbur."

"What you got is ten percent of nothing. That's probably the only fee you're ever gonna get." He grinned broadly, his bladed face silhouetted in the light from his house, and sailed a rock out into the darkness. "Don't worry about that Deitrich kid coming around here, either. His kind was put outside before the glue was dry."

Hopeless.

• • •

I STOPPED AT THE IGA the other side of the intersection and called Wesley Rhodes at his house.

"Get out of town. Visit your relatives in Texline," I said.

"They're in prison. Why you want me out of town?"

"Jeff Deitrich thinks somebody dimed him on the deal with the Jamaicans at the rock quarry."

"Oh *man,*" he said, like someone who had not believed his luck could get any worse.

ON THE WAY BACK HOME I tried to sort out my thoughts and the reasons I felt anger at Wilbur and his wife, and even at my son, Lucas.

The truth was I had no legal solutions for the problems they brought to me. Wilbur had admitted to stealing the historical watch from Earl Deitrich's home office, and hence by implication the bearer bonds, and Kippy Jo had methodically drilled a pistol round in each of Bubba Grimes's eyes. Unless I could bring down Earl Deitrich, there was a good chance both Kippy Jo and Wilbur would go into the system.

Lucas had been stand-up when it counted and had succeeded in putting himself right between the gangbangers and the East Enders. How do you tell a kid that honor has its price and that his father had rather it not be paid?

I felt my palms tighten on the steering wheel. I

wanted to hold L.Q. Navarro's heavy .45 revolver in my hand. I wanted to feel the coolness of its surfaces against my skin and open the loading gate and rotate the cylinder inside the frame and watch the thick, round base of the brass cartridges tick by one at a time. I wanted to feel the knurled spur on the hammer under my thumb and hear the cylinder lock hard and stiffly into place.

L.Q. and I raided deep into Coahuila and killed drug transporters and set their huts ablaze and watched their tar, reefer, and coke flame like white gas against the sky. In that moment all the moral complexities disappeared. There was no paperwork to be done, no rage over our inability to reconcile feelings with legality. Sometimes we would find the dead several nights later, still unburied and exposed in the moonlight, their skin glowing like tallow that has melted and cooled again. I had no more feeling about them than I would have about bags of fertilizer.

The trade-off came later, when I fired blindly up an arroyo and watched sparks fly into the darkness and L.Q. Navarro fling his hands at the sky and tumble toward me.

Brave people kept the fire in their belly out of their heads. Reckless and self-indulgent ones let someone else pay their dues.

The inside of the car seemed filled with a fragrance of roses. My thoughts bunched and writhed like snakes inside a black basket.

• • •

Lucas was sitting on the collapsed tailgate of his pickup in my driveway when I got home. He took off his straw hat and slapped the dust off the spot next to him. Every light in the downstairs of my house was on.

"My office is open. Have a seat," he said.

"You look mighty confident this evening."

"After the show Peggy Jean Deitrich told me to give you a message. I wrote it down. 'No matter how all this works out, I hold you in high regard.' She blows hot and cold, don't she?"

"You could say that."

"She's a pretty thing, I tell you that," he said.

I sat down on the tailgate next to him. "Where we going with this?" I asked.

"You remember her the way she used to be, then you see her the way she is now. It's like you're caught between the woman who's there and the woman who ain't but should be."

"Yes?"

"It's like living in two worlds. Puts a hatchet right in the middle of your head, don't it? In the meantime, you don't need to hear bad shit about people you care for."

"Let me see if I can figure this out. You don't want me pestering you about Esmeralda again?"

"I wish I had your smarts."

"Can you tell me why all the lights are on in my house?"

"Esmeralda is cooking up a monster-big Mexican dinner for us. Enchiladas, tacos, refried beans, chili con queso, she done put the whole garbage can in it."

The moon was yellow over the hills, and in the softness of the light I could see his mother's looks in his face. I cupped my hand on the back of his neck and felt the close-cropped stiffness of his hair against my palm. I saw his embarrassment steal into his face and I took my hand away.

"I bet that's one fierce Mexican dinner. We'd better go eat it," I said.

IT RAINED IN THE MIDDLE of the night and my bedroom curtains flapped and twisted in the wind and in the distance lightning forked into the long green velvet roll of the hills.

L.Q. Navarro sat in my stuffed burgundy chair by the bookshelf, his legs crossed, his Stetson resting on the tip of his boot. He was reading from a leather-bound, musty volume about the Texas Revolution, turning each page carefully with his full hand.

"How's it hangin', L.Q.?" I asked.

"You know how Sam Houston beat Santa Anna? He sent Deaf Smith behind Santa Anna's army and had him cut down Vince's Bridge with an ax. Once the battle started, there wasn't no way out for any of them."

"I'm awful tired, L.Q."

"Sometimes you got to be willing to lose it all. They'll see it in your eyes. It tends to give them a religious moment."

"I'll beat Earl Deitrich in the courtroom."

"His kind own the courts. You're a visitor there, Billy Bob. He fired a gun into the side of his head. You got to admit that was impressive."

"How about taking the Brown Mule out of your mouth?"

"He took Peggy Jean Murphy from you. He durn near killed you with poison. He corrupts everything he touches. Rope-drag him, pop a cap on him, hang his lights on a cactus. I don't like to see what he's doing to you."

"I don't live in that world anymore."

He raised one eyebrow at me over his book, then closed the book in disgust and walked out of the room, the rowels of his spurs tinkling on the hardwood floor.

"L.Q.?" I said.

24

TUESDAY MORNING TEMPLE CARROL CAME INTO my office and closed off the glare of sunlight through the blinds and sat down in front of my desk and opened a notepad on her crossed knee. There was a red abrasion at the corner of her left eye, and the eye kept leaking on her skin so that she had to dab at it with a Kleenex.

"What happened?" I asked.

"I found this ex-con boxer, Johnny Krause, at a pool hall in San Antone yesterday," she replied. "He stuck a pool cue in my eye."

"You went there by yourself?"

"He said he was sorry. He was just nervous around class broads in pool rooms. You want to hear what I have or not?" she said.

She ran through the material in her notebook. Krause had been picked up and questioned in the death of Cholo Ramirez and let go. He drove a cement mixer on and off for a construction company, rented a farmhouse behind a water-bed motel on the outskirts of San Antonio, and spent most of his downtime in Mexico.

"Dope?" I said.

"He draws compo and drives a new Lincoln," Temple said.

"Where's our pool shooter now?" I asked.

WE CROSSED THE BORDER at Piedras Negras and drove down into the state of Coahuila. The sun was hazy and red on the horizon now, and the poplar trees planted along the road were dark green, almost blue, in the dusk. We continued south of Zaragoza and crossed a river dotted with islands that had willow trees on them, then we saw a long baked plain and hills in the distance and a whitewashed village that spilled down an incline to a brown lake. The water in the lake had receded from the banks and left the hollow-socketed skeletons of carp in the skin of dried mud that covered the flats.

A Mexican cop nicknamed Redfish by the Bexar County sheriff's department, for whom he was a drug informant, waited for us in the backseat of a taxi parked in the small plaza in the center of the village. He had jowls like a pig, narrow shoulders, wide hips, and sideburns that fanned out like greasepaint on his cheeks. He wore yellow shades and a mauve-colored flop-brim bush hat, probably to detract from his complexion, which was deeply pocked, as though insects had burrowed into the flesh and eaten holes in it.

"I had to hire my cousin to drive me 'cause we

didn't have no official cars free today. He's gonna need twenty-five dollars for his time," Redfish said.

"Yeah, I can see he probably gave up a lot of fares this afternoon. Tourists flying in for the water sports and that sort of thing," Temple said.

"Your friend at the Bexar sheriff's office? He said you got a hard nose. We don't got no tourists now. But in winter we got *gringos* from Louisiana kill ducks all over that lake. They shoot three or four hundred in a morning. What you think of that?" Redfish said.

"We think we need to talk to Johnny Krause," I said.

"You was a Texas Ranger?"

"That's right," I said.

"One thing to remember here. He ain't been in no trouble in Mexico. He leaves a lot of money in the village. 'Cause he's a countryman don't mean he gets treated without respect."

The wind shifted and Temple's face jerked as though it had been struck. "What's in that lake?" she said.

"Everything from the houses runs downhill here. It don't stink after the rains. The *gringos* come here for the ducks after the rains. They're real proud, drinking wine in the cafe and eating all their ducks," Redfish said.

• • •

REDFISH GOT IN THE FRONT SEAT of the Avalon with me, and Temple sat in back. The sun was an ember on the horizon when we drove deeper into the village and out onto a chiseled rock road above the lake. Caves or old mine shafts were cut back into the hill, and people were living in them. They washed their clothes in the lake and dried them on the rocks around the caves, and cooked their food in pots that gave off an odor like burning garbage. I saw no men, only women and children, their faces smeared with soot, the color of their hair impossible to define.

"They're *gitanos*. They fix dishes with chicken guts. They steal them out of hog pens. You can't do nothing for them," Redfish said.

"Where are the men?" Temple asked.

"A bunch of them got in a fight with knives. The *jefe* got them out at his ranch for a while. Look, *señorita*, this is a house of *puta*. Maybe it ain't good you go in there," he said.

"I'll try not to have impure thoughts," Temple said.

"Johnny Krause ain't grown up inside, know what I mean?" Redfish said to me.

"No," I said.

"Neither do I," Temple said, leaning forward on the seat.

"All the *gitanos* ain't just up in them caves or out at the *jefe*'s ranch," he said, and looked out the window at the dusty surface of the lake.

At the end of the road beveled out of the hill was a whitewashed building that had probably been a powder house for a mining company and possibly later a jail. The walls were stone, the windows inset with bars, the roof covered with wood poles and tin and mounds of dirt that had sprouted grass. The casement of the front door was steel, bolted into the stone, and the door itself, which hung partially open, was cast iron and painted red. The paint was incised with every possible lewd depiction of human genitalia.

The bar and floor were made of rough-planed raw pine scorched by cigarette and cigar butts. The interior was bright with a greasy light from oil lamps, and the smoke on the ceiling was so thick it churned in gobs when someone walked under it. The faces of the customers were besotted and inflamed, their teeth rotted, their skin unnaturally lucent, like lemon rind. A child went in and out of the back door, emptying cuspidors and returning them to the bar and tables. Through the back windows and the open door I could see three pole sheds with burlap curtains hung from the roofs. Under the bottom of the curtains were slop jars and wash pans and the legs of either beds or cots.

"This is hard to take," Temple said.

"It's all right to wait outside," I said.

"I'm talking about *that* right over there," she replied.

A dark-skinned girl not more than thirteen sat at a

table with Johnny Krause. She wore a shift and a faded peasant dress that fit her hips like a sack. On her feet were blue cotton socks that had worked their way down on her ankles and old sandals whose straps were pulled sideways on the soles. Her cheeks were rouged, her mouth lipsticked, and she had braided her hair with glass beads. Her underarm hair looked like it had been touched there by a brush, her small teeth yellow-tinged with early decay. Johnny Krause put his hand on top of hers.

He removed it when he saw us, but not out of embarrassment. His grin stayed in place, his concentration shifting only out of momentary necessity.

"Remember us?" I said.

"Why not? You keep showing up. How's your eye, doll?"

He had pulled his brilliantined hair into a small matador's point in back and fixed it with a rubber band. He grinned at the girl and moved his eyes to the bar and gestured slightly with his head. After she was gone, he lifted a jigger of dark rum by the rim with two fingers and drank from it as though he were tilting a miniature bucket into his mouth. Then he drank from a bottle of Dos Equis and smiled pleasantly at us.

"Her folks are gypsies. They run off on her," he said.

"You did Cholo Ramirez for Earl Deitrich. I suspect this ex-merc, Fletcher whatever, hired you. Earl's going down, Johnny. When he does, the guy who's first in line doesn't have to do the chemical nap," I said.

"That's too bad about that kid Ramirez. The cops talked to me about it. But he was a gluehead, a street mutt, a hype, and a genuine crazoid. If his brains run out his nose, it's because he pulled the chewing gum out of his nostrils. I didn't have nothing to do with it."

I sat down across from him. A box of kitchen matches was stuck in a ceramic holder in the middle of the table. He took one out and struck it on the striker and lit a cheroot cigar. The smoke was like wet leaves burning and maple syrup warming on a stove. The girl returned from the bar and lay her arm across his shoulders and let her thigh touch his arm, her face pouting. He whispered in her ear, then touched the small of her back with his fingers and nodded toward the bar. As she walked away his fingers trailed off lightly on the top of her rump.

"You must have been poured out of your mother's colostomy bag, Krause," I said.

He laughed. His skin was olive-toned and smooth, dry and cool as the surface of a clay pot, as though his glands were incapable of secretion. "You trying to get me to do scut work for you, like drop the dime on somebody, and you call me names? That's why you come all the way down here?"

"No," I said.

The derision in his eyes and grin went away. "Yeah?" he said, and made a rotating motion in the air with his upturned hand. "You got some personal hard-on? Like I know you from somewhere else?"

"You put a pool cue in my investigator's eye. Then you were a smart-ass about it. You feel like a smart-ass tonight?"

He grinned again, then held up one finger at the girl, as though telling her he would be there in a moment. "You want to get fucked up, there's lots of bars in Mexico. But I don't step in nobody's grief for free. You're out of luck, Jack."

Temple squeezed me on the shoulder. "I can't take the smell anymore, Billy Bob. Let's go," she said.

"You're talking about these people's home. Show a little humility, lady," Johnny Krause said.

I stood up from the table and saw my shadow fall across his face. He looked up and waited for me to speak. When I didn't, he sucked a tooth and drank from his bottle of Dos Equis and joined the gypsy girl at the bar. A fat prostitute in a black dress wobbled like a drunk bull out the back door and raised her skirt and urinated into the twilight.

Redfish pushed open the cast-iron door and walked ahead of us toward the Avalon. The hillside where the gypsies lived in caves was speckled with fires. I looked back through the brothel entrance at the plank bar, where Johnny Krause had slipped his arm over the girl's shoulders and was now walking with her toward the back door and the burlap-hung sheds in the yard.

"I left my keys on the table," I said.

I walked past two Indian women at the bar, one of whom was unbuttoning an old man's fly, and picked up a thick, square bottle of mescal, the neck stoppered tightly with a long brown cork, a pale greenish worm floating in the yellow haze at the bottom. The weight was like a short-handled sledge in my palm.

Krause had stopped at the back door to talk to someone. The gypsy girl saw my face and shook his upper arm and cried out in Spanish. Just as Krause turned toward me I whipped the bottle by its neck across his mouth and heard his teeth clank like porcelain against the glass. He stumbled into the yard and bent double and cupped his palms to his mouth. Strings of blood blew in the wind between his fingers. I brought the bottle over my head, the mescal sloshing inside, and hit him again, this time across the ear. He went down in the dirt, where the woman had urinated, rolling out of the light that fell from the open doorway as though he could hide in the shadows.

I kicked him when he tried to get up and swung at his head again and missed and hit his wrist. It was unwinding fast now and I knew I was going to kill Johnny Krause, just as you know upon the pull of a trigger that the hammer is on its way home and you no longer have to make decisions about an adversary's fate.

Then the bull-like woman in the black dress grabbed my hand and thrust a lighted oil lamp in it, saying *"Quémalo.* Burn him, *gringo."*

The lamp was made of glass and tin and was oily and hot in my hand. Its glow shone up into the woman's porcine face. There were dirt rings in her neck and warts that protruded through the makeup on her chin. She punched me in the arm, hard, with the heel of her hand. "Go ahead, *gringo*. Burn this one good," she said.

I stepped back into the light from the doorway, my ears thundering with sound. Someone, Temple Carrol, I think, took the oil lamp and the bottle of mescal from my hands.

Johnny Krause sat up in the dirt, blood dripping off his tongue. He grinned up at me like a carved pumpkin that someone had cracked on a rock. He tried to speak but had to open his mouth and let it drain first. "We're just alike. I saw it in your eyes. You get high on it. We're brothers-in-arms, mother-fucker," he said.

25

LATE THAT NIGHT WE STOPPED IN A REST AREA south of Uvalde and lowered the leather seats back and slept until dawn. In my dream I saw L.Q. and me riding hard down a hill of yellow grass that was lined with flame across the crest. The sky was the texture and color of old bone, and smoke and dust were blowing out of the hills across a sun that gave no heat. Our horses came out of the grass just ahead of the fire, ash and cinders raining upon our heads, then we were on a baked, white floodplain in which our horses' hooves sculpted holes as big as buckets.

But up ahead was a green river, shadowed with willow trees that had turned gold with the season, and in the distance rain falling on hills where red Angus grazed. L.Q.'s pinstripe suit was strung with horse saliva and sweat, his coat blowing back from the Ranger badge on his belt and the tied-down revolver on his thigh.

"Use your spur, bud. They'll cuff us to mesquite trees and cut off our toes and dance in the smoke while we burn," he said.

"He's fixing to go lame, L.Q."

Then I felt my gelding heave sideways under me, slamming me into the soft, baked soil that cracked under my weight like cake icing and powdered my suit with alkali. L.Q. reined his mare and I hit her rump running, vaulting on two hands behind the cantle. I felt her power surge up like a barrel between my thighs, and I locked both arms around L.Q.'s waist and we plunged into the river and down the shelf into deep water.

I saw the alkali and ash and the blackened grass from the fields wash away in the current and felt the water's warmth swell inside my clothes. But something was wrong. The hills on the far side of the river had caught fire, the autumnal gold of the willows now crinkling with flame. Inside the smoke, I could hear cattle stampeding, a roar so loud the surface of the river trembled.

L.Q. had floated out of the saddle and was holding onto the pommel, water rilling off the brim of his hat.

"I think this is the big one, L.Q.," I said.

"It'll take better than them scumbags to do the likes of us," he replied.

"We put ourselves in it."

"In what?" he asked.

"Hell. That's what this is. We've been locating ourselves next to every evil sonofabitch in north Mexico."

"That's the job description, bud. They commit the crime and we splatter their grits. It beats selling shoes, don't it? Stop tasking your innards. The day you lose your humanity is the day you let Johnny Krause's kind have their way."

When Temple shook me awake it was raining only two hundred yards away, like a wet curtain of spangled light that partitioned the land, and the live oaks overhead were green and softly focused against the primrose tint of the sunrise in the east. I could smell cattle in a livestock truck that was parked by the rest station, and the sand flats and the rain dimpling on the Nueces River down below.

"You okay, Billy Bob?" she asked.

"Sure."

"You always have dreams like that?"

A trucker and his wife were eating their breakfast at a stone table under a shed, their faces serene and rested in the cool of the morning, and two little girls were playing on the grass with a big rubber ball. I widened my eyes and opened the car door and felt the flat, dry hardness of the cement under my boot, as though I were touching ground again after having been disconnected from the earth.

"It looks like it's going to be a right nice day," I said.

Temple hooked her elbow over the back of the passenger seat. Her eyes moved over my face with an undisguised affection in them, then she reached out with her fingertips and brushed a strand of hair out of my eye.

THAT AFTERNOON Wilbur Pickett put his hands on his hips and stared at Kippy Jo's dresser and decided he had fixed the uneven drawers for the last time. They hung on the runners and jammed sideways and the threading on the knobs had stripped on the screws. Besides, the paneling on the left side that Hugo Roberts and his deputies had ripped loose searching for the stolen bearer bonds was split diagonally along the face like a long white crack in a mahogany tooth.

So he asked permission first, then removed all the clothes from the drawers and folded them on the bed and hauled the dresser to the barn, where he dropped it upright and began chopping it apart for kindling. On the third blow of the ax the frame cleaved in half and sank in upon itself, and he hooked the ax on the left panel and prised the nails from the warped seam at the top. When he did, the panel cracked apart like a walnut shell, and between the lower portion of the splintered wood and a piece of scrap board that a previous owner had inserted next to the drawer space was the green-and-white-printed edge of a bearer bond.

"They must have planted three of them instead of two," Wilbur said over the phone.

"Did you touch it?" I asked.

"Not with a manure fork, son," he replied.

An hour later he was waiting for me on a wood chair in front of the barn when Marvin Pomroy and I and a fingerprint man from San Antonio and Hugo Roberts pulled into his drive in three different cars. Wilbur's hair was wet and combed, and he had put on fresh blue jeans and a beige sports shirt and a pair of dress boots. He stood up from his chair and extended his hand to Marvin.

"How you do, Mr. Pomroy?" he said.

Marvin hesitated just a second, then reached out and took Wilbur's hand. No one spoke and a bucket hanging on a nail inside the barn door tinked against the wood in the wind.

"I don't hold no personal grudge," Wilbur said.

"I understand you have a piece of evidence that bears looking at," Marvin said.

"It's what them worthless deputies stuck in there and didn't take back out," Wilbur said.

Hugo Roberts screwed a cigarette into his mouth and lit it with his lighter, blowing the smoke out in the sunset.

"If this ain't the silliest waste of time I can think of, I don't know what is," he said.

"If you're going to smoke, do it downwind from me, Hugo," Marvin said.

The independent fingerprint man from San Antonio picked up the bearer bond gingerly with a pair of tweezers and dropped it into a plastic bag.

"Y'all put me in mind of somebody tweezering corn out of pig shit. What in the hell is this supposed to prove?" Hugo said.

"I imagine all your deputies' fingerprints are on file, as well as your own, Hugo. You'll make those immediately available to us, won't you?" I said.

"I don't have nothing else to do. Did your boy smash up a bunch of cars with his stepdaddy's pickup truck?" he replied. He looked out at a freight train crossing a trestle in the hills and held his cigarette close to his lips with two fingers and puffed it uninterruptedly, the skin of his face the same nicotine shade as his fingers in the late sunlight.

I HAD JUST HUNG UP the phone after talking to Marvin Pomroy when Wilbur came through my office door at noon the next day. He continued to stand rather than take a chair, his teeth clamped down on the corner of his lip, his hat held with both hands in front of his belt buckle.

"Hugo Roberts's prints and Kyle Rose's are on the bond. Yours aren't," I said.

"Kyle Rose, the deputy somebody strung a deer arrow through?" Wilbur said.

"That's the guy. You didn't steal those bonds. They were planted, Wilbur. Marvin Pomroy just said as much."

"What's it mean?"

"I have some paperwork to do, then you're going to be out of it."

He sat down in a chair and rubbed the back of his neck, his eyes burrowing into the carpet.

"What about Kippy Jo?" he asked.

"She's still on the hook."

"One deal's part of the other, ain't it? If I hadn't been set up, Bubba Grimes wouldn't have been sent out there to kill me and Kippy Jo."

"I thought you'd be happy."

He got up from the chair, my words never registering in his face.

"I can leave the state now, cain't I?" he said.

"Excuse me?"

"Them boys investing in my pipeline deal down in Venezuela? I showed them that core sample from up in Wyoming. They're ready to rock."

I propped my elbow on the arm of my swivel chair and rubbed the corner of my chin.

"To drill a damn oil well you'd leave your wife by herself?" I said.

"It's money all this is about. She ain't standing trial for killing Bubba Grimes. She's standing trial 'cause her husband's got something Earl Deitrich wants."

"You want to buy and sell him, don't you?" I said.

His skin was still slick with the heat and moisture from outside, and he wiped his throat and looked at the shine his sweat made on his calluses. He wiped his hand dry on his shirtfront and said, "I was one second from being a world champion. Lacking that one second makes me a guy who digs postholes for rich people. You think Ms. Deitrich's a high-class woman. Maybe she is. But when I worked out at their place, she never give me a drink of water that wasn't in a jelly glass. Kippy Jo Pickett is gonna have rubies on her fingers big as bird's eggs, and there ain't nobody in this county, particularly not no dadburn Deitrichs, gonna look down on us."

THE NEXT AFTERNOON I loaded Beau in his trailer and we drove north of the river to the base of the ravine where Pete and I often hunted arrowheads and the flint chippings washed down from Tonkawa workmounds. I hung L.Q. Navarro's holstered .45 and gun belt from one side of the pommel and my rucksack from the other and rode up the incline along the creekbed, Beau's shoes raking dully on the stones along the bank.

The water in the creek was shallow and tea-colored, flowing over green and brown and white pebbles that were no bigger than my thumbnail. The western wall of the drainage was in shadow now, but the east side was of the soft gold texture that light makes when it collects inside a newly coopered pine barrel. The wind blew from the bottom of the ravine and I saw the scrub brush and redbud trees riffle and change tone in the sunlight against the cliff wall, and for just a moment I saw the dark opening of the cave where I believed Skyler Doolittle and Jessie Stump had been living.

I got down from the saddle and lifted the strap of the rucksack off the pommel and looped it over my left shoulder and hung L.Q.'s gun belt from my right and began walking up the path that was barely visible in the pine needles that had been foot-pressed blackly into the soil between the trees.

Just before I reached the cave I threw a pebble at the entrance and watched it bounce off the face of the cliff and roll down the incline. Then I threw a second, this time right through the hole in the rock.

"You guys wouldn't be upset if I visited you, would you?" I said.

But there was no response.

I closed the distance to the cave and squatted down under a redbud tree and took my flashlight out of the rucksack and shined it inside the rock, then stepped under the overhang and stood erect inside the cave itself.

The sleeping bags and canned goods were gone. The vinyl garbage bags that had been flattened on the floor were now tangled and stenciled with silt from the soles of lug boots. The plank that had contained canned goods had been pulled out of the wall and thrown into the back of the cave and the one-gallon molasses can that had held drinking water had been crushed and scoured with scratches on the stone ring around the firepit.

I stepped out of the cave's coolness into the warmth of the afternoon and the breeze gusting up the drainage. The sunlight glimmered on the outcroppings that had been leached clean of soil by the springs flowing out of the hillside and had turned green with lichen. Were Jessie and Skyler buried somewhere along the creek? Had they been covered with rocks or perhaps rooted up and devoured by animals? I doubted it. Whoever had crushed the water can and prised the wood plank out of the wall had taken out his anger on the cave as a surrogate for his intended human victims.

I walked back down the path and mounted Beau and rode over the plates of stone that scraped like slate under his hooves.

I DROVE THE TRUCK, with Beau's trailer wobbling behind it, down the dirt road onto the state highway, then followed the river to the northeast corner of the county, where an oxbow had formed in 1927, then had been dammed up and allowed to become a glistening yellowish-green sump filled with mosquitoes, dead trees webbed with river trash, and shacks knocked together from slat board, tar paper, and stovepipe.

I rode down a dirt street between empty shacks, then crossed a slough and continued up a rise through trees and a break between two low-lying hills that gave onto a glade where a group of California hippies had tried to live in the late 1960s. They had hung tepees and built a longhouse of pine logs and sweat lodges of river stones, dug a water well and root cellars, and carpentered a marvelous cistern on top of boulders they rolled from the fields with hand-hewn poles.

Twenty-five deputized vigilantes burned them out in 1968.

I got down from Beau and lifted the rucksack and L.Q.'s gun belt off the pommel and walked to the foot of the hill on the far side of the glade. Pine trees grew up the slope toward the crest and crows were cawing deep in the shadows. I kicked a bare spot in the ground and made a fire ring from field stones, then gathered an armful of twigs and rotted branches among the trees and coned them up in the fire ring and lit them with a paper match.

I squatted upwind from the smoke, removed a skillet from the rucksack and rubbed the bottom with butter and set the skillet on stones among the flames. When the butter had browned, I lay two large ham steaks inside and watched them fry, then cracked four raw eggs on the edge of the skillet and cooked them next to the ham.

The smoke flattened in the wind and drifted back into the trees on the hillside. A man with a fused neck pushed aside the slat door on a root cellar and stepped out into the shadows. A second man followed him, his face cratered with scars that looked like popped bubbles on the surface of paint.

L.Q.'s gun belt and holstered .45 still hung from my right shoulder. I ladled the eggs and meat onto two tin plates, then toasted four slices of bread in the ham fat and put them in the plates, too. I could see

Jessie Stump's tall, skinny frame out of the corner of my vision and feel his eyes watching me.

"How'd you know where we was at?" he asked.

"You grew up on the oxbow. It didn't take a lot of figuring," I said.

"How come you brung a pistol?" he asked.

"I've always taken you for a serious man," I replied. I picked up the skillet with both hands and drained the last of the ham fat over the eggs and bread and didn't look up.

"Didn't nobody else reckon it," Skyler Doolittle said.

"That's because they searched here first. In the meantime, y'all were in a cave up above the Deitrich place," I said.

"Maybe you're too damn smart for your own good, boy," Jessie said.

"Don't be addressing Mr. Holland like that. He's a decent man," Skyler said.

I stood up and handed Skyler a plate.

"You want to eat, Jessie?" I said.

"I ain't against it," he replied. His black, unwashed hair had the same liquid brightness as his eyes.

"Somebody liked to nailed y'all in that cave," I said.

"You goddamn right they did. They'd a done it if it hadn't been for Ms. Deitrich," Jessie said.

"Come again?" I said.

"She was blackberrying up there. Had three or

four quart jars full," Skyler said. "I think she seen the smoke from our fire. Next day this note was stuck on a pine branch partway up the path."

He unfolded a sheet of blue stationery from his pocket and handed it to me. It read, "This isn't a safe place for you. Leave before your hiding place is discovered. Those who will find you mean you great injury."

"It's not signed," I said.

"Ain't nobody else been up there. To my mind, she's a great lady," Skyler said.

"Mr. Doolittle, I want y'all to surrender," I said.

"That ain't gonna happen, boy," Jessie said.

"He's right," Skyler said.

"They'll kill both of y'all," I said.

Jessie wiped his plate clean with a piece of bread and ate it, then set the plate down on the grass and pulled his shirt out of his trousers. A bloody white sock was tied with a strip of cloth across his top rib.

"That's where some boys in a Jeep notched me with a deer rifle. Next time I'll catch them in their sleeping bags," he said.

"Is this what you want?" I said to Skyler.

"No, sir. I'd like to be let alone," he replied.

I inverted the skillet and knocked it clean on the fire ring, then slipped a paper sack over it and dropped it in the rucksack and hung the rucksack on the pommel of Beau's saddle.

"You gonna turn us in?" Jessie said.

I put my left boot in the stirrup and swung up on the saddle. I felt Beau try to jerk his head up.

"I'm going to ask you just once, Jessie. Take your hand off his bridle," I said.

"Then you answer me. You gonna turn us in or not?" Jessie said.

"He's a river-baptized man, Jessie. He's got the thumbprint of God on his soul. Let him pass, son," Skyler said.

The sun had dropped behind the hills now and the air was moist and heavy and dense with mosquitoes and the bats that fed off them. I crossed the slough and rode back down the dirt street through the row of empty shacks that were encircled by the ugly scar of the oxbow off the river. I felt the thick weight of a bat thud against the crown of my hat, and I kept my face pointed down at Beau's withers until we were up on high ground again.

Peggy Jean knew Jessie Stump had tried to drive a barbed arrow through her husband's head, yet had warned him and Skyler Doolittle so they could avoid capture.

Why?

THAT'S WHAT I ASKED Temple Carrol two hours later while she smacked her gloves into the heavy bag behind her house. She wore a pair of khaki shorts and a gray workout halter and alpine lug boots with thick socks folded down on her ankles, and her thighs were tan and muscular and tight against her rolled shorts.

"Maybe Peggy Jean wants it all. Maybe that's always been her way," she said.

"Pardon?" I said.

She hit the bag again, left, right, left, right, left, and hard right hook, twisting the bag on the chain, ignoring me.

"Will you give it a break?" I said.

"Her first soldier boy got killed in Vietnam. Then she tried a blue-collar kid like you. Then she found another soldier boy with money. Maybe she'd like to keep the money and that monstrosity of a house they live in and have another roll in the hay with you. Feel flattered?" she said.

"Pretty rough assessment."

"Sorry. I'll go scrub out my mouth with Ajax," she said.

She went back to work on the bag. The moon was big and yellow behind the pecan tree in her backyard. Out in the darkness I could hear the wind rattling in her neighbor's cornfield. Her invalid father was inside the house, and I could see his silhouette, in his wheelchair, against the lighted television screen in the front room.

"You mad at me?" I said.

"No, not really. You're what you are. I can't change it," she answered.

I hooked my arm around the top of the bag.

"You've never let me down. They don't make them any better than you, Temple," I said.

"You live with ghosts. I can't compete with them."

"Don't talk like that."

"You don't understand women, Billy Bob. At least you don't understand me."

I put my hands on the tips of her shoulders, even while she was shaking her head.

"I'm hot and dirty," she said.

I touched the pool of moisture in the hollow of her neck and slid my hands down her back and smelled the heat in her hair and felt the tone of her muscles and the taper of her hips against my palms. I let my lips brush against her cheek, and for the first time in our many years as intimate friends I consciously stepped over a line into Temple's life.

She raised on the balls of her feet, her stomach against my loins, as though she were going to kiss me, then her face broke and she walked hurriedly into the house, dropping her gloves randomly into the dust, and closed the door and locked it behind her.

26

WESLEY RHODES WAS STANDING ON THE CORNER of the square, across from the courthouse, in the cool of the evening, watching the junior high school girls go in and out of the Mexican grocery store that had a small soda fountain in back. They giggled and had braces on their teeth and attracted him in ways he didn't understand. Not in a bad way. It was like they were his age, or he was their age, except he knew a lot more about the world than they did and he could take care of and protect them.

He just never could get up the nerve to talk to them. Maybe tonight would be different. He sat up on top of the backrest of a wood bench under a live oak, his hair slicked back, his comb clipped inside his shirt pocket, drinking from a Dixie cup filled with Coca-Cola and crushed ice. The trees were dark green overhead and the face of the clock on the courthouse tower glowed in the sunset, and the streets were striped with shadows now and the girls in front of the grocery marbled with light from the owner's neon signs. Man, summertime was great. If he just had enough nerve to stroll across the street . . .

That's when Jeff Deitrich's yellow convertible,

with the top up, pulled to the curb and Jeff said, "Get in back, snarf."

They chased him for two blocks before they blocked him in an alley and Chug and Hammie and Warren pulled him off a fire escape and threw him in the car.

Crushed between Hammie and Chug in the back-seat, he saw the city limits sign speed past the window.

"What's going on?" he said.

"You're gonna become a deep-sea diver tonight, little buddy. You ever watch those Jacques Cousteau shows on TV? A frog can do it, you can do it," Hammie said. He took the comb out of Wesley's shirt pocket and scratched the purple and burnt-orange tattoo of a butterfly on the side of his throat with it.

"Frog? What's a frog got to do with anything?" Wesley asked.

Just after midnight the convertible turned on a dirt road and a few minutes later Wesley was able to see clearly out the window and recognize the rock quarry, just like someone had taken a bad dream from his life and forced him back inside it.

Wesley climbed out of the car with the others, his heart thundering, his armpits running with sweat. The wind had died and a layer of dust hung in the air and drifted over the mounds of yellow dirt that surrounded the crater.

"Tell them, Warren. I ain't never snitched nobody

off. Even when the gunbulls put me in the hole," Wesley said.

"That's what I've been telling them. You're a righteous, sharp little dude. That's why they're letting you prove yourself," Warren said. He smiled good-naturedly, like the old Warren used to do, square-jawed, his eyes clear, handsome as a movie star.

"Why I got to prove anything? I ain't done nothing wrong," Wesley said.

"Not a good attitude, Wes," Warren said, his face taking on philosophic concern. "You a good swimmer?"

Jeff popped the trunk.

"This is scuba gear, queeb. That's an underwater camera and strobe. You're going to dive that Mercedes and take pictures. The mop-heads had better be inside," Jeff said.

"Why don't you do it yourself?" Wesley said.

Jeff had a rolled magazine in his back pocket. He removed it and used the hard-packed end to hit Wesley on the forehead, biting down on his lip, as though he were on the edge of far greater violence. "Because I don't get in the same water with corpses, zit-face. Want to wise off some more or live out the night?" he said.

Wesley undressed down to his Jockey undershorts and sat on the sand and put flippers on his feet and slipped the canvas straps of the air tank over his shoulders and the mask on his face. Warren hung a rubber-encased light from his neck and placed the camera and strobe in his hands.

"You never had a tank on?" he asked.

"Yeah, he's a regular in the Bahamas, Warren," Hammie said.

"What if I cain't find the car?" Wesley said.

"Don't come up," Jeff said.

Wesley waded out into the water, the rocks cutting his feet, then stepped off a shelf and went under.

It was easier than he thought. The light around his neck turned the bottom of the quarry into a crusted, unthreatening slope that dipped down through the greenish-yellow haze to the Mercedes. Small bait fish and pieces of grass swam at his mask and flanked off on each side of him, and he breathed the air easily from the mouthpiece and even blew his mask clear as Warren had shown him.

Then his light lit up the inside of the Mercedes and he almost vomited into his mouthpiece.

The face of the man on the driver's side looked straight into Wesley's, his lidless eyes like gray marbles, while a fish eel ate his tongue.

Wes aimed through the camera's lens and clicked the shutter five times. Then, with his heart tripping against his ribs, he let the camera float loose on its wrist cord and did something he never thought he would have the courage to.

He prised the back door loose from where it had lodged in the silt, then he was inside the car with the two dead men, his air tank clanging against the roof, their bloated skin brushing against his. A dreadlock wrapped across his mask like a leech, a forehead tipped against his jaw. His hands trembled while he worked, his fingernails and knuckles dipping into what felt like wet cornmeal, then a bilious fluid surged out of his stomach into his throat and he gagged violently and lost his mouthpiece and swallowed water that locked inside his windpipe like cement.

His lungs were bursting, his eyes bulging out of his head when he broke the surface into moonlight and air.

He fell on the sand, gasping, his body shaking, his Jockey undershorts strung with dead weeds.

"You get the pictures?" Jeff said.

"Hang them over your fucking mantel," Wesley said.

Jeff uncapped a bottle of sparkling water and drank it while Wesley stumbled toward the convertible.

IT WAS MONDAY AFTERNOON that Wesley told me all this in my office.

"Who's developing the pictures?" I asked.

"Warren's old man owns some porno places in Houston. Warren uses their darkroom."

"The Costens are in pornography?"

His ruined face, with its harelip and wide-set, reptilian-green eyes, looked into space, as though the question had nothing to do with his life and hence was not one that anyone would expect him to answer.

"What did you do inside the Mercedes?" I said.

"The black guys was mushy and swole up like garbage bags. Like they was full of gas and wanted to float. I unsnapped their seat belts and left both doors open."

A grin scissored across his face, his eyes seeming to separate on the dough pan of his face and dance with light.

Score one for the little guys, I thought.

WHAT HAPPENED that night out at Val's Drive-In started over either Chug Rollins's sister or Jerry Lee Lewis's music, depending on whom you heard it from.

Background: Chug's sister had the same weight problem as her brother, compounded by a notorious reputation for profligate sexual behavior. Two months ago she had made national news when she was prosecuted for the statutory rape of one of her male students at a Fort Worth high school.

It was a fine evening when Lucas Smothers and Esmeralda Ramirez pulled into Val's. The sun had just set below the rim of the hills and the light was draining from the sky as the day cooled. The breeze came up and the neon signs overhead and in the restaurant's windows went on and rippled the cars and pavement in the parking area. Lucas and Esmeralda went inside and sat by the jukebox and ordered, then Lucas dropped four quarters in the slot and began punching in every Jerry Lee Lewis number he could find.

That's when Chug Rollins and Jeff Deitrich and his old girlfriend, Rita Summers, came in and sat down together two booths away. A moment later they were joined by three of Jeff's and Chug's friends, ex-football players from the University of Texas, two of whom had been expelled after a gang rape of a co-ed in a fraternity house. They ordered mugs of draft beer and Rita Summers lit a cigarette under the No Smoking sign. She balanced her cigarette on an ashtray and fixed a clasp on the back of her gold hair, her blue eyes filled with ridicule.

"Look when you have a chance. Lavender spiked heels with embroidered jeans. I think she uses chlorine gas for perfume," she said.

"That's Smothers's hair tonic," one of the ex-football players said. He wore a cap backwards on his head and a white T-shirt that was bursting on his torso.

In the background Jerry Lee sang "I Could Never Be Ashamed of You."

At first Jeff didn't look in Lucas's and Esmeralda's direction, then he seemed to become more and more agitated, his eyes flicking away from the conversation around him, pinning Lucas, then Esmeralda.

"Hey, Smothers, is that your stuff on there?" he asked.

"Yeah, why?" Lucas said.

"It's giving me a headache," Jeff said.

"Jerry Lee Lewis is the greatest white blues singer of our time," Lucas said.

"It's forty years old. It's also garbage. Unplug it," Jeff said.

"Anything else you want? Shoes shined? Car washed?" Lucas said.

Chug Rollins turned his massive weight around in the booth.

"I've still got a major beef to settle with you, fuckhead. Don't give me an excuse," he said.

Lucas dipped a french fry in catsup and ate it and raised his eyebrows innocuously.

"You want to make faces, don't let me see it," Chug said.

Lucas unfolded a paper napkin and draped it with one hand from his forehead and ate a french fry behind it.

"You are seriously pissing me off," Chug said. He got up from the booth and hit the side and top of the jukebox and shook it with both hands until he knocked all of Lucas's selections out of play. Then he dropped a quarter in the slot and punched in a white rap song and reached behind the box to turn up the volume.

"You got a problem with that?" he said.

"It don't bother me if people like to pour shit in their ears," Lucas said.

Chug leaned down on the table. His arms were

enormous, his chest and massive stomach as wide as a woodstove. Lucas could smell the talcum and aftershave lotion and deodorant on his skin, the onions and fried meat on his breath. Chug wadded up a napkin and bounced it off Lucas's chest.

"I see you in here again, you're gonna be taking your meals through a glass straw for six months," he said, then went to his booth.

"Don't say anything else, Lucas," Esmeralda whispered.

Lucas flipped the wadded-up napkin out on the floor by Chug's booth. "All right, let's get out of here," he said.

Lucas went to pay the check while Esmeralda waited, her back turned to Jeff, who sat with one leg out in the aisle, his face disjointed, his eyes on her figure, the rise of her breasts against her form-fitting V-necked shirt. Lucas came back from the cash register and saw Jeff's expression and put his arm around Esmeralda, as though he could shield her from the violation and lust and black radiance in Jeff's eyes.

"Don't be looking at us like that, Jeff," he said.

"What'd you say?" Jeff said.

Lucas and Esmeralda headed toward the revolving side door. Chug got up from the booth and hitched up his scrotum with one hand.

"My ten-inch in your pepperbelly's mouth, Smothers," he said.

"Give it to your sister. She needs it a lot worse than we do," Lucas said, and went through the revolving door.

Chug made a grinding noise deep in his throat and charged toward the door as though he were back on the high school football field, tearing holes in the enemy line like a tank through a hedgerow, his fists balled into hams, his furrowed brow tilted down like a battering ram.

A waitress came through the revolving door just before Chug reached it, spinning the thick, rounded edge of the glass directly in front of Chug's head.

He crashed into it with a sound like someone thumping a wood mallet on a watermelon, then rolled moaning between the partitions, his hands clasped to his forehead. The waitress tried to free herself from being trapped by shoving against the push bar, slamming the door back into his face, mashing his nose against the glass like a pig's snout pressed against a window.

Finally Chug tumbled out on the sidewalk, his clothes spotted with expectorated Red Man and Copenhagen.

"Better put some ice on that bump. It looks like a couple of golf balls," Lucas said.

Jeff helped Chug to his feet while he glared at both Esmeralda and Lucas.

"This is all your fault, Jeff. Don't blame it on anybody else," she said.

"Your mouth's always running. You never shut up. Somebody's going to put something in it," Jeff said.

"You couldn't cut it on the rig and you cain't cut it nowhere else, either. Stop taking out all your grief on other people," Lucas said.

Lucas and Esmeralda walked across the parking lot toward Lucas's pickup truck. The clouds overhead were silver and black in the moonlight, like smoked pewter, the wind rattling the palm trees by the entrance to the drive-in. Jeff's fists curled and uncurled at his sides.

"Don't worry, Jeff. He's gonna be a stump when we get finished with him," the ex-football player with his cap on backwards said.

"Smothers can wait. Esmeralda's asking for a train," Jeff said, his eyes burning into her back.

"You got a sign-up sheet?" the ex-football player said.

Two days later Lucas sat on the top rail of Beau's lot, the heels of his boots hooked on the second rail for support, and tossed chinaberries at a bucket. The morning was still cool, the shadows long on the ground, and Beau was drinking out of the tank by the windmill, switching his tail hard in the shade. I stopped shoveling manure into a wheelbarrow and leaned the shovel against the fence.

"Who heard him say this?" I asked.

"The waitress."

"Maybe Esmeralda should go back to San Antone for a while."

"She don't listen. What do you reckon I ought to do?"

If they try to rape that girl, you blow their damn heads off, I thought.

"Pardon?" Lucas said.

"Nothing. I didn't say anything." I widened my eyes and looked at the clarity of the horizon against the sunrise. A flock of crows was descending into my neighbor's corn, like black ash drifting out of the sky.

I pulled the morning edition of the local newspaper out of my back pocket and flopped it open on the fence rail. At the bottom of the front page was a story about the bodies of two Jamaicans that had been found floating in a flooded quarry outside Waxahachie. "Maybe it's time Jeff Deitrich had some of his own chickens come home to roost," I said.

"He's mixed up with these dead guys?"

"Get her out of town. Let me work on a couple of things."

He dropped down from the fence and scraped a pattern in the dust with his boot.

"The reason I come over is, I was wondering if you might loan me L.Q. Navarro's revolver," he said.

I walked away from him toward the house, not answering him, shaking my head, wanting to flee his words as I would a dark and obscene thought.

27

THAT SAME MORNING I MET TEMPLE CARROL at the office. I hadn't spoken to her since my failed overture in her backyard when she had dropped her speedbag gloves in the dust and gone into the house and locked the door behind her like a slap in the face.

"What's shakin', Slim?" she said.

"You want a taco?"

"Why not?" she said.

We walked across the square to the Mexican grocery and sat at a table in back under a wood-bladed fan.

"Wesley Rhodes told me Warren Costen's father is involved in pornography in Houston. I'd like you to check it out," I said.

"What for?"

"Skyler Doolittle had child porn pictures planted on him when he was arrested. I wonder if Hugo's deputies got the pictures from Warren Costen or Jeff Deitrich."

"Where am I supposed to start?"

"Search me. The Costens are supposed to be an upstanding, pioneer family."

"Yeah, they always let everybody know their shit didn't flush," she said, and bit into her taco. She saw me watching her. She looked down at her clothes to see if something had fallen on them. *"What?"* she said.

"Nothing."

"Why are you staring at me?"

"I'm not. You look great, Temple."

Her eyes fixed on mine, blinking uncertainly.

SHE CALLED ME long-distance two days later.

"I got a tip from a reporter at the *Houston Chronicle* who covers real estate and the zoning board. Costen and several partners run a couple of companies that manage slum rentals in the Third Ward. But during the oil recession in the eighties a lot of property on the west side was sold off to HUD. Costen and his friends bought low and expanded their slum rentals and put in video porn stores in what used to be middle-class and upscale neighborhoods."

"What'd you find out about Costen and child pornography?"

"Nothing. But if video porn is there, so is the clientele for the rest of it. You want me to keep looking?"

"No, come on back up to God's country," I said.

"Just out of curiosity, I went out to Rice University and talked to a history professor about Costen's ancestors. This professor belongs to a historical society that keeps track of all the documents from the Texas Revolution and the descendants of everybody who fought in it. Costen's family was the real thing, friends of Sam Houston and Jim Bowie and Stephen F. Austin."

I felt myself yawning. "You did a good job. Come on back home," I said.

"Hear me out. I asked the professor to check out Skyler Doolittle. Doolittle was telling the truth. His ancestor died in the Alamo with Travis and Crockett and the others. His survivors were given a section of land after the war, which was the promise Sam Houston made to everyone who served with him to the end."

"I'm not with you, Temple."

"You remember describing to me the lunch out at the Deitrichs' place, when Earl Deitrich humiliated Wilbur Pickett at the table by taking that antique watch out of his hand, like Wilbur didn't have the right to be looking at it?"

"Yes."

"You said Wilbur told a joke about his ancestor fighting in the Battle of San Jacinto, except the ancestor was a horse thief and sold horses to both sides."

"Yeah, that's what he said."

"It wasn't just a joke." I could hear her turning pages on a notepad. "Wilbur's ancestor was named Jefferson Pickett. I don't know if he was a horse thief or not, but he survived the Goliad Massacre and was with Houston when Santa Anna was captured on the San Jacinto."

"He received a section of land, just like all the other Texas soldiers?"

"You got it, kemo sabe."

"What happened to it?" I felt my hand tighten unconsciously on the receiver.

"Most of it was sold off. Except for one hundred acres Wilbur's great-grandfather owned outside Beaumont. I'm in the Beaumont public library right now. That one hundred acres was right by the Spindletop oil strike. Wilbur's great-grandfather lost it in a civil suit filed by a Houston oil speculator named Deitrich. Wilbur's great-grandfather hanged himself. This all happened about 1901. Guess which Deitrich family we're talking about?"

I had been standing up in my office, gazing out the window while I talked. Suddenly I felt light-headed, my face cold and filmed with perspiration at the same time. I sat down in my swivel chair.

"You still there?" Temple said.

WILBUR PICKETT WAS inside his barn, grinding the center-cutter for a ditching machine on an emery wheel, the sparks gushing onto his boot tops, when I pulled up on the grass in the Avalon and got out and headed for him without even bothering to turn off my car engine.

I threw my hat at his head. His mouth opened, then he saw my expression and the skin of his face grew so tight against the bone there were white lines, like tiny pieces of string, around his eyes.

"You did it, you lying bastard," I said.

"You stand back from me, Billy Bob."

I started to speak, but I couldn't get the words out. I shoved him in the breastbone.

"Don't do that," he said.

I shoved him again, with both hands, my teeth clenched together, then I pushed him out the back door into the horse lot. He became foot-tangled, off balance, flinching when I came at him again.

"Go ahead, take a shot, Wilbur. See what happens," I said.

His face was the bright red of a trainman's lantern.

"I ain't gonna fight you," he said. He lowered his hands and turned his back to me and hung his arms over the top rail of the fence. His pulse jumped in his neck and he looked at me out of the corner of his eye like a frightened animal.

"Why'd you steal? Why'd you lie all this time?" I said.

"Deitrich rubbed my face in it in front of all them people. I went into his office to bust that watch on the fireplace. Then I seen them bonds in the safe. I started thinking about the oil land his family stole from mine and I looked at them bonds and before I knowed it I had the watch in my pocket and them bonds stuck down in my britches. It was like I was watching somebody else do it instead of me."

He glanced at me to see if his explanation had

taken. He swallowed and looked away quickly. "I got greedy. Is that what you're waiting on?" he said.

"You sorry sonofabitch," I said.

"It wasn't no three hundred thousand. It was fifty. Giving them back wasn't gonna do no good. Earl Deitrich was gonna make money on the insurance claim and come after Kippy Jo's and my oil sand at the same time."

"Does your wife know about this?"

"No, sir, she don't."

"What about the bonds that were in the side of the dresser?"

"They were planted. That's what I been trying to tell you. It didn't matter what I done or didn't do. Deitrich and Hugo Roberts was gonna put me in the pen."

He stared morosely at the windmill blades straining against the lock chain and at his horses out in the alfalfa and the dust and rain blowing out of the hills in the west.

"What'd you do with the bonds you stole?" I asked.

"I sold them down in Mexico. The money's in the oil deal up in Wyoming now."

"You used us."

He pressed the heel of his hand against his forehead.

"I guess this world can be a mess of grief, cain't it?" he said.

"Just stay the hell away from me," I said, and walked back to my Avalon.

I saw Kippy Jo hanging wash on the clothesline. She stopped her work and lifted her head, her eyes focusing on the sky, as though the barometer had dropped dramatically and the environment around her was about to experience a change she had not foreseen.

LATE THAT NIGHT the phone in my library rang.

"Jessie and me has got to get out of here, Mr. Holland," the voice said.

"Mr. Doolittle?"

"I owe you mightily for what you've done. But I need money to get us down to the coast."

"I can't do that. You're an innocent man, but Jessie Stump belongs in a cage."

"Somebody up on the ridge seen us yesterday. He had field glasses."

"Let me surrender you, sir. I'll see that you're protected. You have my word."

"You don't know what it's like for a deformed man in the hands of hateful men. They ain't gonna get me again. You cain't hep me?"

"Not the way you want."

I heard him take a breath through the receiver, as though resigning himself.

"Jessie ain't all bad. I made him give up revenge against Earl Deitrich. That's a start, ain't it?" Skyler said.

"I don't know what to tell you, sir," I replied.

"Goodbye, Mr. Holland. I reckon this is the last time I'll be telling you that, too."

"Good luck, Mr. Doolittle," I said.

He hung up.

THE FOLLOWING AFTERNOON, Saturday, Temple threw a pebble against my library window. I went to the back porch and opened the screen. But she didn't come in.

"This is good right here," she said, and sat down on the scrolled iron bench under the chinaberry tree.

"I've got some lemonade made."

"Another time. I talked with Wilbur Pickett. You're too hard on him," she said.

"Oh?"

"It was there all the time, Billy Bob. You've said it yourself. People will do lots of things for money. Did it make sense that a man who would steal an antique watch would take nothing else with it?"

"He lied."

"He was scared."

"Of what?"

"You, his wife, the kids that look up to him. Come on, stop stoking your own furnace."

"Just dropping by to ladle out some moral insight?" I said.

"No. I did some checking into Earl Deitrich's finances. His place in Montana is up for sale and he's been borrowing on his house here. That's why he grabbed on to this insurance scam after Wilbur stole his bonds. He stands to gain a quarter of a million and he might still end up a partner in Wilbur's oil deal. He probably sent Bubba Grimes to kill Wilbur and Kippy Jo so he could file civil suit against the estate and seize their property up in Wyoming."

"I'm still Kippy Jo's defense attorney, and now I have to put Wilbur on the stand so he can tell the jury how he stole fifty thousand dollars in bonds and lied about it. Does that sound like a credible defense witness to you? You think that will make the jury a lot more sympathetic toward the Picketts? Or maybe I can suborn perjury."

"I can see this might piss you off."

"Thank you," I said.

She walked down the driveway toward her car. Then turned around and came back.

"You got some mint leaves to go with that lemonade?" she said.

TEN MILES FROM TOWN was a drive-in theater left over from the 1950s that opened only on Friday and Saturday nights. High school and college kids got crashed on warm beer and reefer and crystal and purple passion, rat-raced up and down the aisles, accidentally tore the speakers from the stanchions or the windows out of their cars when they burned rubber off the embankments, threw water bombs made from condoms into convertibles, fist-fought behind the cinder-block bathrooms, and stuck firecrackers up the tailpipes of cars in which great love affairs were blooming.

Without the dope the drive-in theater would have been little different in ambiance from its predecessors of four decades ago. In fact, it still had its moments: the smell of foot-long hot dogs and mustard and chopped onions, the palm trees framed against sunsets that were probably the most glorious in the Western Hemisphere, the scrolled purple and pink neon on the concession stand, the strolling groups of short-hair, fundamentalist kids whose piney-woods innocence seemed to insulate them from all the societal changes taking place around them.

Esmeralda and Lucas parked their pickup truck on the second row, and Lucas went to the concession stand and brought back a large popcorn, two hot dogs, and two Pepsis. Lucas was adjusting the sound on the speaker when a skinny kid in horn-rimmed glasses and cowboy boots and a denim shirt with the tails pulled out of his belt and a wallet chain hanging out of his back pocket stopped five feet from the pickup's window and started making frantic gestures at him.

"What do you want, J.P.?" Lucas asked.

"Come over here, man," J.P. said in a whisper, as though Esmeralda couldn't hear or see him.

"Stop acting like a moron. What is it?" Lucas said.

"Jeff's back there with Rita Summers. He was melting coke in a glass of Jack. The guy's out there on the edge, man. When you walked by he give you a look, like . . . Man, I don't want to even remember it. That dude's cruel, Lucas."

"Yeah, thanks, J.P. Don't worry about it, okay?" Lucas said.

A few minutes later Esmeralda said she was going to the rest room.

"I'll come with you," Lucas said.

"No," she replied.

"You don't owe Jeff anything. Don't talk to him," Lucas said.

She tilted her head and feigned a pout.

"He's scum, Essie," Lucas said.

"I'll be right back. Now stop it," she said.

She walked toward the concession, right past Jeff's yellow convertible. She wore a tight white dress with frill around the hem and neckline and scarlet ribbon threaded in and out of the frill. Rita Summers was behind the steering wheel, eating from a paper shell of french fries. Jeff held a tumbler full of bourbon and ice in his hand. His eyes followed Esmeralda, the sway of her hips, the way her hair bounced on her shoulder blades.

He set the tumbler on the dashboard and got out of the car and followed her.

She heard the soles of his loafers crunch on the shale behind her. His face was dilated with booze, his pores grainy with perspiration and heat.

"Go home, Jeff. Get some rest," she said.

"Dump Smothers. We can get it back together," he said.

"You need help. Give therapy a try. What have you got to lose, hon? You'd learn a lot about yourself and see things different."

"Better hear me, Essie. You and Smothers and Ronnie Cross have been sticking it in my face. In front of lots of people. A guy runs out of selections. That's the way it is. Even Ronnie knows that."

"I think you're going to die if you don't get help."

"We had a lot going at first. We can have it back. You want me to say it? I never had a girl like you."

"That's the problem, Jeff. You collect girls. You don't love them. You can't, because you don't love yourself."

His eyes were out of focus. He wiped his nose with his wrist. He seemed to lose balance momentarily, then right himself. "I gave you a chance. But you're just not a listener. It's the beaner gene. Y'all are uneducable," he said.

She turned and went into the women's room. A few minutes later she walked past the convertible again, her eyes focused on the movie screen, her white dress bathed in light. Jeff watched her while he drank from the bourbon tumbler with both hands.

"You're slurping like a pig. Maybe you and the south-of-the-border cutie should still be an item," Rita said.

Jeff took the paper shell of french fries from her

hands and ground it into her face, smearing her eyes and hair and blouse with catsup and salt and potato pulp while she struck blindly at him with her fists, her elbows blowing the horn in staccato.

SUNDAY MORNING SKYLER DOOLITTLE walked up a wooded slope and sat on a boulder that was webbed with lichen and read from a Gideon Bible. The pages of the Bible were water-stained, the thick cardboard cover bleached like ink diluted with milk. The sun was not over the hill yet, and the woods were smoky and wet, the air suffused with a cool green light that seemed to have its origins in the river down below rather than in the sky.

Jessie Stump, shirtless, his belt notched into his bony ribs, was shaving without soap, over a bowl outside a shack that had once been a deer stand. Jessie had packed a duffel bag with their pots, pans, blankets, road maps, clothes, and food. On his belt was a heavy, saw-toothed hunting knife, the edge honed so sharp it cut fine lines in the opening of the scabbard when he slipped it in and out of the leather.

Jessie wiped his face dry with his arm and squatted by a map and counted out their money on top of it. Thirty-two dollars and eleven cents were left over from the money Billy Bob Holland had given to Skyler. Jessie looked down at the map and the lines he had drawn in pencil along all the roadways that led to Matagorda Bay, over which he had written the words "Cousin Tyson's shrimper," as though some-how his hand could create the journey and escape by salt water before they actually took place.

He looked up the slope at Skyler, who seemed consumed by the Gideon he had found in a shack down by the oxbow. So what if Skyler spent his time with that stuff, Jessie thought. It didn't do no harm. Besides, Skyler'd sure been shortchanged in this world and maybe had something good coming in the next. In fact, Skyler was the only decent man he ever recalled meeting, except for maybe Cousin Tyson, who'd been in the pen four times and probably did a good turn for Jessie only because he hated cops on general principles.

Skyler wore a clean plaid shirt and suspenders and gray work pants they had gotten a black man to buy for them at the Wal-Mart. Skyler wet his thumb and forefinger each time he turned a page in his Bible, then he studied one passage for a long time and smiled down at Jessie.

The passage was about John the Baptizer, and John's words seemed to rise off the page for Skyler and re-create the forest around him. The smoky green canopy overhead became the roof of a granary, and wind was blowing through the slats and separat-ing out the chaff and lifting the grain into the sun-light, so that it became as golden as bees' pollen.

Skyler lifted the Bible in front of him to reread the passage, sitting up higher on the boulder. In his mind's eye he was already inside a gilded dome, one in which all the imperfections of the world disappeared, and he did not see the circular glint of glass on top of the ridge.

The soft-nosed .30-06 round tore through the book's cover and half the pages and pierced Skyler through the lungs before the report ever rolled down the hillside.

Jessie Stump ran toward Skyler, his face lunatical, his knife drawn like a foolish wand.

Skyler had slipped to the ground and was on his hands and knees, coughing red flowers on the stones that protruded from the soil. The torn pulp from his Bible floated down on his head like feathers from a white bird.

28

THE SHOOTING WAS REPORTED OVER THE PHONE an hour later by a weeping man who refused to give his name to the dispatcher.

Marvin Pomroy and I drove to the crime scene together. The paramedics zipped up a black bag over Skyler's face and loaded the body into an ambulance and drove away with it, and Hugo Roberts's deputies strung yellow crime scene tape through the trees that surrounded the lichen-painted rocks where Skyler had died.

"You got any fix on Jessie Stump?" Marvin asked Hugo.

"The 911 come in from a convenience store three miles down the highway. A car was stole out of a lady's driveway not far away about the same time," Hugo said.

"Get a warrant on the Deitrich place," I said.

"What for?" he asked.

"To search for the gun that killed Skyler. You might also run a powder-residue test on Jeff Deitrich and any of his friends who happen to be hanging around," I said.

"Right now the number one suspect is Jessie Stump," Hugo said.

"The entry wound was at the top of his chest. The exit wound was in his rib cage. What does that suggest to you, Hugo?" I said.

"That a bullet goes in one place and out the other," he replied, and pared a fingernail with a penknife.

A young uniformed deputy, new to the department, walked down the hillside through the pine trees, holding a .30-06 shell on the tip of a pencil.

"Found it on the crest up there. You can even see the shooter's boot and knee prints in the pine needles. It looks like he fired from the right side of the trunk, which means he's probably right-handed . . . " He paused. "I do something wrong?" he said, looking at Hugo's face.

THAT AFTERNOON I DROVE down the long valley and across the cattleguard in front of the Deitrich home and walked up the huge slabs of black stone that formed the front steps. When no one answered the chimes I walked around the side of the house to the terrace, which was shaded by a black-and-white-striped canopy. Peggy Jean and Jeff and Earl sat at a glass-topped table, drinking daiquiris, while shish kebab smoked on a barbecue pit and young people I didn't know swam in the pool.

Fletcher Grinnel, the ex-mercenary, stepped out of the French doors with a drink tray, paused momentarily when he saw me, smiling either deferentially or to himself, then set down the tray and painted the shish kebab on the grill with a small brush.

"Why don't you invite yourself over?" Earl said.

"Hugo Roberts wouldn't get a warrant on your home. But I thought I should let you know what you've done," I said.

"Sit down with us, Billy Bob. It's Sunday. Can't we be friends for today?" Peggy Jean said.

"Skyler Doolittle is dead. If I had to bet on the shooter, I'd put my money on either Fletcher over there, grimacing into the smoke, or Jeff and his friends wondering if they should go to a swimming party this afternoon or, say, gang-rape a Mexican girl," I said.

Jeff wore a Hawaiian shirt open on his chest. He slanted his head sideways and pushed the curls off his forehead with the tips of his fingers, studying my words with the idle concentration he might show a street beggar. Then he shook his head slowly as though he were bemused by a metaphysical absurdity and let his eyes wander out onto the swimming pool.

"Fletcher, go inside and call the sheriff's office and find out what this is about," Earl said.

"Should I show Mr. Holland to his car?" Fletcher asked.

"That's a possibility," Earl said.

"You know what you've let either this hired moron or your psychopath of a son do?" I said to Earl.

"Skyler Doolittle had gotten Jessie Stump off your case. They were headed for Matagorda Bay, out of your life. But somebody murdered this harmless, gentle man with a .30-06 rifle while Jessie was shaving a few feet away. It looked like Jessie tried to stop the bleeding with his shirt. Skyler's blood was smeared over everything in the area, which means Jessie probably tried to drag him out of the line of fire. That's the man who's probably up in your tree line now, Earl."

Fletcher Grinnel set down the barbecue brush on a white plate and wiped his fingers with a paper towel and approached me, his lips pursed whimsically.

"No," Peggy Jean said, and rose from her chair. She took me by the arm. "You walk with me, Billy Bob. This kind of thing is not going to happen at our house."

She held my arm tightly, almost in a romantic fashion. Her breast touched my arm and her hip brushed against mine as we walked toward the front of the house. When we were around the corner of the building I felt the tension go out of her grip and I stepped away from her.

"You tried to warn Skyler. When this plays out in a courtroom, that'll count for something," I said.

"Whatever do you mean?"

"You left him a note on a pine branch outside the cave he and Stump were hidden in."

"I don't know what you're talking about."

"He saw you picking blackberries on the creek. Why do you deny a good deed?"

"You listen, Billy Bob. My husband has gambled away or mismanaged or leveraged everything we own. After all the years I've spent on this marriage I'm not about to accept a life of genteel poverty in Deaf Smith. I'm bringing civil suit against Wilbur Pickett for the damage he's done to us. Don't you dare lie to me about the theft of those bonds, either. That man stole them and he's going to pay for it."

"Skyler Doolittle was murdered this morning, probably by a member of your household, and you're talking about a civil suit?"

The blood climbed into her face.

"Maybe I'm a victim here, too. Did that ever occur to you?" she said.

"Yes, it did . . ."

"Then why do you treat me the way you do?" She stepped close to me and hit me in the chest with the flat of her fist, then again, desperately, her jawbone flexing. "We could have made it work. Why weren't you willing to try?"

"Because you don't love what we are, Peggy Jean. You're in love with what we were."

Her face crinkled high up on one cheek, like a flower held too close to heat. Then she turned and went into the house, her elbows cupped tightly in her palms, her back shaking.

• • •

MONDAY EVENING RONNIE CRUISE turned off the road into my driveway and parked by the barn, out of view from the front. He was driving Cholo Ramirez's '49 Mercury, and an odor of burning rubber and oil rose from the tires and engine. Ronnie got out of the car and took off his shades and looked back down the drive at the road.

"What are you doing with Cholo's car?" I said.

"I just got it out of the pound. Both our names were on the pink slip," he said.

"Somebody after you, Ronnie?"

"I cruised Val's. Some guys in a roll-bar rig followed me out. I got to sit down. I didn't get no sleep last night."

"What can I do for you?" I asked.

"I'm gonna save you a lot of time. My uncle, the guy who owns the auto shop where I work? He's mobbed-up. Him and Cholo and some other guys, guys out of Galveston, were working the stick-up scam on Deitrich's business friends. There's this old skeet club between Conroe and Houston, except now it's got water beds and chippies in it. Deitrich would steer his friends to the card game, then Cholo and the others would take it down. I got some guilt over this."

"You said you weren't involved with it."

"You not understanding me. Yesterday I saw this dude Johnny Krause with my uncle. I asked my uncle, 'Hey, what are you doing with this guy?' He goes, 'Johnny was one of the take-down artists on the last job at the skeet club.' I go, 'That's the guy who killed Cholo.'

"My uncle goes, 'Cholo wasn't in on that last one, so he didn't know who Johnny was when he run into him at the boxing gym. Too bad it shakes out like that sometimes.'

"Too bad? That's my own uncle talking like Cholo was a sack of shit. I told my uncle to go fuck himself. I hope the cops nail his chop shop and jam a grease gun up his ass."

"You want to come inside?"

"Yeah, I'd like that," he said.

In the kitchen he sat at the table and drank an RC Cola and ate a ham and lettuce sandwich with his face close to the plate. He wore a pair of wash-faded Levi's without a belt and a purple T-shirt razored off below the nipples. His eyes kept studying mine, his lips seeming to form words that he rubbed away with the back of a finger before he completed them.

"What else did you come here to tell me, Ronnie?" I asked.

"Some Purple Hearts got it that Jeff Deitrich wants to do Essie, make her pull a train. The word is he's gonna use some bikers, meth-heads that don't got boundaries. Then he's gonna pop your boy."

"Say that again."

"They're gonna kill Lucas after they get finished with Essie. What world you live in, Mr. Holland? You don't think Jeff and his friends got it in them?"

I was standing up when he said this, and I could

feel the blood pounding in my wrists and temples, and for some reason I wanted to attack him with my fists.

"Here's what it is, Mr. Holland," he said. "I ain't gonna let Jeff get away with this. You remember the two Viscounts who put their hands all over Essie in a movie theater, the ones who took a real bad bounce off a roof? I didn't throw them off, but the choices they had weren't too good. They were either gonna grow new kneecaps or learn how to fly.

"Since that day no Viscount has bothered a Purple Heart or one of our girls. I'm telling you this because I heard about some stuff you done when you were a Texas Ranger, about dope mules that got a playing card stuck down their throats in Coahuila. I don't got any playing cards with Purple Hearts on them, but maybe Jeff and his friends are gonna ask themselves how many funerals they want to go to."

I sat down at the table. The wood felt cold and hard against my forearms.

"You're going to take somebody out?" I said, my words catching in my throat.

"You don't want it to get done, or you don't want to know about it? You rather your boy be killed? Which one you want, Mr. Holland?"

THAT SAME NIGHT Wilbur Pickett appeared in the ESPN television broadcast booth high above an indoor arena in Mesquite, where a rodeo was in progress. Wilbur wore a new gray Stetson with a blue cord tied around the crown and a snap-button silver and blue cowboy shirt that rang like ice water on his shoulders. Kippy Jo sat next to him, wearing dark glasses, her forearm touching Wilbur's.

The broadcaster was a short, wiry, lantern-jawed, ex-bull rider himself, with recessed buckshot eyes and a high-pitched East Texas accent that was like tin being stripped off a roof. His teeth were as rectangular as tombstones when he grinned and pushed the microphone in front of Wilbur.

"It's good to see you, boy. The last time you was here you was coming out of chute number 6 on a bull named Bad Whiskey. That was the only bull on the circuit besides Bodacious could run the clowns up the boards, turn around in midair, and give you a view from El Paso to Texarkana, all in one hop," the announcer said.

"I appreciate being here, W.D. It's a real opportunity for me . . ."

"It's a treat having you drop by to do color for us again," the announcer interrupted. "We're gonna take a break in a minute, then I want your opinion on a bulldogging buddy of yours out of Quanah . . ."

Wilbur sat rigidly in the chair, his right hand clenched around his left wrist. He leaned toward the microphone, the brim of his hat partly shadowing his face, as though he were creating a private space in which he was about to confide a secret to a solitary individual.

"My wife says I got to do this or I ain't never gonna have no peace," he said. "I want to apologize to all the friends and rodeo fans I let down. I was accused of stealing from a man in Deaf Smith. I told everybody I didn't do it, but I lied. I took fifty thousand dollars from this fellow. He says it was more . . . It wasn't but that don't matter. I stole and I lied about it and I'm sorry. Thanks for having me on, W.D."

Both Wilbur and Kippy Jo walked off camera. The announcer stared blankly after them, then said, "I guess we'll go to a commercial now. I don't know about y'all, but I still figure Wilbur T. Pickett for a special kind of rodeo cowboy."

IT DIDN'T TAKE LONG. Earl and Peggy Jean Deitrich were in my office the next afternoon with their attorney, a towering, likable man named Clayton Spangler, who was rumored to own fifty thousand acres of the old XIT Ranch around Dalhart. Peggy Jean wore a white suit and sheer white hose and sat with her legs crossed, her face rouged high up on the cheekbones, so that her whole manner seemed angular and pointed, like the cutting edge of an instrument. Earl had come directly from the hand-ball court at the country club, and his hair was still wet from his shower, his skin glowing with health and the excitement of the moment.

I felt like a mortician presiding over my best

friend's wake while his enemies took the ice from his body and dropped it in their beer.

"It seems like an equitable way of resolving the whole affair," Clayton said.

"All his and Kippy Jo's two hundred acres in Wyoming? With all mineral rights? Forget it," I said.

"How about this scenario instead?" Earl said, leaning forward. "We refile criminal charges against Pickett, sue him in civil court, and take both the Wyoming tract and his place out on the hardpan and get a judgment against everything he makes in the future."

"I'll talk to him," I said, replying to Clayton Spangler rather than to Earl.

"It's good seeing you again, Billy Bob," Clayton said, and stood up and shook hands.

Peggy Jean stood by the window, looking down into the street. Against the shadowy, cool colors of my office her suit seemed woven from light. She brushed at the back of her neck with her fingers, bending her knees slightly to see someone through the blinds, then rubbing her fingertips idly, totally oblivious to the people around her.

She and Earl went out the door, but Clayton Spangler hung back a moment.

"This one has got a personal and ugly bent to it. That's not my way of conducting business. Come back with something reasonable and we'll lock the barn door on it," he said.

"Sounds good, Clayton. Earl and his kind put me in mind of livestock with the red scours," I said.

"I tried," he said.

THAT EVENING, when I came home, Lucas's pickup truck was in the driveway and he was sitting on the tailgate, swinging his feet in the dirt. His straw hat was pushed up on his forehead and his reddish-blond hair stuck out on his brow. Through the kitchen window I saw Esmeralda washing dishes at the sink.

"I took the key from under the step. I hope you don't mind," he said.

"What's she doing at the sink?"

"Straightening up a little bit. Washing your breakfast dishes. Essie likes everything squared away." He twisted his head and looked out at the tank and the wind channeling the grass in the fields and a hawk drifting on extended wings across the sun. He lifted his shirt off his skin and shook it. "It's sure been a hot son of a gun, ain't it? I liked to got fried out on the rig," he said.

"How about telling me what's really going on here?"

"A biker was scouting out my house last night. I seen two more when I come back from work this afternoon."

"You're telling me you want to move Essie into my house?"

"She don't have no folks. She don't want to stay

with Ronnie and his mother. I'll be here, too. I mean if it's okay."

"Why'd Ronnie and Essie break up, Lucas?"

"She told him he had to get out of the gangs."

"You sure it's over between them?"

"It don't matter. I ain't gonna let her down now."

"Y'all take the downstairs. Leave a light on at your house and your pickup in your front yard. You can drive my truck," I said.

"How come you asked about why they broke up?"

"No reason," I lied.

"She didn't want to do this, Billy Bob. She's a brave gal."

I put my hand on his shoulder and we walked toward the back porch. His muscles felt like rocks moving inside leather. Our hatted shadows flowed up the steps as though we were joined at the hip, then broke apart when he opened the screen and waited for me to walk ahead of him.

WILBUR PACED in his living room, his big hands opening and closing. The wind was blowing hard through the screens, popping the curtains back on the wallpaper.

"Give them the whole place in Wyoming?" he said. "That'll be the second time the Deitrichs cleaned my family out. I cain't believe this is happening."

"You confessed on TV. It's good for the soul but usually not for the wallet," I said.

He sat down in a thread-worn stuffed chair. He removed a half dozen color photographs from a table drawer next to the chair and handed them to me.

"That's the kind of high desert it is. The earth don't get no prettier," he said.

The acreage stretched from a winding river up a long hardpan slope to high bluffs that were green on the top against the sun. The slope was in shadow, the sage silvered with frost, and antelope were grazing among cottonwoods by the riverbank.

In the corner of one photograph were two huge pipe trucks, a dismantled derrick streaked with rust, and part of an oil platform.

"What's the matter?" Wilbur said.

"I don't know if I'd want to punch a hole in a place that beautiful."

"Well, you ain't me."

"I'll get everything I can for you. But you have to trust me. That means at a certain point we indicate to the Deitrichs you're willing to go to jail. You have to mean it, too," I said.

"Scared money don't win?"

"Not in my experience."

"I don't think I ever felt so miserable in my life. My mama always said it. Us Picketts has got two claims on fame: My daddy was the dumbest white man in this county and I worked a lifetime to come in a close second."

He took the photographs of his two hundred acres

in Wyoming from my hand and pitched them into the drawer and looked into space.

IT WAS RAINING the next evening, the air dense with ozone, when Chug Rollins left the Deitrich home and drove down the long valley across the cattleguard onto a two-lane blacktop road fringed on both sides with hardwood trees. The landscape was sodden, the corridor of trees dripping, and a green radiance seemed to lift off the crest of the hills into the dome of sky overhead, then disappear into the swirls of blue-black clouds that groaned and crackled with thunder but contained no lightning that struck the earth.

Chug ripped the tab on a Pearl and drank the can half empty in three swallows, then set it in the holder on the dashboard. In his rearview mirror he could still see the sheriff's cruisers that were parked by the Deitrichs' cattleguard. It was all going to turn out all right, he thought. Nobody had tied the drowned mop-heads to him or Jeff, and besides, it was Jeff's grief, anyway. What they needed to do now was straighten out a few people who thought the East Enders didn't have a firm grip on events in Deaf Smith, starting with Jeff's ex and that punk Lucas Smothers and working on down through Ronnie Cruise and any other Purple Hearts who wanted to be deep-fried in their own grease and then finally, as an afterthought, that pimple on everybody's ass, Wesley Rhodes, yes indeedy.

Who paid the taxes here, anyway? Pepperbellies and bohunks?

Up ahead a sheriff's deputy by the side of the road waved a flashlight at him. Chug lifted the can of Pearl from the dash holder and set it on the floor, then pulled to a stop and rolled down the passenger window with the electric motor.

"Give me a ride up to my cruiser?" the deputy asked, bending down to the window. His uniform was soaked through and molded to his thin frame, and water sluiced off the brim of his campaign hat.

"Sure, get in," Chug answered.

The deputy seemed relieved to be in the dryness and warmth of the automobile. He removed his hat and shook the water off gingerly on the carpeting and wiped his face with a red handkerchief.

"That open container you got on the floor don't bother me," the deputy said.

Chug grinned and replaced the can of Pearl in the dash holder. But the deputy continued to study the floor for some reason.

"Where's your cruiser?" Chug asked.

"On up a piece. This rain's a frog-stringer, ain't it?"

"How come you get separated from your car in weather like this?"

"Another deputy dropped me off to check something out, then he went on up to the house," the deputy replied.

"Check out what?"

"A colored man standing by the road. I run him off."

"Is there a reason you keep looking at my feet?" Chug asked.

"Didn't know I was."

"You damn sure were. What's your name?"

"It's right there on my name tag." The deputy hooked his thumb inside his shirt pocket and poked out the cloth and the brass nameplate pinned to it. The plate read *B. Stokes*.

"But what's your name?" Chug asked again.

The deputy was silent. The car hit a depression and splashed water across the windshield, and Chug increased the speed of the wipers, glad to have something to do, to show control of his machine and the environment around him. But why was he thinking like that? he asked himself. The rain spun in a vortex between the line of trees on each side of the blacktop, and the fading, peculiar nature of the light seemed to form a green arch, like a canopy, over the roadway. Chug realized he was sweating and that his breath was coming hard in his chest. He rolled down his window and let the wind and rain blow in his face.

"I'm going to stop at that filling station at the crossroads. You can see the lights from here. Place is full of customers. You can call somebody if you need a ride," Chug said.

He heard the deputy's gun belt creak, then the hollow sound a leather pocket makes when a heavy object is removed from it.

The deputy twisted the muzzle of his nine-millimeter into Chug's neck.

"Turn right at that cut in the trees, then keep going till you see a railroad car," he said.

Chug clicked on his turn indicator, but the deputy slapped it off. After Chug had turned off the road, he looked at the pocked, shiny white face of the deputy, the wired, black eyes, and said, "You got the wrong guy."

"Maybe . . . What size shoe you wear?"

"A twelve," Chug said, his brow furrowing.

"It don't look like it to me . . . Stop yonder."

The sandy road dipped and rose through hardwoods, then ended at an overgrown stretch of railway track on which sat a faded red Southern Pacific boxcar that had rotted into the soft, moldy texture of old cork.

The deputy walked Chug to the lee side of the boxcar and picked up a pinecone and threw it at him, hard. Chug raised his arm and ducked and heard the pinecone bounce off the slats of the boxcar.

"This time you catch it. You drop it and I'll shoot you in the elbow," the deputy said, and tossed the pinecone at Chug underhanded.

"What the hell you doin'?" Chug said.

The deputy worked his handcuffs out of the case on the back of his belt and threw them to Chug.

"Hook yourself up to that iron rung on the corner," he said. "Now kick your loafer off."

After Chug did it, the deputy picked the loafer out of the leaves and pine needles and spread a piece of tissue paper with the penciled outline of a shoe or boot sole on it across the floor of the boxcar and smoothed it with his palm. He held Chug's loafer with the fingers of both hands above the outline, moving it back and forth in space, without touching the paper.

"You're left-handed and got too big a foot. It's your day and not mine," the deputy said.

Chug looked steadily at the side of the boxcar, the blistered strips of red paint, the gray weathering in the wood, the way the rain leaked down off the roof and threaded in the cracks. He gathered the moisture in his mouth so he could speak, but when he did the words that rose from his throat seemed like someone else's.

"I won't tell anybody about this," he said.

"Yeah, you will. You'll tell every little pissant who'll listen. You'll tell your mommy and your daddy and them people at the country club and the preacher at your church and all them little pukes at Val's you hang around with and whatever piece of tail you pay to climb up on top of. You'll be oinking your story like a little pig till people want to stop up their ears. I didn't say look at me, boy."

The deputy brought the barrel of the automatic up

between Chug's thighs, flicking off the butterfly safety and cocking back the hammer.

"Don't mess your britches on me. I'll blow your sack off right now," the deputy said.

But the rings of fat on Chug's hips were shaking, the rain streaming off his hair and face, his eyes wide and his breath sputtering the rainwater off his lips into a spray, so that his head looked like that of a man who had just burst to the surface of a lake after almost drowning.

Chug heard the deputy work open a pocketknife and felt the deputy press the honed edge lightly against the back of his neck, pushing the hair up as though he were going to shave it.

Then the deputy traced the point of the knife down Chug's vertebrae and paused with the tip inside the back of Chug's belt.

"You didn't shoot Skyler but you was part of it," the deputy said, and sliced the knife down through Chug's belt and underwear and the seam of his khaki pants, exposing his enormous pink posterior. "Stop blubbering, boy. A shithog like you wouldn't make good Vienna sausage. Tell the one who done it Skyler ain't here no more to plead for him. Tell him I killed three people no one knows about, people who hurt me real bad. Tell him I done it in ways that made a drunkard out of the detective who worked the case."

Then Jessie Stump scrubbed the top of Chug's head with his knuckles and drove off in Chug's automobile.

29

"WHAT DID YOU DO TO THE DEPUTY YOU TOOK the uniform off of?" I said into the phone.

"Knocked him in the head," Jessie said.

"You called me in the middle of the night to tell me all this bullshit?"

"I want you to lay some flowers on Skyler's grave. Put it on my tab."

"You don't have a tab. You're not my client . . . Hello?"

AT 8 A.M. I WALKED down the first-floor hallway of the courthouse and entered Marvin Pomroy's office right behind him.

"You're going to tell me Jessie Stump got in touch with you after terrifying the Rollins kid?" he said.

"Stump isn't my client. I have nothing to do with him. That's an absolute," I said.

"Three years ago we had him deadbang on a check-writing charge. With his sheet we could have put him away for five years. You discredited an honest witness and got Stump off. How's it feel?"

"I need your help."

"You're outrageous."

"Jeff Deitrich has targeted the Ramirez girl and my boy Lucas."

Marvin hadn't sat down at his desk yet. The heat went out of his face and he moved some papers around on his ink blotter, his eyes lowered.

"You talk to Hugo Roberts?" he asked.

"Waste of time."

"What do you want from me?"

"You have influence with the Deitrichs. They want to stay in your favor. Get them to pull Jeff's plug."

"That's not too complimentary."

"Ronnie Cruise says he's going to take down a couple of Jeff's buds. Maybe cancel their whole ticket."

Marvin brushed at his nose and fiddled with his shirt cuffs.

"That's still not why you came here, though, is it?" he said.

"I've thought about remodeling a couple of those kids myself. Maybe going all the way with it."

"The last portion of this conversation didn't occur. On that note, I'd better get to work," Marvin said, and picked up a sheet of typed paper from his blotter and studied it intently until I was out the door.

THAT AFTERNOON I came home from work and rode Beau along the irrigation ditch at the bottom of the pine-wooded slope that gave onto the backyards of the run-down neighborhood where Pete lived.

To my left was the acreage that Lucas's stepfather, who worked for me on shares, had planted with okra, squash, corn, cantaloupe, strawberries, melons, and beans. I passed the water-stained plank that Pete used to walk down from his house to mine, then rode up on the bench into shadow to a weathered wood shed where my father once kept the tools that his Mexican field hands used.

I let Beau graze along the banks of the ditch and twisted the key in the big Yale lock on the shed door and went inside. The air was warm and smelled of metal and grease. Dust and particles of hay glowed in the cracks of light through the walls, and a deer mouse skittered inside the well of an automobile tire. The door was caught on a wood sled, one with boards for runners that at one time we drew with a mule down the rows when we picked beans and tomatoes into baskets. I propped the sled against the wall, touching the dirt-smoothed and rounded edges of the runners and for just a moment seeing my father framed against the late sun, drinking water from a ladle, then replacing it on the bucket that sat between the baskets. Then I felt someone's eyes on my back.

In the far corner L.Q. Navarro sat on top of a saw-horse, his arms propped beside him for support, his long legs crossed at the ankles.

"Your friend Pomroy is gonna fret his mind till he

takes the easy way home. Which means he's gonna lock up that Mexican gangbanger, what's his name, Ronnie Cruise," L.Q. said.

"Marvin's a good man," I replied.

"He wants to sleep at night, bud. His kind don't win wars. Them kids are scum. You cap 'em and bag 'em and don't study on it."

I began pulling a pile of junk apart in one corner until I found what I had come for. It was made of red oak, and was heavy and splinter-edged, three inches thick, two feet high, and the width of a door. Two screw bolts, with eyelets as big as half dollars, were twisted vertically into the top of the wood. I hoisted it up on my shoulder.

"I'm gonna lock up. You coming?" I said to L.Q.

"You know I'm right."

"I sure don't," I said, and closed the door on L.Q. and snapped the lock into place.

My father had burned the word "Heartwood" into the oak plank with a running iron. He had intended to build a white gate with rose trellises and a cross-beam at the entrance to the drive and hang his sign from the beam, but he was killed that same spring in a pipeline blowout at Matagorda Bay.

I sat in the grass on the slope and wiped the grain clean with an oily rag and scoured the dust out of the branded letters until they were dark and granulated and rippling under my index finger. My mother said she thought it was a bit vain and presumptuous to hang a sign on a farm as modest as ours, and my father's response was, "The only reason it's modest is because the Hollands was honest and didn't steal other people's land during the Depression for four bits an acre."

But I knew my father, the quiet whirrings in his chest, the grace and dignity with which he conducted himself, and the deeply held sentiments he didn't share openly because he lacked the vocabulary to express feeling without sounding saccharine. He loved our home because in his mind it had no equal anywhere on the earth. How many men lived in a three-story purple-brick house, surrounded by poplars and roses and blooming myrtle, with a breezy top-floor view of a barn, horse lot, windmill, chicken run, cattle pasture, plowed acreage with rows of vegetables that ran all the way to the bluffs, a willow-lined tank stocked with striped bass and crappie and bream and catfish, the scars of the Chisholm Trail baked like white ceramic into the hardpan, and a meandering, green river and rolling hills in the distance? We woke to it every day, knowing that everything God and the earth could give to a family had been presented to us with no other obligation on our part than to be its stewards.

I don't think my father was vain at all, and in reality I don't think my mother did, either.

I heard footsteps behind me and turned around and saw Pete coming down the slope through the pine trees. He was barefoot and carried a fishing rod with the Mepps spinner pulled up tight against the eyelet so that it rattled when he walked.

He looked around, his face puzzled.

"Was you talking to someone?" he asked.

"Probably not," I replied.

"Billy Bob, if you was in a conversation and other people was saying a friend of yours was crazy, would you get in them people's face about it?"

"Nothing wrong with being crazy. It gives you a more interesting view. If it was me, I wouldn't debate it with people who don't understand those kinds of things," I said.

"I was thinking along the same lines," he said. "But in my opinion the friend I'm talking about is the best guy I ever knowed." He grinned and nodded to himself, as though taking great pleasure in his own wit and the world around him.

"Why don't we go down to the tank and entertain the bass?" I said.

I got up on Beau, then Pete handed up my father's red oak gate sign and I propped it across the pommel and waited for Pete to climb on Beau's rump. He held me tightly across the waist, his bass lure rattling on his fishing rod, while we rode through a field of wildflowers toward the tank.

SUNDAY MORNING CHUG ROLLINS was still swacked on tequila and downers from the previous night and drove all the way across the border to visit a Mexican brothel. Upon his return to Deaf Smith he cruised Val's and got into it with a carhop who refused to move from in front of his automobile and gave him the finger when he blew his horn at her. The manager, who was six and a half feet tall, walked the waitress inside, then broke Chug's windshield with an ice mallet. By sunset Chug was at Shorty's, out on the screen porch, drunk on beer, wired to the eyes, filling the air with a sweet-sour animal odor that coated his body like a gray fog.

When his friends moved their drinks and food to tables that were at a safe distance, Chug cornered kids who were younger than he, forcing them to drink with him and listen to his rage at the sheriff's department, at Jessie Stump, at Mexican gang-bangers, then at what he called "hip-hop cannibals that crossed the wrong lines."

"You in the Klan or something?" one kid said, a wry grin on his mouth as he tried to preserve his dignity and justify his shame for not fleeing Chug's presence.

"It's like a war. There're casualties in a war. It wasn't my beef, anyway. Hey, I didn't say anything about black people, you got me? I got nothing against them," Chug said.

"That's righteous, man. No problem. I got to use the rest room."

"Bring back a pitcher from the bar," Chug said.

An hour later Chug was picked up for DWI. When

the deputy shook him down against the side of the car, a throat-lozenges container fell from his pocket and broke open in the gutter. A handful of reds glimmered in the mud like beads from a broken necklace.

THE NEXT MORNING I took a chance. No one boiled on alcohol and downers would later remember everything he said and did.

Chug lived in a three-bedroom, one-story brick house, with a wide, cement porch and white pillars that affected the appearance of East End homes which cost much more. His father was a deacon in the Baptist Church, an auxiliary member of the sheriff's department, and a booster of almost every civic group in town, but he wore pale blue suits with a white stitch in them, hillbilly sideburns, and grease in his hair. The lawn was burned along the edges of the walks, and the small concrete pool in back always had leaves and pine needles floating in the corners.

It was there that I found Chug, resting in a deck chair, his eyes shaded with dark glasses, his elephantine, hair-streaked body oiled with suntan lotion.

He raised his head just far enough to see who I was.

"You're getting a burn," I said.

"I'll live with it."

"I thought you might need an attorney," I said.

"My father already got the ticket reduced to reckless driving. The dope I was supposed to be holding was Red Hots. So thanks but no thanks. Who let you in here, anyway?"

"You don't remember what you were telling people at Shorty's?" I asked.

"Yeah, 'Pass the hot sauce.'"

"Two drowned Jamaican drug dealers floated up in a rock quarry. Not too smart to blab it around a beer joint. You talk this over with Jeff yet?"

Chug's glasses were jet black and filled with the sun's hot reflection. His mouth formed a shape like an elongated zero, then he licked the corners of his lips and picked up a glass of iced tea from the concrete and shook the ice in it.

"Maybe you should shag it on out of here," he said.

"No need to be impolite."

Even though I couldn't see his eyes, I recognized the measured change taking place in him. It was characteristic of East End kids, or at least those Chug hung with. They could become whatever you wanted them to be. They just had to discover the role you required of them, the way a water dowser psychically probes the environment around him.

He sat up on the deck chair and wiped the sweat out of his hair with a towel so I could not read his expression when he spoke.

"I'm not feeling too good today, Mr. Holland. We have a family lawyer. I don't know anything about drug dealers or drowned people or why I should be talking to Jeff Deitrich about anything except football," he said.

"You think you can get rid of that kind of guilt by going to a cathouse?" I said.

He saw a man's silhouette go across the sliding glass doors at the back of the house. He got up heavily from the deck chair and walked to the glass and tapped on it with his high school ring.

Chug's father slid open the door, wearing a tan western suit, smiling brightly, his dentures stiff in his mouth.

"Daddy, this guy's being a pain in the ass," Chug said.

"You're Mr. Holland, aren't you?" Chug's father said, still beaming, patting his son on the shoulder as Chug walked past him into the living room. "What can I do for you, sir?"

The skin around his mouth looked like rilled paper against the stiffness of his teeth. He waited for my response, as though I were a customer on the showroom floor at his dealership.

TEMPLE CARROL, WILBUR and Kippy Jo Pickett, the Deitrichs and their attorney, Clayton Spangler, and I met that afternoon in a private dining room at the Langtry Hotel.

As though some cosmic irony were at work, the

hotel's owner had set a silver bowl of floating red roses in the middle of the dining table.

"To settle all claims and grievances, the Picketts are willing to offer Mr. and Mrs. Deitrich forty percent of the Pickett Oil Company. That includes forty percent ownership of all the equipment in place on the Wyoming tract and forty percent of all oil and gas revenues," I said to Clayton.

"Pickett Oil Company? This guy digs postholes and sells watermelons for a living," Earl said.

Clayton rubbed two fingers on his temple. "It's not what we had in mind," he said to me. He looked immense seated next to his client, his flat-brim hat crown-down by his wrist.

"Talk to the geologists who analyzed the core sample. There's a black lake under those two hundred acres. It might extend into two other counties," I said.

Clayton smiled. His eyes were blue, his graying blond hair trimmed close to the scalp. "My favorite line from Golda Meir was her statement about the Hebrews wandering for two thousand years, then settling in the only place in the Middle East that had no oil," he said. "No offense meant, but Mr. Pickett seems to have the same kind of luck. As compensation for real loss, you're offering my clients a chance to gamble. By the way, Mr. Deitrich's employees looked at the equipment on the Wyoming property. It's junk."

"What did you come here expecting?" I said.

"All of it," Peggy Jean interjected.

"You're not going to get it," I said.

Our eyes met across the table, as adversaries, all memories of our youth nullified by financial interests.

"This guy makes good on what he stole, on our terms, or he goes to prison," Earl said, leaning forward, lifting his finger up at Wilbur.

"My wife can go back to the res, so I ain't afraid of jail no more, Mr. Deitrich," Wilbur said.

"There's a complication here you don't understand, Earl," I said. "Wilbur gave me ten percent of his situation in Wyoming. I'm not about to let you rip off both me and the Picketts because you're on the edge of bankruptcy. Here's our best offer. You can buy the property at twenty-five hundred an acre and we retain half the mineral rights. But the drilling equipment and the producer's end of the oil royalties remain ours. You had an opportunity to be a producer rather than simply a property owner. But that offer is off the table. Y'all can't have it both ways."

"You're asking for a half million dollars," Earl said.

"It's a bargain," I said to Clayton. "We'll hold the mortgage for fifteen years at seven percent. The escrow account will be set up right here in town. If this isn't satisfactory to the Deitrichs, they can refile criminal charges against my client and he'll take his chances at trial."

Peggy Jean straightened her back, her chest rising and falling. Earl pulled at his collar; a tic jumped at the corner of his eye.

"We want half the drilling operation," Peggy Jean said.

"Not an option," I said.

"That land's worth a minimum of thirty-five hundred an acre, Mr. Deitrich. For a signature you make an immediate two-hundred-thousand-dollar profit, plus you get half of what may be a huge oil sand. I wouldn't take too long making up my mind," Temple said.

Earl Deitrich looked at his wife, then at Clayton Spangler.

"Why don't y'all have a drink at the bar?" Clayton said to our side of the table.

LATE THAT AFTERNOON I took a half gallon of French vanilla ice cream out of the freezer and put it, a serving spoon, and two bowls and teaspoons in a paper bag and drove down to Temple Carrol's house.

She was wearing moccasins and lavender shorts and a beige T-shirt when she answered the door.

"Sit in the swing with me," I said.

"Where'd you go after the Deitrichs took the deal?" she asked.

"I wanted to get ahold of a Houston homicide detective named Janet Valenzuela. She's working the arson of the savings and loan and the deaths of the four firemen. I told her Cholo Ramirez admitted to being at the fire and was working for Ronnie Cruise's uncle and Earl Deitrich in a take-down scam. I called the FBI, too. Maybe they can squeeze the uncle."

"You left Ronnie's name out of it?"

"He's not a player. You want some ice cream?"

She slipped her palms in her back pockets. They were tight against the cloth and curved against the firmness of her rump. I could feel her eyes studying the side of my face.

The half gallon of ice cream had begun to soften in the warm air, but it was still round and cold in my hands when I set it on the railing of the gallery and filled two bowls. I handed one to her and sat down in the swing. She sat on the railing and ate without speaking. The cannas in her flower bed were stiff and hard-looking in the shade, the bloom at the head of the stalk sparkling with drops of water from the sprinkler.

"Why so quiet?" I asked.

"That deal today? You had everybody in the room absolutely convinced Wilbur was about to punch into a big dome. I don't think he could find oil in a filling station," she said.

"Avaricious people make good listeners," I said.

"What are you up to?"

"I'm just not that complex, Temple."

She raised her eyebrows. I got up from the swing and sat next to her on the railing. Her shoulder and hip touched mine. Her spoon scraped quietly in her ice cream bowl while she continued to eat.

"You want to go to a show?" I asked.

She didn't answer.

"Is your father home?" I asked.

"Why?"

"I thought you might want to go to a show. I mean, if he'd be all right by himself."

"He's at his sister's. They have dinner and watch late-night TV one night a week." Her face turned up into mine.

"I see," I said. I circled my fingers lightly around her wrist and touched her upper arm with my other hand. In the shadows her mouth looked red and vulnerable when it parted, like a four o'clock opening to the evening's coolness.

Then she dropped her eyes and tilted her head down.

"A movie sounds fine. I have to change, though. Can you wait for me out here a few minutes?" she said.

RITA SUMMERS SAT at a table by the window in the restaurant her father owned above the river. This was one of four that he owned in Texas and New Mexico, and she liked to come here sometimes by herself and have a drink in the lounge and watch the boats on the river and think about her day and the men, boys, really, who moved in and out of it without consequence and the protean nature of her relationships that in her mind's eye always ended in a blank place in her future.

There had been a time when she had believed the future was built incrementally, with absolute guarantees of success provided to those who did what was expected of them. You graduated from high school, with all the attendant ceremony, as though it actually marked an achievement, then enrolled at the university in Austin and lived in a sorority house and dated the right boys and kept the right attitudes and learned whom to avoid and whom to cultivate, and one day your father gave you away at your wedding and the pride and love you saw in his eyes confirmed that all the goodness the world could offer had indeed become yours.

But she didn't finish her second year at the university. Her professors were boring, the subject matter stupid, the fraternity boys she dated inane and immature. She began seeing an air force officer who came from old Boston money, even though she knew he had a wife, a Berkeley graduate, in Vermont. They began meeting weekends at the Ritz Carlton in Houston and the Four Seasons in Dallas. The hardness of his body inside her, the tendons in his back tightening under her fingers, filled her with a sense of excitement and power she had never experienced before. Her skin seemed to glow with it when she showered afterwards, and the glow and erotic confidence only intensified when she refused to answer her sorority sisters' questions about the affair she was obviously having.

Sometimes she wondered about the wife, the Berkeley graduate in Vermont. Then she would toss her head, as though dealing with a problem of conscience, but in reality she was secretly happy, in a way that almost disturbed her, at the sexual power she could exert over other people's lives.

But one month she missed her period. She told him this over Sunday breakfast in the hotel. He stopped returning her calls.

The following month, when her menstrual cycle resumed, she sat down at her desk in the sorority house and, using stationery from the Ritz Carlton Hotel, wrote a letter to her lover's commanding officer, detailing the affair, and making particular mention of the lover's statements about his contempt for his wife in Vermont, to whom he referred as "Ho Chi Minh's answer to Minnie Mouse." She mailed the letter to the air base and copies to the wife and to the wife's father, who was the mayor of the village in which they lived.

Rita drank from her gin fizz and was amused at the way her fingerprints stenciled themselves in the moisture on the glass. The gin was cold and warm inside her at the same time, just as the immediate environment around her was. The air-conditioning was set so low her breath fogged against the window, but, outside, the twilight was green, streaked with rain, a palm tree rattling in a balmy breeze. She drank again from the gin and bit down on the candied cherry in the ice, and thought how she was both inside a hermetically sealed air-conditioned world owned by her father and yet part of the greater world, although safe from its elements. In moments like these, in a setting like this, she felt the same sense of control she had enjoyed when she lay down on the bed in the Ritz Carlton and looked at the undisguised hunger in the air force officer's face.

But it was not his rejection of her that bothered her now. It was Jeff Deitrich. And Jeff Deitrich and Jeff Deitrich and Jeff Deitrich, and the fact that two men in a row had used and discarded her and the second one had rubbed food in her nose and hair and eyes while other people watched.

She drank the rest of her gin fizz and ordered another, her jawbone flexing like a tiny spur under the skin.

She heard the car before she saw it, the twin exhausts roaring off the asphalt, the transmission winding into a scream. Then it burst around a line of cars, across the center stripe, a customized Mercury she had seen before, coming hard out of the north, its maroon hood overpainted with a net of blue and red flame, a sheriff's cruiser right on its rear bumper.

A second cruiser came out of the south and slid sideways to a stop on the asphalt, sealing off the two-lane and blocking the Mercury's escape.

The driver of the Mercury shifted down, double-clutching, and turned abruptly into the restaurant's parking lot, flooring the accelerator again. But he spun out of control into a muddy field that sloped down toward the bluffs over the river, showering brown water across his windows, the wheels whining in gumbo up to the axle, mud and grass geysering off the back tires.

Then the engine killed and steam rose off the hood in the rain. The driver, who was shirtless, leaned his head on his folded arms and waited for the two deputies to pull him from his car.

Rita stood on the flagstone back porch of the restaurant, with her drink in her hand, and watched the deputies handcuff the driver of the Mercury and walk him up the slope to the open-air shed where her father's cooks stacked cords of hickory and mesquite wood for the stone barbecue pit inside. The deputies' hair and uniforms were soaked. The deputies tried to dry themselves under the shed, then gave it up and cuffed their prisoner to an iron U-bolt embedded in the side of a chopping block that was chained to the cement pad.

The deputies took off their hats when they addressed her.

"You mind if we clean up inside, Ms. Summers?" one said.

But she knew that was a secondary reason for going inside. They ate free whenever they stopped at the restaurant.

"What did he do?" she asked.

"Oh, he's just a bad Mexican kid wants to give the

Deitrich boy some trouble. Plus he's got a half dozen moving violations against him in San Antone," the deputy said.

Inside, the deputies gave their food order to a waiter and went into the men's room. Rita covered her head with a newspaper and walked down to the shed. Someone turned on the flood lamps in the oak trees, and the mist looked like iridescent smoke blowing out of the leaves.

She leaned against the cedar post at the corner of the shed and drank from her gin glass.

"What's your name?" she said.

"Ronnie," the man cuffed by one wrist said. "You work here?"

"If I want to. My father owns it."

"Impressive," he replied.

So this was the famous Ronnie Cross, she thought. He sat on the cement pad, barefoot, one knee drawn up before him. He had wide shoulders and big arms, Indian-black hair cut short, lips a little like a classical Greek's, and muscle tone and skin that made her think of smooth, tea-stained stone.

"What will they do to you?" she asked.

"Take me back to San Antone on a couple of bench warrants."

His dark eyes never blinked. They were lidless and devoid of any emotion that she could see. But it was his mouth that bothered her. It stayed slightly parted, as though he looked upon the world as a giant, self-serving deception that only a fool would respect.

"You think you're big stuff, don't you?" she said.

"I'm chained up here. I might get county time. These guys will burn me with the bondsman so I got to wait in the bag for my court date. You're drinking gin or vodka with cherries in it. Maybe your shit don't flush, but I ain't big stuff."

"You want a cigarette?"

"I don't smoke no more."

"Anymore."

"What?"

"'Anymore' is the correct usage. You're a lot smarter than you pretend. You're just up here to say nighty-night to Jeff Deitrich?"

He stuck his little finger in his ear and let water drain from it.

"You want to do me a favor?" he said. "I put my car keys under the dash. Keep them for a guy I'm gonna send. Otherwise, some local white bread will chop up my car or these two county fucks will have it towed in."

"I heard you were a piece of work," she said.

"My friend's a wetbrain. But if you'll keep the keys, he'll find you."

"Why trust your car to a wetbrain?"

"In case nobody told you, it's open season around here on Purple Hearts."

"I'll think about holding your keys," she said.

She balanced her glass on a pile of sawed mesquite wood and walked into the shadows, out of the light that shone from the oak trees. She found the ax leaning handle-up against the corner post. The flat sides of the blade were streaked with wisps of wood and dried sap, but the edge had been filed and honed the color of buffed pewter.

She lifted it with both hands and walked back into the electric light. Her shadow fell across Ronnie Cross's upturned face.

"What's the worst thing that ever happened to you?" she asked.

"Dealing with people who are full of shit."

She smiled at the corner of her mouth.

"You ever have a fling with white bread?" she said.

"I'm a one-woman man. Her name's Esmeralda."

"Put out your right hand and close your eyes."

He studied her face, his joyless, dark eyes seeming to reach inside her thoughts. Then his gaze dropped to her mouth, his lips parting indolently. She felt a flush of color spread in her throat, a tingle in her thighs. Her eyes brightened with anger and her palms closed on the ax handle.

"Put your wrist on the stump," she said.

He paused momentarily, then lifted his cuffed right hand so that the left manacle came tight and clinked inside the U-bolt embedded in the chopping block. He spread his fingers flatly on the wood, his eyes never leaving hers. The veins in his wrist looked like purple soda straws.

She raised the ax above her right shoulder, her hands gripped uncertainly midway up the handle, and swung the blade down toward his face.

She felt the filed edge bite into metal and sink into wood.

In seconds he was on his feet, the severed manacle glinting like a bracelet on his right wrist. He paused just beyond the roof of the shed, his face half covered with shadow.

"For white bread, you're a class act," he said.

Then he was running barefoot down the slope in the rain. The iridescent light radiating from the trees glistened on his body. She watched him sprint down the riverbank, gaining speed, and dive like a giant steel-skinned fish into the middle of a rain ring.

30

RONNIE CRUISE CALLED ME AT MY OFFICE THE day after Rita Summers cut his handcuffs.

"I want you to know what can happen when you dime a guy, Mr. Holland," he said. "The two county fucks that nailed me? One of them popped a black guy on a back road and told people he tried to escape."

"I told Marvin Pomroy you might try to take down a couple of Jeff's friends. I'm sorry he sicced those guys on you," I replied.

"What'd you think was gonna happen? . . . Where's Lucas and Essie?"

"Why do you want to know?"

"A friend picked up Cholo's Mercury to give it to Essie. But I drove by their place and they ain't there and neither is the Merc."

"You're in town?" I said.

"Don't worry about where I am." He paused, the surfaces of the receiver squeaking in his grip. "They're at your house, ain't they?"

"Don't bring Cholo's car here."

"That's what you're not hearing. The guy driving Cholo's car is a friend, but he's got yesterday's ice cream for brains. You hearing me on this, Mr. Holland? You fucked it up."

"Meet me at my house," I said.

But he had already hung up the phone.

WHY HAD I ASKED him to meet me at my house? To tell him what? I wasn't sure myself.

That afternoon I began building the trellised, crossbeam entrance to the driveway that my father had wanted to build before he died at Matagorda Bay. The western sky was purple and red, the hills a deeper green from last night's rains, and pools of gray water stood in the driveway gravel. I twisted the posthole digger into the lawn and piled the dirt on the grass, all the time trying to focus on a troublesome thought that hung on the edge of my mind, one that had to do with human predictability.

That's why I had wanted to talk with Ronnie Cruise. He didn't buy easily into illusion and certainly not the subterfuge of his enemies.

L.Q. Navarro stood in shadows, his ash-gray hat low on his forehead, a gold toothpick in his mouth.

"It's that spoiled puke Jeff Deitrich that's bothering you. His threats don't add up. He don't know no bikers. Not real ones," L.Q. said.

"He's got the stash they took off the Jamaicans. He'll use it to hire pros. The Deitrichs cover their

ass. *They don't leave vendettas to amateurs, L.Q.,"* I replied.

"I think you got it ciphered, bud. The question is who's the shitbag he's hiring."

"The mercenary, Fletcher Grinnel?"

"Grinnel works for the old man. Wire up a shotgun out at your boy's place. See whose parts you pick up out of the yard."

L.Q. was grinning when he said it and expected no response.

But neither did he hide what he really wanted from me. He removed his custom-made, double-action revolver from his holster and spun it in his hand, toward him, then in the opposite direction, the yellow ivory handles slapping into the heel of his palm.

"Your great-grandpa Sam could hang from the pommel at a full gallop and shoot from under the horse's neck like an Indian," L.Q. said. *"You're as good a shot as he was. Why waste talent?"*

I dropped two shaved fifteen-foot posts into the holes I had dug, then shoveled a wheelbarrow-load of gravel around the bottoms for support, tamped down the gravel with a heavy iron bar, and added more. I was sweating and breathing hard, my face perspiring in the wind. When I turned around and looked into the shade of the myrtle hedge, L.Q. was gone.

● ● ●

THE PHONE RANG in my library late that night.

"You mind if we fish on the back of your property in the morning?" Wilbur said.

"Help yourself," I said.

"Tomorrow, if you got a minute, Kippy Jo wants to tell you something. I do, too."

After I ate breakfast the next morning I drove the Avalon through the field behind the barn, the grass whispering under the bumper, around the far corner of the tank, and down to the bluffs. The sun was just above the horizon, and the wind was still cool, and leaves from the grove of trees up on the knoll were blowing out on the water. Wilbur and Kippy Jo were down on the bank, fishing in the eddies behind a bleached, worm-carved cottonwood whose root system was impacted with rocks and clay. A knife-shaved willow branch humped with bream and catfish lay in the shallows.

"Tell him what you seen, Kippy Jo," Wilbur said.

She sat in a folding canvas chair and rested her rod across a bait bucket. She wore a pair of blue jeans and a white T-shirt with blue trim on the neck and sleeves. In the softness of the sunrise her hair had a blue-black shine in it and was curved around her throat.

"There won't be an oil well where Wilbur wants to drill. Just a windmill," she said.

"She says I ain't gonna find no oil. Ain't that a pistol? Course, that means Earl Deitrich ain't gonna get none, either," Wilbur said.

"This is what you wanted to tell me?" I said.

Kippy Jo wet her lips. Her eyes followed my voice and fixed on my face. "I've had a horrible vision in my sleep. Several people stand at the entrance to Hell. Or at least one man in the group thinks he sees them there. It's like I'm inside this man's thoughts and I see the entrance to Hell through his eyes. Then there's a gunshot," she said.

"I don't take your gift lightly. But if I was y'all, I wouldn't think a whole lot on what tomorrow holds. The sun is going to come up whether we're here for it or not," I said.

"Yeah, that kind of talk gives me the cold sweats, Kippy Jo," Wilbur said. He cast his bobber out into the current again and picked up a lunch bucket and offered it to me. "Fried cottontail and Kippy Jo's buttermilk biscuits, son. There ain't no better eating."

"I believe it," I said, and then said goodbye to his wife and walked back up to my automobile.

Wilbur caught up with me just as I opened the car door. He wore khakis smeared with fish blood and a black T-shirt with the sleeves rolled up over the tops of his arms. A self-deprecating smile hung on the edge of his mouth.

"I been studying all this time about making money, but the truth is Kippy Jo don't care if I got it or not," he said. "It takes some kind of fool to be so long in figuring out what counts, don't it?"

"I think you're ahead of the game, Wilbur," I replied.

• • •

I DROVE BACK up to the house, brushed out Beau in the lot, watered the flowers in the beds, and went inside to shower and change before going to the office.

Lucas and Esmeralda were eating at the kitchen table. Esmeralda wore a Mexican peasant blouse and a red hibiscus in her hair, almost as though she were deliberately dressing like a Hispanic.

"Running late, aren't you, bud?" I said.

"Our well's a duster. The bossman shut it down yesterday," Lucas said.

"Y'all doin' all right?" I said.

"Fine. I love your place. It's real nice of you to let us stay here," Esmeralda said.

"It's my pleasure," I said.

"We're going down to Temple Carrol's. Her daddy's got an old Gibson she wants me to string. Oh, I forgot to tell you. She called and said she's got to go to Bonham till tomorrow night. Something about taking a deposition for another lawyer," Lucas said.

I nodded, then felt a strange and unfamiliar sense of loneliness at the thought of Temple's being gone.

"Y'all have a good one," I said. When I left the house for the office Esmeralda seemed lost in thought, like a person who has arrived at a destination she never planned.

• • •

LATER, ON THE WAY HOME for lunch, I stopped at the convenience store down the road for gas. While I was paying inside, I noticed a man with a florid, narrow face at the cafe counter. His eyes were a washed-out blue, his hair like a well-trimmed piece of orange rug glued to his scalp. A puckered burn scar was webbed across the right side of his neck. He drank coffee and smoked a cigarette and glanced at his watch.

I stared at him, remembering my last conversation with Ronnie Cruise.

I took my change from the cashier and walked to the counter and sat down next to the man with orange hair.

"You're Charley Quail," I said.

He took his cigarette from his mouth and looked through the smoke at me. "You know me?" he said.

"You used to drive stock cars at the old track out by the drive-in movie. You raced at Daytona," I replied.

"That's me."

"It's an honor to meet you," I said.

His hand was weightless in my grip. I remembered an article from the Austin newspaper, two or three years back, about Charley Quail's long travail with alcoholism, the jails and detox centers, a greasepit fire that turned his body into a candle. He looked at his watch, then compared the time with the clock on the wall and looked over his shoulder at the road.

"You waiting on the bus?" I asked.

"It's supposed to be here at 12:14. I don't know if my watch is wrong, or the one up on the wall, or if both of them is."

"Where you headed?"

"San Antone."

"You know a Mexican kid named Ronnie Cruise? Some people call him Ronnie Cross," I said.

"I just delivered a car for him. I had to look all over the cottonpickin' county for the right house, too."

"Where did you leave it, Charley?"

"None of your goddamn business." He tilted his chin up to show his defiance.

"Sorry. I didn't mean to offend you," I said, getting up from the counter stool. "Is Ronnie a pretty good friend of yours?"

"He was my mechanic. He pulled me out of a fire. You one of them people been giving that boy trouble?" he said.

When I got to my house ten minutes later, expecting to see Cholo's car, the driveway was empty. I looked inside the barn, then behind it, chickens scurrying and cackling in front of me. But there was no sign of the '49 Mercury. The windmill swung suddenly in the breeze, the blades clattering to life, and a gush of water spurted out of the well pipe into Beau's tank.

31

THE NEXT AFTERNOON PETE AND I LOADED Beau in his trailer and hooked the trailer onto my truck, and went to look for arrowheads in the ravine where Skyler Doolittle and Jessie Stump had once hidden in a cave.

The sun was still high in the sky and the cliffs were yellow with sunshine, the air heavy with the smell of the pines that dotted the slopes. I shoveled silt from the edge of the creekbed onto a portable seine with an army-surplus E-tool while Pete picked flint chippings and small pieces of pottery off the screen.

"I heard a schoolteacher in the barbershop say we ain't supposed to do this," Pete said.

"This stuff is washed down from a workmound or a tepee ring. It doesn't hurt anything to surface-hunt," I replied.

"Is digging with a shovel surface-hunting?"

"Matter of definition," I said.

"How you know there wasn't a tepee ring right here?" he asked.

"Would you build your house where a creek could flow through it?" I said. "Say, look at that pair of hawks up in the redbuds."

When he turned his head and stared up the slope

into the trees, I took a flat, fan-shaped piece of yellow chert with a sharply beveled edge from my pocket and tossed it onto the screen.

"I don't see no hawk," he said. Then his eyes dropped to the screen. "That's a hide scraper. It's worked all along the edge. A book at the library shows one just like this."

"It looks like you got a museum piece there, bud."

He rubbed the chert clean with his thumbs, then dipped it in the creek and dried it on his blue jeans.

"It's great to have this place to ourselves again, ain't it?" he said.

"Yeah, it is. You think you can handle one of those buffalo steaks and a blueberry milkshake?" I said.

WE DROVE THROUGH the dusk toward the cafe where we ate breakfast each Sunday after Mass. Fireflies were lighting in the trees along the road, and there was a cool smell in the air, like autumnal gas, even though it was only late summer.

A restless, undefined thought kept turning in my mind, but I did not know what it was, in the same vague way I'd been bothered by the inconsistencies in Jeff Deitrich's threat against Esmeralda and Lucas. The road was uneven, and Pete's head bounced up and down as he looked out over the bottom of the window at the landscape.

"Are you gonna ask Temple to eat with us?" Pete said.

"I don't know if she's back from Bonham yet, Pete."

"I seen her car go in her driveway this afternoon."

"Are you sure?"

"I reckon I know her car. Was she supposed to call you or something?"

"She said if she got back early enough, she might join us out at the creek. Maybe she's a little tired."

"I hope I ain't said the wrong thing again."

"You didn't."

He was quiet a long time.

"What was that gangbanger's car doing in her backyard?" he asked.

I pulled the truck onto the shoulder of the road. A semitrailer with its lights on went past me.

"Which gangbanger's car?" I said.

"That purple Mercury. The one owned by that guy Cholo," he said, his eyes threading with anxiety as he looked at the expression on my face.

I DROPPED PETE OFF at his house and headed up the dirt street, with Beau's trailer bouncing behind me.

Why hadn't I put it together? I asked myself. Ronnie Cruise's wetbrain friend, Charley Quail, had taken Cholo's car to Lucas's rented house in the western part of the county. When he discovered that Lucas and Esmeralda weren't living there, he had probably been told by someone to go to either my house or Lucas's stepfather's. He must have been driving down my road and seen Esmeralda leaving Temple's house after she had gone there with Lucas to string the Gibson guitar for Temple's father.

Charley Quail had assumed Temple's house was mine. He parked the Mercury there and walked down to the convenience store to catch the bus back to San Antonio, thinking he had done a fine turn for Ronnie Cruise.

I went through the stop sign at the end of Pete's street, crossed a wood bridge over a drainage ditch littered with trash and studded with wild pecan trees, and turned out onto the surfaced road that led by my house. The moon was rising now and the sun was only a dirty red smudge inside a bank of purple rain clouds in the west. Up ahead, I saw a plumbing truck parked on Temple's swale. I turned into the driveway and cut the engine. The lawn sprinkler was on and strings of water twirled in the glow of the bug lamp and clicked across the front steps and the hydrangeas in the flower beds. Behind me, I heard Beau nicker and his hooves scrape on the wood floor of his trailer.

The television was on in the living room, but the curtains were drawn. I walked up on the porch and tapped with one knuckle on the screen door. The air-conditioning unit in the window was roaring loudly, and I knocked again, this time harder.

"Temple?" I said.

There was no response.

"Temple? It's Billy Bob," I said, then walked around the side of the house and up the drive.

Temple's car was parked by the shed where her heavy bag was hung, and between the shed and her neighbor's cornfield I could see the dull maroon shape of Cholo's Mercury. The pecan tree above the shed filled with wind, and the heavy bag twisted slightly on its chain, its leathery surfaces glistening in the moonlight.

I leaned over and picked up one of Temple's speedbag gloves out of the dust. A smear of blood flecked with dirt had dried on the flat area that covered the knuckles.

I dropped the glove and walked up on the back screen porch and turned the knob on the door. The door was both key-locked and dead-bolted.

Then I heard voices from the cellar stairway, those of two men who were coming back up to the first floor. I stepped away from the back door and pressed close in to the wall. My hand ached for L.Q. Navarro's revolver.

"We got the wrong place, Johnny. It happens. Write it off."

"I told you, the bitch knows me. So we got to wipe the whole slate. We get those kids down here, then we go home."

"I'm the one she busted in the nose. I say we boogie."

"I'm gonna do the broad. You want, you can have

seconds. But this is her last night on earth. Now give it a rest and fix some sandwiches."

"I'm getting thin. I need something."

"Check in her medicine cabinet. Maybe she's got some diet pills."

"You said it'd be clean, in and out. Just straightening out some punks, you said. She's a cop. We're gonna do her old man, too, a guy in a wheelchair? You know what'll happen if they get their hands on us?"

"Shut up."

The kitchen window was open and I could hear them pulling open drawers, rattling silverware, cracking the cap on a bottle of beer.

Get to a phone, I thought.

No, she could be dead before I got back.

I stepped off the porch, easing the screen shut behind me, and went through the shadows of the pecan tree into her father's old welding shed. On top of a workbench was a thick-handled, grease-stained ball peen hammer, with a head the size of a half-brick.

I went back down the driveway, crouching under the windows, and pulled open the storm doors on the cellar's entrance. The steps were cement and caked with a film of dried mud and blackened leaves. Through a broken pane in the main door I could see a lightbulb burning on the far side of a furnace and the silhouette of a figure whose mouth was taped and whose wrists were tied around a thick drainpipe that ran the length of the ceiling.

I stared impotently through the vectored glass at Temple's back, the exposed baby fat on her hips, the glow of her chestnut hair against the dinginess of the cellar. Only the balls of her bare feet touched the floor, so that her arms were pulled tight in the sockets and her shoulders were squeezed into her neck.

I opened my pocketknife and wedged it into the doorjamb, under the lock's tongue, and began to prise it back into the spring.

A shadow fell across the cellar's inside stairs, then Johnny Krause walked down the steps into the light, his brilliantined hair pulled behind his head in a matador's knot, a five-day line of blond whiskers along his jawbones. He drank from a long-necked bottle of beer and pressed the coldness of the bottle against the side of his face. He wore a short-sleeve Texas A&M workout shirt that molded against the contours of his torso.

"I'm not gonna let them two guys upstairs touch you. But you and me got a date," he said.

Two? Did he say two?

Johnny Krause set the beer bottle down on a chair and grinned and slipped his comb out of his back pocket. He placed the teeth of the comb under Temple's throat and drew them up to her chin. Then he touched her hair with his fingers and leaned close to her and kissed the corner of one eye.

His back was to me now, and I could see a small automatic, probably a .25, stuck down in his belt.

"You want the tape off? Just blink your eyes," he said. "No? I'd like to kiss you on the mouth, hon. Get you off your feet. Come on, think about it."

He placed his hands on his hips.

"This is gonna be quite a rodeo," he said.

"Johnny! Tillman's got the kids on the phone! Get the fuck up here!" a third man hissed down the staircase.

Johnny Krause mounted the steps three at a time. I prised the tongue of the lock back against the spring and scraped the door back on the cement and stepped inside the cellar.

Temple twisted her head and stared at me. Upstairs I could hear Krause talking into a phone.

"That's right. Captain McDonough's the name . . . No, Ms. Carrol will probably be all right, but somebody has to watch her father. Bring Ms. Ramirez with you. I need to ask her about this car of hers that's out back," he said.

I set down the ball peen hammer on the chair and began sawing through the electrical cord that was wrapped around Temple's wrists. Above me the heavy shoes of the intruders creaked on the planks in the floor. Temple's eyes were inches from mine, bulging in the sockets, charged with alarm, then I realized she was not looking at me but at something over my shoulder.

A behemoth of a man in dark blue overalls stood

at the head of the landing, his back to us, his huge buttocks stretching across the doorway. Then he turned to go down the stairs.

I picked up the hammer from the chair and stepped behind the furnace. The insulation on the cord around Temple's wrists was frayed, the bronze wire exposed.

Each plank in the stairs groaned under the massive weight of the man in overalls. His head was auraed with a wild mane of black hair, his neck festooned with gold chains. He was eating a cheese sandwich and his thick fingers sank deeply into the bread and left black marks on it.

He stood in front of Temple, chewing, his eyes roving over her face.

"Hi, girlie," he said.

I swung the hammer into the back of his head and saw the skin split like gray leather inside his hair. He doubled over, his sandwich bread clotting in his throat. An unformed cry hung on his lips, as though he had stepped on a sharp stone.

Then he straightened up and looked at me, his face creasing with both bewilderment and rage. A bright stream of blood dripped from his hair.

I hit him again, this time above the ear. His eyes rolled up in his head, and he struck the cement with his knees, falling sideways into the shadows. My hands were shaking when I sawed through the elec- trical cord on Temple's wrists.

She pulled the tape off her mouth, her breath trembling as she drew air into her lungs. I put my arm in hers and pointed toward the cellar door.

We walked out of the cone of electric light by the furnace, back into the shadows, the door yawning open in front of us, the freedom of the night only seconds away.

Then I heard someone in the driveway, his feet pausing, the gravel scraping under the soles of his shoes. A flashlight beam bounced inside the storm doors I had opened, welling out in a pool on the cement steps that were stenciled with my boot prints.

The man in the driveway eased a foot down on the first step, then removed it and tried to angle the light into the cellar without getting any closer to the door.

I turned the unconscious man on his back and felt his pockets, then inside the bib of his overalls. My hand closed around the butt of a Ruger .22 automatic.

I moved quickly past Temple through the side door and was suddenly standing below the man with the flashlight. Hanging from his right hand was a chrome-plated .45 automatic. His mouth dropped open.

I aimed the Ruger at his throat and clicked off the safety, although I had no way of knowing if a round was in the chamber.

"Throw it away, bud! Do it now!" I said.

He froze, his hand squeezed tightly on the grips of the .45. He had a small, round, tight face and enormous blue tattoos that covered the insides of his arms.

"You can live! Throw it away and run!" I said.

I saw the moment gather in his eyes, the big question that he had always asked himself—Was he really a coward, as he had always secretly feared? Was he willing to risk it all and glide out over the Abyss, with nothing to sustain him except the residue of the last injection he had put in his veins?

He swallowed, the pistol rising upward as though it were a balloon detached from his hand. Then suddenly he gagged in his throat, his face seemed to dissolve, and he flung the .45 into the flower bed and ran toward the road.

I let out my breath and wiped the moisture from my eyes on my shirtsleeve.

Temple came out of the cellar behind me. The inside of the house was quiet, except for the exhaust of the air conditioner and the sounds of the television set. The pecan tree in the backyard puffed with wind, its leaves rising like birds against the moon. I pressed my hand between Temple's shoulder blades and tried to move her toward the road, then felt her stiffen.

"No . . . My father," she said silently with her lips.

But Johnny Krause preempted any more decisions that we may have been forced to make. He came off the back porch, letting the screen slam behind him.

"Where's Tillman at, Skeet?" he said into the darkness.

We stared into each other's face.

He fired with his .25 automatic, the sparks flying into the darkness. The rounds made a dry, popping sound, like Chinese firecrackers. At least two of them hit the windshield of the Avalon and one ricocheted off the curved front of Beau's trailer.

At almost the same time, I raised the Ruger with both hands, my arms stretched out in front of me, and squeezed the trigger. The first round slapped into wood somewhere inside the welding shed, but when I let off the second round I saw his left arm jump as though it had been stung by a wasp.

Then he bolted through the backyard, over a fence and an irrigation ditch, and was running hard through a field toward the river.

"You all right, Temple?" I said.

"My father's tied up in the bedroom. I have to go," she said.

"Are you all right?"

The whites of her eyes were pink with broken veins. Her face contained a level of anger and injury and violation I had never seen in it before, like water-stained paper held against a hot light. She went into the house and did not answer my question.

I cleared the jammed shell from the Ruger and backed Beau out of his trailer and lifted a coil of polyrope off a hook on the wall. I swung up on the saddle and hung the polyrope on the pommel and leaned forward in the stirrups. Beau crossed the yard and irrigation ditch in seconds, then I popped him once in the rump and felt his whole body surge under me.

Beau was beautiful when I let him run. His muscles rippled like water, his stride never faltering. The thudding of his hooves in the field, the rhythmic exhalation of his breath, his absolute confidence in our mutual purpose, were like sympathetic creations of sound and power and movement outside of time. Lightning trembled inside storm clouds that stretched like a black lid on a kettle from one horizon to the other. But electricity or wind or mud and blowing newspaper or desiccated poppy husks rattling in a field never affected Beau, as they did most horses. Instead, he seemed to draw courage from danger, and his loyalty to me never wavered.

Up ahead I could see Johnny Krause running, his face twisted back toward us.

Beau and I went across a ditch and up a slope toward a bend in the river where three cottonwoods grew on the bluff. I widened the loop in the end of the polyrope, doubling back part of the rope in my right hand, and whipped it in a circle over my head.

Johnny Krause turned and fired once with his automatic, but Beau never flinched. I flung the loop at Krause's head and saw it take on his neck and the top of one shoulder. I leaned back in the saddle and wound the rope around the pommel and felt the loop bind around Krause's throat. Then I turned Beau and brought my boot heels into his ribs.

The rope jerked Krause off his feet and dragged him tumbling and strangling across the ground, across rocks, into the side of a tree stump, through a tangle of chicken wire and cedar posts that someone had stacked and partially burned.

I reined up Beau under a cottonwood, freed the rope from the pommel, and tossed the coil over a tree limb and caught the end with my hand. Krause was trying to get to his feet, his fingers wedging under the rope that was now pinched tightly into his throat. I rewrapped the rope on the pommel and kicked Beau in the ribs again and felt Johnny Krause rise from the earth into the air, his half-top boots kicking frantically.

Beau's saddle creaked against the rope's tension as I watched Johnny Krause's face turn gray and then purple while his tongue protruded from his mouth.

Then I saw the lights of a car that had come to rest in a ditch, and the silhouette of a man running toward me.

"What are you doing here, L.Q.?" I asked.

"Somebody better talk sense to you. This might be my way, but it ain't yours," he said.

"He molested Temple. Hanging's not enough."

"Don't give his kind no power. That's the lesson me and you didn't learn down in Coahuila."

Beau tossed his head against the reins and blew air, shifting his hooves and barreling up his ribs like he did when he didn't want to take his saddle.

I released the rope and let it spin loose from the pommel. I heard Johnny Krause thump against the earth, his breath like a stifled scream.

Then I watched Ronnie Cross walk right through

L.Q.'s shape, shattering it like splinters of charcoal-colored glass against the glare of headlights in the background.

"I was with Essie and Lucas at your house when them guys called. We got ahold of some Texas Rangers," he said.

I wiped my hands on my thighs and stared at him silently from the saddle. Then, as though waking from a dream, I looked up at the wind in the cottonwoods and the heat lightning flickering on the leaves, and once again wondered who really lived inside my skin.

THE NEXT MORNING I had my receptionist call Earl Deitrich's house and get the ex-mercenary named Fletcher Grinnel on the phone.

"Last night I hung a piece of shit named Johnny Krause in a tree," I said.

"You're a busy fellow," he replied.

"He just gave you up on the murder of Cholo Ramirez. Check out the statistics on the number of people currently being executed in Texas, Grinnel. You going to ride the gurney for Earl Deitrich?"

"Say again, please?"

32

THREE WEEKS LATER, ON A SATURDAY AFTERNOON, Peggy Jean Deitrich parked her automobile in front of my house and walked across the grass to the driveway, where I was planting climbing roses on the trellises I had nailed up on posts on each side of the drive. I had painted the posts and trellises and the crossbeam white, and the roses were as bright as drops of blood against the paint.

The balled root systems were three feet in diameter and packed in sawdust and black dirt and wrapped with wet burlap. I knelt on the grass and snipped the burlap away and washed the roots loose with a garden hose and lowered them into a freshly dug hole that I had worked with horse manure. I put the garden hose into the hole and watched the water rise in a soapy brown froth to the rim, then I began shoveling compost in on top of it.

"You're right good at that," she said, and sat down on my folding metal chair in the shade.

"What's up, Peggy Jean?"

She wore jeans and shined boots and a plaid snap-button shirt and a thin hand-tooled brown belt with a silver buckle and a silver tip on the tongue. The wind blew the myrtle above her head and made patterns of sunlight and shadow on her skin, and for just a moment I saw us both together again among the oak trees above the riverbank when she allowed me to lose my virginity inside her.

"Jeff's out on bail and still doesn't realize he'll probably go to prison. Earl expects to be indicted for murder momentarily and is usually drunk by noon. He also goes out unwashed and unshaved in public. But maybe you know all that," she said.

"Sorry. I don't have an interest anymore in tracking what they do."

"We're defaulting on the Wyoming land deal. Earl's creditors are calling in all his debts. I think it's what you planned, Billy Bob."

"Earl stepped in his own shit, Peggy Jean."

"I want to hire you as our attorney."

"Nope."

"I can pay. Earl has a half-million-dollar life insurance policy I can borrow on."

I shook my head. "Let me give you some advice instead and it won't cost you a nickel. If you're poor and you commit a crime, the legal system works quickly and leaves you in pieces all over the highway. If you're educated and have money, the process becomes a drawn-out affair, like a terminal cancer patient who can afford various kinds of treatment all over the world. But eventually he ends up at Lourdes.

"That's what will happen to Earl. He'll become more and more desperate, and more and more people will take advantage of his situation. The ducks will nibble him to death and eventually he'll come to Lourdes. If I were his attorney, I'd tell him to negotiate a plea now and try to avoid a capital conviction."

She got up from the chair and gazed at my house, the barn and Beau in the lot and the windmill ginning and the fields that had been harvested and were marbled with shadows and the willows by the tank that were blowing in the wind.

She looked up at the red oak plank I had hung from the crossbeam over the driveway.

"Why did you name your place Heartwood?" she asked.

"It comes from a story my father told me when I was baptized. It has to do with the way certain kinds of trees grow outward from the center."

I sat down in the folding chair and filled a jelly glass with Kool-Aid from a plastic pitcher. My hair was damp with perspiration and in the shade the wind felt cool against my skin.

She stood behind me and her shadow intersected mine on the grass. Then the sun went behind a cloud and our shadows grayed and disappeared. She stroked the hair on the back of my head, upward, as she might a child's.

"Heartwood is a good name. Goodbye, Billy Bob," she said.

Then she was gone. I never saw her again.

• • •

AFTER LABOR DAY the weather turned dry and hot, and there were fires in the hills west of the hardpan, flecks of light you could see at night from the highway, like an indistinct red glimmering inside black glass. I tried not to think about the Deitrichs anymore, and instead to concentrate on my own life and the expectation and promise that each sunrise held for those who accepted the day for the gift it was.

Fletcher Grinnel had given up Earl Deitrich in front of a grand jury and Kippy Jo was off the hook for the shooting of the intruder, Bubba Grimes. She and Wilbur had gone to Wyoming to begin drilling on their property, even though she still maintained that Wilbur would bring in a duster.

Lucas was preparing to return to school at Texas A&M and was talking about Esmeralda joining him there. But Ronnie Cross found excuses to visit my house with regularity and to ask about Esmeralda, and she in turn had a way of dropping by when he was there. In those moments I looked at Lucas with the pang that a parent feels when he knows his child will be hurt and that it's no one's fault and that to try to preempt the rites of passage is an act of contempt for the child's courage.

Temple Carrol and me?

She still said I lived with ghosts.

But even though I told myself each day I was through with the Deitrichs and the avarice and meretriciousness of the world they represented, I knew better. They were too much a part of us, the town, our history, the innocence and goodness we had perhaps created as a wishful reflection of ourselves in the form of Peggy Jean Murphy.

The Deitrichs came back into my life again with a phone call. In a way that would never allow me to extricate myself from them.

A call at midnight from Jessie Stump.

"I THOUGHT YOU'D LEFT the area," I said.

"I been sick," he said.

"Go to a hospital."

"Don't need none. My daddy could heal bleeding and blow the fire out of a burn. He cured warts with molasses and a hairball from a cow's stomach . . . I'm gonna send money to get Skyler's casket moved to a church cemetery."

"I have his personal effects from his rooming house. I'll mail them to any address you want. Why don't you honor his memory and start over again somewhere else?"

"I don't need no personal effects. He give me his watch. The one his ancestor carried at the Alamo. I'm looking at it in the palm of my hand right now."

"It was returned to the Deitrichs."

"Yeah . . ." he began, but did not finish his sentence.

"The Deitrichs gave it to you?" I said.

"I'm fixing to be a rich man, boy. That's all you

need to know. Now, you do what I say about moving that casket."

"You listen to me, Stump. A New Zealander, a man named Fletcher Grinnel, admitted killing Mr. Doolittle. He'll go down for it. So will Earl Deitrich. You stay away from their house."

"You worried about the woman? How long does it take you to figure it out, boy?"

I couldn't sleep the rest of the night.

BUT IN THE MORNING I knew what I had to do. I called Earl Deitrich at his home.

"Jessie Stump's back in the area. I think he aims to splatter your grits," I said.

"What else is new?" Earl said.

"I think someone inside your house is helping him."

"Judas Iscariot is in my midst? You're telling me this because you're a great guy? Okay, great guy, you've done your duty."

"He has possession of Skyler Doolittle's watch. How'd he come by it?"

I could hear him breathing in the silence.

"You're telling me my wife is trying to have me killed? You're a vicious, sick man," he said.

I replaced the receiver gently in the telephone cradle. I couldn't blame him for his feelings.

• • •

I ATE LUNCH with Marvin Pomroy that day at the Mexican grocery across from the courthouse. Marvin listened while I talked, then was quiet a long time. He cleared his throat slightly and drank from his glass of lemonade. His face looked cool and serene and pink in the breeze from the wood-bladed fan overhead.

"Why did you call Deitrich first instead of me?" he asked.

"I gave Peggy Jean a preview of what their lives would be like for the next year. I believe I started her thinking about other options."

He wiped his mouth with his napkin and picked up the check and added up the figures on it.

"You don't have anything to say?" I asked.

"Yeah, maybe Earl Deitrich will finally do something good for a change. Like rid us of Jessie Stump," Marvin replied.

BUT TWO HOURS LATER Marvin called me at the office, as I knew he would.

"Hugo's going to send a couple of deputies back out to the Deitrich place. The next time you orchestrate a train wreck, don't tell me about it," he said, and hung up.

JEFF DEITRICH CRUISED Val's that night in his yellow convertible, alone, the top down. It was a beautiful fall night; the moon was big and yellow over the hills, the air cool, smelling of pine wood smoke and late-blooming flowers. The parking lot was filled, the hand-waxed surfaces of his friends' sports cars and roll-bar Jeeps glowing under the electric lights. He drove up one aisle and down the other, scanning faces and groups of kids who talked with great animation between their parked cars. But no one seemed to look in Jeff's direction, as though he were only a passerby, somehow not a player anymore.

He made a U-turn in the street and came through the main entrance again. Why was it that everyone looked younger? Most of these guys were high schoolers or people whom he had always regarded as barely worth noticing. Where were Chug and Warren and Hammie?

The only empty slot was at the far end of the lot, by a Dumpster that was overflowing in the weeds. He backed his convertible in so he could see everyone who drove by. It was just a matter of time before his old friends would be cruising by, gathering around his car, laughing at all this legal bullshit that a four-eyed fuck named Marvin Pomroy was trying to drop on his head.

Under his seat was a silver cigarette case that contained two tightly twisted joints of Jalisco gage, sprinkled with China White to give it legs.

He cupped his hands around a match and fired one up. He held the smoke down and took the hit deep in his lungs, heard the paper drying and burning crisply toward his lips with each toke, his face warming and growing tight like tallow molding against the bone.

The waitress hooked an aluminum tray on his window. She was cute, in her purple and white rayon uniform, her mouth like a cherry, her bleached hair curled on her shoulders.

"You want to do some Mexican gage?" he asked.

"What's that?" she replied.

"I'll pick you up later. I'm Jeff Deitrich."

"My father takes me home . . . You want to order? I got a pickup getting cold at the window."

She brought him a fish sandwich and an iced mug of beer. Music was pumping out of the speakers on the stanchions that supported the canvas tarps the owner pulled out on guy wires when it rained or during the heat of the day. He walked to the men's room, nodding at kids who should have recognized him but didn't. When he came back out, some kids in a group looked at him quickly, then their eyes slid off his face.

"You got some problem with me?" he said to a thin, crew-cut boy in a red windbreaker and T-shirt who was leaning against a customized van.

"Not me," the boy replied, then grimaced at his girl.

"Sorry, man. I thought you were somebody else," Jeff said, and walked away wondering why he had just lied.

Was he losing it?

He couldn't finish his sandwich. The breeze dropped and a sweet, rotting odor wafted off the

Dumpster and invaded the inside of his head. He put the canvas top up on his convertible and rolled up the windows, then stared through the windshield at a black man in a security guard's uniform locking a grilled door behind the kitchen. The guard twisted a key in the lock mechanism, then rattled the door in the jamb to make sure it was secure.

Jeff swallowed and sweat broke on his forehead and a spasm constricted his stomach, as though someone had raked a nail across the lining.

I'm not going to jail. That's not going to happen. Don't have those kinds of thoughts, he told himself.

He took the roach out of the ashtray and the remaining joint from the cigarette case and rolled down the passenger window and flung them into the darkness.

When he looked back through the windshield he was staring at the side of Ronnie Cross's 1961 T-Bird. Ronnie made the turn at the end of the lot, then pulled into a slot that had just emptied. For no reason that he could explain, Jeff felt a sense of familiarity and friendship with Ronnie he'd never experienced before.

He got out of the convertible and walked to Ronnie's window and leaned his hands on the roof. Ronnie glanced up at him only a second, then rested his palms on the bottom of the steering wheel and looked straight ahead.

"Ronnie, I got no hard feelings. This guy Johnny

Krause is full of shit. I wouldn't hurt Essie for the world," Jeff said.

Ronnie picked up a toothpick off the dashboard and slipped it into his mouth.

"Yeah, uh, look, Jeff, me and Essie and Lucas are gonna meet for some dinner. Maybe you ought to rejoin your party," Ronnie said.

"Y'all are tight, huh?"

"You know how it is." Ronnie played with the toothpick and didn't look up at Jeff's face.

Jeff felt a moist click in his throat, then he heard a voice coming out of his mouth that didn't sound like his own, a voice veined with weakness and fear.

"What's it like inside? I mean, how bad does it get?" he said.

"Inside what?"

"Prison. You hear a lot of stories."

"About guys getting their cherry busted in the shower?" Ronnie said.

"Yeah, I guess."

"I don't know. I was in Juvie once. I never did time. I ain't a criminal."

Ronnie lifted his eyes up into Jeff's face.

When Jeff walked back to his car, he felt belittled, his face tingling. But he couldn't say why.

An hour later he drove across the cattleguard and up the road to his house. The air was dry and cool and he could smell smoke from a fire in the woods somewhere beyond the house. Yes, he could even see a red glow in the sky and ashes rising against the moon, perhaps from the ravine that angled its way down to the river. But surely firefighters were on it and it offered no threat to his home.

He parked the car by the side of his house and decided to stay the night in Fletcher's empty cottage. His stepmother would be asleep by now, in her own bedroom, with the door locked, while Jeff's father walked aimlessly around the darkened first floor, his teeth unbrushed, trailing an odor like a gymnasium, or made long-distance calls to people who hung up on him.

Jeff picked up a half-filled bottle of Cold Duck off a table by the swimming pool and drank from it as he walked to the cottage. Tiny pieces of ash drifted onto the pool's surface and floated like scorched moths above the underwater lights.

From the edge of the woods far above the house, Jessie Stump watched him through a pair of binoculars.

Earl did push-ups in the dark on the floor of his library. One, two, one, two, one two, his arms pumping with blood and testosterone, the tendons in his neck and back and buttocks netting together with a power that he'd never thought he possessed. The moon was full, a marbled yellow above the tree line on the ridge, and it shone through the French doors and lighted the library walls and rows of books with a dull glow like the color of old elephant ivory.

He stripped naked in the bathroom and shaved in

front of the full-length mirror, showered and washed his hair and brushed his teeth and gargled with mouthwash and changed into a pair of loafers and khaki slacks and a thin flannel shirt. While he combed his hair in the mirror he turned his chin from side to side and was intrigued by the way the light reflected on the freshly shaved surfaces of his skin.

She locked bedroom doors, did she? The king of the manor in medieval times would have just walled her up. But he was determined not to be vindictive. Why blame her for her feelings? No matter what they claimed, women were sexually aroused by rich men, and he was no longer rich. But he hadn't believed she would set him up to be killed by Jessie Stump.

Earlier this evening he had found the security system on the back doors shut down. It wasn't accidental. Someone had punched in the coded numbers with forethought and deliberation.

Actually, her level of iniquity intrigued him, caused a vague arousal in his loins in a way that he did not quite understand. No, it was not her wickedness itself, but instead his ability to perceive it, see through and transcend it, to match and overwhelm it in response and deed, that titillated him.

So a pathetic piece of human flotsam like Jessie Stump was the best assassin she could hire? What a joke. But in reality it made sense. She had no money. A fool like Stump could be micromanaged with the gift of an antique watch, then disposed of later.

Maybe he should give Peggy Jean a little more credit.

He walked out the front door and gazed at the constellations in the sky, the glow of a fire beyond the ridge, the long, green roll of the valley in front of his house. He could probably remain in default on his mortgages for another seven or eight months, then this would all belong to someone else. That thought made the veins tighten like a metal band along the side of his head.

He wagged a flashlight back and forth in the darkness and waited for the two deputies to walk from their posts out on the grounds onto the layers of black flagstone that formed the entrance to his house.

"Y'all come in and have some ice cream and strawberries with me. I won't be needing y'all anymore tonight," he said.

"I shined a spotlight up in them trees, high up on the ridge. I swear I seen some field glasses glint up there," one deputy said.

"It's probably a state forester. I think dry lightning started a fire in the ravine," Earl said.

The two deputies looked at each other.

"We didn't hear nothing about a fire in the ravine," one said.

"There's surely one burning. You don't smell it?" Earl said.

"A fire was burning six or seven miles up the river. A lot of ash was blowing around in the wind, but there ain't no fire in the ravine, sir," the same deputy said.

"I'm sure someone's taking care of it," Earl said. He took them inside and fed them at the kitchen table, looking at his watch, feigning interest in the banality of their conversation. After they left he watched through the glass until their cars crossed the cattleguard and disappeared over a rise down the long two-lane road. He went into the library and removed his Smith & Wesson .38 revolver from his desk drawer, flipped the cylinder out of the frame, then snapped it into place again.

He walked into the kitchen, opened the circuit breaker box, and shut down all the floodlights on the grounds and the lights on the patio and terrace and in the swimming pool. The moon was veiled now and the hills that formed a cup around the back of his house rose up blackly into the stars. He threw open the French doors on the patio and smelled the gaslike odor of chrysanthemums and smoke on the wind.

He situated a heavy oak chair where the dining room hallway met the kitchen so he could look out onto the side terrace as well as the swimming pool, then he sat down and rested the Smith & Wesson on his thigh. Bankers and creditors could take his home and his cars, his thoroughbreds and his oil properties, even his fly-fishing equipment and rare gun and coin collections, but Earl Deitrich would leave behind a punctuation mark none of them would ever forget. Neither would his wife.

He had never killed anybody. He had been stationed in Germany and had missed Vietnam; as a consequence he had always competed with the soldier whom Peggy Murphy had truly loved and who had died at Chu Lai. She denied this, but he knew better. She closed her eyes throughout their lovemaking, her lips always averted, whatever degree of sexual pleasure he gave her always muted behind her skin.

He bit down on his molars, his hand clenching and unclenching on the pistol's checkered grips. He was going to love blowing Jessie Stump's liver out.

Then he heard the lock turn in her bedroom door. She stood at the head of the curved staircase, in a white nightgown, her hair brushed out on her shoulders, her bare feet enameled with moonlight.

In his hatred of her he had forgotten how beautiful she could look, even in her most unguarded moments. He started to speak, then he heard the footsteps by the swimming pool. He rose from the chair and looked up the staircase at Peggy Jean and put his finger to his lips, barely able to control the energy and excitement and gloat that surged in his chest.

The moon was behind a black cloud now, but Earl could make out a figure walking across the patio toward the back door. He cocked back the hammer on the Smith & Wesson, wetting his lips, aiming with two hands, trying to steady the trembling sight on the top of the sternum.

He pulled the trigger. It was a perfect shot, right through the throat; he was sure he even heard the hit, a thropping sound like a bullet coring through a watermelon.

Then Earl systematically blew his target apart: a round that hit an elbow, one in the upper thigh, another just above the groin, a final one through the face.

Earl lifted the revolver up at a right angle with both hands, his body canted sideways, his heart thundering with adrenaline. He had never experienced an exhilaration like this one, and he knew for the first time how men could come to love war.

Now Peggy Jean was standing behind him, her face small with fear, her eyes staring into the darkness. Her breath was sour and he stepped back from it.

"Billy Bob Holland ratted you out, Peggy Jean," Earl said.

"What?" she said.

"I killed Stump. I blew him apart. By God, I did it," he said.

He went to the circuit breaker box and began shoving banks of switches with the heel of his hand. When he walked back to the open door, his wife was out on the patio, her skin white in the flood lamps, her fingers pressed against her mouth.

Jeff Deitrich floated facedown in the pool, the blood from his wounds trailing like clouds of red smoke in the lighted water.

33

WE WOULD NEVER BE SURE ABOUT THE EVENTS that occurred next, not unless we accepted the explanation given to us later by Kippy Jo Pickett.

Earl wandered into his front yard, the Smith & Wesson hanging from his hand. The wind was blowing hard now, but his skin felt numb, dead to the touch, as though it were freezer-burned. To his left he saw the fire in the ravine glowing against the clouds and sparks fanning across the sky, drifting onto his roof.

There was no sound anywhere. He opened and closed his mouth to clear his ears and tried to rethink what he had just done. But it was like waking from an alcoholic blackout. The images and voices had become shards of glass that he couldn't reassemble in his mind. Could he have killed his own son only moments ago?

The fire had climbed out of the ravine and was burning through the soft pad of dead grass in the woods, crawling up the trunks of trees into the canopy. The sky was red and yellow now, swirling with ash and smoke, and the heat was as bright and hot on his cheek as a candle flame.

Why hadn't Peggy Jean called the county fire department?

He turned and stared at his house. It looked enveloped in heat, shrunken, the symmetrical lines distorted, smoke rising from the eaves. The black-and-white-striped canopy over the side patio burst into flame, snapping dryly in the wind; the flowers in the beds stiffened and their petals fell like confetti into the baked dirt.

Then he saw her at a downstairs window, talking urgently into a phone.

Finally she did something right, he thought.

The fire truck came hard up the road, sooner than he expected, almost out of nowhere.

He probably looked pretty foolish, standing in the front yard, with a revolver in his hand.

Well, to hell with them.

It was a pump truck, the windows filmed with mud, the running boards full of dark, hatted figures who clung to handrails. The driver pulled parallel to the house and left the engine running and got out and walked around the front of the truck and grinned at Earl.

"Cholo?" Earl said.

"The job's got its moments. Hop on. There's a space next to your son."

"Jeff's there?"

Cholo shrugged good-naturedly, but he didn't speak. The other men on the truck were stepping down from the running boards. They wore slouch hats and bleached, nineteenth-century canvas dusters and laced boots and tightly belted, baggy khaki pants, and Earl realized they were not firemen at all but men who had worked in Africa with his great-grandfather and who carried braided leather whips folded around wood handles in their coat pockets.

"You thought you had me on that first take-down scam, remember?" Earl said. *"You handed me a gun with a blank in it."*

"Yeah, man, you surprised us. It took cojones to stick it up to your head and snap it off."

"I still don't rattle, Cholo. Ready for this? Because I don't know if I popped off six rounds or not."

"Do what you gotta do, man."

"Beaners don't take down River Oaks white boys. You're not a bad kid. You're just dumb," Earl said, grinning.

Earl pulled back the hammer and placed the muzzle of the Smith & Wesson against his temple. He looked directly into Cholo's eyes and smiled again, then squeezed the trigger.

There was no report, in fact, no sound at all, not even the metallic snap of the firing pin against a spent cartridge.

Earl felt a wall of heat from his house baking the clothes on his back. Then the hatted men approached him and took him by his arms and led him toward the truck. Through the muddy window in the cab, he thought he saw Jeff's bloodless and terrified face staring back at him from the rear seat, a bullet hole below one eye.

EARLY THE NEXT MORNING Temple Carrol and I followed Marvin Pomroy out to the crime scene. The sky was a cloudless blue, the air crisp, the trees turning color on the hills. The Deitrich home was half in shadow, the immense white walls speckled with frost. The chrysanthemums were brown and gold in the flower beds, and the zebra-striped canopy over the side terrace puffed with wind.

"His wife said he was hollering about a fire truck. With Cholo and Jeff and dead slavers on it. She came outside and he put a big one right through his head," Marvin said.

"Fire truck?" I said.

"He told two of Hugo's deputies the ravine was on fire. There was a fire way on up the river but none around here," Marvin said.

"Where is Peggy Jean?" I asked.

"Sedated at the hospital. Did I tell you we got Stump?" Marvin said.

"No."

"He fell and broke his leg up on the ridge . . . You bothered about something?"

"No, sir," I replied.

"You dimed Peggy Jean with her husband, so you think you share some responsibility for Earl's craziness?" Marvin asked.

"No, I don't think anything, Marvin. I think we're going to breakfast. You want to join us?"

"Today's Pee-Wee football day," he said.

I walked back to my Avalon. Temple was studying the ground on the far side.

"Look at this," she said, and pointed at the imprints of heavy, cleated tires in the grass.

"There were a bunch of emergency vehicles in here," I said.

"Not with this kind of weight. They don't lead back to the road, either. They go up the hill," she said.

"I think the story of the Deitrichs is over, Temple."

"Not for me," she said, and began walking across the lawn and up the hill.

We followed the tracks onto a rough road that wound up to the plateau and meadow above the house. The ground was heavy with dew and the grass was pressed flat and pale in two long stripes that led up a sharp slope to the edge of the ravine where Pete and I hunted for arrowheads.

"I don't believe this," Temple said.

We walked between the imprints to the top of the ravine. At the edge of the cliff the soil was cut all the way to the rock by a vehicle that had rolled out onto the air and had disappeared. Down below, the tops of the pines were deep in shadow, blue-green, the branches symmetrical and unbroken; mist rose like steam off the water and exposed stones in the creekbed.

"I think we're looking down at the entrance to Hell, Temple. I think Cholo and Jeff came back for Earl Deitrich," I said.

Temple chewed the skin on the ball of her thumb.

"I don't want to remember seeing this. I don't want to ever think about this again," she said.

I studied her face, the earnestness and goodness in it, the redness of her mouth, the way her strands of chestnut hair blew on her forehead, and I wanted to hold her against me and for us both to be wrapped inside the wind and the frenzy of the trees whipping against the sky and the whirrings of the earth and the mystical green vortex of creation itself.

I picked up a pinecone and slapped it out over the ravine, like a boy stroking an imaginary baseball.

"Let's go out and watch Marvin's kids play Pee-Wee League today," I said, and rested my arm across her shoulders as we walked back toward the Deitrichs' home.

EPILOGUE

WILBUR PICKETT DIDN'T HAVE TROUBLE FINDING oil up in Wyoming; he just found it too soon. There was no blowout preventer on the wellhead when the drill bit punched into an early pay sand; the premature eruption of gas and oil and salt water ignited at the wellhead, and the pressurized torrent of flame incinerated the derrick like a tower of matchsticks.

Wilbur and his crew barely escaped with their lives.

After the well was capped, Wilbur squatted on his haunches amid the ruins of his derrick and surveyed the cliffs that rose above his and Kippy Jo's land, the green river that meandered through it, the groves of cottonwoods on the banks, the wet sage on the hardpan, the antelope and white-tailed deer down in the arroyos.

That afternoon he and Kippy Jo drove to a bank in Sheridan and took out a building loan and started construction two weeks later on the dude ranch that he would name the Kippy Jo Double Bar.

For electric power he erected two wind turbines where his drilling rig had been. One morning he hooked his thumbs in his back pockets and gazed at the enormous metal blades turning soundlessly in the sunrise.

"This is a fine spot, Kippy Jo, but it ain't diddlysquat on a rock when it comes to serious wind.

Where's the one place on earth it blows from four directions at once? I mean wind that'll pick your cotton, sand the paint off your silo, and move your house to the next county, all free of charge," he said.

Wilbur went in the house and called the Deitrichs' lawyer, Clayton Spangler, who was rumored to own fifty thousand acres of the old XIT Ranch in the Texas Panhandle.

"Mr. Spangler, Kippy Jo and me would like to invite you trout fishing up at our ranch. I'm talking about rainbows fat as a fence post, sir. I flat got to knock 'em back in the water with a boat oar," he said.

The Wilbur T. Pickett Natural Energy Company was on its way.

THE NEXT SPRING, during Easter break, Lucas and Temple and I drove to San Antonio and had supper at an outdoor cafe on the river, not far from the Alamo. The evening sky was turquoise, the air warm and fragrant with the smell of flowers. Lucas didn't talk anymore about Esmeralda. If I mentioned her name, he always smiled and deliberately created a beam in his eyes that was not meant for anyone to read, lest the dues he had paid be taken from him.

The scene along the river was almost an idyllic one. The gondolas were filled with tourists; mariachi musicians in sombreros and dark suits scrolled with white piping played guitars in the cafes; the fronds of banana trees along the water's edge rattled in the breeze. But I couldn't concentrate on the conversation around me. I kept smelling a heavy fragrance of roses. When Temple and Lucas went into a shop to buy cactus candy for her father, I walked over to the Alamo. The facade was lighted with flood lamps and was pink and gray against the darkening sky, and I sat down on a stone bench and twirled my hat on my finger.

I could never look at the chapel and the adjacent barracks without chills going through me. One hundred and eighty-eight souls had held out for thirteen days against as many as six thousand of Santa Anna's troops. They went down to the last man, except for five who were captured and tortured before they were executed. Their bodies were burned by Santa Anna like sacks of garbage.

But even as I dwelled on the deaths of those 188 men and boys, the smell of roses seemed to be all around me. Was I still enamored with the girl who used to be Peggy Jean Murphy?

Maybe. But that wasn't bad. The girl I knew was worth remembering.

Behind me, I heard the throaty rumble of twin Hollywood mufflers off the pavement. I thought I saw a sunburst T-Bird turn up a darkened street toward the freeway, then I heard the driver double-clutching, shifting down, catching a lower gear, one shoulder bent low as he gripped the floor stick and listened for the exact second to pour on the gas and tack it up.

In my mind's eye I saw Ronnie Cross and Esmeralda Ramirez flying down an empty six-lane highway through the countryside, the chromed engine roaring, the green dials on the walnut dashboard indicating levels of control and power that seemed to transcend the laws of mortality itself.

I thought of horsemen fleeing a grass fire in Old Mexico and civilian soldiers who waited with musket and powder horn at an adobe wall and a preacher who baptized by immersion and created a cathedral out of trees and water and sky. I smelled banks of roses and saw Ronnie Cross speed-shift his transmission and floor the accelerator, tacking up now, the rear end low on the road, the twin exhaust pipes thundering off the asphalt. Esmeralda twisted sideways in the oxblood leather seat and grinned at him, pumping her arms to the beat from the stereo speakers, she and Ronnie disappearing down the highway, into the American mythos of gangbangers and youthful lovers and cars that pulsed with music, between hills that had been green and covered with sunlight only an hour ago.